The Concubine

The Concubine

NORAH LOFTS

ISIS

<u>LARGE PRINT</u>

Oxford

First published in Great Britain 1964
by
Hutchinson

Published in Large Print 2009 by ISIS Publishing Ltd.,
7 Centremead, Osney Mead, Oxford OX2 0ES
by arrangement with
Author's Estate

British Library Cataloguing in Publication Data
Lofts, Norah, 1904–1983.
    The concubine [text (large print)].
    1. Anne Boleyn, Queen, consort of Henry VIII,
King of England, 1507–1536 - - Fiction.
    2. Henry VIII, King of England, 1491–1547 - -
    Fiction.
    3. Great Britain - - History - - Henry VIII,
1509–1547 - - Fiction.
    4. Love stories.
    5. Large type books.
    I. Title
    823.9'12–dc22

ISBN 978–0–7531–8330–4 (hb)
ISBN 978–0–7531–8331–1 (pb)

Printed and bound in Great Britain by
T. J. International Ltd., Padstow, Cornwall

For Barbara, to whose encouragement
this book owes its being.

Contents

CHAPTER ONE

"It was devised that the Lord Percy should marry one of the Earl of Shrewsbury's daughters — as he did afterwards. Mistress Anne Boleyn was greatly offended with this, saying that if ever it lay in her power she would work the Cardinal as much displeasure as he had done her."
Cavendish. *The Life of Cardinal Wolsey*

BLICKLING HALL, NORFOLK. OCTOBER 1523

The serving woman went and knelt by the hearth and busied herself with the kindling of the fire. Every movement, every line of her body, proclaimed that she was making a concession to unusual circumstance. Fifteen years and almost as many small promotions lay between her and such a lowly task: but the room, the whole house except for the kitchen, was as cold and damp as the grave, and what was left of the household was in that state of disorganisation possible only to one caught unawares in the moment of relaxation following a visit from its master who has just departed and unlikely to return for some time. So Emma Arnett, a practical woman, was lighting the fire.

She had, after all, been specially charged to look after her new mistress, the pale, thin girl, stony-eyed with

1

misery, who now stood, still in her damp riding clothes, staring out at the lashing rain. It had rained almost all the way from London, and the state of the roads had added at least two days to the miserable journey. Unless the girl were soon warmed, and coddled a little, she'd come down with a cold, and to judge by the look of her, she was in no state to shake off even the most trivial indisposition.

"Even the wood is damp," Emma said. "Or I've lost my knack."

It was as well to draw attention to the fact that she, Lady Lucia's personal body-servant, was down on her knees, blackening her hands, doing a kitchen slut's work.

"It doesn't matter," the girl said in a dull, indifferent way. "We can go to bed."

"That we can't do, yet. Apart from the servants' pallets there's not a bed in the house fit to sleep on. Those Sir Thomas and his company used, that might have been aired, are all out in the barn, emptied and being picked over. He complained that they were lumpy, as I've no doubt they were. That slit-eyed rogue that calls himself steward is as fit for the job as I am to be Master of Horse."

The window rattled under the onslaught of wind and rain; what little smoke had gathered in the chimney gushed out again and drifted about the room.

"A fine home-coming," Emma Arnett said.

The girl brought her hands out from under her arms and began to rub them together.

2

"It's not my home. It's just one of my father's houses. I haven't had a home for years. And now it looks as though I never may again."

Emma turned her head and gave the girl a cautious, almost apprehensive glance. Would it come now, the inevitable breakdown, the moment she'd been dreading ever since she had been set this task? She hated weak tearful women, and one of the things which irked her now that she had achieved her ambition to be lady's maid was the emotional demand ladies so often made of their servants. They'd smile and hold their heads high, and conceal their sufferings both of mind and body, right up to the door of the bed-chamber. Once within, with the loosening of the stays, the letting down of the hair, would come the collapse. To you, Emma, I can show my hurt; from you I can ask pity. The trouble was, she had none to give; and to be asked for it was as embarrassing as being accosted by a beggar when you yourself were penniless. Poverty, misfortune and exploitation had made her hard, through and through, and she disliked acting the hypocrite though she did it, frequently and successfully.

If the girl, upon those woeful words, broke down and wept, Emma would pat and make clucking sounds, and find something hopeful and consoling to say; but the pretence at sympathy would kill the genuine and quite lively feeling towards the girl which had been building up, hour by hour, over the last six days. For, although Emma was incapable of pity, she could be moved to admiration by any evidence of fortitude and hardihood,

3

which were her own virtues. And so far the girl had behaved with a remarkable and surprising gallantry.

For there was no doubt that she had taken a heavy blow, all the worse for following upon what seemed to be a piece of quite astonishing good fortune.

Satisfied that the dangerous moment had passed, Emma turned her attention to the sulky fire while through her mind ran again, on a well-worn groove, everything that she knew about Mistress Anne Boleyn.

She had come home from France where she'd been in the service of Queen Claude, because there'd been a disagreement between King Henry of England and King Francis of France which looked as though it would end in war. She'd very soon been given a place among Queen Catherine's women which was natural enough, for her father, Sir Thomas, was one of the King's favourite errand-runners, place-fillers, a kind of gentleman lackey.

In her new sphere the girl had been noticeable, but for all the wrong reasons. Queen Catherine — now in her thirties and a little faded, her figure ruined by ill-fated pregnancies — had once been beautiful and still showed a preference for good-looking women about her, just as she liked fine clothes and jewels. Anne Boleyn had no looks to speak of, no bosom even. One of the Court gallants had dismissed her with the words, "All eyes and hair," and that was a truer saying than were most such slighting remarks. Her hair and her eyes were noticeable, but they were black, and at Court brunettes were out of fashion. And out of fashion, too, was anything French. Mistress Anne, who had lived in France since she was nine years old, had brought home a marked French accent. This, with her colouring and a certain, indefinable freedom of manner, regarded as typically French, had led a number of people to think that she was not wholly English. Any levity was noticeable at Court, Queen Catherine was, after all, a Spaniard, and Spanish Court manners were known to be the stiffest, most formal in all the world. There was another thing which weighed, in the scales of public esteem, against the plain, lively girl; her elder sister, Mary Boleyn, had been for a time the King's mistress. For a King, a man married to a woman some years his senior, Henry had led a comparatively chaste life, so his lapses were noted, and remembered.

There she was; sixteen years old, with no advantages whatsoever; the Cinderella of the Queen's ladies, and, it seemed, about to turn the fairy-tale into real life. For she had caught the eye of young Harry Percy, heir to the Earl of Northumberland; a young man who by blood and wealth would have been a suitable match for any woman outside the closest kin to royalty. And even when you considered royalty's close kin, you must remember that Charles Brandon, Duke of Suffolk, with a lineage much inferior to Percy's, had married the King's sister and weathered the storm of the King's anger. Harry Percy could, in fact, have married almost anyone; and he proposed to marry Anne Boleyn.

It was a nine days' wonder and the gossip reached Emma Arnett, busy with the wardrobe, the jewels, the hair-dressing of Lady Lucia Bryant, one of the women closest to the Queen. This, said gossip, is a love affair which will link all the Johnnies-Come-Up-Lately with those of the real nobility who survived the Wars of the Roses. Sir Thomas Boleyn's grandfather had been a tradesman, mercer, saddler, corn-chandler, who remembered exactly what? He'd been Lord Mayor of London and made a pile of money. But William de Perci had come over with William the Conqueror; and young Harry Percy's namesake, nicknamed Hotspur, had been on shoulder slapping terms, boon companion terms, with Henry V, hero of Agincourt.

People began to say that there must be more in the thin, sallow, sloe-eyed little girl than appeared on the surface. What was it? Nobody could say. It was a mystery. It was a little like those old, discredited tales of the alchemists who could turn base metal into gold. From plain Mistress Anne Boleyn to Lady Northumberland . . .

And then, from the centre of his enormous, complicated web, from open negotiations with the Emperor, secret negotiations with the French, from his buildings, his law suits, his multitudinous ecclesiastical concerns, the great Cardinal, Thomas Wolsey, son of an Ipswich butcher and now called, not entirely in jest — though jesting words often hold unpalatable truths — "the King of Europe", moved. Harry Percy was attached to his household. One evening he was called in and told, pleasantly but bluntly, that his notion of marrying Anne Boleyn must be abandoned.

Wolsey was a practical man and he gave good practical reasons for his order. It was not a suitable match. Sir Thomas Boleyn was a toady, a lackey; Mary Boleyn was a whore. Daughter of one, sister of the other, Anne was unworthy of a Percy's attention.

The Cardinal was, at that moment, at the zenith of his powers. He was the friend and confidant not only of the King of England, but of the Emperor of the Holy Roman Empire, of His Most Christian Majesty, Francis the First of France, and of lesser rulers, Regents, Dukes, Margraves, throughout the whole of Christendom. He could make or break alliances; he could plan war or peace. The King of France and the Emperor were little boys, sitting on opposite ends of a see-saw; Wolsey, with a flick of the hand, could set the thing swinging.

Nobody yet, except in the debased market-place of diplomacy where "No" merely meant "What bid?", had ever said "No" to Thomas Wolsey. But on this evening, the great silly handsome boy, Harry Percy, in whom under the silk and velvet of this later, softer age, the blood of Hotspur ran, said "No" with a firmness which the Cardinal recognised. Harry Percy said that he did not intend to be dictated to; he'd chosen the woman he wanted to marry and he meant to stick to his choice. His Eminence could say what he liked about Sir Thomas, and about Mary; he wasn't proposing to marry either of them.

In Court circles there was a great buzz. There were plenty of people who would have been delighted to see the Cardinal defeated, even over so minor an issue. But they were in an awkward position, standing on one foot, as it were. For they were the very ones who were against "the new men" and who would willingly have seen Thomas Boleyn also cut down.

Taking sides, not taking sides, awaiting the outcome, curious, avid, people who had never bothered to give Anne more than a passing glance, now studied her carefully, and missed the quality that Emma Arnett was so soon to recognise. Through those critical days the girl moved almost as though unaware that her fate was in the balance; stared at, she was neither embarrassed, nor defiant; she seemed to be deaf to gossip, and when questioned by those whose curiosity outran their mannerliness, she returned answers that were masterpieces of evasion.

The situation lasted only as long as it took the Earl of Northumberland to come roaring down to London. The Cardinal had never yet suffered defeat on a domestic issue, and it was not to be for Harry Percy, doughty fighter as he was, to score the first success. The Cardinal and the Earl had been closeted together for an hour; then the Earl emerged and found his son and informed him that he seemed to have overlooked the fact that he had been betrothed, in his early youth, to a daughter of the Earl of Shrewsbury, and that nothing short of expensive and long-drawn-out legal procedure could set him free to marry anyone else. The Cardinal sent a messenger to the Court, and before the day was out Emma Arnett, hitherto a mere listener to gossip, had been assigned an active part.

She was removing her lady's head-dress when the lady, who had said little and seemed thoughtful since she entered the room, said,

"Emma. Mistress Anne Boleyn is to leave Court tomorrow and go to her father. She has no woman of her own and the Queen, who feels sorry for her, suggested that I should lend you to accompany her and stay with her as long as needs be."

In Emma, the cold, sluggish resentment that passed for anger stirred. You worked and watched, copied and learned, and by sheer determination pulled yourself out of the kitchen of a remote Norfolk manor house into the bed-chamber of a palace; but it made no difference. You were a chattel still. Something to be lent about, like a piece of clothing. Less important. Lending a sable-lined cloak a lady would say, "Treat it carefully". No such words had accompanied this lending, she'd warrant.

She was mindful to keep her face impassive because of the mirror; and no sign of her discontent sounded in her voice as she asked,

"Who will take my place with you, my lady?"

"Agnes Fieldman. I can manage with her. I shall miss you, Emma, but Her Grace looked straight at me as she described the position. Someone reliable, responsible and kind, she said, and waited for me to offer."

In truth, the Queen had not had to wait at all. Lady Lucia had made the offer with a promptness that was almost unflattering to Emma, and there was reason for that. Emma was reliable and responsible and skilled, but she was forty years old and set in her ways. Naturally she always did exactly what she was told — she'd have caught a buffet otherwise — but somehow anything new, any innovation suggested by her ladyship, seemed to go wrong as soon as Emma took it in hand. It was possible to have one maid too long. Lady Lucia would be very happy to be served by Agnes — who was adaptable — for a change. Another thing which made Emma, for all her virtues, less than perfect as a bed-chamber acolyte was her tendency to receive anything of which she disapproved with silence. It left you at a disadvantage, complaints and protests would be answered and quelled; you couldn't very well chide a maid for saying nothing; yet there were times when Emma's silences were more eloquent and offensive than words. This was one of them.

"One reason why I made the offer," Lady Lucia said almost peevishly, "is that she is bound for Blickling, in Norfolk. I thought it would be pleasant for you to visit your family and friends."

Trying to make an imposition seem like a favour, Emma thought, laying the head-dress away with delicate care. But her quick ear caught the note in her lady's voice and she said, as a good servant should, exactly what was expected of her,

"It was kind of you to think of that, my lady."

Her own inner voice said — Kind! Family and friends? It's more than twenty years since I was in Norfolk; twenty-four since my father's farm was turned into a sheep-run and he died, empty-bellied and broken-hearted, and my mother, the best butter-maker in five parishes, had to go to work at a wool-merchant's as a picker and baler, and was dead in a year of the cough.

Gently she loosed and removed the lady's gown, gently unlaced the iron-stiffened stays.

"Of course, I began at the wrong end," Lady Lucia said. "I should have explained *why* Mistress Anne is bound for Blickling."

Emma had heard already. News spread quickly in palaces which were, in effect, small towns. But she listened with the required politeness, and was rewarded by hearing one thing that had not been mentioned over the goffering irons.

"The Cardinal's intervention," Lady Lucia said, "is regarded as being very strange. And so is the fact that no-one, no-one at all, has, until today, heard a whisper about the betrothal between young Percy and Lord Shrewsbury's girl. One would have expected the father, not His Eminence, to have made the first protest. In fact, the whole thing appears to be a political move. A blow aimed at Sir Thomas Boleyn who, many people think, is getting beyond himself. So the poor wench must suffer, and you, Emma, must be kind. And patient. Remember, all her hopes are shattered."

Emma had been prepared to take charge of a tearful, perhaps hysterical girl, who in this moment of crisis would show her lack of breeding. The serving woman recognised two kinds of breeding, that of the truly great, that of her own peasant class. The outstanding example of the former kind was the Queen herself who had borne, without self-pity or bitterness, repeated disappointments in her effort to provide England with an heir. One living child, the Princess Mary; a son who had died while the celebrations of his birth were still in progress, still-born children, miscarriages. And never a whimper. Catherine was the daughter of Isabella of Castile, the Warrior Queen, and she battled against ill fate with the same dogged courage as her mother had shown against the Moors. That kind of courage was admirable. And so was that of the hard, tough peasant stock from which Emma herself came, the courage of patience, of endurance, of a fundamental hopelessness. Between these two extremes lay the middling sort of people, which included those seemingly great ladies who showed a brave face to the world and then cried on the shoulders of their serving women.

Emma had been prepared for tears and swoonings all the way from London to Blickling.

On the first day she'd thought the girl was stunned, not yet aware of what she had lost — just as they said that in battle a man could receive a disabling, or even fatal wound and feel nothing for a while. Hatfield; Stevenage; Baldock; Royston; the weather bad, the inns poor, the two man-servants surly; Exning; Thetford; Aylsham; and then the arrival at the almost-worse-than-deserted house. And still not a tear. Not even now, when she commented upon her homelessness in the past and the likelihood of being homeless forever.

This behaviour showed quality that Emma Arnett recognised; it spoke of something hard and strong; something with which she was akin.

She rose from her knees.

"That Rhys," she said, "looked me as straight in the face as his eyes would let him, and said he had no key to the cellar. I told him that if that was so, he should take a hatchet to the door. If he hasn't, I will."

Anne said, "He'll have found the key."

"I'll find out," Emma said, and gave the fire a last look, you *dare* go out! and went from the room, the old, dirty rushes crackling under her feet.

Left alone, Anne bent her thumb and put it between her teeth and bit upon it hard. Seven days now; a whole week, and never one moment in which to cry. Lady Cuddington had taken her aside, into the embrasure of the window, and broken the news; and she and the others had expected a storm of tears, a swoon, a fit. But they were all too small, too ordinary things. Women cried over toothache, swooned if they cut a finger, had a fit at the sight of a mouse. What she had wanted to do, when Lady Cuddington had kindly and hesitantly said what was to be said, was to wave her hand and destroy everybody, to call down the fire that had consumed Sodom and Gomorrah and watch them all burn. But she couldn't do that and, raging against her impotence, she had done the only thing left to do; held her head high, kept her face mask-like, compelled her voice to be steady.

"If I am to travel tomorrow I should ask leave to retire and make ready."

She crossed the room, every eye upon her, to the other window where Catherine and two ladies noted for their nimble needles were busy embroidering an altar cloth. She made her perfect, French-style curtsey and begged permission to withdraw, "Your Grace will know upon what cause."

The Queen said quietly, "Yes, I know." She would have liked to have added, "And I am sorry for it," but she did not add those words. Not because she dared not; upon any matter of principle, any matter of right and wrong, Catherine's courage was boundless. But to express, openly, at this moment, her sympathy with Anne, whom she regarded as a silly young girl, misled by a boy almost as young and even sillier, would have implied criticism of the Cardinal, and might easily be misinterpreted. The Cardinal's spies were everywhere; Lady Lucia Bryant, Lady Cuddington even, might be the one to run and tattle, saying that the Queen had questioned the rightness of his decision with regard to Mistress Anne Boleyn. And just now, when the great Cardinal seemed to have changed sides and to be against France and for the Emperor, who was Catherine's nephew, she was anxious to be upon good terms with him, outwardly at least. So she contented herself by saying,

"I hope you have a safe and pleasant journey." And then had done her best to ensure the girl's comfort by making certain that on the journey she should be well served. A Queen's life was largely made up of such compromises.

Anne had gone, consumed with rage and misery which must be concealed, to the large room that she shared with three other maids of honour. Two of them, with their women, were there, half naked, trying on the

14

clothes that they were to wear at the Masque in two days' time. No place to cry.

They'd have believed that she was crying from thwarted ambition, for the title and the wealth and the position which would now never be hers. "Love" was a word much used in the poems and songs and masques, but in real everyday life about the Court it means nothing. There wasn't one person who would have believed her had she cried, "My heart is broken; I love him." But it was true. Harry Percy, big, handsome, a little stupid, had arrived in her life just at the moment when she passed the line between childhood and womanhood and she had given him all the stored-up, hitherto untapped love that was in her, love which girls who had grown up at home had dispensed unthinking to their fathers, brothers, cousins, friends. His name, his wealth, his status meant nothing to her; she would have felt the same about him had he been a groom, a forester, a farmer. Merely to look at him across a crowded room made her feel dizzy, boneless, breathless; a glance from him, a chance touching of hands sent all her pulses leaping. She was in love with him before he noticed her, and in her inexperience thought that it would be impossible that anything could ever increase that love; but when he began to single her out for attention, always choosing her as his partner in any dance or game, contriving excuses to get her alone, gratitude and wonder, even a kind of awe were added to her love. In her mind he assumed almost god-like proportions; in choosing her he had elevated and honoured her. The jealousy of the other ladies, openly displayed or masked by congratulatory phrases, was like incense.

He was older, infinitely more worldly-wise, much more prey to urgent physical desires. He would gladly enough have made her his mistress — at least not that exactly, since he intended to make her his wife — but there were evenings, in that summer of 1523, when he would willingly have anticipated the marriage ceremony. Two things prevented it. One the simple but bothersome business of lack of privacy; he was attached to the Cardinal's household, she to the Queen's, which meant that neither had a room where the door could be locked or bolted; neither was free to disappear for any length of time without explanation. But such handicaps had been overcome in the past and would be again in the future; it could have been contrived but for the other preventive, Anne's surprising prudery; surprising because she was so gay, so frivolous, so French, so eager to attract, and having attracted, up to a point so responsive. Harry Percy, like almost everyone else, had preconceived notions about the French, and the French King's lechery was a by-word. Hardly anyone knew, or being told would have believed, that Queen Claude was almost fanatically chaste and had imposed upon her ladies a standard of conduct more suitable to a nunnery than a court. Years of such training, experienced in pliable youth, were not without effect. Also, of course, there was always Mary to remember. Mary hadn't suffered; when the King had tired of her he had found her a husband, and her behaviour had, in general, benefited her family, but Anne was liable at any critical

16

moment to find herself thinking — Just because Mary was easy, don't imagine that I . . .

So when the blow fell there was just a little extra sting to it; it was unjust to be so punished when she had behaved so blamelessly. And under that there was the deeper hurt of privation, of a loss that could never now be made good. She had loved him, she had saved the ultimate expression of that love as something to be enjoyed on her wedding night. Now she was never to have it. Lady Mary Talbot would. It was a childish comparison — but childhood was, after all, only just behind her; it was as though, served with cherry pie, she had saved the cherries until last, mumbled the crust and then seen the fruit snatched away and given to another.

Never now, never never, in the whole of life, would she and Harry Percy lie together, naked in a bed. And it was that, not the wide acres, or the wealth, or being called Countess of Northumberland, that had mattered to her.

Upon that thought she pressed her arms to her waist and bent over against the pain that slashed her, as real and savage as though it derived not from a thought, but from a physical cause. This empty, gnawing emptiness, how long can it last? Until I die? I'm only sixteen, and women sometimes live to be old.

She straightened herself as Emma Arnett re-entered, but she looked so ghastly that the serving woman recalled a few instances of particularly stubborn people who had died, literally, on their feet. Suppose she died, Emma thought, remembering how little the girl had eaten in these six days, or slept. They'd blame me. They'd blame me for pushing on, for not seeing the state she was in, for not stopping at Hatfield and sending for a doctor. I was given full charge.

"Are you well, mistress?" she asked, setting down the tray she carried. It bore a tarnished silver candlestick, a lidded jug and a tall cup.

"Well enough," Anne said.

"Come to the fire; there's heat in it now. Let me take your cloak. There! The wine will hearten you. That Rhys found the key when I mentioned the hatchet, and they've heated it right, warm enough to be a comfort and not hot enough to lose goodness." She poured some into the cup and handed it to Anne who took it and cradled it in both hands.

"They're making the supper," Emma said. "It's a poor one, I'm afraid."

As she spoke Emma Arnett who lived in the same skin rebuked her. A *poor* supper? A duck taken straight from the pond, plucked, dressed and spitted; followed by marigold eggs, a rich confection of custard and apples. Poor? When to thousands of people two such dishes in conjunction would constitute a feast, suitable only to a wedding or a christening. When there were thousands more who had never in their lives tasted either, people who lived on bread and porridge, with two or three times a year a taste of salt pork or stockfish. When there were other thousands, beggars, who on many days ate nothing at all; who counted themselves lucky to be thrown a crust, or to be allowed to delve into a bucket of pigswill in the hope of

18

dredging up some eatable morsel. There were at this moment more beggars in England than there had ever been, and not idle rogues, far from it; decent labouring men, thrown out of work because the acres they'd ploughed and seeded and scythed had been turned into sheep-runs. One man, they said, could tend the sheep that grazed an area which, properly farmed, had employed twenty; and what happened to the other nineteen Emma Arnett knew only too well. So she felt it wrong to decry the meal now being prepared, though her common-sense told her that for a young lady straight from Court, where between twenty and thirty dishes were commonplace, it *was* a poor meal.

Anne said, "Whatever it is, I'm not hungry."

"But you must eat, sometime." Emma spoke earnestly, but without the coaxing manner most women in her position would have employed. "Every meal so far, you've just pecked and pushed away — I grant with good reason most times — but you can't go on this way."

"No, because I might die. And what a pity that would be!"

"There're easier ways," Emma said drily. "Besides, mistress, you're young. It was a bad knock, and painful, but time will ease it, as it does most things. One day you may look back and laugh — I hope you will. But to do that you must keep alive."

"I shall keep alive. Anger alone will do that for me." She stared across the wine-cup, into the fire. "It was such an unfair way to treat us," she said, speaking more quickly and in an agitated manner. "Are we expected to

19

believe that Harry had grown to this age and never been told that he was betrothed? When he came to London, wouldn't his father have said, 'Mark you, Harry, you're not in the market for marriage, Mary Talbot has her brand on your flank?' Or even if he had overlooked so mild a precaution, wouldn't he have found Harry and told him, himself, the moment he reached London? But oh no! First he must spend an hour, alone with that great bloated red spider, and then, out he comes with this tale all ready in his mouth. And why? God's Wounds, I rack my brain trying to think *why*? Even if, to all Wolsey's monopolies and all his duties had been added the arranging of marriages, why should *this* one so affront him that he must interfere?"

Lady Lucia, Emma remembered, had said much the same thing. Probably no one knew the reason, nor ever would. The Cardinal's methods were too subtle to be understood by anyone but himself.

"He's very sly," Emma said. "If ever he fell out of favour he could earn a living at fairs, with three thimbles and a pea. Drink your wine while it's warm, mistress."

"Put the jug on the hearth," Anne said, "and fetch yourself a cup. You've had a long, cold ride, too."

During her spectacular career — upon which, although she did not know it, she had already started — she was to have virulent enemies, some devoted friends; arguments about her behaviour, her motives, her personality were to go on and on down the years, but those who actually served her in a menial capacity

20

never wavered in their good opinion of her, never had anything but kind things to say. "She was always considerate and just." "To me she was a good mistress." "She was easy to work for."

Fetching the second cup Emma said to herself — That was thoughtful, with all she has on her mind, too. And she remembered how often, in her own hard life, a furious resentment had been all that had kept her going. She understood, and therefore sympathized with Anne's anger, far more than she would have done with any softer emotion.

When she had poured wine into her cup she lifted it a little and said formally, "Good health, mistress; and better fortune."

"I wish you health and happiness," Anne responded. The wind whined and threw rain against the windows, but the fire was hot, the candles bright and the erstwhile dreary room was cosy, a safe, warm refuge.

They had missed dinner in the effort to reach Blickling before twilight and upon empty stomachs the mulled wine, spiced with cloves and cinnamon and ginger, and sweetened with honey, was a potent brew. Under its influence each woman lowered guard a little and when a sudden thought struck her, Anne spoke aloud.

"Do you know, I believe, I truly believe that the Cardinal knew that my father had gone from here. That was another trick. My father has no great fondness for me, he is not a man given to fondness, but he is ambitious and my being cast off in this manner will displease him. Had he been here he would have heard my story and carried it to the King — he has his ear, at times, when the Cardinal is not whispering into it. He'd have asked for some proof of this former betrothal. And the Cardinal needed time. So I was sent here, because my father is at Hever. Oh, I was a fool to have left so meekly. I did everything wrong. Even the Queen . . . if I'd thought . . . if I'd had my wits about me, I shouldn't have asked leave to retire, I should have flung myself at her feet and asked her to plead for me."

"With the King?"

"Who else?"

"It would have been to no purpose," Emma said, flatly. "Whatever influence Her Grace ever had upon the King is outworn. That marriage, mistress, is fourteen years old and has not given His Grace what he wanted, a sturdy son. You may ease your mind there, nothing that you could have said to the Queen could have bettered your case. And to have pleaded, fruitlessly, that, later on, would have burned you to remember."

Anne looked at Emma and saw, for the first time, the woman within the servant.

"Yes," she said. "It would." And her mind took a sideways skip and she thought — At least I have done nothing to be ashamed of. So few minutes before she had been regretting that on those warm, rose-scented evenings she had withstood the demand of Harry's urgent lips and hands, and of her own newly wakened, clamorous senses. Now she was glad. It was humiliating enough to be cast off as she had been; to have been

22

abandoned *after* . . . Yes, that too would have burned her to remember.

The rest of what Emma had said slid through her mind almost unremarked. She had seen the King often enough; huge and handsome, in every way just a little more than life-size; the most powerful monarch in the world, the best knight in a tourney, the most skilful handler of the lute, the best — or almost the best — maker of songs. There was no visible sign of the Queen having lost influence over him, but possibly Emma knew best about that. She herself had been too much engrossed in her own love affair to give much heed to other people.

She thought — Fourteen years; if Harry and I had been allowed to marry, would our marriage have been outworn in fourteen years? It seemed impossible to imagine, as impossible as imagining snow and ice on the hottest summer day. No. Ours would have lasted, because it was a love match. The King and Queen had been thrust together by an arranged marriage, just as Harry and Mary Talbot were being thrust together.

And so, here she was, thinking the same thoughts, over and over, driving herself mad. It was as though her mind had been locked in a little stone cell, without door or window, and with nothing to do except go round and round.

She lifted the cup and drank, forgetting for once to be careful of something the concealing of which had become almost second nature; and suddenly she was aware that Emma was regarding it. Instead of whisking it away out of sight as she always did on those rare occasions when she had exposed it, she spread it out against the firelight; her slender, long-fingered left hand with its hateful deformity. Growing out from the little finger, near the nail, was another tiny fingertip.

"Yes," she said, "you see aright. And you should cross yourself, Emma. People do, if they glimpse it. They call it a witch mark."

"I'm not superstitious," Emma said. As soon as the words were spoken she wished them back, or wished that they hadn't sounded so abrupt and final. She had cultivated that way of speech; the fewest words, the least revealing, but she shouldn't just at this moment have clipped a subject off so short. While the girl talked she wasn't brooding; and she should have kept her talking until supper came; then maybe she would have eaten with some appetite.

With an obvious air of beginning again, she said, "It's always seemed to me that if those who're called witches could do a half of what they're said to do, they could do more for themselves. But they're always poor and ugly and old, and if their neighbours turn against them, they let themselves be taken and ducked, or swum, or pricked, as helpless as sheep."

"You speak as though you had known a number."

"There's one in every village, and I had country jobs until about eleven years ago. In the country, until a cow dies or somebody has a bad accident, people take the whole business as natural. In fact country children play at being witches the same way they play at being married and keeping house."

"Do they? I was a country child, too. I lived here, most of the time, after my mother died; but I hardly ever played games. I had a governess, a Frenchwoman, named Simonette, and with her it was lessons, lessons all the time. She was a very serious woman. I've been grateful to her, since. In France it made things easier for me, and once, when the other English maids of honour were sent home, I was allowed to stay because, speaking both tongues, I was useful."

Was that good or bad? If I'd come home sooner I might not have met Harry at all; or I might have met him sooner and perhaps the Cardinal might not have noticed . . . All her past life, back to the lessons with Simonette, seemed like a path leading straight to this stony cell out of which she could not break, where her thoughts went round and round. She made another effort.

"Did you ever play at being a witch, Emma?"

"Well, I never had much time for play, either. My father had a little farm then and my mother was always busy and wanted all the help she could get. And even when there was time . . ." Emma heard herself making this confidential statement with some surprise, for it was something that she had always kept to herself, for you never knew who might listen and play a trick that they might think funny but which would be too loathsome to contemplate . . . "I never could abide frogs or toads," she said. "So I never could play properly. But I have gone so far as to give our yard dog a secret name, 'Owd Scrat' I used to call him, when we were alone; and I've well-wished people with a bit of cherry blossom, and I've pricked more than one name on a laurel leaf with a thorn. And nobody a bit the better or worse and the dog no more heedful of me, in fact less than he was of my father who called him 'Nip' and lammed into him if he didn't do what he was bid."

Round and round inside the small stony cell; this time, if I were a witch, or even playing at being one, I know what I'd wish, good and ill. God's life, if I could just have power for five minutes . . .

You see, she said, addressing herself, there is no escape; your thoughts always come back to the same point, as a mariner's compass always comes back to the North. I can't even sit and talk about my serving woman's childhood games without relating them to me and my situation.

She made another attempt to break through.

"You say you've pricked names on laurel leaves, Emma. How? Could you write when you were young?"

"Not then. I've learned since. Maybe," the slow, dry self-derogatory humour of her breed brought a smile to Emma's craggy face. "Maybe that's why nobody was ever the worse for our pranks. We just named the leaf and pricked along the veins, and then kept it next to our skin till it was cooked, as we called it. When it was cooked all the prick-holes were brown. Then we buried it and said, 'Within nine days, as this leaf rots, so will you,' and we said the name of the person we meant. Once, I remember, we did it to try to get our own back on a man who'd closed a footpath and made us trudge all the way round, another two miles, to get to church."

"And what happened to him?"

"He was knighted," Emma said, and the smile showed again. "And if that wouldn't cure you of being superstitious, what would. Young children at one end, old women in second childhood at the other; and that, mistress, to my mind, is all it is."

But the truth was that Emma Arnett's lack of superstition, like her tendency to silence, her sense of responsibility and the unspoken disapproval of which Lady Lucia Bryant had been aware, stemmed from causes far removed from childish games. Emma's first job in London had been as nursemaid to a family named Hunne. Richard Hunne was a prosperous merchant tailor who, because of his dealings with the Netherlands, where new ideas were rife, was what a hundred years earlier would have been called a Lollard. He was anti-clerical; he read the New Testament. He was "a new man" of a very different kind from Thomas Wolsey and Thomas Boleyn and hundreds of others, who were new where their own importance was concerned, and everywhere else strongly conservative. Amongst his other advanced ideas, Richard Hunne held that in an ideal society everyone should be capable of reading the Bible; and finding, in his new nurse-girl, a woman of some intelligence, who admitted to a desire to read and write, he had taken pains to teach her. Before Emma's studies were very far advanced, the child whose birth had been her occasion for joining the household had died, and over his funeral his father had decided to make what he called "a test case". The officiating priest had claimed the coffin cover, a good one, worth four shillings, and Richard Hunne, to whom the value of the cover meant less than nothing, had refused to give it up. It was, he said, just one more example of how priests acted as extortioners; in this case the cover didn't matter, but what of a poor family, where a dead child might be wrapped in the best perhaps the only, blanket, or a cloak?

There'd been a lot of fuss and argument, some of which ordinary people like Emma could understand, some of which was far beyond their comprehension. The priest had sued Master Hunne and then Master Hunne had turned about and claimed that the priest, in suing him, had been acting for a foreign power — to wit, the Pope of Rome. The word "praemunire" had been tossed about. But Richard Hunne had been taken off to gaol, and there found hanged. It was said that he had committed suicide because he feared trial for heresy. That, no-one believed; he had gone out of his way to *invite* trial; and the most sinister feature of the case was that the gaoler had run away as soon as he knew that there was to be an inquest. A great many people, and especially, of course, his family, believed that Richard Hunne had been murdered, was a martyr.

Emma Arnett, busy with her upward climb, had entered the Bryant household, and was, within a year, to achieve her ambition of being personal maid to a great lady. But she had never forgotten Master Hunne, or his teachings, not just the mastering of the reading and writing, but his general attitude towards things. When she said, "I'm not superstitious," she meant a great deal more than that she could regard a deformed little finger without horror; she meant that she did not believe that at Walsingham one could see the milk of the Virgin Mary, still liquid after more than fifteen hundred years, or that at Canterbury St Thomas's bones still had shreds of bleeding flesh attached to them, or that you could go to the tomb of St Edmund at St Edmundsbury and in return for a sizeable gift be cured of the lame leg or crooked back which had hitherto crippled you. Master Hunne had denounced all this as nonsense; and she, without knowing it, had already been in a state of mind open to conversion. There were in England many thousands like her, sound, hard, practical people who felt that something had gone wrong; who could, however obscurely, sense the gulf between Jesus of Nazareth who had owned nothing, whose only mount had been an unbroken donkey, and His self-styled heirs and servants; Thomas Wolsey for example, who rode like a prince, who, though professedly celibate, had a son and a daughter, at whose table every day nine hundred idle or sycophantic persons ate their fill.

Anne said, "Nonsense it may be, but everyone isn't sensible, and they look askance at me if they see my finger. That is why my gowns are made with trailing sleeves, which several ladies, I have noted, are beginning to copy."

She spoke from the surface of her mind for Emma's last words had set something astir. Young children at one end, old women at the other, playing . . . but suppose someone in neither category, someone in the prime of life, someone actuated by the deepest hatred, someone who bore not merely one but two of the supposed signs . . . She touched with a finger of her right hand the heavy gold and enamel necklet which hid the dark, protuberant mole on her neck. Suppose . . .

Of course, it was all nonsense, and the idea that she could injure the Cardinal in any way, by means natural or supernatural, was really as absurd as the idea that she could destroy his great palace of York House with her embroidery tools. Quite, quite absurd but wonderful to think about. It was as though a ray of light had been let into the little stone prison where her thoughts went round and round; a sinister light, concentrated upon a laurel leaf upon whose glossy green surface the brown-edged holes spelled out the name of Thomas Wolsey.

CHAPTER
TWO

"Whereas the King for some years past had noticed in reading the Bible the severe penalty inflicted by God on those who married the relicts of their brothers, he began to be troubled in his conscience."
Letters and Papers of the reign of Henry VIII

YORK HOUSE. OCTOBER 1523

The cardinal's plump, well-cared-for hands tidied the papers as he said, "Your Grace may safely leave it all to me." They were the words which had first endeared him to the King and during the past thirteen years he had repeated them uncountable times. Henry had always hated paper work and any kind of administrative detail, mainly because he lacked patience: he was fully as able as his minister, his mind, if it lacked Wolsey's subtlety, having a greater capacity for assessing a situation at a glance. He found it tedious to be obliged to explain to slower-witted persons, to persuade those who didn't immediately see eye to eye with him. Wolsey had a passion for detail, a talent for explanation, an outstanding gift for persuasion. They made an almost perfect team. The King said, "It would be as well if . . ." "I would like . . ." "We should . . ." and the Cardinal said, "Your Grace may safely leave it all to me." For thirteen years the association between them had been as close, as smooth working as the association between a man's mind and his hands and feet. And this way of working had another advantage besides setting the King free of the routine which in a few years had turned his father from a knight-errant into a furrow-browed, round-shouldered book-keeper; it didn't merely give him time to hunt and dance and make music; it provided him with a scapegoat. When, as sometimes happened, the thing that Henry thought "it would be well", "I would like", "we should", went wrong, all the blame fell upon Wolsey. Even when an expeditionary force, years ago, had first been defeated, and then mutinied and come home, the fiasco had been called "Wolsey's War". Beyond all question Thomas Wolsey had been very useful to Henry Tudor and he had been commensurately rewarded.

How, Henry asked himself, is he going to take *this?* And instead of, as usual, rising and making off as soon as the Cardinal had said the releasing words, he settled himself more firmly in his chair.

"There is," he said, "another matter."

The Cardinal gave a little inward groan. Once upon a time, as several people could testify, he had had such control of his body, as well as of his mind, that he could sit for twelve hours on end at a table, working away, undisturbed by the necessity to relieve his bladder. But those days were over and gone; he was fifty-one years old. He'd been in some discomfort for the last ten minutes, within a few more he would be in misery.

And the strange thing was that although he could have explained his need to retire to anyone else, he couldn't do so to Henry. There were a number of reasons. They were close, very close, but the King after all was the Lord's anointed and one didn't, to one's Sovereign Lord, mention a physical function. And there was always the fear — common he supposed to all *employed* persons — of revealing any weakness which might be regarded as a sign of age. A fine thing it would be, wouldn't it, if the King left York House this afternoon thinking to himself, Wolsey is getting so old that he can no longer hold his water.

But it would be equally bad if he went away thinking that Wolsey had been hurried, or inattentive to this other matter.

He rose to his feet.

"If your Grace will honour me, I have a very special wine; from Burgundy, and this moment ripe. I saw to its laying away and I would like to point it out to my butler, so that there is no mistake."

On almost any other day Henry would have made some light-hearted remark about the advisability of labelling one's wine, of having a butler one could trust; or he might have asked, in the voice which he did now and then use to Wolsey, the reminding, the calling-to-heel voice, who it was who had sent a gift of special wine to the servant and not to the master. But this afternoon he had other, more heavy matters on his mind and merely said,

"I shall be glad to sample it with you, Thomas."

He was almost glad to have a moment or two alone, to shake off the memory of the state affairs which had been under discussion and to remember the cogent arguments, the telling phrases which had formed in his mind during a series of wakeful nights. Of Wolsey, as Wolsey, he was entirely sure; he was Thomas; he was My Lord of York; he was Chancellor, Ambassador, Privy Councillor and trusted friend; but, and this must never be over-looked, he was also a Prince of the Church, and Papal Legate; as such he owed some allegiance elsewhere, and there was no doubt that the subject about to be mentioned could lead to a conflict of allegiances. Still, the subject must be broached.

Wolsey rustled back into the room, followed by a page who poured the wine into gold cups, richly chased and studded with jewels, presented them, kneeling, and withdrew.

Henry sipped appreciatively.

"As you promised, a sound, ripe wine. When next your friend is in a giving mood I should be a not-unwilling recipient."

"Your Grace, I was only waiting your word of approval before sending it to you." It was, like many of his statements, a lie only by its timing. He was lavishly generous — not only to those who could in turn be generous to him — he liked giving; and beyond all he liked to give to his master.

"I would accept, with thanks," Henry said, graciously. "But we'll leave it in your cellar. For one thing a move would hardly improve it; for another, to drink it will sweeten our discussion. And as you will hear, by the time this business is fully threshed out, we shall be down to the dregs."

It was unusual, out of character for him to beat thus about the bush. As a rule, both in giving an order and in stating a wish, he was brisk and forthright. Wolsey felt that this was one of those times when a direct question — ordinarily impermissible — might be welcome, so he said,

"And the business is, Your Grace?"

"Let formalities rest, Thomas. This is a talk between men."

And still he hadn't said what it concerned. A little glumly Wolsey made a guess. Something he knows will not please me; most likely another and more serious attempt to get his only son, Bessie Blount's bastard, recognised as heir presumptive. Completely unfeasible; the English would never accept it, and it would break up the Princess Mary's betrothal to the Emperor. *He* has agreed to marry the future Queen of England, not a dispossessed girl whose base-born brother sits on the throne.

"It is," Henry said, forcing himself to frankness, "a matter of my conscience."

They were words which were presently to echo and re-echo around the known world; loaded, dangerous words which were to bring down many seemingly unassailable institutions and ruin many men, Wolsey foremost among them; yet he heard them now, for the first time, without a premonitory pang.

"Your conscience, sire? Then it must be a trivial matter, for there's not a man in Christendom that can claim a clearer one!"

"You're wrong, Thomas. I have — and have had for some time past — a very heavy burden upon my conscience." He looked his minister full in the eye. "I've lived in sin, with my brother's wife, these fourteen years."

For a second Wolsey felt nothing save genuine astonishment. Nothing that the King or any other man could have said would have surprised him as much. He was seldom surprised; he regarded all men as venal; he could draw up a water-tight treaty and at the same time speculate upon how soon, and in what manner, it would be broken. But now he was surprised; and then, as his powerful mind reached out and grasped every implication of Henry's words, inside his stoutening body his heart halted, and then with a jerk beat on.

He said, quite cheerfully,

"What a freakish fancy! The Pope himself declared your brother's marriage null and void. It was never consummated. Your union with Her Grace is as legal in the sight of God and man as it would have been had your brother never existed and you had married Her Grace when she arrived from Spain. Rest assured of that. I do beg you not to let such a doubt darken another moment."

"I have told myself these things, on many a wakeful night. They are things that a man would *wish* to believe. But I can't. All the evidence points the other way."

"Evidence? What evidence?"

"My children," Henry said heavily. "My children, all stillborn or dead before their navels had healed."

"Not all. The Princess Mary . . ."

"I should have said my sons. For a King to have no son is to be childless, Thomas; you know that as well as I do. You know the history of your own country; only once has the throne gone to a woman, Matilda. And what did that lead to? Civil war, with such famine and widespread misery that men said Christ and His Saints slept. Is that to happen again? Can you sit there and contemplate, with an easy mind, the prospect of my leaving no heir but Mary?"

"We have, in a manner contemplated it, ever since Her Grace's last miscarriage. Not with an easy mind, I agree. But we have contemplated it, and as far as possible prepared for it by arranging her marriage to the Emperor."

"And that I never liked! Charles already has more territory than he can handle properly, and married to Mary he'll have England, too. This England, yours and mine, Thomas, will be just one more unimportant bit of fringe on Charles's great Empire; within twenty years it'll be known as the Outer Isles or some such slighting name. And as the last-comer to the conglomeration, England would always get the dirty end of the stick, in every bargain, every market. It just so happens that at the moment the Emperor and I are allied against France, but it'd be madness to believe that there is any fondness between the Spaniards and us." He drew a deep noisy breath. "Why must I give away England as part of a wench's dower? It's as unjust as though I claimed your manor of Tittenhanger simply because my bull had served your heifer!"

"It's been done from time immemorial."

"So have many other regrettable things. It isn't what I want for England."

He spoke with sincerity. Even in his most light-hearted moments he had always remained aware of the responsibilities that were a part of Kingship; England and the English belonged to him; he was head of the State and Father of the People. But he was only a mortal man, and one day — a day so far ahead that it could be viewed calmly — he must die. What then?

It was a question that he asked himself more frequently and more urgently as the years crept by. His marriage was fourteen years old; with the ordinary amount of luck, and God's blessing on a pious man, he should by now be the father of a son moving from boyhood to manhood, a strong, handsome Prince of Wales, effortlessly acquiring from his father's example skill in the use of arms, cunning in the management of men, the secret of maintaining personal popularity without sacrificing self-will. Blessed with such a son, he could, when the time came, die knowing that England was safe in the strong hands of Henry the Ninth. But there was no boy; the heir to England was a little girl, a grave, intelligent, lovable child, most satisfactory as a daughter, but viewed dynastically, a disaster.

Wolsey said,

"All that you say is true, and it is regrettable. But, Sire, I see no alternative."

Henry said, rather heavily

"I do." Wolsey waited for the mention of little Henry Fitzroy, and braced himself. But the King went on, "I'm thirty-two, Thomas, and I have proved that outside this cursed, incestuous marriage I *can* breed a boy. And if I can, I should. You would agree that the provision of a successor could be reckoned part of a monarch's duty?"

One of those questions to which neither yes nor no was a safe answer.

Cautiously, Wolsey said, "What does your Grace propose?"

"Pope Julius annulled my brother's marriage to Catherine and gave me leave to marry her. Events have proved him to have been in error. I propose that we ask Clement to look into the matter, find some flaw in Julius's ruling and retract the annulment. That would make me free to re-marry and try again."

Except for a whitening of his nostrils Wolsey's face gave no sign of the disturbance he felt. This was worse, much worse than any suggestion of legitimizing and recognising the bastard son; because basically Henry *knew* that to be impracticable. This new proposal was practicable, it had a kind of deadly logic; but oh, how difficult, how dangerous! And it could not be kept, as discussion of Henry Fitzroy's fate could be kept, within these four walls.

He was aware that he must say something and say it promptly; Henry was eyeing him with some eagerness, and behind the eagerness there was calculation. When the difficulties and the dangers proved too much it would *never* do for the King to be able to swing round and say, "You were against me from the first."

He said, "It sounds simple enough; but it would be, I don't say impossible, few things are impossible, but it would be fraught with such difficulty and likely to lead to such unpredictable results that it is not a thing to be lightly undertaken."

"I am not undertaking it lightly. Nor hastily. I have even taken into consideration Catherine's feelings. She has been a most excellent wife to me, Thomas, and I am fond of her; but she is of royal blood, she will realise the *necessity*."

"Will His Holiness? Is Clement the man to set a precedent by revoking an opinion given by his predecessor? In theory the Pope's judgment and wisdom are infallible, his edicts inspired. If Clement says Julius was in error, where does Clement stand? And then, even suppose that it could be proved that when Julius issued his brief he had been misinformed in some particular so that the pronouncement was legally invalid, what of the Emperor? The Queen's Grace is his aunt. Would he welcome a pronouncement that declared that she had eight times conceived out of wedlock? And even could he stomach that would he not gag on the notion of the Princess Mary being made a bastard?"

"He'll gag, and more, at the thought of losing England, but why should that fret us, Thomas? I gag at the thought of his having it as a marriage portion. As for the Pope — I'm a good churchman but I can say to you, surely without offence, you high clerics are skilled in dealing with awkward situations; slippery as eels, all of you. And by Holy Cross, the Papacy owes me something. I was the one who took up cudgels against Luther."

"That is true." Wolsey shifted ground. "We must also bear in mind the common English people. On the whole they dislike foreigners but from the first, in their unpredictable way, they took the Princess of Aragon to their hearts and never once, in all the time that she has been Queen, has she acted in such a way as to diminish her popularity. Every time she had been brought to bed every woman in the land has hoped with her, suffered with her, and shared her disappointment. To say now that she was never your lawful wife will, I fear, incense all your female subjects — and all the men whose own marriages have brought them less than they hoped for in children, goods or simple comfort. That must be thought of."

"I, too, have some popularity," Henry said, touched in his vanity. "And naturally if anything comes of the matter it must be presented in an acceptable form. Every man with a conscience will recognise the claims of mine, and every man with his own good at heart will be concerned for the succession."

"And the French, of course, would welcome it, as they would welcome anything that caused a breach between us and the Emperor," Wolsey said, musingly, his mind leaping forward. The French would gladly provide some plump, nubile princess to take Catherine's place in Henry's bed.

"Has your Grace some Princess in mind?"

"God's fingers! No! You go too fast, Thomas. The ground must be tested. I've thought the matter over and convinced myself. I've now asked your opinion. And you have mentioned the Pope, the Emperor and the common people. What does my own Lord Chancellor think?"

It was one of those moments, frequent enough in Wolsey's complicated life, when truth and common-sense dictated one answer and expediency the direct opposite. He wanted to say — Leave it alone, it can only lead to enmity abroad and rebellion at home; expediency urged that he give the pleasing answer. Also to expediency was added a genuine fondness. It was hard on a man in his prime, a strong, lusty man, to be tied to a woman six vital years his senior; it was even harder on a devoted King to be without a son to succeed him.

"Your Grace knows that in this as in all things I have no other wish than to carry out your will to the best of my ability."

"That," Henry said, "is a smooth answer and worthless. And you know it. Save your evasions for those who trade in such things. Give a blunt man a blunt answer. What do *you* think?"

The basic, rock hard, East Anglian realism that neither his friends nor his enemies ever gave its due came to Wolsey's aid,

"I think — in fact I know — that it will be difficult to bring about, and it will take time, more time than you imagine. But there is this . . ." Behind the massive brow the brain which even his most virulent enemies admitted to be formidable was already working; cog engaged upon cog. "The whole thing could be eased and accelerated if Her Grace could be persuaded to co-operate. She is a pious woman; she is of royal blood, she understands the need this land has for a prince. If she could be brought to agree that the marriage was no marriage, that His Holiness decreed it void, she might withdraw and retire to a nunnery. That would lift all shadow of blame from you. Your Grace, that is my concern — that you emerge scatheless, that you and Her Grace should seem in equal measure to have been victims of a Papal error."

"As we were. But you're right, Thomas. This hinges on the Queen." He imagined himself facing Catherine and mentioning the matter, and recoiled. "Not yet," he said hastily. "Time enough to tell her when we have the Pope's decision."

Wolsey nodded. "And that will not be yet. I suggest a careful preliminary approach by as secret a channel as can be found; then, in the event of failure there need be no gossip, no embarrassment."

"The means I leave to you," Henry said simply. "They missed a rare chance, Thomas, when they failed to elect you for Pope, though for my own part I can't help but be thankful."

Wolsey's face remained impassive, though his casual reference to the greatest disappointment of his life hurt him. He had come very near to being chosen in 1521 when Leo X died, and had tried again eighteen months later upon the death of Adrian VI. His hopes, his dreams of being Pope — now shelved indefinitely —

had given him, through anticipation, some insight as to what being Pope involved and he was able to think now that if *he* were in Clement's place it would take something of a cataclysmic nature to induce him to revoke a bill of annulment granted by one of his predecessors. Yet, at the same time, thinking of his thwarted ambition he was reminded that the Emperor, Charles V, had promised to use his influence to get him elected. How far, how vigorously had he kept that promise? Wolsey, always pro-French at heart, would welcome the annulment, could it be obtained; and welcome, too, the French marriage which must almost inevitably follow. There was a Princess named Renée . . .

He said, "Your Grace may rely upon me to give this matter great and careful thought, and to do my utmost to gain you what you desire."

"Then that is all for the moment," Henry said, and rose. He glanced at the piled papers. "Everything seems to be in order here; I think, since the weather has cleared, I'll have a few days' hunting down at Hever."

"I trust Your Grace has good sport," Wolsey said.

A few minutes later, when the King had been seen off and Wolsey was back in his room, in the act of handing the papers to one of his secretaries he stopped suddenly and stared into space.

Hever. That brought Thomas Boleyn to mind and that slant-eyed slip of a girl who was his daughter. The King had said, "Break off, as soon as you can, this affair between young Percy and Tom Boleyn's girl. I have other plans for her. She can marry Piers Butler and that will settle that old dispute. I'd sooner not appear in this business because I have not yet made up my mind about the titles and wish to rouse no false hopes on either side." Wolsey had said, "I can say, with truth, that she is no match for Northumberland's heir." "Good," Henry said. "and get her away from the Court for awhile. Send her to her father."

Sir Thomas was then at Blickling, so the girl had been sent there. Now she'd be at Hever. And Henry, besides going there to hunt, would be arranging her marriage to Butler, and it looked as though, arranging it there, when he was Sir Thomas's guest, he had decided to give Boleyn the title after all. And Thomas Boleyn, en-nobled, would be more unbearable than ever.

There had been a time — not so long since — when the King would not have made such a move without consulting his chief minister; he'd have said, yes, as lately as a year ago, "Which shall it be, Thomas, Butler or Boleyn?" and Wolsey, after a pretence at pondering, at impartial judgment, would have given some good reason for passing over Boleyn whom he disliked and distrusted, and the King would have taken his advice. Now, without even discussing the matter, off he went to Hever, lightly mentioning a few days' hunting.

Well, it was inevitable, Wolsey supposed. "If the lion knew his strength who could rule him?" To a degree Wolsey had looked upon Henry as his son, and even the most beloved, the most amenable sons grew up and delighted in a show of independence. Trotting off to Hever to promise Thomas Boleyn a title without having consulted Wolsey probably gave Henry a pleasing feeling of standing on his own feet.

But it was, nonetheless, a little straw which indicated the way the wind blew. For a moment Wolsey was thankful that there were larger, non-domestic issues which only he could handle. Yes, Henry could make Thomas Boleyn, that assiduous toady and climber, Viscount Rochford without either help or advice from Thomas Wolsey; but he needed him still, and would need him for a long while if one Pope's ruling was to be set aside by another.

He came out of his reverie, gave the secretary his instructions and sent him away and then sat down to give his whole attention to what, in his own mind, he had already named The King's Secret Matter.

He propped his chin on his hand so that the stone of his great Cardinal's ring pressed into the thickening flesh.

And suddenly his mind, instead of working in its usual smooth, logical, sensible fashion, chose to turn freakish, allowed itself to be taken over by the memory of an absurd happening which had taken place years ago and which he would have said he had forgotten.

It was in his Court of Star Chamber; a complicated legal case concerning some property, and one of the claimants was a woman. He had given — as he always did in that Court — a just, an impartial verdict, against the woman who had felt herself aggrieved. She had jumped up and begun to shout some hysterical nonsense accusing him of being unfair to a woman and threatening that some day in the future another woman would make things even. "You sit high," she had screamed, "but a woman will bring you down!" He had ordered her removal from the Court and calmly proceeded to the next case. Why think of her now?

He knew the answer to that. This new, heavy, dangerous business which the King had just flung into his lap was concerned with a woman, Catherine the Queen. If she chose to be obdurate . . .

Nonsense, he rebuked himself, superstitious nonsense, but he sighed and knew a moment's envy for Henry who could broach such a subject, say "The means I leave to you," and then go off, light-heartedly, to hunt at Hever.

CHAPTER
THREE

"There is reason to believe that Anne was tenderly attached to her stepmother, and much beloved by her. After a period sufficient to allow for the subsiding of ordinary feelings of displeasure had elapsed, the King paid an unexpected visit to Hever Castle."
Agnes Strickland. *Lives of the Queens of England*

HEVER. OCTOBER 1523

Sir Thomas Boleyn's second wife was a plump, pleasant woman, who left in her proper social sphere would have been competent, a little managing, and as fully-self-assured as a woman of good sense and virtue had a right to be. As the wife of a great man and mistress of several large establishments she suffered painful moments of self-distrust.

It was not that she felt inferior; she came of sound Norfolk yeoman stock and was proud of the fact, but she did often feel misplaced. Sir Thomas had met her, fallen in love with her and married her during one of his visits to Blickling where he had gone to sulk after suffering what he considered to be a slight at Court. He was consoling himself by playing the part of a rather bucolic squire, a shrewd judge of cattle, knowledgeable about crops. He had spoken of retiring from public life and settling down in Blickling. And Blickling she could manage; what was it, after all, but a magnified farm? They'd been married less than a month when an urgent messenger had summoned him to London; and there was the London house, and new dresses, and there was Hever, and there was Sir Thomas saying, "My dear, I realise that nobody can cure a ham as you can, but I cannot have you ruining your hands."

Then there was this business of being stepmother, of its very nature, an awkward, thankless role. If the children had been babies, she would have tended and reared them, and loved them like her own — she was just too old to expect children herself. But even Anne, the youngest, was fifteen, a maid-of-honour in France; Mary and George were fully adult. And Tom's attitude towards them all kept Lady Boleyn constantly conscious of a difference in behaviour between classes. The great put their babies out to nurse and that act was symbolic; there was none of the cosy family life such as she had known. George and his father got along very well, two worldly men, with common interests. Mary her father seemed to dislike, which was understandable; she had disgraced herself twice, even before becoming the King's mistress for a short time; but she was now respectably married; and as Lady Boleyn had once tried to point out, she had lacked a mother's guidance at the time when a girl needed it most. Tom had said, "God knows what she'd have done *with* it! Elizabeth was a trollop."

That did sound rather a dreadful thing for a man to say about his wife who was dead, but there again, great people looked at things differently; and Tom was so truly fond and loving one couldn't help feeling that if he spoke so of his first wife she must have led him a dance.

Lady Bo — George had given her that name, being, as she shrewdly guessed, unwilling to call her "Mother" yet thinking "Lady Boleyn" too formal — was pleased, and ashamed of herself for being pleased, when Anne arrived at Hever, utterly miserable and suffering from the worst cold Lady Bo had ever seen. They'd come from Blickling and the hard-faced, short-spoken woman, Norfolk born by her speech and therefore to be trusted absolutely, had given such a shocking account of the state of the house there, that Lady Bo bitterly blamed herself for not accompanying Tom on his last visit; but he was only planning to stay for a day or two, and wanted her to go from London to Hever.

"She wasn't fit to travel," Emma said, "I could see *that*. But there wasn't a decent aired bed in the house, the chimneys all smoked. And she was very anxious to get to her father."

Anne — and really despite having been in France and then one of the Queen's maids-of-honour, she was nothing more than a child, a sick child — had been put to bed with hot bricks wrapped in flannel, with possets hot with ginger and cinnamon and clove, with linseed plasters on her back and chest, with a cup of honey and vinegar to ease her throat and restore her voice. Lady Bo had been in her element and quite happy until Tom came home from Edenbridge and was told of his

50

daughter's arrival and said, "In God's name, why was she sent home?"

"That I can't tell you. She can't speak, and the woman didn't say, even if she knows. She did say that Anne was anxious to see you. But you're not going into that room yet! Colds like that are as catching as measles. And you know what happened with your last cold; deaf for a fortnight."

"My dear, I must risk the cold or have a sleepless night. Girls aren't sent home from Court in October for nothing. There's something behind this, and I must know what it is."

"Then I will make you a pomander, and you will hold it in front of your face all the time. Wait here."

She ran up the main staircase, holding her skirts high, looked into the room where Anne lay and said, "Take the honey and vinegar, child, because your father wants to talk to you," and then ran down the back stairs into the kitchen, where she took a fresh orange and pressed cloves into its skin and then, as an extra precaution made a little posy of lavender, rosemary and borage. Presenting these to her husband she said, "Ask just what you must and then come away." She added, under her breath, "God shield you!" for he was dear to her, and when his last cold had deafened him he had been extremely worried, saying, "His Grace would never send a deaf man on an errand; one needs sharp ears in his service."

He was with his daughter for about fifteen minutes and when he emerged from the room Lady Bo was certain that despite all her precautions he had taken the cold. He looked ghastly. But that was soon explained. He said,

"They've gone behind my back again, God damn them!"

She knew by this time who "They" were. His enemies. And first and foremost amongst them was the Cardinal. Lady Bo found that very awkward; Thomas Wolsey had always seemed to the middling sort of people a triumph for their kind, and particularly to those of East Anglia, a justification of their claim that there were no people to match the East Anglians.

The son of a butcher and grazier at Ipswich, with nothing but his own wits and merits to aid him, he had climbed to the very top of the tree. Nothing but foreign prejudice had prevented him from being elected Pope. Lady Bo, like all her kind — except a few near heretics who mattered little — had been, until her marriage, very proud of Wolsey. Then she had learned, rather sorrowfully; that he was one of Them, the people who were jealous of her Tom; and he was so mighty, so paramount in importance, that when Tom burst out with his complaint, she said,

"Oh dear, what has he done now?"

"Broken off . . . no prevented her betrothal to Lord Harry Percy. Northumberland's heir."

That was one thing that had come easily to Lady Bo, this nominating of men by their lands; in Norfolk, when you said "Ten Acres" you meant John Bowyer, when you said "Pond Farm" you were speaking of Will Riddle; so she knew instantly what Tom's mention of a county implied.

"That would have been a match indeed — if she liked him."

"From what I gather, she did. Not that that matters. What worries me is *why*. The Percies never concern themselves with affairs. They're not courtiers. They sit there in their stone fortress, guarding the border and think themselves little kings, like Darcy and Dacre. Why, in the name of God, should Harry Percy's choice of wife matter to anyone? Still, no doubt about it; the Cardinal acted; and the blow was aimed at me. But I'm damned if I can see why."

Lady Bo surreptitiously crossed herself; to say I'm damned, or damn me, was to invite disaster.

"How did they prevent it?" she asked. Sir Thomas told her, and she said, as soothingly as she could,

"Perhaps that is the truth of it — that the young man was already betrothed to this Mistress Talbot."

"My dear, she is not plain Mistress Talbot; she is the Earl of Shrewsbury's daughter and a betrothal between two such families would not have been unremarked." He frowned and pulled at his beard. "No, this is a move against me, and may I be — sorry, my dear — blessed if I can see its purpose. But I shall find out. His Grace is on progress, working his way back, he'll be at St Albans or thereabouts. I shall go and see what I can find out."

Lady Bo sighed; she always felt apprehensive when Sir Thomas ventured into a world largely peopled by his enemies. She thought of them as wolves. Lurking, ready to spring. And suppose he had taken Anne's cold and fell ill in a place where there was no one to tend him properly.

"How long will you be away?"

"That depends," Sir Thomas said darkly; then he added fondly, for he loved his wife,

"No longer than I can help, you may depend upon that."

He was back, safe and sound, in less than a week and the moment she saw him she knew that in this latest brush with the wolves he had got the better of them. He looked pleased with himself, almost sleek. And he was unusually willing to discuss the business with her.

"I never bothered you with all this before," he said, "but my mother was a co-heir to property and titles, my claim to which has been long disputed by my cousin Piers Butler. His Grace has decided that the best way to end this old quarrel is to marry Anne to Piers and leave the property in their hands, but to confer the titles — now in abeyance — upon me. That is why he asked the Cardinal to break off this other arrangement; and I must say, I think it was a wise decision. Anne will be well provided for. And you, my dear, will be a Countess."

She was one of the few women in the world whom the prospect dismayed rather than pleased, but like a dutiful wife she concealed her feelings and pretended to share her husband's delight.

"Though I'm well enough as I am," she said. "What I can't understand is why the Cardinal couldn't give his real reason and save you all the worry. And Anne too," she added, remembering some of the events of the last few days. "If he'd just said that he was acting by the King's order . . ."

"Ah, but that is diplomacy. My unbeloved cousin is going to be taken by surprise. If he knew what the King intended he'd run straight out and marry someone else, from spite. He's always regarded himself as heir to the property *and* the titles. So not a word of this to anyone, my dear. We get the wench on her feet again and His Grace will indicate to Butler what he wishes. And all will be well."

It seemed to Lady Bo's simple mind a bad beginning to a marriage.

"I don't like these arranged matches," she said. "Such things should be left to chance, and liking. Nobody said a word or lifted a finger for us, and we . . ."

"Fit like hand and glove. But we were come to years of discretion — at least, I had," he said gallantly. "Now, tell me, how have things been here?"

"She's better now; but for two days and nights I was sorely worried. Every breath creaked, and she raved. Thomas, some of the things she said frightened me. I lay in her chamber myself, not wishing the servants to hear, though that Emma she brought with her seems a very decent sort of woman. But her hatred of the Cardinal, and some of the names she called him! It was horrible. I shouldn't have thought a gently reared girl would have known such words, even."

"But you recognised them," Sir Thomas said, teasingly.

"Of course. Well, on a farm. I mean I wasn't gently reared and never pretended to it. I heard carters and ploughmen and drovers."

"Just as Anne has heard pages and ushers, grooms and ostlers."

"This was different." But she knew that she could never make him understand. "That great dog that came with her and she will have him by her bedside. She's changed his name."

"Quite right too! He had a French name, and we want nothing French in England just now."

"But his new name is Urian."

"Well?"

"That's another name for Satan."

"Then I consider it a good choice. I can see you've had a very trying time. Come and sit on my knee. I saved one piece of news till last. His Grace is coming to visit us. Not part of his progress, just a friendly visit, to hunt a little. No formality, he said, and no ceremony."

"Oh dear, oh dear," Lady Bo said.

She was still saying it, mentally, days later, when the royal visit was almost at an end. It was all very well for Tom to say no formality; the truth was that wherever the King went some formality was bound to follow. And there was this everlasting worry of how to entertain him during the evenings.

She had counted upon Anne for that. Even while she was sitting on Sir Thomas's knee, with the announcement of the visit still in her ears, she had had a comforting thought. Here under the same roof was a young woman, daughter of the house, experienced in the ways of Courts, and reputed to be a musician of more than average ability. Anne would know just when, and to whom to curtsey, who should sit where, and why; and she could provide entertainment. Coming, as she did, direct from Greenwich, she would know the latest songs, and His Grace's personal preferences.

Anne had been no help at all. She said, "I've done with all that," and pleading her cold as an excuse, had refused to make an appearance.

On the afternoon of the last day of the visit, Lady Bo went to make one final plea.

"Your father hasn't noticed, I'm thankful to say, but then I don't think men do notice things about people. I can see that every evening His Grace gets uneasy and fidgety. He seems discontented, somehow. I think it is the music. Lady Forsyth lent us her musician and I hired some as well, and they seem to me to play very sweetly. And that young man who goes everywhere with His Grace — Groom of the Stole, they call him — Norris is his real name, he sang extremely well. But something is lacking. Anne, please, come down this evening and bring your lute and sing some of his own songs. Wouldn't that be a pretty compliment?"

"I can't sing, Lady Bo. You can hear for yourself, I am as hoarse as a rook."

"Oh no. Just a little husky. To tell you the truth, Anne, I think it is rather attractive. You'd be doing me such a favour. I feel so awkward you see. If he'd come to our farm and been hungry or anything, I'd have fed him and done anything I could to please him. But here it is different. He has a *right* to expect Lady Boleyn of Hever Castle to entertain him and I simply haven't any accomplishments at all."

"You have many. And a talent for music isn't an accomplishment, it's like — like blue eyes, you either have them or you haven't."

"And you have — not blue eyes, the talent. Anne, if you'd come down this evening and help entertain him, I'd let you have anything out of my jewel box that you fancied. Or my marten cloak . . ."

"You don't have to bribe me. I'd do it to oblige you, if I could. But truly, I don't feel like singing. And lute music is always a little sad. I might break down and cry."

"You'd feel a great deal better if you did. I sometimes think that God knew women had such hard things to bear that He gave them tears for comfort. I never liked to mention the matter outright," she said, a little shyly, "but I do think it was harsh. You must try not to grieve, though. Sometimes, you know, things that look bad . . . When I was young I lost my heart. He was a sailor and he was drowned, the last voyage before we were to be wed. I thought I'd never fancy anyone else again, and I didn't, for years and years, not until your father stopped at our place that day. And we're very happy. So you see." Her mind came back to the present and its problem. "The one thing I *dread* is that one day he should notice the things I fail at and wish he'd chosen somebody with more airs and graces. That is why this music does so worry me."

"I'll come down," Anne said impulsively. "Not to supper, not into the hall; but on to the gallery, out of sight. And I'll play my best, and sing if I can."

"Oh bless you! Sweet Anne. I can never be grateful enough," Lady Bo cried, and she leaned forward to kiss her stepdaughter, who then dismayed her by leaning against her, shaking like an aspen, and laughing and crying at the same time.

Lady Bo thought — Hysterical! and thus diagnosed an ailment which was to puzzle many people. Had the girl been her own flesh and blood she would have slapped her smartly on the face, but a blow from a stepmother could be ill-taken; so she shook her instead and said, "Stop it, Anne. Stop, dear." Then, under pressure of distress, her mind slipped back a little and she called as though to a restive horse, "Whoa!" At that the sobbing stopped and only the laughter was left, laughter in which Lady Bo joined.

"Country talk will out," she said.

"It was just what was needed," Anne said, wiping her face. "I've been a fool, torturing myself with hope. When Father went to London and when the King came here, I thought they might have put things right after all. But I don't suppose even the King can go against the Cardinal. Or perhaps, angry though he seemed, Father didn't dare mention the matter."

"Oh, but he did," Lady Bo said, rushing to Tom's defence, and then realising with horror that she was on the brink of a breach of confidence. "He did look into it. And . . . and the betrothal with Miss . . . with the other young lady was in order, and must stand."

"That I shall never believe. Still, it's over and done with now. Let's think of other things, plot and plan. If I

sing, my voice being so hoarse, I'd better sing as a boy.
I've done it before, in a Masque."

"And you'll sing some of His Grace's own songs."

"I'll decide that later."

She would not. They were too closely associated with
happy days in Greenwich; for Lady Bo's idea of what
would be a pretty compliment was far from being
original; every Court lady had had it.

"Which page-boy's clothes would you most fancy?"

"The cleanest. The fit doesn't matter. Nobody will
see me closely"

Supper was almost over and Lady Bo was still saying to
herself, Oh dear, oh dear! She'd been wrong about the
music. Anne in her hidden place had played beautifully,
varying the instruments, harp, lute, rebec. And the
tunes had all been merry or sad in a pleasant way, sad
like the scent of cowslips or violets when you were
grown up and picking them for practical purposes, the
cowslips for wine, the violets to crystallise, and to smell
them reminded you of how eagerly you had gathered
them just for themselves, when you were a child.

So far Anne had not sung a word, but that was
understandable; nobody who valued her voice would
sing against so much clatter and the coming and going
behind the screens.

The King still fidgeted and had that faintly
discontented air.

Actually, for a man labouring under a sense of woeful
disappointment, Henry was behaving very well.

He'd come, hotfoot to Hever, eager as a boy, imagining himself to be about to enjoy four days in the company of the fascinating young maid-of-honour whom he had noticed during the summer. When he went out to hunt, she would stand by, admiring the way he sat and controlled his great horse; when he returned, she would admire his trophies. In the evening she would sing and play for him, and he would sing for her, a good deal of tender meaning could be infused into a song. Then he would suggest dancing and she would be his partner.

Nothing had been as he had imagined. On his arrival he had been told that she had suffered a heavy cold, not yet shaken off, and was still confined to her room. Well, he knew a sovereign remedy for colds, and one which couldn't be commanded by just anyone. Fresh fruit. A courier had been sent posting back to Greenwich to bring oranges and melons, grapes and pomegranates from the hot-houses.

She'd be better tomorrow.

But she was not; and now the last evening of his visit was dragging its weary length along, and Henry was trying to hide his boredom and displeasure out of consideration for Lady Boleyn, who did try so hard and was so aware of something not being as it should. Every now and then Henry would see her eye him anxiously and then look at her husband. He had an impulse to pat her on her firm square little shoulder, as one would a pony, and say, "Easy, then. Easy." She had done her very best and it wasn't her fault.

Of Tom Boleyn the King was less sure. He'd been complaisant about Mary — it had paid him to be; it was possible that he realised that in Anne he had a more valuable asset; it was also possible that he was resentful over the short duration of Mary's sway and the fact that she had been dismissed without much reward. Tom Boleyn didn't know how Mary had behaved at the end, the tears — and he hated women to weep — the tirades, the pleadings and the refusal to take anything from him. For whatever reason, Tom always backed up his wife's excuses for Anne, "Very poorly, your Grace, very poorly indeed, I'm sorry to say."

Henry was deeply puzzled by his own attitude towards this heavy cold — assuming it to be genuine. He hated any kind of illness, had a morbid horror of it, and the thought of a woman with a heavy cold should have been utterly repellent; coughing, hawking, blowing the nose, wiping the eyes. Any kind of physical disorder in a woman must, by a simple law of nature, repel a man. You pitied them, you did what you could to relieve them, you pretended, but you kept away. And yet, if he could, with any decency, have been admitted to Anne's sick room, he felt that he would have left his fastidiousness outside the door. He'd have lent — yes, he would — his own handkerchief!

The meal was ending, the top-cloth was being withdrawn, and the clattering dishes had been collected. On the stiff starched, lace-inset undercloth only the wine flagons and glasses, the dishes of fruit and nuts remained. The hall was suddenly quiet.

Into the quiet broke a voice, sexless; the voice of a boy just broken; the voice of a girl not yet fully recovered from a cold. Henry stiffened and looked towards the gallery, whence the voice came. He could see nothing; behind the heavy carving it was in darkness.

"Your Grace, ladies and gentlemen all, if it be your pleasure I will now sing for you."

Henry looked questioningly at his hostess who gave him one of her anxious, deprecating half-smiles, and then looked at her husband. Henry glanced at him too. Sir Thomas was busy, probing a walnut. Poor dear, he thought, this is all a sad trial to her. It hurt him to see her look so anxious. Yet if he had stepped in and said he would arrange the entertainment she would take it as a criticism of her efforts, and even for the King's approval he would not risk hurting her feelings. And however badly this half-fledged boy in the gallery performed, it would just have to be borne.

Anne began with a merry ballad, well known to Lady Bo and to anyone else who had been near a field at harvest time, for on account of its rhythm it was very popular with reapers. It was, like most ballads, a little bawdy, not quite what a young lady should sing, but that didn't matter this evening, because no one knew that it was Anne singing. What did matter was that the King was pleased. At its end he shouted in a voice accustomed to issuing orders in spacious places."

"Come down, boy! And be rewarded."

Oh dear, oh dear, Lady Bo thought. Now they would know. Tom would learn that she had entered into a plot without telling him, and the King would know that Anne's cold had just been an excuse, and everyone would know that those saucy insinuating words had been sung by a young girl. Oh dear, oh dear.

The voice from the gallery said,

"I thank your Grace, but I am already rewarded — by your attention."

Now *would* a page-boy have said that?

The music began again, and then the singing. This time a sad song.

"When we two are parted, all the world is grey,
Hope and joy and comfort, go with you away.
Away, alas, with you away.

Not a flower will blossom, not a bird will sing,
Lacking that sweet summer you alone can bring.
You, alas, alone can bring.

When we two are parted, all my heart is numb.
And it will not waken, till again you come.
Alas, alas, you cannot come.

More than seas divide us, worse than death doth sever,
I am now alone, love, alone, my love, forever.
Alas, alone forever."

The lute made its plaintive, dying outcry and was silent. Lady Bo did not look at the King, or at her husband; their approval no longer mattered. She looked down to hide the tears that stung her eyes. It was more than twenty years since she had lost her Johnny, and life had mended itself, and she loved Tom; but the song affected her because it so exactly recalled how she had felt when the news came. Alone forever.

In the hall there was a perceptible silence. The song was a love song and the audience was largely composed of people to whom romantic love meant little or nothing. Possibly the most genuinely romantically minded person in the hall was the King himself, and even he had been furious when his sister Mary had made a love match with Charles Brandon and thus deprived England of a useful pawn in the diplomatic game. But to the English love songs were new; until lately there had been solemn church music, merry marching tunes to keep weary men in step, and ballads; so purely sentimental songs were making their first impact upon people who, through lack of immunity, were particularly vulnerable. Lady Bo was far from being the only person with moist eyes. Tomorrow the men who were blinking and the women who were dabbing their lower lids would unhesitatingly arrange advantageous marriages, if they could, for themselves, or for their children, and give no thought to any heart-break involved; but for the moment they were touched, and paid the singer the compliment of silence before the outbreak of applause.

Henry shouted through the noise,

"A sweet song, well sung. Come out and show yourself."

For answer Anne plunged straight into a ditty with which hired performers often ended.

"Gentles all, within this hall, we wish you now
     goodnight,
If aught that we have here performed, hath pleased
     you, 'tis your right.

Our Lord the King, past everything, we wish you joy
     in store,
We wish you all you wish yourself. What could we
     wish you more?

Ladies, we hope your lovely eyes may evermore stay
     bright,
And never see a worser scene than they have done
     tonight.

Nobles and knights, to our good nights, we add a
     hearty greeting
And pray that all goes well with you, until our nextest
     meeting.

May we remind your hearts so kind, that though it
     gives us pleasure,
To sing for you, we like to eat, and corn is sold by
     measure?

So give, we pray, not charity, but what you think our
     due.
Thus gentles all, within this hall, we take our leave of
     you."

The lute twanged its final flourish; there was the sound of light footsteps, and then the slam of a door.

Henry said, "Did I not *know* otherwise, I'd have said that was your daughter, Tom," and waited for Sir Thomas to laugh, reveal the trick and congratulate him upon his perspicacity. But Thomas Boleyn's face showed nothing except surprise.

"My daughter? But as your Grace knows, she's in bed with a cold, and hoarse as a crow"

Henry looked at Lady Boleyn who blushed and said too quickly, too eagerly,

"It was a page-boy, your Grace. Very young, very shy. I had great difficulty in persuading him to sing at all." The firmness with which she brought out the last words merely emphasised the flutteriness of the others.

For a second Henry hesitated. He was King. He had only to say that he'd like a closer look at this page-boy who sang so well. That'd teach them to play tricks on him! On the other hand it was rather an engaging trick, and it was hers, he'd warrant. She had a gay and lively look. Much as he longed to see her he wouldn't spoil her little masquerade. So he said,

"I heard your daughter sing and play, once, at Greenwich; the boy's voice and his handling of the lute reminded me. Perhaps she schooled him. And whoever he is, he went off unpaid, after singing so sweetly. Give him this, with my thanks."

With one of the great royally generous gestures in which he so delighted he pulled from his little finger a ruby ring, the red stone the size of a thumbnail and all set around with diamonds. Lady Bo eyed it with apprehension; no woman could possibly look at it and not wish to wear it; so Anne would wear it and Tom would know that she had connived, behind his back!

"Your Grace, it is much too fine a gift. I will see to it that the boy is rewarded — adequately."

Sir Thomas looked at the ring with green jealousy and fury. Typical! Throw to some scruffy little page-boy a ring worth a small fortune, grudge to a faithful servant the title he longed for, the title to which he had a right. All through this visit he had waited for the King to refer to the promise he had made at St Albans.

Henry said, a little too gently, "Lady Boleyn, I asked you to give this trinket to the singer."

The girl would understand, he thought; just as he had understood the burden of her songs. The saucy ballad had informed him that she was no prude. The love song and the passion she had put into it had said — Look how I can love. The professional entertainers' song at the end had been part of the joke, and the subtle changes in it had been meant for his ear alone. "Joy in store," she had wished him. And he would have joy, for he was in love again. Wonderful, marvellous. She'd receive the ring and know that he understood; and he'd come back, and when he did . . .

He began immediately to prepare for that next visit, overwhelming his host and hostess with thanks and praise. Seldom, if ever, he said, had he received such hospitality; and nowhere in the world was there such ham as at Hever.

Lady Bo gave her husband a look which said — There you are! That was a ham that I cured myself before you became concerned about the state of my hands! And it said, in true Norfolk fashion — All these elaborate messed-about dishes, made to look like something other than what they are, and the King, the King himself singled out my ham!

But the ring weighed heavy in her hand. Before she slept she must make a clean breast of it to Tom. Never mind her promise to Anne. Husbands and wives should have no secrets from one another. In law they were regarded as one person; in the rubric they were called "one flesh", and so they were, twice a week at least, when Tom was home, in the big tester bed.

So, in the bed, she told Tom everything, and he said, "Maybe it was as well. She isn't pretty, but she is lively and taking and we don't want Mary's tale over again. I'm sick and tired of the notion that I rose to favour, not of my own merit, but on my daughter's supine body. Untrue. Unfair. I was of sufficient importance to be one of those chosen to carry the canopy at the christening of the Princess Mary, years before our Mary caught the King's eye. And I am still hoping for my rightful titles. I don't want my enemies to say that I bought *that* with a virgin sacrifice."

"The things you say!" said Lady Bo, so greatly relieved by the way he had taken her confession that she felt she could afford to be a little admonitory. Even now, even in the big bed . . .

CHAPTER
FOUR

"But Mary was the fairest, the most delicately featured, and the most feminine of the two."
Agnes Strickland. *Lives of the Queens of England*

". . . his cast-off mistress. Mary Boleyn."
Garrett Mattingley. *The Life of Catherine of Aragon*

BLICKLING HALL. JANUARY 7th, 1524

Christmas that year had been spent at Blickling, to Lady Bo's extreme delight. Ever since Anne had described the state of the house there, her housewifely fingers had itched to get busy. Also she liked the idea of spending the merriest festival of the year in her own countryside, where the voices, even of the gentry, had a homely, familiar sound.

It had promised to be, as Christmas should be, a family affair, for George was to be in Norfolk too. His Grace had half-promised him the manor of Grimston, and he was anxious to look it over. Lady Bo, in those busy days between their own arrival and Christmas Eve when George was expected, had acted upon a piece of information which Sir Thomas had once let fall in a fit of anger, and prepared two bed-chambers, one for

70

George and one for Jane, his wife. They were unhappily married and no longer shared a bed. Lady Bo quite liked her stepdaughter-in-law, who always took pains to be civil to her, and who was so much more serious a person than George. George was frivolous and had a way of making mock of so many things and so many people that Lady Bo never felt quite at ease with him. However, Anne had cheered up considerably at the prospect of having George for company and Christmas was, in any case, a light-hearted season.

It had given everybody a surprise, almost a shock, when George arrived bringing with him, not Jane, but his sister Mary.

A daughter of the family had come home to spend Christmas and no one was pleased to see her.

Lady Bo always suffered a conflict of emotion when in Mary's company; she found it impossible not to be censorious; and equally impossible not to feel straight-laced, countrified, old-fashioned and unkind for being censorious. There were the facts; Mary had established for herself a reputation for easy virtue even when she was in France; then she had been the King's mistress; but the past was the past, and she was now respectably married, and she had, for all her elegance, such a sweet, almost simple way with her. Sometimes Lady Bo wondered whether Tom were not right in saying that Mary was half-witted. You couldn't really look at her and believe that her wicked behaviour had been deliberate. Lady Bo had always imagined that bad women, kept women, women who became men's mistresses were hard-eyed, cynical, brash.

Sir Thomas regarded his elder daughter with disfavour for a number of reasons. It angered him, as it would have angered any able and ambitious man, to know that in the eyes of the world a good deal of his success was due to a pretty daughter's frailty. It simply was not true, as he often said, with oaths. Hadn't he, he would demand, been one of those chosen to carry the canopy over the Princess Mary when she was christened; wasn't that a sign of high favour, and back in 1516 before the King ever looked at Mary? That he had bought his way by being complaisant was just another of the damnable lies put about by his enemies. At the same time it angered him to think that Mary had made so little of the vast opportunities she had been offered. For a little while — not long, but long enough — she had held the King's heart in her hand; and what had she got out of it? Nothing. Not a house, not an acre of land, not a penny of money. All that shame and gossip and nothing to show for it. Lesser men's mistresses went flaunting away with damned great manors, with monopolies in wool or wine, with pensions. Mary, after all the scandal, had got a husband, a plain Mr Carey who was one of the gentlemen of the King's bed-chamber, and would never be anything more. It was the *waste* that most irked Sir Thomas's thrifty mind. Fair-haired, blue-eyed, with a pink and white skin unflawed by the pox, and a voluptuous figure, what couldn't she have made of herself? No spirit, that was her trouble.

Anne's feelings towards her sister were more complicated than Lady Bo's, more vehement than Sir

Thomas's. In the far distant past she had adored Mary, looking up to her as elder, more worldly wise, more elegant and more beautiful; as far as possible, in her very early days she had modelled herself upon Mary, regretting equally that she lacked her looks, and that she could never match her placid good nature. And then, just when she herself had reached the most vulnerable, fastidious, idealistic and intolerant age of thirteen, she had learned the truth about Mary. And the truth was that not only had she just become the King's mistress, but she had, while in France, gained a bad reputation, memories of which this most recent scandal revived. Mary who always looked so fresh, so clean, so pure, Mary whom she had loved.

Mary, who during her own time in France had suffered from her father's extreme parsimony and never had any money for clothes, and now remembered, in her new prosperity, her little sister, sent across to Paris a parcel of clothing, all of rich material, hardly worn, and still smelling deliciously of the scented sachets which Mary always hung or laid amongst her clothes. The young Anne had at the sight and scent of them suffered a feeling of such revulsion that she was nauseated. A few hours of work — and she was clever with her needle — would have made them fit her more slender figure, and there was a long hooded cloak, lined with fur, and some stockings and gloves which needed no alteration at all; but she had given everything away. And although she was as handy with a pen as with a needle she had written no letter of thanks. And when, not long after, the news had seeped through that Mary had married William Carey, she had not written to wish her well. And Mary had understood.

Back in London, during all her time in Catherine's service Anne had dreaded coming face to face with her sister; it had never happened; and to Anne Mary had remained just a fallen idol and a horrid warning, a warning which had always sounded whenever Harry Percy had been a little too ardent.

Always that small, poisonous thought — Just because my sister Mary . . . At the same time being in love brought a new understanding and softened the fierce intolerance of the just-nubile. Having suffered the onset of temptation herself Anne began to see that Mary, with no example of a sister's fall to warn her, had found it easy to succumb. Even that measure of understanding did not, however, make her wish to see Mary again; as adorer and adored they had come to an end, and any other relationship would be sad.

Yet, brought face to face with Mary, against the background of the old, loved home, it was impossible to believe that she had been anything but silly and too easily persuaded; in appearance, in manner, she had scarcely changed at all; she still looked pretty, fresh and pure; she was still gentle and softly spoken; she still had no defence against the taunts which Sir Thomas launched twenty times a day in some form or another.

He professed himself surprised that she should come visiting without her husband.

"George I can understand, his domestic ties gall him, but yours, my dear, was a love match, or so I was given to understand."

He commented upon her obviously well-worn gowns. Anne had noticed them, too.

"It is curious," he said, addressing nobody in particular, "how rapidly married women become dowdy. A hanging up of weapons on the wall, I suppose."

His obsession with titles obtruded itself; he would have thought, he said, that the King would have knighted William by this time. And he mentioned innumerable instances of women, less favoured than Mary, who had married well, gaining either status or wealth.

Mary bore it all, answering when she could, otherwise remaining silent; she explained that George had suggested her making the visit because William was to be on duty all through the Christmas season; she admitted that she had had few new clothes since her marriage, "but I didn't look for them; I knew that William was not rich." Over the matter of William's knighthood she merely looked unhappy.

Sir Thomas's open antagonism had the effect of welding his children into the close, self-supporting group that they had been in their childhood, after the death of their mother. George, forced on two occasions to go to Mary's defence, said two things that made matters much worse. A knighthood, he said, no longer meant so very much — there was Thomas Wyatt, their cousin, a prime favourite with the King and still plain Mr; and there was Harry Norris who had been knighted and was still called Mr as often as not. Sir Thomas, though discontented with his own title, valued it and did not welcome such remarks. George's second attempt to help Mary was even more unfortunate; he hit his father's most sensitive spot by saying, "After all, but for her, we shouldn't be where we are . . ." Sir Thomas repudiated that suggestion hotly, and mentioned all the favours he had been shown, all the missions with which he had been entrusted, "before Mary had sense enough to blow her own nose". He reminded George that he had carried the Princess Mary's canopy, and asked him to remember to whom he was speaking. George then became prey to a conflict of feelings; he was fond of Mary, he was sorry for her, he wanted to be loyal, but there was expediency to be considered. He and his father were closely associated in several enterprises, were likely any day to be sent together on some business of the King's; a quarrel would be most inadvisable. So the next time Sir Thomas eased his spleen by baiting Mary there was no one to support her except Anne. The subject was, once more, Mary's ill-advised and unprofitable marriage, her lack of status, her shabby dress.

"But, Father, if she loved William she couldn't have married anyone else. And if you mind so much how she looks, buy her a new gown and I'll wear what I have for years and years, until . . ."

Almost gleefully, Sir Thomas swung round to attack his youngest daughter.

"You'll do that in any case, my young madam. I thought you were settled. You could have been at Court, costing me nothing, but you must go and get yourself entangled with a man already betrothed. And let me not hear any more bleatings about love. You've only to look at her, to see where that leads. Or look at yourself for that matter. I must say my daughters do me fine credit; one with a bad name married to a pauper, the other thrown back on my hands, like a sheep with the foot-rot."

He was wreaking upon them his anger with circumstances. Nothing had come of all that the King had so blithely promised in October; the girl's marriage to Piers Butler had never been mentioned again, the titles were still in dispute. When he thought how happily he had ridden back to Hever, carrying with him those promises, that delicious hint of intrigue against Butler, he felt quite sick with disappointment.

Mary wilted under the combination of bad name and pauper in a single sentence, but Anne stood her ground and said in a meditative way.

"I don't see why you should so decry love, Father. I don't know about our mother, but you love Lady Bo and you married her."

She had hit her father in his second most vulnerable spot. Sensible, cool-headed, calculating man who had pulled himself out of the mere middle class by his first marriage, what had happened to him one late summer afternoon in Norfolk? A lapse, a total contradiction of all that had so far governed his actions. And it had brought him happiness, he'd never for a moment regretted it. But it was not to be mentioned in the same breath as easy, bed-bound goings on of his elder daughter, or the silly vapouring ideas of his younger —

which might, at some crucial moment in the future, prove awkward.

He said furiously,

"Keep her name out of this, if you please. It's a different thing altogether. I pleased myself. When you're my age and have made as much out of as little, and with no help or encouragement from your family, you'll be entitled to do the same. Go away, both of you!"

Half-way up the stairs Anne said,

"Come to my room. There'll be a good fire there. Emma sees to that."

The invitation was a sign of total acceptance. Anne's feeling of revulsion towards her sister had vanished within an hour; Sir Thomas's behaviour had resurrected the old loyalties; but the years of silence, the unacknowledged gift, the good wishes withheld had made a barrier between their new relationship and the former close intimacy. That barrier had now fallen, and as they entered Anne's warm room, she said,

"It hurts me to hear him taunt you so. Why don't you answer him back? You're not dependent on him any more."

"It'd only worsen matters," Mary said, holding her hands to the fire. "And you mustn't quarrel with him on my account — though it was sweet of you to take up for me, just now. I had no notion that he would still be so . . . spiteful. In fact," she gave a little rueful laugh, "I actually came with the intention of asking him to lend me ten pounds."

"Ten pounds! That is a great deal of money."

"I know."

"He never would."

"I know. I asked George first, but you know George; he's in worse case than I am, though not so shabby. He said that to give me ten pounds in cash he'd either have to sell something, or borrow. But he was kind and said that if he gets Grimston he'd give me what I wanted immediately, but that would be too late; William will have found out before then."

"Found what out?"

"That I've been playing cards with money he gave me for other purposes. You see, it wasn't enough. William is not a pauper, as Father says, nor is he miserly." She raised her beautiful eyes and gave Anne a disarming smile, "I'm a bad manager and no matter how often I add up reckonings I never get the same answer twice. But now and then I am lucky with cards, so I hoped . . . But it was just the other way."

She spread her hands helplessly and Anne had a strong feeling that the people with whom she had played cards had cheated, or inveigled her into playing some game with whose rules she was not familiar. Mary's looks and manner, everything about her, Anne thought shrewdly, evoked in all ordinary people either the desire to protect or the intention to exploit.

Hers was to protect. She said,

"I have something. I don't know its worth, but it would help. And you're welcome to it; it's of no use to me whatsoever."

"I can't take anything from you, darling. You heard what Father said just now. No new dress for years and years . . ."

But Anne had turned and gone to the little leather-covered box which held her few worthless trinkets and the King's ring. Holding it in her hand she came back to Mary and pressed it into her hand and closed her fingers over it.

Mary thought — her ring, her poor little scrap of silver and amber, worth ten shillings at the very most; and the facile tears sprang. Without looking at what was in her hand she put both arms around her sister and kissed her, a warm, wet, tear-flavoured, sachet-scented kiss,

"Thank you, dear Anne. Dear Anne. But I couldn't possibly deprive you of . . ."

"You haven't even looked at it," Anne said.

Mary brought her hand up and opened it, and the ring lay there, the ruby as big and as red as a raspberry, the diamonds winking their rainbow colours, the solid, richly chased gold setting gleaming.

She'd seen that ring a hundred times; she knew it so well that looking at it she could see the hand, surprisingly shapely and delicate-looking for so large a man, whose little finger it had adorned.

Anne had been watching Mary's face, joyfully expectant of an expression of astonishment and delight, for who would have dreamed that she, poor Anne Boleyn, had such a gift to give? But Mary's face blanched and shrivelled, in her eyes the pupils widened until they looked as black as Anne's own; her expression indicated a dismay, verging upon horror.

"Mary!"

"Where," Mary asked, raising her hand a little, "where did you get *this?*"

"I earned it, quite honestly. Well, almost. By a trick really. You see . . ."

"Henry gave you this?" For the first time in her life Mary Boleyn cut in upon another person's speech.

"Not me; a page-boy . . ." Anne hastened to tell the whole story, wondering as she spoke why Mary should look so shocked. So ill. Surely she didn't think . . . or was it jealousy?

At the end of the story, Mary said,

"But he knew who was singing. He must have known. He is generous when it suits him to be, and he can be impulsive, but even *he* wouldn't have sent this to a page-boy, however pleasingly he had sung."

"He did. Ask Lady Bo if you don't believe me. She tried to bribe me to sing and I wish now I'd taken something from her and then you could have had it as well as the ring."

Mary, whom everyone regarded as a fool, heard in those words the ring of clear innocence. And innocence must be guarded.

"Of course I believe you. Has he been back?"

"No."

"He'll come, with the better weather and the harder roads. Anne, listen! When he does, be firm; have nothing to do with him. Dearest, forget everything else; believe this; if I were now on my death bed and had only enough breath to say a few words, these are what I would say. Don't have anything to do with him. I know. I can tell you. He's dangerous. There's something," she paused, hampered by her inborn inability to express herself in words, "something *twisted* about him. Half of him is just a simple, lighthearted boy, greedy and selfish as boys are, but there's another side, dark and ugly, like the Devil. He wants to be loved, he really does want to be loved, but anyone who loves him he is bound to despise. It's like . . ." she paused again. "In the lists, it is the same; he always wants to win; but if an opponent lets him win, he despises him for evermore; if an opponent puts up a fight and beats him, then he hates him for evermore. I do know what I'm talking about; I could give you a hundred examples. Only I'm so bad at explaining things. Take the Cardinal," she was so intent upon her analysis that she did not notice Anne's sudden stiffening. "Henry loves him, calls him his True Thomas, heaps favours on him, and for one simple reason, only, he *knows* that Wolsey in his heart esteems the Pope more. Henry would deny that and so would his True Thomas, but they both know it, and it holds a kind of balance. Women can't do that. He is so handsome and so charming, and then . . . Oh I know that Father thinks I managed badly not to have got something out of the loss of my good name; but in the beginning it would have seemed like selling what I was only too anxious to give, and at the end . . ." She gave a small, convulsive shiver. "I couldn't *ask*," she said.

"You loved him, Mary. I think you still do."

The colour which had fled from Mary's face flowed back.

"Don't think," she said hastily, "that that is why I spoke as I did. He's finished with me, long since; and what he does is no business of mine. But I wouldn't wish to see any girl, least of all you, dearest Anne . . ." She left the sentence unfinished, and then, after a second said, very definitely, "He's cruel. Not always. Not often. But it is there. I do beg you, keep out of his way. If you can, though of course, with Father . . . That is what is so unjust; he speaks now as though I had disgraced him, but at the time he was delighted. And if it happened again . . . Oh, Anne, isn't there anyone you could marry, quickly?"

Anne had listened to the admonition, but hardly heeded it, since it seemed to deal with a situation which existed only in Mary's mind. What did interest her deeply was that Mary was still in love with the King, and yet had insisted, against her father's counsel, on marrying William Carey.

She said, "No one has asked for me, yet. And if someone did I think I should be more vexed than pleased. You see," she coloured a little, "I've been . . . I am . . . in love, too."

"Harry Percy?"

Anne nodded.

"I was sorry when I heard," Mary said. Then she went on, in a more worldly wise manner, "Still, you mustn't spend your life grieving over that. One falls out of love, as well as in."

"Yet you just admitted that you still love the King."

"That didn't prevent me from marrying William, and being very fond of him. And being happy. Besides, there is a difference. I have lived with Henry and he isn't like any other man. Yours was just a romantic, boy-and-girl affair."

"Like yours, in France, when you were my age!"

"Oh don't!" Mary cried. "When you're angry you sound just like Father. I didn't mean to annoy you. I was trying to encourage you. This," she held up the ring and the firelight caught the great ruby which blinked at them balefully, "bodes no good. I *know*. And you should marry anyone, darling, anyone who is kind and decent and who could keep you. There're worse things in the world than wearing the same gown three years running. He'd hurt you far more than he hurt me, and that was bad enough. You're not so . . . pliant. Or so experienced. In fact . . . I'd sooner see you in a convent."

"Me?"

"You'd be safe. And you're so clever; you'd be an Abbess. Nunneries are the only places where women really count for anything. Had you never thought of that? I have, often. Everywhere else in the world it's what your father is, or what your husband is. I thought about it the other night, at supper; all the women seated according to their husband's ranks, and mine a low place; and I thought if I had been a nun, home for Christmas from Ramsey, I should have been near the top of the table, and treated with great respect."

Anne forgot that a moment earlier Mary had annoyed her, and only thought, with a pang of pity —

She *minds!* She forfeited all claim to respect long ago, and didn't make the grand marriage which would have thrown a cloak over the past, and she pretends not to care, but she does. Anyone who wishes she were a nun must be in a low state of mind indeed.

She said,

"Such respect has its price. I should think that unless you had a real vocation it would be unbearable. Always the same dull clothes, only sacred music, a life governed by bells, prayers at midnight and no pets, nothing of one's own. I think you would have to be very pious to bear so bleak a life."

"The rules aren't always kept. I know at least one nunnery where they lead gay lives. The Abbess is said to have had two children."

"I should dislike that kind of establishment just as much; or even more."

Mary said mildly, "It was only a suggestion. I'm just so afraid that if when Spring comes you are still at home, he'll come. He'll flatter you and charm you and you'll be fascinated. And then . . . then suddenly it is all over. The things you did and said, that used to please so much, no longer please. And then, for a long time, maybe forever, life is like . . . like a banqueting hall next morning, early, in winter, all cold and grey."

"Is that how life seems to you, Mary?"

"Sometimes. And I would hate it to happen to you."

"About that you need not worry. It has happened already. But I don't want to talk about it. And I think you attach too much importance to the ring. I did sing very well; and he had been royally entertained; I think he just snatched off the first thing that came handy. He has plenty of others. Do you think you could sell it for ten pounds?"

"I don't think I could even try," Mary said, laying the ring on a table. "It was *his* and I should feel . . ."

Anne entertained three thoughts almost simultaneously. The first was that Mary was incurably sentimental; the second was that she herself might well feel the same way if confronted with something that had belonged to Harry Percy: and the third was that she would give the ring to George and ask him to dispose of it and give the money to Mary, he'd certainly strike a better bargain.

"You will remember all that I have said?" Mary asked, earnestly.

"If I ever need to," Anne said.

CHAPTER
FIVE

"He in the end fell to win her by treaty of marriage, and in his talk on that matter took from her a ring, which he ever wore upon his little finger."
Sir Thomas Wyatt

HEVER. JUNE 1524

By mid-summer of 1524 Lady Bo had ceased to be shy in the King's presence, or worried about the standard of her hospitality. She had a graver cause for concern. Henry had paid, in all, four visits and in the intervals he had sent letters and valuable presents. Lady Bo had no doubt at all that his object was to seduce Anne, and her sturdy, yeoman-class standard of respectability was outraged by the very thought. Mary had been bad enough, but that was in the past, when the family had been drifting without a feminine hand at the helm. If it happened now, under her eye, under her roof, she would be ashamed forever.

Talking to Annie was useless; she had tried it. Anne had said, "I never ask him to come." And that was true. It was true, also, that she never — at least never in public — seemed to give him any encouragement at all. She adopted a stiff, grand manner which aged her by several years; she never looked at him with any expression but that of grave attention when he addressed her directly; she never matched his wit — which Lady Bo knew she was well able to do if she chose; and she always had to be persuaded, almost compelled, to play for him.

But Lady Bo had an uncomfortable feeling that this demure, touch-me-not manner was only a façade. There was a good deal more in Anne than met the eye. And if, when they were alone, she behaved as she did in public why, why, why did he persist in paying her attentions?

On this particular evening, having seen the two of them vanish between the high dark walls of the Yew Walk, Lady Bo turned to her husband, and in a voice she did not often use, sharp, a little shrill, demanded,

"And where is all this going to end? Tell me that!"

"My dear, I might as well ask you."

"You should put a stop to it. You're her father. You once said yourself that you didn't want her to go the way Mary went. You should do something!"

"And what would you propose? Am I to look my sovereign lord in the eye, and say — Sire, you are not welcome in my home; I suspect you of having designs upon my daughter? Are you really anxious to see me clapped into the Tower on some trumped up charge or other?"

"Of course not. What a question! But there must be some other way. She should be married."

"I seem to remember your professing a distaste for arranged marriages. And have you seen her cast a single favourable glance on any man, all these months? The

Butler match has never been mentioned again, and it is not for me to re-open the subject. And nothing has been done about those titles. Sometimes, when my gout keeps me awake in the night I wonder whether the King isn't playing a crafty game with me. Perhaps he thinks that I should put some pressure on the girl; but I shan't, after the shabby way he treated Mary. Besides, I think the next move should be his. Also, I doubt whether, even if I wished, I could persuade her against her will. I don't think His Grace yet realises what kind of cat he has by the tail."

"And what does that mean? You know, Tom, I never could understand parables."

Sir Thomas looked round cautiously.

"I mean, my dear — and I wouldn't for the life of me breathe a word of this to anyone but you — I shouldn't be surprised if the wench isn't prepared to hold out until he's on his knees offering a wedding ring in one hand and a crown in the other."

"Tom!" For a moment she could say no more; the enormity of the suggestion took her breath away. When she regained it, she said, "But that is mad. Her Grace is alive and in better health than ever, they say, now that her child-bearing days are done."

"I have heard otherwise. There's talk of dropsy. In a woman hard on forty, that could be . . ."

"Tom! That is wicked talk. Waiting for dead women's shoes! Oh dear, now I don't know what to think." For which was worse, to let yourself be seduced, or to set out for some objective that could only be reached over a dead body?

"Whatever we think, whatever we do makes no difference. That I know from hard experience. Anne is the only one of my children to take after her mother." He seldom thought of his dead wife these days and mentioned her even more rarely. "Not in looks. Mary has her looks, watered down, and George has her ability, but Anne has her . . . her . . ." Even his facile tongue could not find the right word; he never had been able to. It was a quality which in a wife could be, had been, exasperating in the extreme, but in a daughter who had a King suing for her favours, might be of incalculable value. "All or nothing, that's their way. And if it turns out to be nothing, then they laugh."

"I'd grown fond of Anne," Lady Bo said, rather miserably, her mind still upon the two alternatives. "And at least," she added more cheerfully, "she isn't greedy or grasping. His presents don't mean much. That necklace he sent her — the one with the great B for a pendant — she wanted to give me that. B for Bo, she said; and laughed."

Sir Thomas, accustomed to being sent on diplomatic missions where in a chance talk the mere inflection of a word might mean a great deal to a sharp ear, narrowed his eyes. B was for Bo, for Boleyn, therefore it was not for Anne because she intended . . . But how? Was this rumour of the Queen's dropsy more well founded than most rumours? Was she more ill than anyone, save Henry, knew? Was she in fact very ill, and the fact being kept secret for political reasons?

"I'd give a good deal to be able to hear one of their conversations when they are alone together," he said.

"You can't. They use the seat by the sun-dial and the hedge is so wide and high, you can't hear a word. I tried, last time he was here." She realised that she had confessed to eavesdropping and said, "Oh dear," and put her hand to her mouth and turned very red in the face. Blushing, she looked like a sweet rosy apple. Sir Thomas laughed,

"I shall have to inquire whether the Cardinal has a vacancy for a most unsuspicious-looking little spy," he said. "Come and sit on my knee!"

Trapped in the high hedges of the rectangle in which the Yew Walk ended, the day's heat still lingered. The sun-dial, in shadow now, no longer told the time, but offered only the engraved admonition, "Watch Well The Hours." The words irked Henry every time he saw them. God knew, he was well enough aware of the passage of time. A year this very month since he had first seen her, a new face amongst those of Catherine's ladies. Just one glimpse. Slim and dark and with some indescribable grace which made mere prettiness seem cheap and vulgar. It was as though, hunting red deer in Windsor forest, he'd caught sight of some mythical creature like the unicorn.

Nose down, a hound on a trail, he had pursued his inquiries; learned her name, learned that she was almost betrothed to Harry Percy; put a stop to that; thrown her father the promise of the Butler betrothal; waited for the wounded girlish heart to forget. And then he had gone through all the routine of seduction; the compliments, the gifts, the looks of longing and of lechery, and all he had so far received was a firm, unequivocal "no", sweetly spoken, but in a way that showed that she meant what she said. Once — on the visit before this — he had lost his temper and roared out that it would be a long time before he came riding this way again. She had replied to that with the slightest, only just perceptible shrug of a shoulder. No words could have conveyed as eloquently her indifference as to whether he came or not. He'd carried his anger back with him to London and deliberately cherished it for a day or two; then it had faded and he'd begun to ask himself what right had he to be angry because she was chaste. Wasn't modesty a virtue in a girl? So he'd sat down and written a slavish, loving letter, saying that to please her was his one aim, and signing himself her servant. And at the first possible opportunity he had come himself. And here he was.

He frowned at the sun-dial and passed on to the stone seat.

"We'll sit here," he said, and then added hastily, "if it pleases you." He was learning; and one thing he had learned was that he must take nothing for granted, not even her assent to his choice of a place to sit. She sat down, spreading her skirts wide, so that in order not to crush them and bring a rebuke upon himself, he was obliged to keep his distance. He had always been spoilt and flattered and treated with exaggerated respect and to be in awe of someone was a new experience; not entirely agreeable, but with a certain titillation.

He made a few remarks of no importance and then mentioned once more his great desire that she should return to Court.

"I haven't changed my mind," she said.

"Why won't you? You never give me a reason."

"You know it. Those who can't afford a loaf are fools to stand by the bake-house door."

He thought that over and decided that it was the most promising thing she had yet said to him. It sounded as though she wanted to give in, and was afraid that subject to his company for long enough she would give in.

"But we can afford the loaf. If only you would come to London, I would so arrange it that you had your own apartments. I could be with you every night."

"My father is not over generous; I shall have a small dowry, but part of what I take my husband will be my virginity. I do not intend to be your mistress."

"Then you don't love me!"

She intended to say, "I never pretended to do so." But when she spoke she said.

"How can you know? You've never tried me."

And there it was — it had happened again. As though some other woman had taken possession of her. That seemed the only possible explanation of the inconsistency of her behaviour. She'd spend an hour behaving coolly and prudently, and then in half a minute undo the hour's work by some remark of a frivolous nature, faintly tinged with lasciviousness to which he instantly and extravagantly responded. He now reached out and snatched at her hand.

"Whether you love me or not, I love you, sweetheart. Come to London and let me show my love. Is it the thought of scandal that deters you? I can impose my will, you know; and I shall make it abundantly clear that I expect everyone to honour and respect you as I do."

"And how long would that last? No man hunts the hare he has caught."

"I shall love you forever."

"You think so now. Men tire of their wives." A mischievous note came into her voice. "But a wife still has rights. A mistress can be thrown away like an old shoe."

"You're thinking of Mary."

"Who wouldn't?"

"But I swear to you, there's no likeness between the two cases, no more likeness than there is between you and her. She was . . ." he was about to say, "the plaything of an hour", but one never knew; some sisters were fond of one another; "very sweet," he said, "and I was fond of her; but I was not devoured by love, as I am for you. Every man by the time he reaches my age, has had his passing fancies and indulged them if he could. But a love like this comes only once in a lifetime. I tell you I see no woman but you; I think of no other. I live like a monk. Soliman the Great could parade his harem before me, half naked, and I should know no flicker of desire. Whereas the sound of your voice in another room, or your step on the stair, even the thought of you . . . On all my visits here I doubt if I've slept more than an hour at a stretch, knowing you so near, yet so unattainable. I ache with longing . . ."

She too had had her wakeful nights, thinking of Harry Percy and Mary Talbot together in a bed.

"Time will cure it," she said, and gave him a sad little smile. "I think it would be better if you stayed away. We have no future. Your wife I cannot be, because you are married already; and your mistress I will not be."

She had said much the same thing last time and he had been infuriated; she expected him to let go her hand, get up and stamp away in a rage. And she thought that for the ache of thwarted love anger was no bad remedy. And she thought, too, of Mary.

But Henry had learned another lesson. Complaisant or otherwise, she was necessary to him. When she said, "We have no future," he'd looked ahead and seen a long dark tunnel of years stretching from where he sat to the grave, with no joy in it, no hope. Appalling. Not to be borne. He tightened his hold on her hand and began to work his against her palm.

"If I were a free man, a bachelor, and could offer you marriage, what then would your answer be?"

Something new in his voice, the sensuous movement of his thumb, the question itself, caught her unawares. It was like one of her worst dreams, the one where she found herself taking part in a Masque without being prepared, not knowing what to say or do, but conscious of being watched by a hundred avid eyes.

"But to answer that would be a waste of breath," she said, forcing herself to speak lightly.

"Waste it then. God knows I've wasted breath enough on you!"

She tried the oldest trick of all to gain time, repeating his question.

"You ask me whether, if you were free and offered to marry me and make me Queen, I'd say yes, or no."

He said violently, "I *am* free. I've yet to prove it and that may take a little time; but prove it I will. Listen, sweetheart, and I'll tell you something I've mentioned to no one, except Wolsey. I am not, I never have been, lawfully married. A man may not marry his brother's widow; that is God's own law and a few words written by the Pope can't alter that law. And don't think that this is something I have invented out of my love for you — though I would invent more than that for your sake. This is sober fact and I can prove it. The Emperor's own lawyers, when my daughter Mary's betrothal to the Emperor was first mooted, questioned her legitimacy and spoke of her being the child of an incestuous marriage. Other lawyers said otherwise and she was betrothed, but the fact that the question was ever raised is evidence in my favour. Julius, mistakenly, gave a dispensation, which I shall ask Clement to declare a mistake. And the moment I am free, I'll marry you."

She remembered standing in the embrasure of the window at Greenwich, listening to Lady Cuddington's quiet, deadly voice and longing for power, power to destroy them all. And she remembered standing in the cold, smoke-filled room at Blickling and feeling the uprush of — not power exactly, but its crazy sister

96

thing, the ill-wish magic of the otherwise helpless. And now this!

"If you'll have me," Henry said, awed again because she seemed so unmoved.

"How long would it take?"

"In Rome the wheels, however well-oiled, move slowly. If I remember rightly it took Rome fourteen months to decide that the marriage between Arthur and Catherine was no marriage. With Wolsey at work, Clement might do his part in a year. Wolsey will throw his heart into this; he's always been against the Empire and for the French, and he'll think that once I am free he can marry me off to some French princess. He'll get a sad shock when he knows the truth, but it will be too late then."

The small hand that he was fondling suddenly turned so cold that the chill ran up his arm and set the hairs on end. They had sat here too long, he thought, all compunction. He was warm enough, even sweating slightly, but she was vulnerable to cold being so small, so delicate. He could link his two hands about her waist, span her neck with one, and the hand he held was as fragile as a flower.

"We should go in," he said, "unless you would sit closer and let me warm you."

She shook her head. She could not at that moment have stood steady on her feet. Silly childish games, Emma had said. But she herself had sensed the possibility of real damage to be done by the channelling of virulent hatred; and she had pricked the laurel and buried it. And nothing simple or straightforward had resulted; Wolsey hadn't fallen from his horse, or been stricken with sickness or suffered any of the things one thought of as bad luck; the vengeance was to be far more subtle, something — her mind hesitated and then drove on — something that Satan might well have contrived. The great Cardinal, working away to set his master free to make the French marriage he had always wanted for him, and then having the sad shock of discovering that all his efforts had been directed at making a Queen of Anne Boleyn!

For a moment she had a terrifying glimpse of the dark currents that move hidden behind all the busy little lives of men; and she would have crossed herself, had not Henry taken her other hand as well and said,

"You still give me no answer."

She said carefully, "If it could be so arranged, openly, lawfully. Why then, of course I . . . But the Queen! What of her?"

"Catherine is a woman of great piety; whatever the Pope decreed she would not question. She will see herself as my fellow-victim of a Papal error, and be equally anxious to put things right. I shall provide for her, and for Mary, royally. Catherine is not my wife, and I love you. I shall regard her as my sister."

And that, for him, settled the matter. He felt as though he had won a great victory, and careless of her dress, moved closer and took her into his arms, and clasped and kissed her as he had been longing to do for a year. The kisses were different from Harry Percy's youthful, ardent ones, but for a moment they reminded her of him and something in her shrank, affronted.

Then, under the searching, hungry mouth and hands her flesh stirred and she'd learned another of the sorrier lessons of growing up — that it was possible to respond to another's need, regardless of your own. She kissed him, and he grew bold.

"A year is all too long," he murmured against her neck. "We could be happy now. Let me come to you tonight, sweetheart."

She stiffened and drew away. Just like a yokel and his wench, she thought, lying among the haycocks. I'll marry you after harvest Nan, Peg, Polly, but let me have my way tonight. So women were seduced and bastards begotten. And perhaps the whole story, Wolsey, Catherine, the Pope, had been fabrication, a net woven to snare her.

"No," she said, "not tonight, nor any other night until we are married. I am your true, loyal subject and it pains me to refuse you anything, but this I must."

He was disappointed, but not wholly displeased. She was unique amongst women, and for her he could wait a year. All that part of him that was romantic and took pleasure in song and story, in pageantry and the outward form of chivalry rose to the surface. He'd serve his apprenticeship, as Jacob had served for Rachel, but — God be merciful — not seven years! This was a challenge, and he would meet it nobly; he'd be patient, considerate, undemanding.

But for the moment he felt the need for some gesture, something to put a seal upon this evening, and, casting about in his mind, he found it. He bent forward and kissed her gently, and then stood up and taking her hands, pulled her to her feet.

"You are a maid," he said solemnly, "and I regard myself as a bachelor. Let us plight our troth. I swear by Almighty God that as soon as I am free in the eyes of the world, as I am now in my own, I will take you for my wife."

This, following immediately upon her latest rebuff, made that fleeting suspicion seem unworthy; she wondered, for the first time, how she would have felt towards him had she not met Harry Percy first, had she not been Mary's sister.

"You must answer me," he said.

"I promise that when you are free, I will marry you." His spirits soared suddenly and he said, boisterously, "Now we must exchange rings."

He pulled at the emerald which had taken the place of the ruby upon his little finger and slid it on to the third finger of her left hand. It was so large that only by bending her finger quickly was she able to prevent it sliding off again.

"Had it fallen, it would have boded us no good."

"I'll wear it on my biggest finger, the middle one of my right hand." She moved it. "That will save explanations, too."

"I never thought of it," he said. "That is how it is, Anne. When I am with you, I feel that we are alone in the world.

She believed it; he looked at her with the eyes, spoke to her with the voice, kissed her with the mouth of love. She thought for a moment, drearily, of all the people in the world who were in love with people who did not return that love. Mary loved Henry, Henry loved Anne, Anne loved Harry Percy. Were there any happy lovers, anywhere? Harry and I could have been, she thought fiercely; that was where we were different, and that is why we couldn't be left alone.

"You must give me your ring," Henry said, prompting her again.

She took off the little silver and amber thing that she had bought for herself, in Paris, liking the colour.

"It's a poor exchange," she said.

"Of all my jewels, the most precious. Dearer to me than any in my crown." He kissed it and pushed it on to his little finger where it stuck at the second joint.

"I'll have it made bigger tomorrow. There, now we are properly plighted. You are my dear betrothed."

He remembered then that this time he had come down to Hever determined to make her his mistress. But it was better this way. She was altogether too rare, too wonderful to rank with his lights-o'-love. She was Queen of his heart, and for her there was but one fitting place.

"I shall go back to London tomorrow and set Wolsey to work. Handled vigorously this business should take no more than a year."

It was to drag on for twelve.

Harry Norris, except on his rare off-duty times, slept in the King's chamber. It was a custom left over from the old troubled days when a King was not safe in his bed. At each day's end, Norris, with the remote, impersonal look of a priest at a ritual, pushed his sword twice under the bed, opened every press or closet in the room, said, "All is well, your Grace, and I wish you a good night," and then went to his own bed which was always placed between that of the King and the door.

He was a man of the world and he had never imagined that Henry had come to Hever for his health, or to enjoy the scenery or the company of Sir Thomas and his lady. He was far too discreet to mention the matter to anyone, but he had little wagers with himself about how long Mistress Anne would hold out. This, he thought, would be the crucial visit; the King and the lady had quarrelled last time and the King had ridden off in a rage; this time they would make up and the siege would be over. But the King had gone glumly to bed on the first night of the visit, and glumly on the second, and Harry began to wonder: if the first flush of reconciliation didn't move her, what would?

On this, the third night, the King came to bed in a jubilant mood; all through his disrobing and preparing for bed he was making jokes, slapping shoulders and humming tunes. Norris drew his own conclusion and was astonished to find that as the King's spirits soared his own declined.

It was inevitable, wasn't it? It was a wonder the girl had resisted so long. Nobody to support her. A father who would sell his own mother to Turks to gain a smile from the King; a stepmother, an amiable little nobody.

But it was a pity. It was a shame.

People who gossiped about these visits to Hever declared themselves puzzled to know what the King saw in Anne Boleyn. North knew. Those great dark eyes, so bright, so fascinatingly set with the little tilt at the outer corners, the clear line from cheek to chin, the mouth that changed shape so easily, the wealth of black hair that seemed too heavy to be carried upon that slender neck; the low, velvety voice, the grace that touched every movement. Not pretty, people said; and it was true; she was beautiful. But apart from that, she had something other than beauty, something that would have made itself felt if you dropped a sack over her head. She was made to be cherished, and that was precisely what she would not be now: the King took these little passing fancies, but fundamentally, Norris thought, he was devoted to Catherine. When he rode in the lists he had for his title "Sir Loyal Heart", and by and large that was true. Considering his looks, his position, his boundless opportunities, he'd been singularly faithful. And that was right, of course; very admirable. But it was hard on the women he pursued and charmed and then abruptly abandoned. Mary Boleyn, Anne's sister, had almost died of grief, it was said, and she was a light-minded, easy-going creature, very different from . . .

How do you know? he asked himself.

And it was none of his business; the King's pleasure was; and Kings, like other men, asked the impossible — that their lecheries should be secret; they tasted better so. Norris should busy himself, not with pitying a girl many women would envy, but with thinking up some good reason for making himself scarce, so that the King could go to his rendezvous thinking himself unobserved.

He performed his senseless ritual and said,

"All is well, your Grace, and I wish you a good night. I should like to ask leave to absent myself for a while."

"Ha!" Henry said, "I thought you were very thoughtful. Did you *promise*? Because if so, run along. One must never disappoint a lady. But you've chosen an inconvenient time. I've had two bad nights and I feel like sleeping, and I want to start out for London early. So I warn you, if you come blundering in and wake me, I shall be displeased."

Taken aback, Harry Norris said, "In that case, Your Grace, I'll . . . I'll let it go. It was only a . . . a tentative arrangement."

"They're never any good, Harry, believe me. Hop into bed. And for the love of God, don't lie on your back and snore. Last night I had to get out and throw you on to your side and I stubbed my toe in the dark. If I weren't the soul of good nature I should have given you a buffet. Tonight I will. Good night."

He settled into the pillow and fastened his right hand around the little finger of his left where the poor little amber ring had stuck. His mind had the same clean, comfortable feeling that his body knew after a bath and change of linen. Tonight he had taken a great decision, of all the decisions that life had demanded of him, the most important. He was glad, glad in the last recesses of his heart and mind, that Anne had resisted his attempts to seduce her. That would have been a bad start to the new life which he planned. He was glad that his conscience had troubled him, and that he had mentioned the matter to Wolsey before he had had any serious intentions concerning Anne. When he'd talked to Wolsey he'd been thinking of the succession, and away at the back of his mind, unconnected, had been his — well, in his own bed a man could be honest — his lust for a maid-of-honour who had caught his eye. Now the two had come together; he'd be done with his old, cursed marriage, and he'd marry his little love, and she would give him sons. God was rewarding him, he thought, for his fidelity to Church and Pope. He'd lived in sin and time after time God had called his attention to the fact; he'd taken heed. And from now on everything would work for his good. He gave a great sigh of contentment and fell asleep.

Harry Norris thought — It's over. She didn't give in, and he's taken his defeat like the stout fellow that he is. She'll probably marry some gentleman of Kent who'll never get over his sense of being favoured and will coddle her as he would an orange tree. And that is how it should be. I wish him joy, though I envy him. We shan't, I think, be coming to Hever any more, and maybe that is just as well, I might, all too easily, fall in love with her myself.

Anne knew that Emma missed nothing. The emerald ring was easily explained, just another of the King's gifts. But the absence of the amber one might rouse curiosity.

She said, "In the garden this evening the King had cramp in his leg. He said he was subject to it and I told him he should always carry a piece of amber about him. He'd never heard of that remedy. But it is old and tried. You've heard of amber as a cure for cramp?"

"Jade," Emma said. "Or better still, bloodstone."

"Then I've wasted my dear little ring, and have in exchange this, which is far too big for me."

Emma eyed the emerald coldly. Another piece of bribery and corruption. Oh, she thought, he may have taken her poor trinket in exchange, but who is deceived by *that*? Emma knew what was afoot; she had noted Sir Thomas's complaisance, Lady Boleyn's helplessness; it was a simple, ordinary situation, except for Anne's behaviour. Emma thought that Anne was holding out for some secret reason of her own, making some condition which, up to the present, the King had been unwilling to meet. He would; he was hopelessly infatuated, and since Mistress Boleyn would never give in, he must. He'd give in, and Mistress Boleyn would yield, and on the day when she did, Emma Arnett would quit her service. She had no intention of being a participant in a back-stairs intrigue.

She had only stayed at Hever to suit herself. Once she had brought Anne there her work was done, but she had stayed to help nurse her through her cold, and by that time country life had made its appeal to her country blood. And Lady Lucia, rather surprisingly, had not seemed anxious to have her back. So she had stayed on, never quite settled, telling herself that she might move after Christmas, or in the New Year, and then deciding that Hever Castle was as good a place as any in which to winter.

Then one day she went into a haberdasher's shop at Edenbridge, where the haberdasher's wife, in the act of measuring off a yard of ribbon, suddenly threw it down, said, "My gingerbread!" and fled to the living quarters. When she returned she apologised and they began to talk about cake-making and presently Emma was invited into the room behind the shop to taste the new gingerbread and drink a glass of small beer.

People of the same breed have methods of communication that have little or nothing to do with words; within ten minutes both women felt that they had found a congenial friend and by their third meeting they knew that they shared their beliefs. Emma found herself introduced to a small circle in which the name of her old master, Richard Hunne, was not only remembered but revered as that of a martyr, in which the Pope and all Cardinals and most priests were ill thought of, in which the Bible in English was read by those who could read to those who could not, and was regarded as the final arbiter on every question of belief and behaviour. With these people Emma was instantly at home and in their company she was happier than she had been since the dispersal of her family.

In Hever, especially after the King became so frequent a visitor, she was less happy. She, like Norris, felt that the outcome was inevitable, and deplored it, not from any feeling for Anne, but on moral grounds.

Yet even she was puzzled. Tonight, for instance, there lay the great emerald, a gift too costly to have been promoted by any good motive; and there were many others, for which Anne seemed to care little, and which she only wore when the donor was expected. And here was the recipient of such gifts, going in good time to her maidenly bed.

Of the ring she said, "Put it away, it is too big for me."

Probing, Emma said, "But His Grace will expect you to wear it. It could be made smaller, mistress."

"I don't think the King will visit us much in future. He is going to be much occupied by affairs."

She spoke with as little feeling as though mentioning tomorrow's weather, and Emma, even more puzzled, put away the emerald and took up the brush and began to brush the long black hair. From her position she could catch, now and again, a glimpse of Anne's face in the glass. It told her nothing. The eyes wore their look of seeing something far away, and there was sadness in them, but then there always was, even when she was gay and smiling. Under Emma's hands the hair sprang, warm and lively, and below it was the narrow little skull which housed, whatever knowledge, thoughts and feelings the girl had. What was she thinking?

It had started with the words, "too big for me". All this talk of great matters, appeals to the Pope, the supplanting of Catherine; even the weight of Henry's passion seemed too heavy . . . She thought — Oh, I would so much rather have been Harry's Countess than Henry's Queen.

CHAPTER
SIX

"If the Pope be slain or taken, it will hinder the King's affairs not a little."
Letters and Papers of the Reign of Henry VIII

THE CASTLE OF SAN ANGELO, ROME. MAY 1527

At the end of the hot May day which had seen the overturning of the world, the Pope lay on a bed in a high room overlooking the Tiber. In the streets of Rome the Emperor's German troops, drunken and completely out of control, were sacking the city more thoroughly than ever the barbarians had done in ancient times.

Clement himself was safe enough. The Castle of San Angelo, built thirteen centuries earlier by the Emperor Hadrian, had proved, before this, to be an impenetrable fortress; and it had food and water for a year. So he lay there, safe in one stony cell in a honeycomb of masonry, with the outer rooms filled with his Cardinals and chaplains and, secretaries and chamberlains, and with every entrance and doorway guarded by Swiss soldiers, the most reliable mercenaries in the world. But he could not be thankful, even for safety. He wept, thinking of the Hell let loose in the streets, and of his own helplessness; he, the Pope, the direct successor to

109

St Peter whom Christ had adjured to be a shepherd to his sheep; he lay here, safe, while the wolves ravaged the flock.

His self-esteem, at no time a very sturdy growth, wilted and died. Why had he failed? He could truly say, even in this stripped-down moment, that he had done his best. He had recognised that these were dangerous times, and one of his first acts as Pope had been to issue an appeal to all the Kings and Princes of Christendom to live in peace, as brothers. Much good that had done! Greed, jealousy and hatred, ambition, rivalry, stupidity and sheer wickedness had made peace impossible.

And what could any man, however clever, however well-meaning, do to manage a world where what was called the Holy Roman Empire contained such discordant elements as Spain, most conservatively pious of all countries, and the German states where the Lutheran heresy had spread like plague? Charles V, head of this grossly overgrown Empire had let his troops loose in Northern Italy, acting out of rivalry with Francis of France who also coveted that territory. Clement had written to him, sharply one day, appealingly the next, but Charles had done nothing and in the end, when Florence, his birthplace, was threatened, it had seemed to Clement not only good sense but the only possible policy to ally himself with France, and with England, against the Emperor. The King of England had recently been angered by Charles's breaking of his troth with the Princess Mary and marrying instead another of his cousins, Isabella of

Portugal — a mercenary act, for Isabella had a dower of a million ducats.

So it had come to war and the French had been defeated by the Emperor's forces. And the English, where were they?

Lukewarm from the beginning. And Clement knew why.

Tossing uneasily on the bed the Pope admitted that where Henry of England was concerned, he might possibly have managed things better. Henry was a good churchman and very orthodox; in Leo's time, when Luther first published his protests and criticisms, Henry had written a book which refuted his arguments and Leo had rewarded him with the title Defender of the Faith. He might, in this war, today so disastrously ending, have done more to live up to that title if Clement had been more obliging.

It was almost two years now since the Pope had first received the information that Henry Tudor believed his marriage to be incestuous and wished to have it annulled. And the request could not have come at a more awkward time, for Clement was then still hoping to make a settlement with Charles, and Charles was nephew to the woman whom Henry wished to put away. It would have been insane to *provoke* Charles while trying to negotiate with him.

And there was another aspect too; less obvious, but fully as important. With heresy spreading every day, it would surely have been a fatal move to admit that a former Pope had been wrong to allow Henry and Catherine to marry. That would have started the so-called reformers screaming that dispensations and annulments were like pardons, on sale to anyone who could pay.

He'd had all the relevant papers brought out of the archives and studied them carefully. Arthur Prince of Wales, and Catherine of Aragon had been young, he fourteen, she fifteen, and the boy already sick of consumption, so fragile that the records hinted at advice given that the marriage should not be consummated for a year, or two. Clement could not blame Julius for deciding, on the face of such evidence, that Catherine was free to marry Arthur's brother; he'd have done the same himself.

So to Henry's pleas he had returned noncommittal answers, wishing to anger no one; and as a result, when it came to war with the Emperor he'd had little help from the English.

He was sorry for that, now. A company or two of English archers might well have turned the tide of the battle today. Still, he did not see how he could have acted otherwise.

Presently he began to think about the future. In the long history of the Church there had been one almost exactly comparable incident, when, more than two hundred years ago, Boniface VIII had quarrelled with the French King and had been taken prisoner. For the next seventy years the Papal Court had been not in Rome, but in a dusty little French provincial town named Avignon. Clement very much doubted whether, if he left his safe refuge and surrendered to Charles, he would be allowed to set up his Court in some dusty little Spanish town. There was less respect for the Church, less chivalry in these days. Besides, those seventy years had been immensely troubled; at times there had been two Popes. A repetition of that kind of thing could be fatal just now.

He contemplated staying inside the safe fortress of San Angelo for a year; that would give him twelve months to negotiate and hope for a change in the general situation; but what a year it would be; a state of siege, every message having to be smuggled in or out; the constant watching for signs of the pestilence which invariably appeared when too many men were crowded together for too long. And outside, the world going on without a Pope. Imagine the gloating joy of the heretics! No Pope for a whole year, they would say, and who had missed him?

No, he must get out. He must get out and contrive, with God's help, to placate Henry Tudor without too grossly offending the Emperor.

The often-used, pious phrase, "with God's help" slid through his mind and then turned and came back and leered at him. Where had God been all day? Where was He *now* while the drunken Lutheran soldiers raped the city and the Vicar of Christ cowered helpless? To face such things with a steadfast mind demanded the faith of a saint; and even the saints had known their moments of black disbelief and despair. One must believe that what happened on this earth was permitted to happen by God's will; yet who could believe that this overthrow of holy things, this bloodshed, this triumph of evil was in accord with the will of God?

He should pray; he knew that, but in these last months he had prayed with the utmost fervour; the set stylised prayers of the Rubric and the other sort, the simple humble appeals from the heart. Yet this had happened . . .

He rose, slipped on a thin silk robe and prostrated himself before his Prie Dieu.

Some long time later he stood up, still uncomforted, and knew that it was useless to go to bed again. So he rang a bell and sent someone to look for Cardinal Campeggio, who was one of those who had fled with him to San Angelo; that in itself proved Campeggio's allegiance; several Cardinals, in sympathy with the Emperor, had thought it safe to stay in the city. Clement liked Campeggio, a singularly level-headed man, capable alike of silence and of outspokenness.

"If he is awake," Clement said, considerately, "I wish to see him. If he is asleep, leave him be."

Campeggio was not asleep. In the whole of Rome that night the only people who slept were babies so young that the security of their mothers' arms was enough for them, and such of the invading soldiers to whom drinking mattered more than loot or rape and who had by this time fallen into sodden stupor.

In the safe, if not very comfortable room, the two men sat on hard stools and talked; first about the day's disaster, about which there was nothing new to say; and then about the future which was so vague and speculative. Campeggio, having taken the measure of

114

Clement's mood, racked his brain for some consoling words, and presently said,

"I am as certain as one can be of anything that this is not the Emperor's doing. This is the work of the Duke of Bourbon and the Prince of Orange and the rabble who call themselves their followers but refuse to be controlled by them. Charles is a faithful son of the Church, and when he knows what has taken place in Rome this day he will be appalled, and rightly." He paused for a moment and then added, "The Empire is so vast and so varied; I think it would be wrong to allow those few dissident German states to colour one's view of the whole. For myself, I sometimes doubt if they were ever converted at all. They were the last people to renounce paganism, and now infected by Luther they have reverted. But they are *not* the Empire."

"You think I should hasten to make peace with the Emperor?"

"I think that the well-being of the world depends upon the unity between the Papacy and the Empire. They are *natural* allies. The French are frivolous and unreliable; and the English have only one interest in Europe — their unrealistic dream of regaining France. The fact that the Turks are in Hungary affects them less, I am sure, than the price of mutton."

Clement remembered that during his predecessor's reign Campeggio had been sent to England to ask Henry's support in a crusade against the Turks. The mission had been a failure, but Campeggio had made himself agreeable, and had been given an English bishopric.

He said, "I have been thinking about the English. You know them. Do you understand them?"

"No. Nobody does. They do not even understand themselves. Of all people they are the most unpredictable — and the most hypocritical. Their King is typical of them all."

"He failed to send the help he promised," Clement agreed.

"I was thinking rather about his pious whimperings with regard to his conscience; he doubts the legality of his marriage yet he continues to co-habit with his wife."

"So he should," Clement said, gently but firmly. "Until the marriage is declared unlawful he would be wrong to put her aside."

"Things come to my ears," Campeggio said, "rumours with which no one would trouble your Holiness. And the latest thing I heard from England is that it is less a matter of his conscience than his liking for another lady — one of his wife's maids-of-honour."

"Oh," Clement said. Rumour could never be relied upon, nor could it be discounted; there was often a grain of truth in the wildest story. "But even so — Kings allow themselves a good deal of latitude in such matters without attempting to overturn a marriage of long standing."

"And so, no doubt, would he," Campeggio said drily, "but the lady has some say in the matter. And her ultimate intention is surely signified by the fact that she has for three years resisted all his attempts to seduce her. Or so gossip says."

"And that is a very unusual form for gossip to take! Do you know her name?"

"She is Anne Boleyn, daughter of Sir Thomas Boleyn, an upstart. On the distaff side the girl is well-connected. And one thing I do know about the English. If the King were ever in a position to marry her, they'd accept her. They think so highly of their Englishness that they'd regard an English commoner as more than the equal of any foreign princess."

Clement was regarding the thing from a different angle.

"Boleyn. No friend to Wolsey."

"Wolsey," Campeggio said, "has no friends. He has hench men, and tools and sycophants and partisans. But that is by the way. Wolsey is a sound churchman, he is opposed to any change. Thomas Boleyn, like all his kind, would welcome any change which brought them ten pence."

"Lutheran?"

"No-o-o. That wouldn't suit the King. He's shrewd enough. He can see, as any sensible man would, that the logical end of heresy is anarchy. Throw down the Church and how long would the throne stand? This, going on outside there . . ." the noise came up to them, muted a little, but still clearly enough, for the screams of the victims to be distinguished from the drunken yells of the victors, "that is Luther's work. Begin by treating your parish priest with contempt and you end by ignoring the orders of your own leader in war. Henry knows that. There'll be no Lutherans in England while he sits on the throne. But there are many changes, short of that, which might come about if new men like Thomas Boleyn ever had, say, half the power Wolsey now holds. The English," he hesitated; he had no wish to depress Clement any further; on the other hand an hour of gossip and mere academic discussion might help to divert him. "The English have never, I feel, been fully integrated; they're Christian, some are even pious, but their Englishness gets in the way; they have this ancient law against receiving instructions from any outside power; it has never been repealed and could at a moment's notice be considered to apply even to a Papal Bull. There was that London tailor, Richard Hunne, who if he hadn't lost his nerve and hanged himself before his trial, was prepared to sue his parish priest under that old law, you may remember. They resent paying what they call Peter's Pence; they resent the payment of annates; they troop in their thousands to the shrine of St Thomas à Becket, and one out of every two boys born in England is named for him, but if the same situation arose again and the King fell out with a Bishop — they'd take the King's side to a man. A very curious people; one has only to watch them keeping Christmas to realise that."

"And how do they keep Christmas?"

"With a Mass in the church and the old Druid sacred plant, the mistletoe, in the hall; with evergreens, holly and ivy, sacred to woodland gods even farther back in time, and with twelve days of undisiplined revelry that is more like the old Saturnalia than anything I ever saw or heard of."

118

All very interesting and informative, but Clement's mind insisted upon coming back to his present situation.

"When they hear of this," he moved an eloquent hand, "what will their reaction be?"

"Mixed, as their reactions always are. They'll say — We're glad we weren't there; and — If we'd been there things would have been different; and — Serves him right for falling out with the Emperor. Never forget, Your Holiness, the Netherlands are part of the Empire and it is in the Netherlands that the English sell their wool. The French they hate, and I have no doubt that it was the idea of fighting alongside the French and not against them that has made them such feeble allies for you in this war."

He should have said, "for us". He realised that as soon as he had said the other thing; but Clement seemed not to have noticed.

"To make peace with the Emperor seems to be my only hope," Clement said. "Spain is the stronghold of the faith, and the heart of the Empire. And that brings up again the problem of the English marriage, now more important than ever if what you tell me is true."

"It is a matter of time," Campeggio said. "The King may tire of being repulsed; the lady may give in. The Queen is said to be dropsical — though that is denied in other quarters. Given time anything could happen. Henry has reached the age when men have a roving eye; it might easily fall upon someone less obdurate. Let us hope . . ."

He broke off as a series of screams, more piercing than any hitherto heard, rose through the din. Clement shuddered, and his heart reproached him anew. How dismally he had failed. He broke into womanish tears.

"They are my sheep," he said, "and I can do nothing to protect them."

Campeggio said, not callously, but as a plain statement of fact,

"Your Holiness is their *spiritual* shepherd. On the physical plane there is but one defence for sheep — they must learn to fight back. In any given situation they always vastly out-number the wolves."

Clement was not exactly comforted by these comments, but he sensed in Campeggio a detachment which he himself did not possess, and he made another attempt to control his tears.

"You were speaking about time."

"Oh yes. I was thinking that the French having proved no match for the Emperor's troops and the English having failed us, our only hope is to come to terms with Charles. I'm no seer, but I think that Henry will do the same; his wool-merchants will see to that. And while this peace is brought about, such trivial extraneous things as whether Henry is married or not should be . . ." He realised that he was on the brink of proffering an unasked-for-piece of advice. "I am sorry, your Holiness; it is not for me to advise you."

"If you can, do."

"The matter should be delayed. Not shelved, that would anger Henry. Merely delayed for as long as is

120

possible. There are methods of delay well known to lawyers."

"If I am free to use them," Clement said, coming back to his own immediate future. He then voiced the thing which troubled him most, "I think I was wrong to allow myself to be persuaded to come here. I should have stayed, robed and in my chair. That was my intention. At the lowest it would have been an assertion of faith, and it would have left me with some authority."

"If you had stayed, you would now be dead. Of that I am certain!"

"You think they would have dared . . ."

"They are drunken and mutinous; they would re-crucify Christ given the chance. Your Holiness must . . ." There he was doing it again.

"Must what?" Clement asked mildly.

"Escape from here. Throw yourself under the Emperor's protection. Unless I am much mistaken this day's work is going to make a breach between the real Empire and the German principalities. The Emperor and the Empire will be on your side. After all, Charles has not yet been crowned. Who else could do it?"

So the hideous night ran its course and the talk in the high room ran hither and thither, touching upon many things. Before the year was out, Clement was to follow Campeggio's advice and, dressed like a workman, with a sack on his shoulders, escaped to Orvieto. He was to carry with him inerasable memories of the rape of Rome, memories which strengthened his determination never again to fall out with the Emperor; and adhering to the memory of that one particular night, as barnacles cling to a ship's hull, some of the other things that Campeggio had said; that Henry was a staunch churchman, unlikely to turn Lutheran if offended, that Henry must not be offended; that it would be against the interest of the Church for Anne Boleyn ever to be Queen of England; that only time was needed to solve everything.

He was to carry also the conviction that Campeggio was far-sighted and reliable, and very knowledgeable. If, in the years that lay ahead, so unsafe and so uncertain, he ever needed a man for any particularly delicate mission, Campeggio was the one he would try first.

CHAPTER
SEVEN

". . . she showed neither to Mistress Anne nor unto
the King any spark or kind of grudge or displeasure,
but took and accepted all things in good part, and
with wisdom and great patience."
Cavendish. *The Life of Cardinal Wolsey*

GREENWICH. JUNE 1527

When Henry entered, Catherine rose and greeted
him with grave respect before giving any sign of the
immense pleasure which his visit gave her. Even to
herself she would not use the word neglectful, but it
was impossible to overlook the fact that lately she
had seen less and less of him on private occasions.
She told herself that he was busy, much occupied
with the affairs of state, and of that, she, daughter of
Ferdinand of Aragon and Isabella of Castile, fully
approved. Rulers should take their duties seriously.
She had often thought, and occasionally in the past
gently hinted, that Henry left too much to Wolsey.
Such dependence, even in its most innocent aspect,
was bad, since Wolsey was twenty years older than
his King, and must one day die, or sink into useless
senility. It was better that Henry should learn to do
without him.

She had almost brought herself to believe her own explanation of Henry's withdrawal from her: but she was not a fool, and she knew very well that any man, however preoccupied, can make time to spend with the woman who holds his interest. She had lost Henry's; that she admitted to herself, sadly, but with resignation. It was no one's fault; it was inevitable; it was due to the dates of their births.

Just six years difference, so little, so much, so *variable*.

Six years had made an unbridgeable gap between a boy of ten and a well-developed, marriageable girl of almost sixteen; and it was across this gap that they had first looked at one another when he gave her his hand and led her along the aisle of St Paul's Cathedral where, at the altar, his brother Arthur awaited her. She had thought him very handsome, had even entertained a fleeting hope that her first-born son might inherit the sturdy physique of his young uncle Henry, rather than that of his delicate-looking father.

After that, with every passing month, the gap between them had narrowed, until he was a great lusty fellow of eighteen, almost full-grown of body and in mind rendered precocious by the respect that had been paid to him, and the demands made upon him since the death of Arthur had made him heir to the throne. Between such an eighteen-year-old and a young woman of twenty-four, who since the death of her husband, after a few months "marriage" had lived an almost nun-like life, there seemed no gap at all. They were married; they mourned together over their first still-born child, and in the next year rejoiced — oh, with what fervour — over the birth of a living son. Completely at one in joy, they had organised the celebrations to mark his birth, completely at one in sorrow, they saw him coffined before the gay decorations were down.

Then, a man of twenty-five, a woman of thirty-one they had leaned over the cradle of another living child, a daughter this time, a small, not very thriving child, but she lived and that was a good sign. They were still young; there was still hope that they could breed another boy, who would live.

All too soon the gap began to yawn again; Henry was in his prime, Catherine moving into middle-age. Repeated childbirth had thickened her body, repeated disappointment had sobered her spirits. There was still no child but the one daughter. Catherine had prayed to God and to the Virgin and to the Saints until sometimes she felt they must be weary of her; she had made pilgrimages to shrines and paid for prayers to be said for her, she had been charitable, and patient, and always on guard against despair, for despair was sin . . . And now, on this brilliant June morning in 1527, Henry was thirty-six, handsome, shapely, hard-muscled, sexually at the height of his powers, while she was forty-two and had known for several months that her child-bearing days were done. The six years' gap was wider than it had ever been.

Under her determined cheerfulness and resignation to the will of God, a persistent sense of failure gnawed. She had failed as a wife, for every man, even a peasant with nothing but his name, an old donkey and a scythe to bequeath, wanted a son, how much more so the King of England . . .? She had failed England, too; that curious and in some ways uncouth country, where foreigners were ill-esteemed, had taken her to its heart and had looked to her to provide it with an heir. Still, even the feeling of failure had its palliatives. What happened was according to the will of God. And there was Mary. After all, Catherine's own mother had been Queen in her own right, and a better ruler the world had never seen. Why should not Mary be as good; she had all the qualities, young as she was, gravity, intelligence, integrity and courage.

When Henry said, "I have a matter of some importance to discuss," Catherine thought instantly of Mary.

Henry spoke pleasantly, addressing Catherine, but looking at her ladies, all as gay as flowers in their summer dresses. Catherine — he gave her her due — was not as dowdy as many pious women were, nor did she surround herself with women so old or ill-featured that by comparison she might look younger and more comely. There were, indeed, amongst the women who went fluttering and chattering away, more than one who might have attracted him, had his heart not been fixed.

But his heart was fixed, and this next half-hour, which he suspected would be the most uncomfortable half-hour he had ever spent, must be regarded as the breaking of a barrier between him and his heart's desire. It must be regarded as one of those ordeals

126

which qualified a man for knighthood. It was, more simply, just something that must be done.

God's life, though! How he wished it were something that he could do, could bear, could achieve, either by himself or in contest with other men. Catherine would be hurt, and he hated hurting a woman.

He told her to be seated, sat down himself, got up again and looked out of the window. He had said, "a matter of some importance", yet his remarks, for several minutes, dealt with trivial things. Like Wolsey, on a former occasion, Catherine found this behaviour uncharacteristic, and like Wolsey, she was anxious to be helpful.

"I think," she said, "that I can guess what is on your mind. The betrothal of our daughter to the Dauphin of France. My Lord, I have considered it well and am now assured that it is for the best."

That should please him, she thought.

There again she was putting a brave face against a crushing disappointment. Mary had been betrothed to Charles, King of Spain, Emperor of the Holy Roman Empire. The betrothal had satisfied Catherine's strong family feeling, and it promised to link the two countries she loved best, her native Spain and England which had so kindly adopted her. But Charles had decided not to wait for Mary, but to marry instead another of his cousins, Isabella of Portugal. And then Henry and Wolsey, throwing their weight on to the French end of the European see-saw, had thought of betrothing Mary to the Dauphin of France. France, the ancient enemy of England and Spain.

It had taken some time and much effort for Catherine to resign herself to that idea, but she had done so, and now she held out her acceptance of it towards Henry, like a posy, trusting that he would be pleased.

He said, with awkward abruptness,

"I didn't come here to talk about Mary. I came to talk about us.

"About us?" The rather sombre lines of her face lifted. Perhaps he, too, had been aware of their drifting apart; had realised that outside of bed there was a good deal that a man and a woman, well-disposed, could give one another. Lately she'd prayed for this; perhaps at last one prayer was about to be answered.

"Yes," he said. And then it was as though at one minute she had been standing on a safe sunlit terrace overlooking a flat sea, rippling hyacinth and sapphire and jade, and the next minute a great cold, slate-grey wave had come up and engulfed her, swept her down, battered her against sharp rocks and then thrown her back, dying, but not dead, limp, broken and breathless on some strange and desolate shore.

She could never recall afterwards exactly what words he had used, or how long he took to say them, but his meaning reached her. He and she had never been married; they had lived in sin; they'd broken God's law; she wasn't his wife, she was Arthur's; and all those precious babies, miscarried, still-born or soon dead, were a proof that God had cursed their incestuous union.

128

When at last she could speak she heard her own voice, a faint mewling, the last cry of somebody being strangled.

"But, Henry . . . the Pope. He gave . . . a special dispensation. He knew . . . everybody knew . . . poor Arthur and I . . ."

I must, I must collect myself and speak firmly. This is nonsense; it must be refuted.

"Arthur and I," ah, that was better, her own voice. "We were married; there was the ceremony; and for a few nights we shared a bed. But he was a child, and sick, even then. I shared a bed with a sick child. And knowing that, the Pope gave us leave to marry."

"We were deceived, Catherine. The Pope had no right to issue such a dispensation. Of that I am now convinced, and so are many learned men of whom I have asked counsel. Ours was an unlawful marriage, and its results condemn it."

"The children? Henry, you know, babies are born dead, or die in every family. We have Mary. Is she not living proof of our marriage being good. It says — I know it too — that the man who marries his brother's wife shall be childless. You are not childless. And I was never, never, your brother's wife. You know it. You must know that I came to you virgin as I was born."

After all these years, in a moment of stress, her voice, the way she used her hands, betrayed her Spanish origin. Once he had thought her accent, her gestures, fascinating; now they revolted him, as a dish, once loved, eaten to surfeit, will ever more revolt. And the mention of virginity, coming from a woman who was

129

ageing, growing stout, and labouring under emotion, that was revolting too. A kind of disgust held him speechless.

"Your father and mine," Catherine said, "two of the wisest princes in Christendom; they were satisfied that the dispensation was good."

"No," Henry said, feeling firm ground beneath his feet at last. "My father had a doubt and spoke of it on his death bed."

That was true, and he leaned back against the memory of that moment as a man might lean against a strong wall. Henry VII, who for years had kept the young widow in England, who had once even thought of marrying her himself, because his miserly nature hated to part with her dowry, who had extracted from the Pope the permission for her to marry his second son, had, in the final hour of his life, seen the worthlessness of material things. He had mumbled out a few words which Henry had chosen then to ignore.

Henry, the second born, bigger, stronger, in every way save age Arthur's superior, had always envied his brother. He had coveted Arthur's heritage, and later Arthur's princess. She had been, then, every boy's dream, plump, pretty, amenable, and despite her Spanish blood, blue-eyed and golden-haired; her grave and stately Spanish manners gave her the charm of the exotic, and her curiously accented English was pleasing to the ear. He'd led her to her wedding, wishing all the time that he stood in Arthur's place. And when, eight years later he stood by his father's death-bed and heard the warning, issued in a thready, failing voice, he had

130

thought — He's failing, he does not know what he says; he asked for the dispensation and Julius gave it; and I shall marry her; why not?

But it was useful now to mention his father.

"He knew it was wrong. I was young and headstrong and chose to ignore his warning. Now I know that he was right. Wolsey has approached the Pope, with no result so far, for reasons that we know of; but Wolsey and Warham have had a discussion upon the matter and came to the conclusion that our marriage was open to question. So there we are."

All this and not a word to her.

She remembered often during the last few weeks, coming upon a group of her ladies, chattering like magpies, and then falling silent as she approached. They knew! Wolsey had his own channels to the Pope, his discussion with the Archbishop might be kept secret, but things of such importance had a way of brimming over all such precautions. Her ladies had known; she had not. Unkind! Unkind, she thought, and then hastened to exonerate him.

"You have been badly advised, my Lord."

Neither of them realised it then, but Catherine in seven words had expressed her belief and nothing was ever to move her from it. Henry, left to himself, was, she was sure, incapable of thinking along such lines, or of acting so unkindly. Theirs had been an unusually happy marriage and he had never been anything but kind to her. A little inconsiderate perhaps in bringing his bastard son to Court, and making him Duke of Richmond, but it was natural for a man to love his son, even it he were a bastard. He'd been unfaithful to her twice that she knew of; people whispered about a third time, long ago, but those whispers she had ignored, and that for a King with unlimited opportunities and so many temptations was a remarkably clean record. All this made the blow which he had just dealt her more wounding, and at the same time convinced her that he was not really responsible.

It was Wolsey.

Wolsey had always aimed at a firm alliance with France, and he was infinitely cunning. He'd worked on Henry's wish for a son, and was now, this minute, over in France, bargaining for some buxom, bright-eyed girl with a quarter of a century of child-bearing years before her.

The awful inescapability of the years' damage confronted her fully for the first time; a woman was nubile, fruitful, barren, subject to a progress as fixed as the passage of the sun across the sky.

Abruptly she began to cry, taking Henry by surprise, for she wept seldom. The tears welled up and spilled over, quietly, as though they were her life blood seeping away.

"Don't," he begged her. "Catherine, don't cry. I had no intention of making you cry."

He felt like a great clumsy boy who, romping round, had unintentionally hurt his mother.

"It will make no noticeable difference," he assured her. "It is some time now since we . . . since we lived as man and wife. This means only the separation of our households, for the sake of appearance. You can have any house, any of my houses that you care to choose. You shall be shown every honour and consideration. You can keep what state you wish, and be known as the Princess Dowager."

(Yes, I know, I was clumsy and hurt you, but don't cry. Have a bite of my apple, borrow my top, but please don't cry.)

She pressed her hands to her mouth and willed the tears to cease, her mouth to stop trembling. There was so much she must say, clearly, positively, firmly, before this nonsense went any further.

"Henry, I am your wife. Nothing can alter that. The present Pope would never dream of retracting a proper dispensation given by his predecessor. I don't care where I live, or what state I keep, but I am your wife. I have been for sixteen years and shall be until I die." She saw the shame-faced expression change to sullen displeasure. "If it is . . . if it is a question of another woman . . . I will be discreet. I know that I am growing old and no longer attract you. If some other woman could make you happy, I would accept that, and pray for you both. But to treat our marriage as though it had never been, that I could not do. It would be impossible. It would be wicked."

"Wicked to put right a grave wrong?"

Her own voice came back to her, deep-toned.

"Wicked to pretend that I have been nothing but your mistress and that Mary was born out of wedlock."

"Pretend! Pretend! Anyone would think that this was some game I had invented for my own amusement. You speak of Mary. Isn't it true that when the business of her betrothal to the Emperor was discussed the lawyers, Spanish ones, brought up the question of her legitimacy. It came up again over the French betrothal. This isn't something I made up out of my head. It's fact. If it were merely my fancy wouldn't Clement have told me I had no case? Do you think Wolsey and Warham would sit in solemn session and say the marriage was open to doubt were it not so? There was an error and we suffer for it; Mary too; but it must be put right. Come now, once accept the situation — as I have — and it will not seem so bad. I'm fond of you, and of Mary, as well you know. I shall treat her as I always have, and you as . . . as my favourite sister."

She knew that if she gave in now she would have his friendship for life. Something would be salvaged from the wreck — his goodwill. If she made things easy for him, he would make things pleasant for her. But it wasn't only of herself she must think.

It never had been. All her life long it had never been Catherine first. The English marriage which would be good for Spain; the long, wretched time of waiting after Arthur's death, while her father and Henry's brooded over her dowry and the choice of a second husband for her; marriage to Henry which had, by mere chance, brought her happiness, though when it was arranged nobody cared whether it did so or not. And now this. Even now Catherine mattered hardly at all. Mary was the one who mattered.

She said, "As long as I live I shall regard myself as your wife and shall call myself Catherine the Queen. And Mary will be your one legitimate child. You have gone, behind my back, which was unkind, to the Pope and gained no satisfaction. I shall ask him to consider my case. I will write to the Emperor, too. The original dispensation that Julius gave is either in Rome, or in Madrid. They can get it out and study it and see if there is a flaw that would justify this troubling of your conscience, after so many years. You are my husband, my King, my lord, under God I owe you obedience and in any other matter that you could name I would obey you. But when you ask me to accept something which denies the Pope's ruling, and the sacrament of marriage, and the legitimacy of our child, then you ask too much."

Knowing her as he did he knew that further words would be wasted. The tears had made her eyes swell, and with her jaw set in that obstinate line she looked like a bull-dog.

"We shall see," he said, and turned and went out, setting each foot down more heavily than usual.

He was still far from being the tyrant that he was to become in later life, but he liked his own way and was accustomed to getting it. And at the moment Catherine's attitude mattered. The Pope was the Emperor's prisoner and it would have been of inestimable value if the next emissary could have carried some proof that Catherine had agreed to the annulment. Her orthodoxy and piety were everywhere acknowledged, if she would have admitted to a qualm of conscience, too, there'd have been no more argument about it.

Now it would go on and on.

What a fine way to repay his years of devotion and the patience with which he had borne all her mishaps in child-bed. Never once had he reproached her, never once allowed his disappointment to exceed her own.

It was the waste of time that irked him most. Of the final outcome he had no doubt. The Pope needed him and in the end would settle for his terms. But there'd now be the pretence of studying Catherine's case. And another summer was well on its way and here he was, a man, strong, healthy, lusty, with on one side a woman of whom he was tired, and on the other a woman he wanted as no man, surely, had ever wanted a woman before. Both stubborn women, too. One clinging to a marriage which, as he had just explained to her, was no marriage at all; the other demanding marriage as the price of surrender. Of the two he had, being in love with her, more sympathy with Anne. To a woman her good name mattered. Catherine's good name was in no danger, everyone would regard her as the unfortunate victim of a mistake; she was merely being proud and disobliging.

The first thing to do — he thought — was to prove to her that he meant what he said. And he knew a very agreeable way of doing that, if only it could be brought about.

His face brightened; his step grew lighter and swifter.

Within ten minutes he was mounted, and riding hard for Hever.

CHAPTER
EIGHT

"Mistress Anne Boleyn was called back into Court, where she flourished afterwards in great estimation and favour."
Cavendish. *The Life of Cardinal Wolsey*

HEVER. JUNE 1527

June again, with the cuckoos calling in the Kentish woods, and the roses blooming in the garden at Hever; lovers' weather again, and nothing changed, save that he was more in love than ever, and growing impatient, and aware of the time slipping away.

He was renewing his pleading that she should return to Court.

"I can't forever be coming down to Hever, darling, yet I count every day when I don't see you, wasted. I *need* you in London. Why won't you come?"

"I did," she said, "in May, and you sought me out so openly that had I stayed out the week, scandal would have been busy."

"It was May Day," he said humbly. "Everybody makes merry then."

"That saved us, perhaps. I don't think even the Queen had any real suspicion. But if I came back, and it happened again . . . Henry, I hate the thought of

137

people talking in corners, watching, making up tales; and I hate being sly and furtive, and in the wrong."

"But everything is changed now. I've been frank with Catherine; I've told her that I no longer regard her as my wife, and . . ."

"Did you mention me?"

"No. It was not the time for that. She was very upset. She . . . she . . . I don't care to think about it. But I am a free man, and I intend to act like one. Wolsey is now in France and when he returns I want him to see that I do not intend to marry this Renée he has picked for me. I want him to see you beside me. I want it all out in the open. I have chosen you, and as soon as a few legal points are settled we shall be married. What is there in that for people to talk over in corners?"

"When you put it like that, nothing. But I would rather remain here until those legal points *are* settled. They take so long. Last month the Cardinal and the Archbishop were to look into your marriage and declare it void. And that all came to nothing."

"That was a stroke of foul luck," Henry said with a touch of impatience in his voice. "How could anyone foresee that while they were actually sitting we should get news of the Pope being taken prisoner. His is the ultimate sanction, so there was nothing Wolsey and Warham could do but what they did, which was to say that the marriage *was* open to question. They said that, the two highest authorities in England. And that justifies me. The news from Rome was a shock. But things are settling now and it may well be that the Pope's captivity may even be of benefit to us."

138

She looked at him questioningly.

"In two ways, or one of two ways. A helpless man — and Clement is that if ever a man was — is always eager to find an ally. As soon as his slow mind takes stock of his position he'll see that his only hope is for me and Francis of France to go to his aid; and he'll know what my price is! Francis can make his own bargain. Or — and this was Wolsey's inspired idea — it would be feasible to argue that a Pope who is a prisoner is incapable of fulfilling his proper function and therefore his authority devolves upon his Legates in the various countries. Here that means Wolsey, and Wolsey would free me like that!" He snapped his fingers.

"To marry Renée of France, not me!"

"Trust you, sweetheart, to put your pretty finger on the nub of the matter," Henry said dotingly. "But he *said* it. He admitted that the marriage was open to question, he said that in certain circumstances he could assume Papal powers. He can't go back on that. He can't turn about to me, his King, and say — I'd free you to marry the Frenchwoman, but not the woman you love. By God's throne, if he did that, I'd have his head!"

The very thought turned his face plum-coloured, made his eyes bulge.

"Not that he would. Wolsey's aim is to please me. It always has been. I've set him very high and in his heart he is grateful. He'll grumble a little; he has always had this leaning towards France, and he's getting old and set in his ways; he'd like to see me make a French marriage. But when he knows that my mind and heart are set on you, and that I'll not budge, he'll give in. He's rather like . . ." Henry fumbled in his mind for an apt simile and found it, the fruit of his long rides about the countryside where he would talk to farmers and shepherds and blacksmiths and millers and ploughman, talks which had established the toughest roots of his popularity with the common people. "He's rather like those old horses that in their last days are set to turn a mill wheel. They have to be blindfolded at first, otherwise they turn dizzy and stagger; later on they become accustomed and the cloth can be taken away. Thomas, blindfolded, has started on the round that will set me free, and I think the time has come to uncover his eyes. When he comes back from France I want him to find you by my side, and to know the truth."

"And that," she said in that light, frivolous manner which always took her by surprise, "is why you *need* me at Court."

"How you love to tease me. One day," his voice thickened, "I'll tease you!" He thought of the form the teasing would take; the two of them, naked in the wide bed. He'd take his sweet, sweet revenge for all the times when she had laughed and he had not known why, for all the openly mocking words like those she had just spoken, and for all the more subtle things, looks, words with which she had tightened the chain that bound him to her. One day his devotion, his patience, his unswerving allegiance, his love, would have their full reward.

He answered her solemnly.

"No; that is not why. It is a reason, but I have another, more urgent. You should understand it, for you have, and rightly, a concern for your good name. *And so have I for mine.* I know what people will say. Henry of England has tired of his old wife and fallen in love with a pretty face. Simple people always reduce everything to their own simple measure. They'll laugh at the mention of my conscience. It'll be a rare man who can understand the full truth, that my conscience is troubled and that I love you and that the two things are separate. I think that no man has ever been placed as I am. There is my conscience, but many with worse settle things with their confessor, and I could, if I wished, take refuge in the thought that Julius sanctioned my marriage. Then there is my lack of an heir. Nothing remarkable in that. Other men suffer the same and fold their hands and murmur about the will of God. So we come to the naked truth. My conscience, my heirlessness, maybe I could bear, had I never seen you. I'm ready now to turn the situation to my advantage, but I did not *create* the situation, though they will accuse me of that. And sometimes, when I think of the calumny, the arguments — yes, I'll be honest, when I think of Catherine's hurt, a black moment comes upon me. And I am in London, you are here; it isn't possible for me to run here every time I am downhearted." His face lost a little of its healthy colour, the pupils of his light eyes widened. "So I think of you, and, sweetheart, sometimes you seem so near, so close that I can smell the scent of your hair; but there are other times when it seems that I'd fallen in love with a woman I'd dreamed about, or read of. I say your name, Anne, Anne Boleyn, and it is just a name. I'm like a man who has left his safe warm house at night to follow the will-o'-the-wisp that dances two steps ahead and will lead him on, over the quick-sands, and will still dance on, over the place where he has gone down —" He broke off, stared into her face and said in a different voice, "Don't look at me like that! In God's Name, I don't want your pity, or your concern. I want *you*, close to hand, in London, so that when the black dog sits on my shoulder I can see and touch you, hear you laugh. Is that too much to ask? At best, being a King is a lonely business."

The last feeling that she had ever expected to feel for him was pity; pity was for the small, the weak, the ill-done-by, not for the great, the rich, the powerful. Also, she realised suddenly, she had never, until this moment, given him much consideration as a person; as a King, yes, as a man, yes, but not as a mere human being, capable of feeling frightened and lonely.

She said, "I'm no will-o'-the-wisp, Henry. I'm real enough. I gave you my word and as soon as this troublesome business is settled and I can decently come to London, I will do so, gladly enough."

"But I want you there *now*. I shall want you when I face Wolsey. I shall get my way with him in the end, but he'll produce a thousand reasons why I should not follow my heart. And Catherine, stubborn as rock; nothing will shift her until the Pope gives his verdict. The worst part lies just ahead, Anne; and I mean it when I say that I need you."

142

She heard the warning, clear as a trumpet call. One of these days, when the black mood was on him, when Wolsey argued and Catherine wept, and she seemed no more than a woman he'd dreamed of, he'd give in. He'd go running to Catherine, put his head on her motherly bosom and say he was sorry and let all be as it was before, love. He could do it tomorrow, all too easily. As yet he had given no reason for his desire to deny his marriage, save the pricking of his conscience, and he could say that Wolsey or Warham had managed to set his conscience at rest.

Thoughtfully she twirled the rose she was carrying. She often carried a flower or a trinket, for apart from the marred little finger her hands were of exceptional beauty, long and slim, the colour of cream, and toying with some object — the little finger tucked away — was a means of drawing attention to them. This evening, however, she moved the rose without any conscious design, and was hardly aware of breathing in the scent set free by its movement. But into her indecisive mind the fragrance sent a pang of memory. Four years now since she and Harry Percy had kissed in the Greenwich gardens; the wound healed, the scar sensitive in certain weathers, like the arm and leg stumps of old warriors. And to think of Harry brought Wolsey to mind; Wolsey, so devilishly skilled in finding reasons why one shouldn't follow one's heart. To retire now, to let consideration for her good name weigh against the ultimate advantage, would be to let Wolsey triumph yet again.

And she thought — I'm twenty, no longer really young; I might never get another chance to marry; and my father, very tolerant now because he sees in me a way to favour, would, should that favour be withdrawn, show quite another face.

Yet still the thought of the greedy, hard-glinting eyes, the flicking, forked serpents' tongues, was horrible.

Until marriage — however long that may take to attain — nothing but a few harmless caresses; and if anyone says otherwise I shall demand a panel of matrons to refute the slur.

The thought was so fantastic that she laughed and Henry, waited anxiously, looked at her in amazement.

"I'm laughing," she said, "at *you*. Asking for what you could so easily command. You have only to order me to be at Greenwich on such a day, at such a time, and I should be there, careful to be punctual."

He said, with an earnestness that was almost pompous,

"I should never dream of giving you an order, as you should know by now. You are my lady and I serve you, hoping that in return you may grant me some small favour. I promise you that if you will come to London I'll ask nothing more, make no demands, never embarrass you in any way. All I need is your presence. You shall have your own apartments, your chaplain, train-bearer, everything. In all but name, you shall be Queen. And that, too, before long."

She said,

"I will come."

He began to babble. "Bless you, my sweet Anne, bless you. You strengthen and hearten me. Now I can fight them all. And never think that your position will be in doubt. You shall at all times, and from everyone, receive the respect that is due to my bride-to-be. I thought," he said thickly, "that I loved you as much as a man could love a woman, but for your kindness I now love you a thousand times more."

He leaned forward and kissed her in the way he had mastered, passionately, but with passion hard held in control. And she kissed him, coolly, but with infinite promise. Oh God, he thought, how long?

Sometimes it worried him a little. He loved her so much, he longed for her, with every nerve and fibre of his body, yet always his mind must rein his flesh. He'd set himself to wait — and four years had gone by. What did four years of celibacy do to a man? He imagined a man, accustomed to feeding full, fond of his food, cast away on one of the desert islands sailors told of, or clapped into gaol. Would the appetite shrivel, fit itself to hard circumstances and make him unable to eat well when at last the full board was spread before him? The thought had so troubled him that once or twice he had thought of taking another woman, some almost anonymous female body, as a kind of medicine. But he knew that it would be useless. In all the world there was only this one woman; and though half of him grieved over her refusal to allow him to become her lover, the other half rejoiced. Chastity was a virtue; and she was compounded of all the virtues. On the whole, willingly he kissed the rod.

Anne thought — Presently we shall go into the house and I shall tell my father and Lady Bo that I am going to London and they'll hold me cheap.

She said,

"There is one thing, so silly and small that I hate to mention it to you, because, born royal, you can never understand how hard other people must fight for precedence. But I have been at Court before. It would amuse you to know how strictly we were graded. As a mere knight's daughter, for example, I should not be allowed stabling for my own horse. And that comes all the harder because my father has claims, not yet recognised, to higher titles."

"The Butler dispute," Henry said, coming back to earth. "I'll make him Viscount Rochford immediately, and presently he shall be Earl of Wiltshire. Does that content you?"

She was still aware that up to a point she had given in; the awareness was there, raw and touchy. Presently her cousin Thomas Wyatt was to write to her, "And wild for to hold, though I seem tame," and he knew her well. Temper flared.

"Content me? Content me? Henry, if you threw your hound a bone for which he begged you might ask that. But if you eased his collar, too tightly buckled, would you use those words?"

"You are right. I should have said — Will it ease things for you?"

"Not that neither. You should have said that you were sorry not to have observed sooner that the collar pinched."

For as long as he could remember nobody had said to him "You should . . ." His father could have done, would have done, but there was never any need, he had always been a dutiful son; and at eighteen he had been King of England and any advice or admonition offered him had been tactfully wrapped about — If your Grace would consider . . . It would be well if . . . Perhaps I should point out . . .

He said, "You are right, sweetheart. I should have advanced your father before suggesting your return to Court. I was thoughtless."

She smiled at him, twirling the rose. He thought that one of the first things he must do, once she was established in London, was to get her portrait painted. In a picture which must stay as it was and could not be forever changing, he hoped that he might find some clue to her elusive and bewildering charm which had so little to do with any accepted standard of beauty. Her brow was broad and high, her eyes widely spaced and beautiful, and then the face sloped away to a little narrow jaw and chin. Her mouth varied. There were times when the top lip seemed full and sharply curved, hardly able to cover the small childish teeth; there were other times when it seemed thin and taut and the lower lip dominated, slightly protruding, kiss-inviting. Yet none of this meant much; he could, any day, look around and find inside the immediate circle of his Court a dozen women prettier. Except for the eyes. And even their charm was due less to colour and size than to something there was no name for. Expression did not serve, for their expression was constantly changing; one thing remained constant, though, a curious far-seeing look, it was there when she laughed, when she looked thoughtful, when her eyes flashed with anger. As though, Henry thought, with the poet in him coming uppermost, some part of her sight was always directed at some far spread vista, seen by her alone.

He said, "Look at me, sweetheart." She looked, smiling, and the smile hung there, as real, as visible as the necklace she wore, and just as little part of her.

"What are you thinking?" he asked, almost querulously. "I never know what you are thinking."

She said, "I was wondering. About the future. Suppose the Pope never agrees to declare you a free man."

"But he must," Henry cried blusteringly. "He's hedged, and learned his lesson. He needs me now." He looked at her, drawing his eyebrows together. "Driven too far, I'd make Wolsey act. But I don't want that. Clement is a weak, vacillating, pusillanimous fellow, but he is Pope, the supreme authority on all spiritual matters; and marriage, being a sacrament, is a spiritual matter. I want his admission, made known to all the world, that I was never Catherine's husband. Our marriage must be perfect, sweetheart, proof against all question, legal beyond all doubt."

148

CHAPTER
NINE

"Even if hostility towards the Church did not assume the proportions of a national revolt, it was still there to be reckoned with . . ."
Charles Ferguson. *Naked to Mine Enemies*

EDENBRIDGE. JUNE 1527

After a long pause during which the haberdasher was plainly giving the matter his undivided attention, he spoke.

"To my mind, Mrs Arnett, you'd do a sight better to go along and stay close. She's young, she might be shaped. And she's going to be mighty powerful. The cause could do with a friend in a high place."

"You hadn't gone and give in your notice already, had you?" the haberdasher's wife asked anxiously.

"Only in my own mind," Emma said. "I've seen which way the wind was blowing for a long time now, and I always told myself that if she left home, and took up with him in that way, I'd have nothing to do with it. I like things decent."

"But you said she said . . ."

"I know what she said. And I daresay she meant it. But what chance would she stand? Once she's there, and the King so set on his own way." She looked into their faces, noticing the innocence of their eyes. What could they know of the ways of the Court? But *she* knew. Only too well she knew, from first-hand experience, what it meant to be involved in an illicit affair; the lies that must be told, the messages to be smuggled out, or in, the candles set in windows as a sign. She knew it and loathed it; and the haberdasher's answer had surprised her; she'd expected that he would say that she, as a decent woman, couldn't possibly lend her countenance to such goings on.

"And what can I do?" she asked, "by staying, I mean. Ladies don't set much store by their servants' notions."

"Ah, that's where you're wrong," the haberdasher said. "There's more than one case mentioned in the Scriptures of servants bringing their masters to the truth. A word here, a word there; and always the *example*. You'd be a fine example to any belief, Mrs Arnett, if I may say so. If you was a Turk and lived and talked and behaved as you do, always so decent, I should feel bound to ask myself if there wasn't *some* good in whatever it is Turks hold with."

"And so should I," his wife agreed. "Why, the first time you ever set foot in the shop I said to myself — There's a decent woman, and right-minded, if ever I saw one."

Such tributes were gratifying, especially as the haberdasher and his wife and their friends had become more and more the ruling influence in Emma's life.

She said deprecatingly, "I was brought up to be decent. And then I had that one good master. And this bothers me. I don't like the idea of being mixed up in . . . well, anything shady."

"But you can't say that yet, Mrs Arnett. You have to take the long view. The way I look at it the King's no more married to her we call Queen than he is to . . . to my missus here, or you. There it is, plainly writ in the Bible, a man must not marry his brother's wife, which she was, and nobody can deny that. And who gave them leave to marry? The Pope at Rome, and he's got no more power to set aside God's given law than I have. We no more believe the Pope can alter God's law than we believe in pardons and relics and images, do we now? All right then, we don't reckon the King is a married man. Nor, according to what I hear, straight from my brother in Milk Street, do he. He've asked, so they say, quiet like, to be set free; and mark my words, if he ain't *set* free, sooner or later he'll *get* free. And your little lady'd be Queen most like."

Two rings, one of emerald, one of amber, shaped themselves before Emma's inner eye. Troth-plighted? Just for once she found herself regretting that Anne was not garrulous, easily confiding or even girlishly naïve. What had she said about the rings? Amber was good for cramp, she'd got the better bargain, the emerald was too big for her. And these simple people thought that she, Emma Arnett, could influence a young woman capable of such cool behaviour, such secrecy.

"Even so," she said, "I don't see that I can do much."

"You could *try*," the haberdasher said sternly. "After all, it's us God work through and it look to me He put you just in the right place. Say for instance what my

151

brother say is true and the King have asked to be freed and the Pope dilly-dally, couldn't you every now and then edge in a word so she could see that he was no friend to her. That'd be something to start with. And suppose you could get her, just once, just for curiosity to look inside an English Bible and then next time some poor chap was in trouble for reading in it she could say to the King, well, what's wrong with that, I read some myself. That's the kind of thing. Nothing much, just little things, but they'd mount up. I tell you what, Mrs Arnett, I only wish I stood in your shoes and had the chance. Like they say about pitch, you can't touch it without getting yourself black, and the same is true of the truth; if you're in touch with it, as close as she must be when she's being tended by you, then some must rub off. Stands to reason."

He spoke with fervour and confidence and a certain rough eloquence.

"So you think I should go to London?"

He gave a little secret sigh; women, how stupid even the best of them could be; what did she think he'd been talking about all this time.

"I think it's your duty, no less."

And although she had, when she laid her problem before him, hoped for the opposite answer, she was conscious of a feeling of relief. She was, after all, a little old to go looking for another job in an overcrowded market, and Mistress Boleyn was easy to serve; it was only that her conscience, her liking for everything to be clean and orderly and above-board, had made her feel

152

that she didn't want to serve a light woman, even the King's.

"If you put it like that," she said. "And of course I'll do what I can. But she's a very strange . . . at least not like anybody I ever worked for. After all this time about the only thing I really know about her is that she hates the Cardinal."

"Well, there you are! What better start could you have? So do we, don't we? He's the enemy on the doorstep. No getting hisself picked to be Pope of Rome, he's doing his best to be Pope of England. You work on that, Mrs Arnett. And now, if you're bound for London I'd better tell you how to find my brother. He'll make you welcome, and through him you'll find a lot of friends. Down here the cause is only just finding its feet, up there it's flourishing. More people think like we do than you'd ever believe."

"I shall be glad of friends," Emma said, "for I shall miss you all."

On her way back to Hever she reflected upon the strange turnings life took. After the break-up of her family she had been dreadfully lonely; then, for a brief time, in Richard Hunne's household, she had fallen into place, been happy, felt at home. Then had come another upheaval and she had been lonely again. She had held to certain ideas, some inculcated by her dead master, some the result of her own observation and good sense, but nowhere, until she entered the haberdasher's shop, had she found, or even hoped to find, anyone whose ideas ran alongside her own. Then she had found that far from being an oddity, she was one of a group, small as yet, and nameless, who were confident of ultimate victory because their beliefs were taken directly from the Bible, the Word of God.

And she'd gone into Edenbridge today prepared, hoping to be told that she should leave Anne's service. The very opposite had happened, and the haberdasher in charging her to put in a word here, a word there, had set her a task the magnitude of which he, in his rustic innocence, had no notion.

Yet, going back to Hever, she was far happier.

To the real reason for this happiness her stern, puritanical eyes were sealed.

CHAPTER
TEN

"... my physician, in whom I have most confidence,
is absent at the very time when he could have given
me the greatest pleasure. Yet for want of him, I send
you my second, and hope that he will soon make
you well."
Henry VIII in a letter to Anne Boleyn

THE KING'S HIGHWAY. JUNE 1528

As he rode — not hurriedly, but keeping a good steady
pace — Dr Butts mused over the mystery of the
Sweating Sickness and over the exact interpretation of
the Hippocratic Oath, and over the state of things in
England, and over his master's infatuation; and the four
subjects, diverse as they might sound, were all one.

The Sweating Sickness was a form of fever which
Englishmen sometimes called the Picardy Sweat, and
Frenchmen called the English Sweat. In France it was
endemic, a few cases here and there all the time; when
it broke out amongst English people, even inside the
Pale of Calais, it was always in the form of a horrifying
epidemic. It would decimate towns and villages, bring
business to a standstill and then vanish completely, and
perhaps there would be no other case for twenty years.
Unlike most other forms of sickness it chose most of its

155

victims from the upper classes. Its onset was sudden, a little pain in head or belly, burning fever, the prodigious sweating that gave it its name, coma, death. It was not, as some uninformed people averred, a form of the plague, for it left no outward sign upon the body. There was no known cure, and almost no palliatives.

The King lived in mortal dread of it; and this Dr Butts did not find strange; it settled upon the well-fed, the well-clothed, the well-housed, the well-born; therefore the King was its natural target. The moment it was known that the Sweat had broken out in London, the King had fled; and his behaviour since leaving London had been that of a man trying to elude a conscious human enemy out to kill him with a sword. He'd moved from manor to manor, making his moves suddenly, with no warning; and therein he showed wisdom, for in each abandoned house somebody had died of the Sweat almost as soon as the King had left. As though the enemy, finding Henry gone again, had slashed about with the sword indiscriminately. I've missed the King, so I'll kill you Carey, Poyntz, Compton . . . For a moment Dr Butts thought sadly of the dead.

For himself he had no fear, and he did not find that either surprising or praiseworthy; he'd known his moments of terror when he was young; but no doctor could pursue his vocation for long unless he could bring himself to believe that he was immune to disease. Doctors did die, of course, but chiefly as very young or very old men; it was remarkable when you considered the risks they ran, how few doctors between the ages of twenty-five and sixty died, or even had poor health. St Luke, their patron Saint, was watchful and powerful.

Dr Butts fingered his little golden medallion of St Luke; and breathed a little prayer of which he was almost, but not quite, ashamed, as soon as his mind had framed the words.

"Let her be dead before I arrive."

And that violated the spirit, if not the actual wording of his Hippocratic Oath. A doctor promised to do his best for his patients. And if Mistress Anne Boleyn were alive when he reached Greenwich he *would* do his best to keep her alive; see that she was wrapped in wool to counteract the chill which often followed fever, see that she drank quantities of liquid to replace what she had lost by the sweating. And that, he knew from experience, was really all that could be done. All the other nostrums, herbal, animal and mineral, he had proved to be quite ineffective.

News that the lady had fallen victim to the Sweat had reached the King at Tittenhanger, one of my Lord Cardinal's manors where he was making a temporary visit. (The Cardinal, staunch, admirable man, had stayed in London, keeping things together and ignoring the sickness. Quite possibly he had a secret faith in his low birth; a disease which could pick out an Englishman in Amsterdam, and which was unknown in Ireland, and stopped its ravages on the Scottish border, would have discrimination enough to see the butcher's son under the Cardinal's robes.) Henry had sent forthwith for Dr Butts and told him to ride hard to Greenwich and use his best endeavours to save the

157

lady's life. He'd been so near distraught that Dr Butts had ventured to offer a word or two of advice, telling him that mental distress could be a traitor opening the door to the enemy. "Above all things, your Grace must be of good heart and not fret."

God and His Holy Mother knew that this woman had done enough damage already without casting the King into a low state of mind which might invite the sickness.

Henry had said,

"I shall be calm and trust you, my friend. And you will send me word; three times a day. And carry this letter which I wrote in haste."

Dr Butts had thought then — If she dies, as she well may, it will be a heavy blow for him; but death brings its own anodyne as I know, having seen it a thousand times. And what a good thing for England!

Dr Butts, like the vast majority of people in England, had not been at all pleased with what had happened lately. He was fond of the King, as was almost everyone who came into close contact with him, he wished him to be happy, he wished that he had had a son to be Henry the Ninth. But he deplored an action which aimed at making good Queen Catherine nothing more than a harlot — after nineteen years of blameless marriage — and the Princess Mary a bastard. The King claimed that his conscience was uneasy and that had seemed feasible, until last year, at the end of the summer, when Mistress Anne returned to Court and the truth was out.

They said that when the Cardinal knew the truth he went down on his knees and stayed there for two hours, weeping, beseeching the King to abandon his insane plan to marry the Lady Anne. Take her, he was said to have urged, take her as you took her sister, and Bessie Blount, but in God's name I beg you, do not look to make her Queen.

The common people had been of the same mind, We want none of Nan Bullen. "Nan Bullen shan't be our Queen," they had shouted at street corners and tavern doorways whenever Mistress Anne ventured abroad; and by contrast, whenever Catherine went about, which she did now much more than formerly, they greeted her enthusiastically. "Long live *Queen* Catherine!" "God save the *Queen*!"

Anybody except the King, Dr Butts reflected, would have trimmed his sails to the prevailing wind. But Henry had not. And oddly enough, slow inch by inch, the tide was beginning to turn. Here and there a man would say, "Well, I married the wench I fancied, Pope or no Pope, and why shouldn't he do the same! The other was a rigged up job." Even Dr Butts, completely orthodox, couldn't help feeling a slight admiration for a man who could stick to his point in the face of so much opposition, so much argument, so much well-meant advice, and such long-drawn-out waiting.

People said that Anne was already Henry's mistress, but Dr Butts, who knew a good deal about human nature, and about Henry, found that hard to believe. It was the desire to possess, not the possession, that drove the King on. Earlier this year he had sent two of his bishops to argue out his case with the Pope, and in the end the Pope had agreed to send a Cardinal Campeggio to England to sit with Wolsey to decide whether the King and Queen were truly married or no.

Here Dr Butts broke off his train of thought to spare a little pity for this Cardinal Campeggio who was said to suffer most cruelly from gout, not only in his feet — common enough, but also in his hands. His progress across Europe was being slowed down because there were days when he could not hold his horse's reins. Dr Butts hoped that he would get an opportunity to look at those gouty hands. Perhaps, while Cardinal Campeggio was in England he might be persuaded to try drinking the waters at Bath, or Epsom, or another place, far to the north, in Derbyshire. There were known cases where they had brought definite relief to gouty subjects.

But it would be best for all concerned if Mistress Boleyn could die; then Campeggio could turn about and go back to Italy and a lot of woeful dirty scandal would be averted. If she died, Henry would go running to Catherine and weep on her bosom and she would comfort him. She still regarded herself as his wife and she still had a fondness for him; everyone said that she never spoke, or listened to, a word of criticism with regard to his behaviour; she would only say that Henry had been ill advised by his ministers, particularly the Cardinal, and bewitched by Anne Boleyn. (That, of course, was a mere figure of speech; Dr Butts, a religious man, did not believe in witchcraft and he was certain that the Queen, a religious woman, must be equally sceptical of it.) The Queen, God bless her, would comfort the King as a mother would comfort a child whose toy has been broken. Henry's own mother had died when he was only twelve and Dr Butts was one of the few people who realised that in a manner Catherine had slipped into her place. There'd been a brief time when the six years of difference in their ages hadn't seemed to matter much, but the pattern had been set long ago, before they were married, and it was quite possible . . .

Dr Butts hesitated upon the threshold of this far-flying fancy, and then went on. It was quite possible that the King had always looked upon the Queen as upon his mother and that when he spoke of an *incestuous* marriage, though he honestly believed he was referring to Catherine having been Arthur's wife, he was putting into words a thought too deep even for his own understanding.

As indeed my thoughts will be unless I take them in hand . . .

He looked at the fields on either side of the road. Winter and spring had been very wet, and the summer, so far, not much better; the corn was in poor shape and there was murrain amongst the cattle. Could there possibly be a connection between the outbreaks of murrain and outbreaks of the Sweating Sickness? That was a subject that would bear a little investigation. A poor harvest, a shortage of meat, and people would naturally say that the wrath of God was being visited upon the land.

And suppose the patient to whom he was travelling lived — a certain number of stricken people recovered — and the Cardinals got together and decided that the King and Queen had never been husband and wife in the eyes of the law, and that he was free to marry his paramour. A fine uproar there'd be. Or suppose the Cardinals decided otherwise; would the King then dare to attempt to do some of the things which in moments of anger he'd been known to threaten? Cut England off from the Pope and all things Papal? That was Lutheranism. It had happened in Germany. Could it happen here? God forbid. The way the drunken Germans amongst the Emperor's forces had behaved in Italy last year when the Pope was taken prisoner was enough to make any Christian man shrink from Lutheranism; monks had been stood against walls and made targets for arrows and knives and any other kind of missile that came to hand; nuns had been raped; Cardinals' houses had been stripped of all valuables and what couldn't be easily carried away had been smashed. People who knew said that the Germans had done more damage to Rome in one night than all the barbarian invasions had.

Tittenhanger was only twenty miles from London, and with his mind so occupied Dr Butts found the journey short; soon the countryside began to change, to become more populated; traffic on the road increased, though even so it was very light for the time of year; nobody went abroad on an unnecessary errand when the Sweat was about. He realised that the final stage of his journey would be made through the narrow streets and crowded hovels and tenements on the south side of the river, and since he had ridden almost twenty miles and breakfasted lightly, he began to look about for some decent hostelry where he could drink some red Burgundy wine — which he reckoned a great fortifier — and eat some bread and bacon. No beef or mutton while the murrain was raging; too many farmers were inclined to kill off a beast in the first stages of the disease and sell it as sound flesh.

Without turning his head Dr Butts raised his hand, a signal which his servant, riding respectfully at a little distance to the rear, with a box of medicaments strapped to the back of his saddle, understood and responded to, hurrying up alongside.

"We'll stop at the next decent inn, Jack. Do you know a likely one?"

"I do, sir. *St Peter and the Keys*. Three furlongs ahead, sir, with a great chestnut tree afore the door."

"Ride you on, then. Order me red Burgundy wine, bread and bacon; ale for yourself and water for the horses. That will save us time."

But he was doomed to waste time, not to save it; and maybe there the hand of God was at work. Maybe it was intended that somewhere in Greenwich Palace Mistress Anne Boleyn, burning with fever, would throw off her covers and, with no one to warn them, her attendants would let her lie and take a chill; or she might be in the hands of some ignorant doctor who still held to the old-fashioned theory that a sickness could be discouraged by denying it sustenance; so she would be kept without the water she needed, and so die.

163

Those were his thoughts when he reached the inn and found his servant under the chestnut tree, carrying on a shouted conversation with a woman who stood at an upper window. The door of the handsome inn was closed and a wisp of straw was nailed to it. That was the law in London and for a radius of four miles, a wisp of straw to mark every stricken house, and if anyone from one such must venture out he must carry a white-painted stick so that other people could keep their distance.

"They're smitten," Jack said, laconically. He had no fear for himself, he'd carried that black, brass-bound box into too many dangerous places not to be sure that he shared his master's immunity. "I keep trying to tell her we don't mind."

"It's against the law," the woman said. "There's a *law*. Any public place where there's a case of Sweat must close. You should know that."

"Who is sick?" Dr Butts asked.

"My man. Looks like he's dying."

"I am a doctor," Dr Butts said. "You can let me in, and my servant."

She gave a wordless cry and vanished from the window. Within a few seconds the bars of the door squealed and it opened. The woman, who had been firm and controlled when she spoke of the law, was now incoherent and babbling, with her thanking God and calling down blessings on Dr Butts and her declaration that it was a miracle which had brought him to her door.

"I can't work miracles," Dr Butts said; he then added, with a touch of professional pomposity, "I can advise. I shall give you precisely the same advice as I should give the attendants of his Grace the King should he, which God forfend, take the sickness. Are you alone here?"

"Why, no. My husband's sister is in the kitchen and her boy is in the yard."

"Then ask the other woman to make ready what I want." He told her briefly what he wanted and said that the boy should draw water for the horses. Then he climbed the stairs and found, as he had expected, the sick man lying almost naked on a bed soaked with his own sweat.

"Wrap him close, in your best woollen blanket," he said.

"And him so hot already!" the woman said in astonished protest.

"Do as I say. And give him plenty to drink, water, milk, ale, anything."

"But, good sir, it'll all run out again as sweat. This is the Sweating Sickness!"

"Are you instructing me?" Dr Butts asked coldly. Then, more kindly he said, "Wrap him warm and let him drink to replace the liquid he is losing, and he may live. Disobey my instructions and he has no chance at all."

He then went downstairs, and in the manner which he had learned as a young man, put the sick man out of his mind and applied himself heartily to his wine, his bread and bacon. Then, the meal almost finished, he remembered that he carried a letter. The King's letters to his sweetheart, in the past had been a matter of some speculation. Some people said that for a year or more, until she reappeared at Court, he had written to her every day. That was clearly an exaggeration. Nobody had ever seen one of the letters, not even the lady's father Sir Thomas Boleyn, beg his pardon, Lord Wiltshire; and that at least indicated that Mistress Anne was discreet and no show off. Some people said that she simply dared not show them, because they were couched in terms that contradicted her own statement, and the King's, that they were not lovers in the accepted sense.

So much mystery, so much gossip, and here was William Butts, by nature and profession a searcher out of truth, with one of these letters in his possession. Unsealed, too, being written in such haste; merely folded and the ends tucked in.

He looked around quickly. The sick man's wife was upstairs, his sister had gone back to cry in the kitchen, Jack had taken his bread and bacon and ale out into the yard and was talking to the boy of the house in the watery sunshine.

Without any great feeling of guilt, since the human mind is capable of entertaining only one predominant emotion and his at the moment was curiosity, Dr Butts unfolded the letter.

Sentences leaped up at him.

"The most displeasing news that could occur came to me suddenly at night." "I would willingly bear half of what you suffer to cure you." (Not the whole, part of Dr Butt's mind observed; well, at least Henry was

166

honest!) "My physician in whom I have most confidence is absent . . . from want of him I send you my second, and hope that he . . ."

Dr Butts read no further.

He was always warning people about the dangers of rage which could send a red mist swimming before the eyes, set the heart battering, swell one's brain, lead, uncontrolled, to death; but now his own rage was ungoverned.

"My second." In God's name then, who was his first. Wotton? Cromer? Yes, Cromer the Scot, the bumptious oaf; just because he'd done part of his training in Paris. It was nothing short of disgraceful, it was disloyal. Everybody knew that Scots and Frenchmen always joined together against Englishmen. Every time England went to war with France, the Scots came over the border, raiding and burning. The Battle of Flodden Field was only now sixteen years past. It was abominable to think that a Scot . . .

It was no comfort to Dr Butts to have his money refused, to be told that at any time whenever he passed the *St Peter and the Keys* he was welcome to the best the house could provide.

He rode in rage towards Greenwich and was almost there before he could think, wryly, of the old proverb that said that eavesdroppers never heard any good spoken of themselves. Likewise people who opened other people's letters deserved to take a knock on the nose. But all the way his horse's hooves seemed to beat out the hateful rhythm, my second best, my second best, my second best.

CHAPTER
ELEVEN

"Beauty and sprightliness sat on her lips."
Sanders

GREENWICH. JUNE 1528

Dr Butt's careful balancing of his professional integrity against the welfare of England had all been wasted. Mistress Anne Boleyn had passed the crisis when he arrived. She was alive, she was conscious, she had been handled wisely. She was covered with a warm, light blanket and on a table near the bed stood a tall jug of water and a Venetian glass goblet. And one of those middle-aged, hard-faced, short-spoken women who, in Dr Butts's experience, made the best nurses of all, was in attendance.

The lady looked, naturally, very ill still, and he addressed her in the soothing voice the situation demanded.

"His Grace sent me, my lady, as soon as he had word of your sickness."

Anne moved her head a little, and the fraction of the pillow thus exposed showed dark and damp with sweat.

"Emma!" The single word held accusation.

The woman said, "Yes. Yes, I did. It was only right he should know. You're mending now, thanks be to God, but suppose . . . With everything so disordered I took it on myself."

Anne said in a small thin voice, the words separated by indrawn breaths,

"I was afraid that he might feel that he should come. And he has such horror of any sickness."

"His Grace recognises his importance to the state," Dr Butts said, almost rebukingly. Then he remembered that he was addressing a patient and changed his manner. "His Grace will be delighted to hear that you are recovering."

A great many people in England and in other places would be sorry, he thought; and wondered again at the mystery of things; strong lusty men struck down and dead in a few hours, a creature as frail seeming as this surviving. Though of course it was early yet to tell; there was always the chest . . .

He said,

"If your woman supported you, could you bear to be raised a trifle? Half a minute, no longer."

So Emma held her while he laid his ear to her chest, and then to her back, alert for the little crackle, like a piece of paper being crumpled, which would betray the most dreaded complication of all, one which often killed people who had survived the sweating and the coma. There was no sign of it.

Emma said, "If you could hold her for another half minute, sir, I could slip in a fresh pillow; this one's drenched."

169

So, for half a minute Dr Butts held between his hands the body which had caused such an upset.

He'd seen her often enough, but never close to, and never without the ornate clothing, the jewels, the head-dress which lent bulk and importance. He was amazed to see how small she was. He allowed for the dramatic wastage of this disease and judged by the bones; they were like a kitten's, or a bird's; and her neck! He'd only once seen a neck so slender, and that was on a ten-year-old who was dying of the lung rot, and was not so long by two inches. Dr Butts, whose personal taste ran to plump, buxom females, wondered anew what a great hearty man like the King could possibly see in this woman. And if his true aim in all this tom-foolery was to get himself a good strong boy he could hardly have picked a less likely breeder.

Emma slipped in the fresh pillow, and almost gratefully Dr Butts released his hold and moved towards the foot of the bed.

"You will recover, my lady" he said. "The worst is over. I shall prescribe certain strengthening and heartening medicines; and you must keep warm, and quiet, and eat and drink well. I shall stay for a day or two, just to keep an eye on you."

"Will you let His Grace know that there is no cause for anxiety?"

"Indeed I shall. He bade me let him have news three times each day."

Then he remembered the letter.

He was tempted, really tempted to take it away and dispose of it. "My second best." Cruel, undeserved

170

humiliation. Where was the need to have said such a thing? Why not, "I send you my physician", or "one of my physicians", or "Dr Butts"?

Horribly mortified, he produced the letter and said, curtly,

"He sent you this."

And he thought — William Butts, if you hadn't pried this bad moment would have been spared you. And a worse moment might be on its way; suppose she asked him to read it to her! In what voice, with what manner did one announce one's own second-rate status?

He laid the letter within reach of her hand and would have made for the door, but the weak voice halted him.

"Wait, please. There may be something which should be answered, and if so, you could send word with your other message. Emma, lift me again."

He turned to the window and tried to think sensible thoughts. It is *something* to be second physician to a great King. Better that than to be first physician to the Duke of Norfolk. But he failed to convince himself. The truth had been spoken centuries ago by some Roman whose name Dr Butts had forgotten. Standing in some small provincial Italian town, the man had said that he would sooner be first man there than second man in Rome. And he had spoken. for all men, at all times, everywhere.

He heard the sound of paper being handled; he heard Anne's voice say, "Lay me down." Now he must turn. His face felt stiff and there was a stinging sensation at the back of his eyes.

She said,

"Dr Butts."

He turned.

"Thank you for waiting. There is a message. Tell the King that I am recovering, that I hope his health continues good and say that I thank him heartily for sparing me his best physician at such a time."

His best! But the letter clearly said "my second", and she couldn't know, unless she was the witch that people said she was, that he had read the letter and been so hurt. She couldn't know . . .

He looked at her and noticed her eyes for the first time. Beautiful, wonderful eyes, looking at him with apparent candour, but behind the candour there was depth upon depth of mystery, and secrecy and understanding, and something else, a distant-seeing look, as though she saw more, knew more . . .

He pulled himself together and said in a harsh voice,

"My lady, either the King mis-wrote or you mis-read. Dr Cromer holds pride of place. I have the honour to be His Grace's second physician."

She smiled and he realised that she had a beautiful mouth as well.

"Who can judge of that? Does it go by seniority? No matter. To me you are first, and will be, always."

His natural vanity — the thing which must be fed from without or it will turn and devour the inner man — seized on the word "seniority". That explained all. Those other words, "in whom I have most confidence", might never have been written; he wanted to forget them, and he did, promptly. Of course, everything in and around the Court had to be governed by some form of protocol or another. Seniority! And he'd never even thought of it. He'd worked himself into a stupid rage over nothing, nothing at all. He could have brought on an apoplectic fit!

He forgot that she was the cause of all the turmoil; that all the way from Tittenhanger he had hoped to find her past aid. He forgot everything except that she, lying flat and exhausted, had hit upon the magic, restorative word. Seniority. When he came to make the medicines that would fortify her, he would see that they were well-flavoured and palatable.

And he no longer wondered what it was that the King saw in Mistress Anne Boleyn, because he saw it himself. All the way down the stairs he tried to put a name to it. And failed.

CHAPTER
TWELVE

"I will do my utmost to persuade the King though I feel sure it will be in vain."
Campeggio in a letter to Salviata

"It is useless for Campeggio to think of reviving the marriage."
Wolsey in a letter to Casale

SUFFOLK HOUSE. OCTOBER 22nd, 1528

Henry was coming to supper with Anne in her fine new house. Having an establishment of her own gave her immense pleasure, not lessened by the knowledge that the house itself had been one of the Cardinal's possessions. He had offered it, Henry said, and in that offer there was a hint that at last her position was being recognised, and that even Wolsey found it expedient to please her.

The joy of entertaining in her own house was still new, and this evening was, in a way, a celebration. Cardinal Campeggio had at last arrived in England, and now things would move. Disabled by his gout and exhausted from the journey, he had taken to bed immediately upon arrival, but today he was to have had his first audience of the King who was now so confident of success that he was talking of being married within a year.

Henry arrived in a glum mood, one of those which he had himself, speaking in the garden at Hever, described as black. Such moods were more frightening and more difficult to deal with than his more frequent roaring rages, which, like bonfires, quickly burned themselves out.

She was relieved to feel, from the warmth of his kiss and the force of his embrace, that she was in no way the cause of his gloom, and set herself to cheer him, but without her usual success.

At last she said,

"Something is troubling you. What is it?"

"One of my headaches." But that, she knew, was not the full explanation. He was subject to severe headaches, from time to time, but ordinarily when thus afflicted, he was rather pitiable, childishly suing for sympathy and for comfort, pleased to have his head rubbed and stroked, and to be offered a sniff of her hartshorn or to have a cold wet handkerchief held over his eyes.

He ate hardly any of the special supper she had ordered, throwing so much to Urian that finally even that greedy dog was sated and flopped down in a corner with his stomach bulging like a whelping bitch's.

"What is the news?" she asked, at one point.

"No news. There's a joke though. I'll share it with you later."

She dared warrant that the joke would be a sour one.

It was.

They were alone, by the fire, and she was just about to break the heavy silence that had settled, when he said,

"I gave audience to Campeggio this afternoon. Do you know what he did, the moment he had kissed hands and gone through the formalities? He said — and he spoke as though he were offering me the sun, the moon and all the stars to play with — that Clement was prepared to make good whatever was lacking in Julius's dispensation, so that I could go back to Catherine, with an untroubled conscience."

And he'd taken the offer; that was why he was so surly. He was dreading the task of breaking to her the news that he could now never keep his promise, or make good his troth. She was, after all, to be flung aside, like Mary.

"After all this delay," Henry said, still in that dull, heavy voice, "when at last I thought Clement was moving on my behalf, he sends me this indubitable proof of what he thinks of my case. And the man who has come all this way to act as an impartial judge reveals his bias the first time he opens his mouth. A fine, fair trial that promises, doesn't it?"

So there was still to be a trial! He had not accepted the offer.

"What did you say?" she asked. Her voice had gone small and thin.

"I said that even tailors knew that a botched job couldn't be mended by a bit more botching. I said I should await the verdict of the Court."

Relief from fright made her speak vehemently,

"You should have sent him home. Straight back to Rome. As you say, it promises a fine fair trial when one of the judges is the Pope's man, and brings such an offer! It might as well never begin!"

Henry winced and put his hand to his head.

"It's not quite as bad as that," he protested. "It'll be an English Court, composed of English clerics. And Wolsey has equal power with Campeggio. This may just have been Clement's last attempt to evade . . . He can now assure himself, and the Emperor, that he has tried everything."

"Oh no!" she said. "Oh no! He'll have another trick up his sleeve, and after that another and another. While we sit here and grow old!"

The last words rang out with a passionate intensity. She had developed such a preoccupation with the passing of time, with the waste of time, that she dreaded each change in the name of the month, thinking, there's June gone, thinking, yet another November. And New Year's day was always so sorry a festival that she could take no pleasure in her presents. Another year!

The last two years, outwardly so glittering and gay, so enviable, had been years of strain, a walking of a tight-rope whose end receded as one approached it. Always just a little longer to wait. Hope, disappointment, hope, delay. It had been such a great day when the Pope had agreed to send Campeggio to judge the case in England; and then Campeggio had made the journey more slowly than ever a man had made that journey in the whole history of time. Now this!

And Catherine was still at Court; still proud and stubborn; still calling herself Queen, and being treated as such by everyone save Henry.

And there were the London crowds, watchful, jeering, uncivil.

There was the sharp division of all those about the Court; two parties, hers and Catherine's, and one would have to be very blind or very stupid not to see that of the two Catherine's was the more devoted, the more steadfastly loyal. Catherine's party was rooted in solid rock, tradition, personal affection, her own upon the shifting sand of Henry's favour and political expediency.

And always there was Henry himself. Up to a point he had tried to keep his promise about not demanding anything; but as time dragged on she could see that he often regretted it. Day after day she had faced the almost impossible task of making herself attractive enough to hold him, but not attractive enough to inflame his passion. This called for constant vigilance and self-control on her part, and those did not make for beauty. Often she wondered whether others saw the change in her that she saw when she faced her glass.

Henry heard in her voice a new note, a shrillness that displeased him.

It made him say, perversely,

"Oh no! That was Clement's last shifty little trick. It didn't work, he won't try any more."

"He will. He must. What Campeggio offered you today shows what the Pope wants, what they all want — your reconciliation with the Queen."

"She is *not* my Queen. She is the Princess Dowager."

"What does it matter how you name her? Let's face the truth for once. In the eyes of the world yours was a good marriage and only the Pope can annul it. He hasn't any intention of doing so. He daren't. The Emperor would box his ears or stand him in the corner. If you wait for the Pope to free you, you'll wait forever."

"What else can I do?"

"Send Campeggio packing. This is an English matter and you are King of England. The English bishops are anxious to please you. They'd give you the verdict you wish for. If indeed that is your wish. Sometimes I wonder."

"And what in God's name do you mean by that?"

"You say you are free, you also say that the one person who can set you free is the one person who will never do it. You must know by now that you cannot have me and the Pope, yet at every turn you choose him." The relief of speaking frankly at last was as intoxicating as wine. "Why not accept the Pope's last generous offer. Catherine has waited for this; go back to her. I shan't hold you to anything you promised me. All I ask is to be left in peace and have done with this everlasting waiting and promises that are as empty as blown eggshells."

Railing at him as though he were at fault. And she knew he had a headache. She hadn't sympathised with him, or tried any remedy. She was a screeching virago!

He stood up and flung at her the most hurtful words he could muster,

"In all our time together, Catherine never spoke to me like that," he said, and went away.

Anne did not recall her ladies but went through into her bed-chamber where Emma Arnett was placing freshly-laundered linen in the press, with little scented sachets between the layers.

Anne ignored her, went to the bed and flung herself face down, took a handful of the quilted cover in each hand and wrenched it and ground her face into the pillow, trying to hold back the screaming.

Emma, who had seen her face, thought, not without irony, that the moment had come at last; the moment when the bedroom door closed and restraint gave way. But at least *this* lady did not demand a shoulder to cry on.

In any case, Emma was fortified now; she was still devoid of pity, and any words of sympathy that she might use would still be dictated by expediency rather than feeling, but it was no longer an expediency concerned solely with her own situation; there would be purpose behind whatever she said. She had been warmly welcomed by the reforming group that centred around the shop in Milk Street, and its members had provided her with verbal ammunition to be used when occasion offered. This might be one such occasion; you never knew.

She went softly to the bedside and asked, "My lady, are you in any pain?"

"No. I'm frantic."

And that was all. This was a thing which Emma's advisers could never understand — the Lady's ability to keep things to herself.

"Don't bother," Anne said into the pillow, "to put away that linen. We're leaving London tomorrow."

"For long, my lady?" That was a permissible question.

"Forever!"

Emma was dismayed. What of the Cause? Queen Catherine had the support of the Pope, therefore it followed that Anne, whether she chose or not, must be the rallying point of the anti-Papal party. Emma's friends, and hundreds more, hoped that Anne would maintain her hold on the King and that the situation would develop in one of two ways. Either the Pope would give Henry an annulment and thus bring the whole Papacy into further disrepute; or that Henry would tire of waiting and act upon some words he had once said in a rage, "In England I am the only ruler." Either way would open the door to the Reformation. And for either thing to happen Anne was essential.

Emma made no protest, asked no question. She merely said, deeply cunning,

"The Cardinal *will* be pleased."

Anne heaved herself over and sat up, propped on her elbows, her eyes enormous in her white face.

"You would say that!"

"Is it not true, my lady?"

"Of course it is true! And not the Cardinal alone. I could count on my fingers the people who will *not* be pleased."

"No. There you are wrong, asking your pardon. Very wrong. You have friends, hundreds of them, whose faces you never see, whose names you do not know. Hundreds of them who" — her natural caution warned her not to say too much — "who hate the Cardinal. If you leave London and leave him triumphant there'll be many a sore heart tomorrow."

"Then they must bear them. My heart is sore, too. I have no wish to please the Cardinal, but nor do I wish to play in this mummery any more. The longer it goes on the sillier I shall look in the end. They mean to keep him tied to the Queen, lured on by false hopes until he is too old to care. He can't see it, or won't, and tonight, when I pointed out the truth . . ." Even now she hesitated for a second, but what did it matter any more? She broke through her habitual reserve and told Emma what had happened. "So what is there left to do but to retire with what small dignity is left to me?"

A bad decision, Emma thought. After an ordinary lovers' tiff it might not be a bad policy to withdraw for a while; but the King's parting words held a bitterness, a threat. If the lady left now he might remember her only as a nagging scold, he might take the easy way and go back to Catherine.

She said,

"Why don't you sleep on it, my lady? Things often look different in the morning."

"Sleep! I feel as though I shall never sleep again."

Emma thought for a moment and then said, diffidently,

182

"One of my friends has a friend who is an apothecary and last spring, when I had that arm that ached so and kept me awake, he made me up some syrup. He swore there was nothing nasty in it." Emma's loathing of reptiles extended to snails and earthworms which often found their way into medicines. "He said it was made of poppies, not like ours that grow in the corn, but poppies from somewhere far away. It is pleasant to taste and it does bring sleep. I've proved that. Would you try a dose?"

"Anything so as not to lie awake all night, thinking."

Emma went to her own low bed and pulled from under it the wooden chest, iron cornered and banded, which was one of her most cherished possessions. She had left home for her first post with all that she owned packed in a rush basket and she had saved for years in order to buy a chest with a lock, a serving woman's only stake in privacy; it represented her home. When she locked it, it was like locking the door of her house.

There was the wooden bottle, and when she shook it the liquid gurgled. She poured a careful dose into a cup and handing it to Anne said,

"May you sleep well, my lady."

It tasted of honey and then of something bitter.

Anne handed back the cup and said,

"Poor Emma! In addition to all else you have to be my confessor and my physician."

Emma thought — but without emotion — that it was a rare lady who was aware of the demands made upon her body-servant.

"You should get to bed now; it's quick working," she said, and set about the business of unrobing Anne, grumbling all the while in her mind. The idle lady attendants had gone off to play cards or make music as soon as supper was over. They'd came rustling back when all the work was done and pretend that they had not heard the King depart, or had been waiting for the bell to ring. In Emma's opinion all waiting ladies were lazy and frivolous and those attached to Anne at the moment were worse than most because they recognised the insecurity of her position; nobody wished to become too closely associated with one whose future was uncertain.

By the time that she was in her bed-gown and Emma was brushing her hair, Anne was feeling the effects of the dose. A great peacefulness; not truly sleepy yet, but so relaxed, uncaring, almost happy that she knew that when she did lie down she would sleep. The taunt about Catherine had lost its sting, it might have been said to someone else, long, long ago.

When, from the outer room, there came the sound of tramping feet and men's voices, she felt neither surprise, nor alarm nor interest.

"See who it is, Emma, and send them away."

Emma went briskly out, and came briskly back.

"My lady, it is the King and Sir Harry Norris. His Grace has brought you a gift."

Emma Arnett, the reformer, was delighted that the King had come back with a peace-offering. Emma Arnett, the servant, was less pleased. The Lady already had two dogs, Urian, growing old and incontinent, and Beau, presented by the French Ambassador, young and incontinent.

Anne tried to think what Henry's returning with a gift must mean. Reconciliation. But rocked on the soft opium tide she could neither think nor care.

"I'm sleepy," she said. "I can't talk."

The real, the dominating, managing woman in Emma came uppermost.

"You can say 'Thank you', surely," she said, and snatched up Anne's furred velvet robe, wrapped her in it, and spread her hair, a shimmering cape of black silk, over it. "Just thank him. You'll like what he's brought."

She led Anne to the door and hovered for a second until she was safely down the steps into the outer room.

Henry tried to cover the fact that he was ill-at-ease and unsure of his reception, by adopting a boisterous, blustering manner.

"I had to come. I couldn't wait to show you. Show her, Norris, show her!"

Norris spread wide the piece of velvet he carried and revealed a tiny puppy which might have been made out of the same material. Its domed head was wrinkled like a bloodhound's, its amber eyes were at once utterly innocent and full of ageless wisdom; everywhere its soft coat was a little too large for it.

"I spoke for it long ago and it arrived not an hour since. The Spanish Ambassador once mentioned the breed to me. Brave as lions, yet small enough for a lady's lap. All the way from Augsburg. The only one in England. I hope you like it."

"How could I not?" She took the puppy and held it against her. It put out a pink ribbon of tongue and licked her chin softly. "I love it."

"All right, Norris. You may go," Henry said. Norris said his good nights and withdrew. He was one of those who knew that the relationship between the King and the lady was, so far, blameless, and as he blundered down the stairs his admiration for his master increased. In that soft robe, with her hair all loose! What iron control the man must have.

Left alone neither Henry nor Anne spoke for a moment. She because the effort seemed not worth making; he because he knew he must apologise, and apologies never came easily to him. He brought it out at last,

"Sweetheart, I am sorry. I ask your forgiveness for speaking as I did. I'd had a trying day and my head ached, and then you pained me by calling my promises egg-shells. Then, as soon as I was back I found this little creature. I'd ordered it to please you; and I could have wept, Anne, I could have wept; it is so suited to you and to nobody else. So I brought it. Say I'm forgiven."

"There was nothing to forgive. I daresay what you said was true."

He stared at her. That was about the last thing in the world that he had expected her to say, and her manner of speaking, so remote and detached, alarmed him. It sounded as though there was nothing to resent because she no longer cared.

"It was an unforgivable thing to say. But I implore you to forgive me."

186

She stood holding the little dog, her head bowed over it.

"Promises," he said, a little wildly. "You said I broke promises. Anne, tell me, what promises did I ever make to you and not keep?"

She should have said, would have said, that no specific promise had ever been broken and that she had spoken in anger and disappointment. But the poppy syrup moved like Lethe water in her veins and the little dog lay warm and soft against her breast. All she could think of was sleep.

"It doesn't matter," she said.

And again it sounded as though she had done with him. He felt that had his present been anything but a dog, had it been a rope of pearls or some similar thing, she'd have let it fall to the floor.

"Of course it matters," he said violently. "You and I are troth-plighted; I am your servant. If ever I break a promise made to you I am unworthy of the name of knight, let alone King. Tell me, what promise? To make you Queen! Is that it? Sweetheart, haven't I tried? God's teeth! Do you think I like this delay? You said I chose the Pope. That isn't true. I use him. I must. Ours must be a proper marriage."

The little dog licked her again and she looked down at it with doting, dreamy eyes.

Paying *me* no attention at all, Henry thought; she's cast me off, she's no longer interested in what I am saying.

"Look at me! Listen to me! I'm going to make you a promise that I'll keep if it costs me my crown. If

Clement won't free me, I'll defy him. You are my one true love and I mean to have you, Pope or no Pope. Well? What do you say to that?"

She lifted her drowsy eyes and looked at him, and tried to find some words. She should have felt jubilant at this forthright statement of intention; and glad that he had taken their quarrel so much to heart. But she could feel nothing, except, far off, a faint obligation to make some response. So she smiled.

"Do you disbelieve me?" he demanded. "For God's sake, Anne, don't punish me this way. I've said I was sorry. I spoke in anger. Now I'm speaking in sober earnest and you *smile*. I tell you that for your sake I would break with the Pope if he forced me."

She made a great effort.

"I hope not. You're a Papist. If it came to that you'd hate me."

"Hate you? How could I? I could as soon hate myself. Here . . ." He snatched the puppy from her so roughly that it squealed a little, and set it on the floor. "I love you, I love you," he said, and took her in his arms and kissed her face, her throat, her breast, greedily and with mounting passion, in a way against which she was usually on guard. Tonight even her vigilance was lulled and for one wild moment he thought that she was on the point of surrender.

He saw, in that moment, all his brave thoughts about serving and waiting for what they were, trimmings hung out to hide the stark truth. This was the woman he wanted to bed with.

Only just in time she began to push him away with limp, helpless-feeling hands.

"You promised," she said.

"But, sweetheart, I want you. And you want me."

She wanted nothing but sleep, to give herself up to the cloudy, peaceful nothingness that drew closer and closer. To speak, to think was almost a pain. But she must.

"What I want has nothing to do with it. What I *don't* want is a child out of wedlock. *My* child must sit upon the throne."

She had hit upon the only argument that would, at that moment, have restrained him.

Right, of course, he thought, half-peevishly. And in a year, or less, he'd have her for his own. He must, should, *could* wait just that little more. He loosened his hold, kissed her once more in the manner that she approved and said,

"He shall!"

He bent and picked up the puppy.

"Let him lie against your heart and keep the place warm for me. Late as it is, I'm going to see Wolsey and warn him against that damned tricky Italian. So, sweetheart, good night. Sleep well and dream of me."

CHAPTER
THIRTEEN

"In the beginning of this yere, in a greate Hall within the Black Friars of London was ordained a solempne place for the two Legattes to sit in . . ."
Hall's Chronicle

BLACKFRIARS. JUNE 18th-JULY 23rd, 1529

Everyone was in his pre-arranged place and all was ready. George Cavendish, Wolsey's gentleman-usher, turned his eyes without shifting his head and looked about and thought that in this one measureless, static moment before the procedure began, the great hall at Blackfriars looked like a scene set out for a Masque. Only the music was lacking. From some hidden place the musicians should be plucking their strings, louder and louder in a crescendo which would end in a silence into which the first player would speak the words he had conned. But there was no music, merely the hushed sound of a number of people gathered together and waiting, the shoe scraping the floor; the small quickly smothered cough, the rustle of silk.

This was no Masque; this was reality; the culmination of all the talk that had been going on for years, all the speculation, all the negotiations, the appeals, the waiting and the worry. This was the

Cardinal's Court which was to investigate the reasons for the King's doubts as to the validity of his marriage to Catherine, and to decide whether the marriage was legal and must stand, or illegal and could be treated as though it had never been. It was in order to sit here, in judgment upon that issue, that Campeggio had made the painful journey from Rome; it was in preparation for what was to take place here today that Wolsey had sat up at night, studying, praying and fretting.

Cavendish loved his master; into this moment of waiting he breathed a little prayer, to Almighty God, to the Blessed Virgin, to holy St Thomas of Canterbury for whom Wolsey had been named, and to St George, his own patron saint — *Let things so order themselves that my master shall suffer no damage.* Then he amended it. *No further damage.* For he, so close to Wolsey, knew how much damage was already done by broken sleep, by sleepless nights, by loss of appetite, by anxiety.

No one would guess, Cavendish thought with pride; Wolsey looked well this morning, calm, stately and impregnable. His appearance benefited from comparison with that of his fellow Cardinal. Campeggio was seven years the older, and his face was marked by ill-health and pain. And even at his best, he had never had Wolsey's presence. Cavendish, himself a Suffolk man, derived immense satisfaction from the fact, the indisputable fact, that the son of a Suffolk butcher could outshine in appearance, in intelligence, in style, any other man in the world. Cavendish did not even except his King. Henry was handsome — but he was younger than Wolsey; he was very able — but Wolsey had schooled him; and on this vitally important morning he had a fidgety, uneasy manner which contrasted ill with his chief minister's calm. A scolding woman, Cavendish reflected, could work more havoc with a man than anything else in the world, which was why every decently run village had its ducking stool, or its scolds' bridle for the punishment of women who let their tongues run wild.

Wolsey, settling into his place, felt far from calm and impregnable. That halt, flutter and jerk on of the heart which he had first experienced almost six years ago was now a permanent affliction. He could only thank God that it was not plain for all to see, like Campeggio's gout. Only he knew about it, and so far he had hidden it well; but it was there, and occasionally it made him so short of breath that he was hard put to it not to open his mouth and gasp like a landed fish. And sometimes it seemed to shake the cage of his chest so that he longed to press his hands there and steady it. And there was, too, his other wretched, squalid little affliction which he had mastered in the only way he could; one small cup of water in each twenty-four hours all the time the Court had been sitting — and it had begun its preliminaries on the last day of May. Once the verdict was given, he'd drink a gallon, straight off, cold water, straight from the well.

In this suspended moment, he, like Cavendish, turned his eyes without moving his head and looked at his fellow Cardinal. Typical Italian, slippery as an eel. Civil, smooth, revealing nothing. The moment he had arrived in England he'd gone, without a word to

Wolsey, and infuriated the King by telling him of the Pope's offer to make good anything lacking in Julius's dispensation. The King had then sent for Wolsey and stamped and raged. "I want no more tricks like that. I want freedom, and you must get it for me, by hook or by crook. Or by God's Wounds, I'll find somebody who will! I heard the other day of some humble cleric with a good head on him. He thought of something none of my favoured advisers had hit on. Canvas the Universities of Europe, he said, and ask their opinion of this marriage. His name's Cramer, Cranmer, Canner, something like that; and by God he has the right sow by the ear."

It was disturbing to learn that some unknown little man had thought of a move which he himself had overlooked; but there was nothing irrevocable and ruinous about that. What bothered Wolsey far more than anything else at the moment was Catherine's attitude.

Either she had been very shrewdly advised or she had been inspired by the quintessence of feminine guile; she refused absolutely to approach the problem from the legal point of view, refused to admit that the solution lay in the validity or otherwise of Pope Julius's dispensation. She had taken her stand upon the contention that she and Arthur had never been man and wife, that their marriage had never been consummated. This meant that the Cardinals' Court would be forced to abandon the strictly legal ground and venture on to the quaking morass of a personal, very intimate relationship; most distasteful. And potentially dangerous; for though a legal document could be studied and argued over, clause by clause, and some rational conclusion drawn, nobody in this world could truly decide whether a marriage had been consummated or not — especially after a lapse of almost thirty years.

Wolsey was worried about Catherine. He was also troubled by a suspicion that Campeggio carried secret orders from the Pope; perhaps even a relevant document. Campeggio, since his arrival in England, had discussed the case with Wolsey, with a seething frankness and co-operation, saying, "We must see that . . ." saying, "It would be well if we . . ." saying, "Our contention is . . ." But always Wolsey felt that Campeggio held some thing in reserve, knew something, or planned something which he did not propose to divulge. And to ask a point-blank question would be undiplomatic, and useless since it would merely provoke a lie. His sense of something being hidden from him had slipped from his waking thoughts into his dreams, and his short snatches of sleep were often troubled by dreams in which he was searching for something immensely precious and important, hidden in some filthy place which he dreaded to explore and yet must.

All in all, these last few months had imposed strain enough to kill a cart-horse. Thank God the end was near.

For now the static scene sprang into life.

First the solemn proclamation of the Court's commission from His Holiness Pope Clement VII; then the crier calling, "Henry, King of England, come into the Court." The King from under his royal canopy, replied in a firm, loud voice, "Here, my lords." His fidgety, uneasy manner was the result of impatience rather than of lack of confidence. He was certain that his cause was good; he had attained his wish in having the case brought to open trial in his own country; and he had refused what he was sure must be Clement's last pathetic attempt to compromise. Now he wanted the whole thing over, finished, done with, as soon as possible.

The crier raised his voice again, "Catherine, Queen of England, come into the Court."

This was the last time — or one of the last times — that she would be addressed thus, Henry reflected. The Court would move slowly, high-ranking clerics were adept at making everything seem solemn by acting with great deliberation; but within a few days his claim to be a free man would be acknowledged, and he would be able to keep his promise to Anne. Queen Anne. It sounded well. He thought of all the work the stonemasons and the wood carvers and the embroideresses would have to do, removing all the C's from the places where they now stood, entwined with the H's, and substituting the A's.

Catherine, instead of replying, played a typically female trick. She stood up, gravely crossed herself and began to move towards where the King sat. She had aged and altered lately and could now well have been in her fifties instead of forty-four; her shoulders had bowed and her neck shortened, which gave her a dogged, stubborn look; but she had dignity, too. Her dress was in the Spanish style, sombre in colour, rich in fabric and she wore a good many jewels. She moved with assurance.

As she neared him, Henry gripped the arms of his great chair and looked to left and to right, as though meditating flight and seeking a way of escape. If that had been his intention he thought better of it and settled down to face her with a set, hard look. She knelt down before him and made a long speech, pitiable or irritating according to the inclination of the listener. The pretty broken-English which had been one of her attractions long ago had almost vanished, leaving only an oddly accented word here and there. Her voice was deep, at times almost gruff.

True to her plan, she made no mention of Pope Julius, or of the dispensation. She addressed herself to Henry as a supplicant, trying by words to stir a sentiment long since dead.

"Sir, I beseech you for all the love that hath been between us, and for the love of God, let me have justice and right, take of me some pity and compassion, for I am a poor woman, and a stranger, born out of your dominion. I have here no assured friends, and much less impartial counsel. I flee to you as to the head of justice within this realm . . ."

Ill-timed, Wolsey thought, coolly assessing; and out of place. This was a Court of law. What could she hope for by publicly putting the King in such an embarrassing situation? Surely there was no man in the place, not even Fisher, Bishop of Rochester, her most

196

confirmed supporter, who did not at this moment share the King's discomfiture.

It went on, grew worse.

"This twenty years or more I have been your true wife and by me ye have had divers children, although it hath pleased God to call them out of this world, which hath been no default in me. And when ye had me at the first, I take God to be my judge, I was a true maid without touch of man."

That was open to question; there were witnesses who would presently swear to the contrary.

She mentioned the King's father and her own, "They were both excellent kings in wisdom and princely behaviour." They and other men of good judgment had thought the marriage good and lawful.

She ended by what was tantamount to an insult to the Court, saying that it could not be impartial since it was composed of Henry's subjects, "and dare not for fear of your displeasure, disobey your will and intent, once made aware thereof". She begged that this Court should be dismissed and she be given time to consult her friends in Spain. "And if ye will not extend to me so much impartial favour, your pleasure then be fulfilled, and to God I commit my cause."

By the time she had reached the end she knew that she had failed. The healthy colour in Henry's face had deepened and spread into a flush of embarrassment, but there were white patches over his jaw muscles where the clenching of his teeth made them bulge against the skin. His eyes were as cold and hard as pebbles at the tide's edge. No hope.

She rose, made a deep curtsy and then turned and moved away, not towards her former place, but to the door.

Henry stirred and spoke, "Call her back!"

The crier repeated his call. Griffiths, Catherine's gentleman usher, offering his arm, said, "Madam you are called again." In a loud rough tone which carried back into the farthest corner of the Court she said, "I hear. But that is no court of justice for *me*! Let us go on."

Let us go on, also, Wolsey said to himself.

Everybody in the Court shifted a little in his place.

There was no such moment of drama on any of the ensuing days. They were largely spent in the hearing of evidence whose nature proved that Wolsey's misgivings, and his dreams of having to deal with filth, had been prophetic.

Catherine did not come to Court again, yet she dominated it, for it was her attitude which had shaped procedure. A woman, in her personal life modest to the point of prudishness, she had, by refusing to base her case on the validity of the Papal dispensation and choosing to fight instead upon the ground that she had gone virgin to Henry's bed, stirred up the very elements which any ordinary woman would have striven to suppress. The clear stream of justice was forced into many muddy little side channels.

What had Arthur meant exactly in 1501 when he said, "Tonight I have been in Spain"? How could one overlook his calling for wine and saying, "Marriage is thirsty work, my masters"? At what age was a boy capable of consummating a marriage? There was no lack of witnesses ready to declare that they themselves had been no mean performers at an earlier age than fifteen. And even if old waiting women came forward to swear that in all Catherine and Arthur had only bedded together for twelve nights, what did that prove? A virgin could be deflowered in an hour.

To Wolsey the whole business was unutterably distasteful. He'd urged from the first that the Court should concern itself with law, and law only, not with old men's lecherous memories and old dames' gossip. But, though disgusted he was not unhopeful. Catherine had said a true thing when she said that this Court dare not do other than declare for the King. Fisher would certainly declare for Catherine, Ridley almost certainly; there were a few dubious ones, but the majority would be ruled by the King's known wish, and confirmed in their decision to do so by the case Wolsey had prepared, with its careful repudiation of Catherine's absurd claim.

The days dragged on, each one warmer and stuffier than its predecessor; the air grew steadily more polluted, past the help of the little posies, fresh each day, to redeem.

Campeggio, giving no sign at all, must have seen, as Wolsey had, the way the Court was tending. On July 23rd he acted, abruptly, in obedience to the secret orders which Wolsey had always suspected him of having received. Wolsey could imagine the very words Clement had spoken — If it looks as though the

English will themselves declare the marriage good and valid, by all means let them do so: if they veer the other way, advoke the case to Rome; that will gain us time.

At exactly the right moment Campeggio rose and said that the legal issue was far from being decided, but procedure had gone as far as it could in England. This was a great matter, one upon which all the eyes of the world were fixed and nothing must be done in haste. This was a case for the Courts of Rome, and thither it must be advoked.

There was a second's stunned silence and then the sound of heavy footsteps moving fast. From his place in the gallery where he had come, on this last day of the trial to hear a decision in his favour, the King of England went stamping out.

The butcher's son from Ipswich, grown so tall, a man on two stilts, one his King's favourite, the other the power of his Church, faced, without a second's preparation, the most agonising, the most desperate decision of his whole life.

His treacherous heart betrayed him; it began to gallop and thunder, shaking his chest, deafening his ears. Sweat broke out on his forehead and neck. All the astonished, angry faces moved together in a pale blue which began to go round and round, dizzyingly before his eyes.

Yet within this physical collapse his mind was steady; it stood, as the chimney-stack of a burned or ruined house will often stand when all else is gone. He could still think, coolly and clearly. He knew he had a choice of actions.

He could stand up, now, and declare firmly that this was an English Court, called to consider a matter which concerned England, and that he, as an Englishman, intended to proceed. He could ask Cardinal Campeggio to retire, and go on alone, ask for a decision and have it, within five minutes.

That was what the King wanted, expected of him. And he could always justify himself to himself by remembering that had the Pope remained a prisoner in San Angelo, he would have conducted this Court alone and accepted its verdict.

But not now.

Not now.

He was a Prince of the Church, and the Head of that church was the Pope, who was still performing his functions — the presence of Campeggio proved that. The Pope had given Campeggio his orders, and by implication, they were orders to Wolsey too. And he must obey. For he, too, was a good churchman and throughout his long career had never yet done anything to undermine the authority of the Church, the one, holy, indivisible Catholic Christian Church. Within it he might scheme and spar, jostle for position, debate and demur, but always inside it. He could never over-rule or ignore a direct order from St Peter's successor, the supreme authority, the Pope.

It might, almost certainly would, mean personal ruin; but greater issues were involved.

He had thought so rapidly that there seemed to those watching and listening no more than a breathing space between Campeggio's last words and Wolsey's smooth utterance,

"Then this Court is adjourned."

The decision once taken, his heart steadied, he had his hearing, his sight. The blur of faces broke up into their individual identities and here was one, coming forward, insolent and angry. Its owner banged his hand on the table behind which the Cardinals sat.

Charles Brandon, Duke of Suffolk.

He'd gone, years ago, to bring back to England, Henry's sister, the young widowed Queen of France. They'd fallen in love and married and Henry had been furiously displeased; but he had yielded in the end to family feeling, accepted and advanced Suffolk, who now saw a chance to repay, to prove his loyalty. But he was a stupid, witless fellow and all he could do in this moment of crisis was to bang on the table and shout,

"Things have never gone well in England since we had Cardinals amongst us."

Campeggio slightly turned his head and looked at Wolsey as though to say — I defined my position quite clearly; you deal with *this*.

Wolsey said,

"My lord, we are but commissioners, and our commission does not allow us to proceed further without the knowledge and consent of our chief authority, which is the Pope."

Campeggio in his speech had spoken of his conscience, his soul, of his age and his sickness. Wolsey, the butcher's son, scorned such irrelevancies.

Campeggio looked at Wolsey with grave approval. (In his final talk with the Pope he had asked, "And if I am compelled to make this announcement, how will the English Cardinal take it?" Clement had said, "Correctly. He has that respect for my office only possible to one who has entertained hopes of occupying it." Campeggio had thought then that Clement was a little over-optimistic, but he had been right. Under all that fumbling, bumbling manner Clement was shrewd, and it was a great pity, Campeggio thought, that he had never met Henry of England. That fanatical intelligent eye, that bull neck, that curious blend of manner, familiar, formidable. Now that the case was to be advoked to Rome, perhaps the two might meet and Clement would see that behind the petulant boy who wanted his own way, there was a rock of a man who intended to have it. Face to face with Henry, Clement would give way. It was only a matter of a little more delay. The Roman Courts reopened in October.)

The two Cardinals rose, bowed to one another, and then to the assembly, and in a rustle of silk, retired.

Wolsey expected to be met at the door with a peremptory summons to wait upon his King. But there was no messenger and he passed along and went to his great house, York Place, tasting, for the first time, the loneliness of those who fall, suddenly, from high places.

CHAPTER
FOURTEEN

"The Lady is all-powerful here, and the Queen will have no peace until her case is tried and decided at Rome."
The Spanish Ambassador to Charles V

"Mark Smeaton, a performer on musical instruments, a person specified as of low degree, promoted for his skill to be a groom of the chambers."
From the indictment for high treason

SUFFOLK HOUSE. JULY 1529

She knew by the look on Henry's face that it was over and the verdict bad, so when at last he became coherent enough to make a straightforward statement it came as a relief. At least no judgment was yet given.

"I was so angered by the trick the damned Italian played," Henry said, "that I came out. Then I stopped. I thought to myself, Wolsey knows what I want and here is his chance to give it to me. So I waited, and next thing I knew, they were telling me that he had agreed to adjourn the case and we're back as we were. Except that now I know the truth about *him*! I've treated him better than most men treat their brothers; gifts, favours, preferments! There's not a King in Europe, there never was a King anywhere who let a subject swell so large. But he'll learn, the jumped-up jack-a-nape. I made him, and I can unmake him. I can't take away his bishopric, or his rank as Cardinal, but everything else I'll strip him of. Ungrateful dog!"

He raved on in that manner for several minutes, repeating himself often.

She thought of an angry, impotent child burying a laurel leaf.

She said,

"He was always my enemy."

"He called himself my *friend*, I called him my true Thomas! But Christ Himself said it, no man can serve two masters, and Wolsey is the Pope's man. I see now how I have been fooled. But that's over. I've been ill-served by Cardinal Facing-both-ways. I'll replace him by somebody who can bring Clement to heel. And I'll go ahead with Dr Cranmer's suggestion for canvassing the opinions of the Universities. I haven't shot my last bolt yet. Far from it."

"You'll let them take the case to Rome?"

"Oh, most certainly; if only to show that I am serious. That's half the trouble. Nobody yet has taken this thing seriously. They thought it was an idle fancy I'd taken and if they made me wait long enough, I'd give up. The original brief of the damned dispensation is still locked up in the archives at Rome or Madrid. We'll have that out and know why it wasn't produced before. Cheer up, sweetheart. We shall win."

Between threats and plans he had talked away the worst of his hurt and disappointment, and when two pages hurried in bringing the dishes of cherries and sugar-strewn raspberries which Anne had ordered to be served on his arrival, and the Rhenish wine that he loved, nicely chilled from being hung down the well, he was ready for refreshment. It was some moments before he realised that she had been very silent and that her look of seeing something invisible to others — and not much liking it — was more than ever in evidence.

Wiping his sugary lips on the back of his hand he said,

"You're downcast. So was I until I put my thoughts in order. And Wolsey did *betray* me."

The fury in her wanted to cry — And if you let the case go to Rome, *you'll* betray *me*! The night you brought the little dog you promised that if things went wrong you'd break with the Pope.

Angry words which it would be bad policy to utter burned in her brain. More waiting! And she was twenty-two, already; no longer young by any standard, and worn sharp and thin by waiting, by constant vigilance, by the dreadful insecurity of her position. In a man, of course, it mattered less, but the years were not improving Henry either. Denied one fleshly pleasure he indulged too freely in those he could command, he both ate and drank too much. Look at him now! He was growing thick and heavy. And he was thirty-eight.

She thought, with a sudden burst of spite, of Catherine, stubborn, impervious and arrogant. Catherine, who, having failed to give Henry an heir was doing her best to make sure that no one else should. Catherine had behaved throughout as though she were the whole garrison of a beleaguered city: she would not even discuss terms of surrender; she was sure that eventually her allies would come to her aid. And so far no pressure had been brought to bear upon Catherine at all; a few feeble arguments which she ignored.

Anne had mastered the art of suggesting things to Henry. So now, concealing her true feelings, she said in a musing, almost dreamy way,

"Yes, Wolsey betrayed you; but Catherine also served you ill, I think. She took her stand upon something impossible to prove or disprove, instead of upon law. All things considered I think your magnanimity towards her does you great credit."

"Sometimes I wonder at myself," Henry said, smoothed and flattered. "The truth is, sweetheart, that I find it difficult to be harsh to a woman. And much as I deplore her attitude, I understand it. She for twenty years regarded herself as my wife and Queen of England. She finds it hard to let go."

It might seem crazy, but it flashed upon Anne that the truth was that deep down he took Catherine's behaviour as a compliment to himself. It was as though she had tired of Urian's surliness and incontinence and had tried to give him away and he refused to settle in any other place, kept coming back, shoving his head into her hand and saying wordlessly, "But I belong to you!" Henry honestly wished to be free of Catherine, but her refusal to let him go made an appeal to his vanity.

She said, "There are people who find it hard to cross a stream by way of stepping stones. If it is a stream that *must* be crossed, it is sometimes necessary to give them a little push to start them going."

"And what little push, sweetheart, could I give Catherine? I've argued, pleaded. All to no purpose."

"You could begin by separating her from the Princess Mary. They are of like mind, they hearten one another. And if that failed of its purpose you could . . ." But why should she suggest every detail? "You know how to show displeasure. If the Queen could be brought to see reason, the Emperor would no longer feel he must support her, nor Clement feel fear of the Emperor."

"Why do you insist upon calling her the Queen? I've remarked it before."

She said, sweetly reasonable,

"Most people do still so call her. And surely it would ill become *me* to be the first to deny her the title."

Henry laughed. "You have an answer for everything. And you are right about her. I've been too indulgent. But things will be different from here on, I promise you. With Wolsey out of the way, and Catherine brought to her senses — separation from Mary, even for a month, will do *that*, and I wonder I never thought of it before — and with Cranmer at work, it shouldn't be long . . ."

He looked at her, and the lust which he had learned to control in his speech, his hands and lips, shone in his eyes. He was so blindly in love that he saw no difference between this woman and the girl who had caught his fancy six years ago, the girl he had thought too good for young Percy. For him she represented the not easily attainable and he meant to have her at all costs. The long waiting, the forced celibacy, the scandal, and today the loss of his oldest and best friend, what did they matter?

As on all but the one occasion, he left her strengthened and heartened and in a better mood than that in which he had arrived.

Anne had no support; nothing but her own pride and ambition, both in such thwarted moments prickly props indeed. And today, to disappointment and the appalling prospect of another period of waiting, there was added a curious little fear. Not superstitious exactly, but tending that way. She had cursed Wolsey; today he was ruined and no one could deny that she had been instrumental in bringing about his ruin. Suppose that were all? The end of the story. Suppose that life was like a masquerade where some people had major parts and others minor, contributory ones, of no importance in themselves, only as they affected those who mattered. She could imagine the summing-up of the chroniclers — *The King, falling in love with one, Anne Boleyn, desired the annulment of his marriage, which the Cardinal failing to obtain for him, he fell from favour.*

That was a thought truly unbearable; it made her nothing. It denied the very existence of the girl who had been young, capable of happiness, whom the Cardinal had smashed, as one might smash a glass beaker, and whom circumstance had put together again, not quite in the same shape, but alive and sentient. No longer young, or gay, or capable of loving any man as she had loved Harry Percy, but a creature with a boundless ambition, a future Queen of England, mother of the next King. Wasn't she important? Wasn't hers the central story?

She knew that if she remained alone, thinking these roundabout thoughts, she could drive herself distracted. She could go and fling herself on her bed and be fussed over and ministered to by Emma Arnett, who secretly despised her. Or she could call in Mark Smeaton.

Smeaton was a country boy who had joined her household in a menial capacity but had proved himself to be a most skilful musician. Fond of music, and able performers themselves, she and Henry had gathered about them some gifted singers and players; but Smeaton, out of the kitchen, surpassed them all. The lark, the nightingale, as opposed to the thrush and the blackbird.

Often, when he played for her, Anne thought of the story of King Saul and the shepherd boy, David, in the book of stories known as the Old Testament, which had now been translated and smuggled into England, following upon the New Testament. Emma Arnett had introduced a copy into Anne's apartments, saying, in an off-hand way, "My lady, I found it entertaining, and I wish someone with more learning could tell me why it is forbidden reading." Anne had found it entertaining, too, though some of the stories were horrible. The King Saul whom she remembered every time Mark Smeaton played for her, had suffered from possession by an evil, melancholy spirit and David, by playing the harp, had been able to exorcise it.

Now, with her own evil, melancholy spirit set ravening by the outcome of the Blackfriars trial and the prospect of further waiting, she sent for Mark.

He was a shy, awkward young man, with a peasant's blunt features, slow speech, big hands and feet. Nobody who had not heard him perform could have believed that those hands could be so delicate, so nimble, so expert. In other ways, too, his bucolic appearance was deceptive; he was excitable, easily moved to tears or laughter, and very vulnerable to pain. He would cry like a child if a tooth ached.

What she said to him that morning was said partly from kindness, but in far greater measure from a need to assert herself.

She said,

"Mark, I should like you to play for me. And before you begin, I want you to know that in future you are to be my own, personal musician. What other tasks you have hitherto performed are ended. You may get yourself fitted for a black velvet suit and rank as one of the gentlemen of my household."

It was his wildest, most impossible-seeming ambition come true. He broke down and cried, protesting his undying gratitude, his loyalty and service forever. He used the words, "When you are Queen . . ." which none of those who knew her mind ever did; and he said it would give him joy to die for her. She made allowance for his delight and surprise, and for the over-enthusiasm that so often went with great talent, but even so it was tedious. She said, coolly,

"I trust that will not be necessary, Mark. And now, please play."

He then looked at her with the baffled, hurt expression of a dog that has been chided and wonders why.

CHAPTER
FIFTEEN

"Then the King took my lord up by both arms . . .
and led him by the hand to a great window, where
he talked with him"
Cavendish. *The Life of Cardinal Wolsey*

GRAFTON. SEPTEMBER 14th, 1529

Dr Butters had been sufficiently sensitive to the
atmosphere prevailing in London not to have bothered
about any suggestions for the relief of Cardinal
Campeggio's gout. Something, it seemed, had gone
wrong with the first interview between the King and
the Italian, who thereafter had been treated with the
exact amount of respect to which his rank and
commission entitled him, but with no sign of favour.
So, when Cardinal Wolsey and Cardinal Campeggio
rode out on a bright September morning to go to
Grafton where the King and the Lady were staying,
Campeggio's swollen hands still shrank from the touch
of the reins, his feet from the pressure of the stirrups.

Horse-riding was indeed so painful to him that he
had tried using a litter, but the jolting had put his
whole body in misery. There was only one comfortable
means of transport for him, and that was by water. As
he rode along, he reflected, without rancour, that had

he given Henry the verdict he desired, the King would have taken pity on his wretched state and ridden back to London so that the formal leave-taking could have been performed at Greenwich or Westminster or Windsor, places all accessible by barge. In a covert kind of way Campeggio was being punished, and knew it, and conscious that he had merely carried out his orders, bore the misery with fortitude.

Wolsey, jogging alongside, envied Campeggio, who was going back to his master to report a job well done; who knew where he was going, and what kind of reception he would get; where, in fact, he stood. Wolsey knew none of these things. The last seventy days had been wretched beyond his fears: not on account of what had happened but because so little had.

Hour by hour, since leaving the hall in Blackfriars, Wolsey had expected to be summoned into the presence and denounced, scolded, raved at, punished. But once face to face with Henry he would, sooner or later, have been given an opportunity to state his case and to explain his reasons for siding, at the critical moment, with Campeggio. He had a good case, and his reasons were valid.

The King had sent no word. Wolsey's messages, written and verbal, had been ignored. It was as though for Henry, Wolsey had ceased to exist on that hot July day.

And not for Henry alone. Wolsey had made one attendance, in the usual manner, to his Court of Star Chamber and found it deserted save for officials and ushers. The empty space cried aloud that men no longer came to him for justice, no longer looked upon him as arbiter. Yet he was still in office, still held the Great Seal of England in its velvet bag. His ancient enemies, the Dukes of Norfolk and Suffolk, had made one attempt to take it from him; they had arrived, late at night when he was abed, and demanded that he yield it up. He asked, as a matter of routine, to be shown the authority, direct from the King, which was the only thing which legally could oblige him to relinquish the Seal and was greatly surprised — because this was the kind of development which he had hourly expected — to find that they had none. He had then said, with that calm so often decried as insolence, that he had received the Seal from the King's own hand, and could only deliver it to someone who brought an order for him to do so, signed by the King. They had gone, furious, away; and they had not come back. And so, on this September morning, though the King had ignored him for seventy days, he was still Chancellor of England and the Keeper of the Seal.

And he was on his way to see the King; on a necessary errand, the escorting of a visiting dignitary to his formal leave-taking.

When he thought of meeting Henry he had the old bother with his bumping heart and his breathing. It was a thing which few people in this cynical world would either believe or be able to understand, but he was, in reality, devoted to Henry in a way which had nothing to do with ambition or policy. He was twenty years older than his King, he had trained him in state-craft and taken great pride in his budding ability; to a large degree his feeling towards Henry was paternal, but their relationship was almost infinitely complicated, Henry being his King, his patron, his master and his friend, as well as being, physically, the man Wolsey, or any other sensible man, would wish to be, and mentally an equal. They shared, too, a sense of style, a liking for ostentation, for the grand, generous gesture, and their love of England.

Their attitudes upon the latter point, were, Wolsey admitted to himself, subtly differentiated. What he himself had done at Blackfriars, un-English upon the face of it, was in the long run, and would be seen to be eventually, for England's good. To have proceeded with the business and defied the Pope, would have been to divorce Henry from Catherine, certainly, but also to divorce England from Christendom and reduce her to the level of those wretched little German states which had gone over to Lutheranism.

And, Wolsey said to himself, he had saved Henry from a disastrous marriage.

He was shrewd enough to have seen, long ago, that Mistress Anne Boleyn — Lady Anne Rochfort as they now called her — was different from any other woman in one thing only — her ability to say "no" and to go on saying it. And what did that prove? Merely that she had no true feeling for Henry and was as ambitious and self-seeking as her father and brother. And her uncle, Norfolk. Wolsey could see, in a way, what had happened to Henry; he'd accepted the challenge; for to a man who could command anything, a single repulse, such as any other man would dismiss with a shrug and the

216

reflection that there were as good fish in the sea as ever came out of it, must be a challenge. And *fish* was a very apt word. She was cold as a fish. No normal woman, with warm human blood in her veins, could possibly have held out against such a wooing as the King had made to her all these years. She'd said "no" once and got a diamond bracelet or some other trinket, and with true Boleyn cunning she'd decided that by saying the same thing enough times she'd get the Crown.

And Wolsey did not *blame* Henry. He remembered his own youth, his hot pursuit of Joan Larke, his non-canonical marriage. It was something that got into men and rendered them not fully responsible; there'd been times when, had Joan Larke stipulated any fantastic conditions before admitting him to her bed, he would have moved heaven and earth to comply with them. He remembered, and remembering understood.

Maybe the exercise in the open air just at this briskening season had something to do with it, but whatever the reason, the optimism without which self-confidence is impossible began to rise in him anew. He reflected that had Henry intended to disgrace him publicly, he would hardly have waited seventy days, he'd have done it in the full flush of anger. It was just possible that the silence and the withdrawal had another cause, Henry might be having trouble with the Lady, who must have seen, by the result of the Blackfriars trial, that the road to the Crown was not as easy as maybe she had supposed. There'd been no public outcry, for one thing. The sycophants and the self-seekers had followed the King's example in

217

shunning Wolsey — that was only to be expected, but the ordinary common man of the London streets had accepted the advoking of the case to Rome without protest. He didn't want Anne Boleyn for his Queen, and she would have to be very stupid not to realise it. She wasn't stupid, Wolsey granted her that. She had indeed a very pretty wit which he acknowledged, even though it had occasionally been exercised at his expense. He had not forgotten his return from France, in the summer of 1527. During his absence she had returned to Court and been established in her anomalous position, neither wife nor mistress: and he, returning from a mission to a foreign country, had sent the formal message to the King, announcing his arrival and asking where he and the King should meet, so that he might make his report. The Lady had replied to the messenger, before the King should speak, "Where else should he come but where the King is?" And that was, of course, the actual true answer, though not couched in diplomatic words. Everybody had found it vastly amusing . . .

Wolsey pursued his own train of thought for some time, and then looked sideways at Campeggio. He didn't like the man, and considered that his action at Blackfriars had been unfriendly, though proper enough, but they were still upon good, if not intimate terms. He might risk some plain speech now. So he edged his horse a little closer to Campeggio's slow-paced mount, and said,

"When I come into the King's presence it will be for the first time since the Court rose, as you know. I

218

displeased him and he may be short with me. It would ease matters if I knew the answer to one question. You have the answer, or should do. Would His Holiness be more disposed to grant the annulment, when the case comes up in Rome, if His Grace were minded to take for his next wife some lady other than the Lady Anne?"

Campeggio said, after a small pause for thought,

"The case will be tried upon its merits. I am not a seer, nor am I conversant with His Holiness's intentions; but I think it would be safe to say that he will take into consideration the ultimate good of all concerned and such consideration must include the future of this country as part of Christendom."

It was answer enough for Wolsey, with his long experience of circles where nobody ever said a plain yes or no. He said, musingly,

"She is not — and when I say unfortunately I mean from the practical, not the moral standpoint — his mistress. In some respects her behaviour may be open to criticism, but her character is not."

"Had she been his mistress this situation would hardly have arisen."

"There I must disagree. The phrase, 'the King's conscience', may be becoming a joke, but I assure you that it was active long before this infatuation befell him. And the Princess Mary's legitimacy was being questioned before Anne Boleyn had all her second teeth."

"Not openly, nor with quite such vigour. That doubt exists is undeniable, otherwise why am I here?" He shifted his rein and flexed his painful fingers. "The

219

Roman courts will find an answer," he said, with an air of dismissing the subject.

"If the King should ask you whether their verdict will be in his favour or not, what would you tell him?"

"His Grace would never ask me such a question," Campeggio said reprovingly. "I have done what I was sent to do, and now I come to take leave. No one has ever suggested that the King of England is lacking in manners."

Only people of low birth pressed questions likely to embarrass.

"He will ask me — if we have any conversation at all."

"If you are wise you will say what I just said, that you are not a seer."

Clearly, Campeggio had no idea of what he had done, of what he had compelled Wolsey to do. One answer like that, at such a tricky time, could land a man in the Tower!

Shortly after, he wished that he *were* in the Tower. There was at least a certain dignity about an arrest, on whatever trumped-up excuse; and the Tower was private. Yes, he would have found it easier to walk in by the Traitors' Gate than to suffer the public humiliation in the courtyard of Grafton manor house.

Like many of its kind, Grafton had grown gradually, with rooms added as the need arose, each set with its stairway. One stairway, and the apartments to which it led, had been prepared and set ready for Cardinal Campeggio's occupation. When the Cardinals' cavalcade came to a standstill in the courtyard, men had come forward, some to take his horse, some to escort him to his stairway, some to carry his baggage, some to show his servants to their quarters.

For Wolsey nothing. No welcome, no accommodation. Only the sly gloating in the many watching eyes, the air of waiting to see what he would do now.

They expected him to break down. There was, he knew, a supposed difference between the behaviour of the well-born and the lowly in moments of crisis, but Wolsey had lived long enough and seen enough of the world to know that subject to the right pressure men of the highest lineage could crawl and fawn and weep. The butcher's son from Ipswich was determined to show, in this moment of ordeal, an example of that ground-level fortitude which kept poor men alive.

He sat on his mule — thankful that he had not alighted, and with his own dismayed little retinue behind him, he watched Campeggio being received. His expression revealed nothing; he might have been a figure cut from rock and painted and garbed to look like a Cardinal. His mind was made up. So long as the mule could stand — and mules had great powers of endurance — he would sit here. When the mule dropped he would stand until he fell, too. He had a right to be here; to escort the visiting Cardinal to his leave-taking was part of his duty; and if he were made to look like an unvited guest, that was not his fault, or even his concern.

He did not believe that the King had ordered matters in this fashion. Henry was angered, yes; but he was incapable of retaliation in this petty, malicious way. This was the work of the Lady, that night-crow who sat on Henry's shoulder and whispered. She, even more than the King, had been angered by his behaviour at Blackfriars, and her revenge was this attempt to keep him out of the King's presence. She imagined that, rebuffed, he would turn and ride away. Norfolk-born herself; Wolsey thought wryly, she should have known a Suffolk man better; the stubborn refusal-to-be-shifted quality of East Anglians was a by-word.

Firmness was rewarded. After ten agonising minutes that seemed like half a lifetime, out came Sir Harry Norris, the King's favourite, the Groom of the Stole; and he must have come direct from the King. He said,

"My lord, this house is very small, and Cardinal Campeggio, a stranger in the land, was offered the only available accommodation. If you could bear the inconvenience, and make shift with my own apartments, I should be honoured."

"I accept gladly, Sir Harry, weary and soiled from riding as I am. But I have no wish to put you about. If I may borrow your chamber briefly, Cavendish here will ride around and find some place for me to spend the night."

Had the offer come from anyone else it might have been attributed to pity, or to spite, an underlining of his lack; but coming from Norris it could mean but one thing, that the King, as soon as he was acquainted with the situation had taken immediate action to make amends. Otherwise Norris, so close to the King, would never have dared make such an offer.

He dismounted gladly; and hope was again renewed.

He was washed and robed when Campeggio came to join him. If the Italian were aware that there had been anything lacking in Wolsey's reception he gave no sign. In mind and spirit he was probably already far away, back in the temporary Papal Court in Orvieto where the problem of the English marriage was one of many problems. As he himself had said, what he had been sent to do was done; whereas for Wolsey another stage was just about to begin. His heart resumed its rattle, quietened a little and then began again, more violently, when Sir Harry Norris came to announce that the King was ready to receive the Cardinals.

They made their slow and stately progress to a sizeable hall which had been made into a presence chamber by the erection of a canopy and the placing of a chair at its further end. The place was full, for in addition to the officials, courtiers and friends who followed the King on his progresses there were many local landowners and gentry of the kind whom Henry loved to meet, and impress, during his country visits. It was his manner to such people which had gained him a name for being bluff.

Entering the hall Wolsey was miserably aware that every man there would have heard of his humiliation in the courtyard and now be speculating upon the manner in which the King would receive him. It was an ordeal to move amongst the crowd, greeting those he knew, and behaving as though the past seventy days had never been; but he managed it, governing his hammering heart, keeping voice and hand steady, meeting the eyes, curious or hostile, with a level impassive stare.

Then the King entered and took his place under the canopy: Wolsey and Campeggio advanced and knelt.

In Wolsey all confidence, all hope, suddenly ebbed away. Norris's offer lost its significance; the seventy days of silence, the unanswered letters, the messages ignored, loomed large. Perhaps the King intended to ignore him in the face of this crowd . . .

If he does, Wolsey thought, I shall die here, die of shame, on my knees. Perversely, the contrary fear afflicted him too; if Henry spoke, he would never find breath enough to reply.

Henry extended his hand to Campeggio who bowed his head over it, released it and stood up. In the tense silence Henry turned towards Wolsey and extended his hand. Wolsey bowed his head and then raised it and looked directly into the beloved face. The shared experiences of twenty years were relived as their eyes met. From great things like foreign policy and subtle plans for England's welfare, to small things like jokes and meals enjoyed together: all bonds, not easily cast off.

Wolsey attempted to stand, but his legs were flaccid and trembling. Henry took him by the elbows and heaved him to his feet, saying genially,

"You're still stiff from the saddle, Thomas."

Stare, Wolsey thought, stare and listen, all you who thought I was finished. Listen to that, my own heart, lately so down cast that I was prepared to die in the courtyard beside a foundered mule!

He said,

"Your Grace, I am cured of my worst ill, the lack of seeing you."

Henry said,

"I have missed you, too." He put his arm over Wolsey's shoulders and drew him aside into the embrasure of a great window.

Campeggio, watching, reflected that this was one more instance of English unpredictability. Two months of sulky silence because Wolsey had done the only thing possible for him to do, let the poor man arrive to find no place where he could wash and change his clothes, and then, brought face to face with him, show him every sign of favour. Well, it was good to see Wolsey forgiven, he was a sound churchman, and had proved it. The Pope would be pleased to hear of this.

That his own reception had been restricted to the most formal, stylised ritual fretted Campeggio not at all. He knew that he had annoyed Henry at their first meeting after his landing; in the old days monarchs cut off the heads of those who brought bad news; and Clement's offer to bolster up the King's marriage had been bad news. In a just world, Campeggio thought wryly, he would have been better treated by the King, for in three interviews with Catherine he had done his best — as had Wolsey — to persuade her to give in. He had quoted to her the case of a French Queen who had entered a nunnery in order to allow her husband to re-marry. That had moved Catherine as little as his arguments. On his second visit to her she made her confession to him, and had solemnly declared that although she had bedded with Arthur in all twelve nights, she had been virgin when she married Henry, therefore, whether the dispensation were in order or not mattered little; she was Henry's legal wife. Undoubtedly a good, pious woman, but excessively headstrong; and by all accounts this Anne Boleyn upon whom Henry had set his heart, though different in many ways was equally self-willed.

One could almost be sorry for the man, set between two such unmanageable females.

In the window Henry said,

"I was so maddened by disappointment that I hated the thought of looking at anyone concerned with it. I've thought of you as a traitor — until a moment ago. I realised then that no traitor ever looked so at the man he had betrayed. Judas only kissed Christ. I doubt that he looked Him straight in the eye!"

"I could have sat on and the Court would have decided for you, your Grace. By verdict of an English Court, from which the Pope's commissioner had withdrawn, you would have been declared a bachelor. But in the eyes of the world your subsequent marriage would have been bigamous, the issue of it tainted with bastardy. I *knew* that that was the last thing your Grace really wished."

"You were right — in a way," Henry said reluctantly. "If I wished to *act* the bigamist I should have done so long since. Bigamist in fact I could not be, never having been legally married."

"And that is the point upon which Clement has yet to be convinced." Wolsey hesitated. Was this quite the moment to mention that Clement would be more easily convinced if only the King would choose some other lady? A man in love . . . And seventy days, during which many things might have happened. He compromised. "Campeggio," he said, "is a close-mouthed fellow. He sat side-by-side with me all those weeks and never gave me a hint of what, in the last resort, he had been ordered to do. But on our way here he let fall one significant remark which I noted to report to your Grace."

Henry would have liked to hear it there and then, but he had promised Anne that as soon as he had received the Cardinals he would dine with her. So he said,

"Everybody is hungry, and you, Thomas, must be hungriest of all. I see they're bringing in the tables. We'll have further talk after dinner."

He went striding away, thinking how good it was to be talking to Wolsey again. He'd allowed anger and disappointment to blind him to the real issue; but Wolsey, even at the risk of offending him, had kept his eyes fixed upon it. Wolsey knew that above all things he *needed* the Pope's verdict in his favour, needed it personally because he was a good Catholic, and in a wider sense because he wanted to be proved right in the sight of the world. If Wolsey had sat on at the Blackfriars Court the marriage with Anne could only have been a hole-and-corner affair, and his son's legitimacy would always have been in question. It was far better this way.

Wolsey took his place, as Chancellor, as Keeper of the Seal, as Cardinal, at the trestle table set crossways above those set lengthways in the hall. And he came straight from a confidential talk with the King who had received him with marked favour. His enemies were confounded, his few friends pleased; and his faithful gentleman-usher, George Cavendish, leaned over from behind his chair and murmured that he had found him a lodging, comfortable and suitable to his estate, in a house called Euston, just three miles away.

For the first time in many days he felt an appetite for food.

After dinner he went to Henry's own apartments, and there, after a few preliminaries, said,

"Campeggio indicated very clearly, sire, that Clement would take a more favourable view of your case were you not determined to marry the Lady Anne."

Henry's demeanour altered immediately.

"There you have the clearest admission of the weakness of their case that I have yet heard! Either Julius's dispensation was good and I'm married, or it was not, and I am free. That's the ground we're fighting over, Thomas, and all else is irrelevant. If I'm free, I'm free to marry a Turk or an Ethiopian provided I could get her to be baptised. Is that not true? Is that not the law?"

"Upon the face of it, yes. The whole trouble with this matter has been, all along, that so much outside the law is involved. Three-quarters of the time spent at

228

Blackfriars was wasted on discussion as to whether Her Grace came to you maid or matron, which was no concern of the law. Clement is Pope and in theory above all personal preferences, and when the case goes to Rome he should be governed by law; but he'll have human feelings too, which will sway him."

"Then he's a damned rogue! He knows nothing whatsoever about the Lady Anne, except a lot of evil gossip, garbled at that, sent him by Catherine's friends. I wouldn't judge a horse or a hound on such evidence."

"Horses and hounds are not so important as Queens, your Grace. I think I know what Clement fears."

"From *her*?"

"From what she represents." Wolsey's voice took on a heaviness. "Her father, his friends. All who are known as 'new men'. You, your Grace, know that as well as I. Clement fears — and not, I think without reason — that those who take easily to new ways in secular matters eventually tend to new ideas where religion is concerned."

"Clement fears his own shadow. I detest Luther and all his notions. They'll never take root here while I rule. By God's Blood, how often have I wished that I could tolerate these so-called reforms. When I think of how I have been treated by the Pope, who should have been my friend. When Luther began to spit his venom I was one of the first to defend the established faith; and what did I get? From Leo an empty title! And Leo's successor refuses me justice. That is all I ask. I get no justice; I get inquiries and commissioners and insolent advice and now that they can think of no further shifty trick, they attack the woman I love, who is as good a Catholic as I am. *And* have the audacity to hint that they'd free me of Catherine if I'd promise to marry someone of their choice."

His voice had grown loud; his face was dark crimson, the whites of his eyes, red. Wolsey knew, however, that the rage was not directed at him, and that if he sat quietly the storm would blow itself out.

"It's enough to make a man lose faith," Henry went on. "Sometimes I think I'll cut loose, thumb my nose at the Pope and all connected with him. I'm damned if I know what holds me back. No, I do know. I've no wish to line myself with those little German princelings and archdukes and electors, nun-rapers, image-breakers. It's almost a thousand years since Augustine set foot in England and made it part of Christendom. Must I break away, merely because Clement is a weak, frightened fool? I'm not forever on my knees, but I *believe*, Thomas. I believe that when the Host is elevated, Christ is there, in the flesh. But I'm trapped; and sometimes the only way out that I can see is the gate that would take me into the camp of those who hold that the bread is still bread, the wine, wine. You'd best tell Campeggio to warn Clement; he'd better not drive me too far! And he can tell him at the same time that Anne is no heretic; there are no heretics in England."

"Clement will find for you, in the end. But we must remember that he has the Emperor to consider. That is one good reason for allowing the case to go to Rome; a verdict there will be more likely to satisfy the Emperor. And in the meantime . . . After all, your Grace, the

230

Roman Court opens next month and the work on the case is largely done. It could be over by Christmas. If you could bring yourself to allow the Lady to be a little less . . . prominent. Perhaps even if a rumour of a rift could be spread abroad . . . It could do no harm, and it would ease Clement's mind."

Henry considered the suggestion for a moment.

"I'll think of it," he said. "After all, Clement has not played straight with *me*. It would serve him right. Yes, I'll think of it."

"Campeggio might carry back some hoodwinking tales," Wolsey said. God knew that this kind of thing was abhorrent to him, petty, sordid stuff for a man to bring his brains to; but the King had taken him back into favour and he must do his best to be of service.

"Still my wily old Thomas," Henry said. "We'll talk more of this tomorrow. I must go now and be seen by my guests."

They parted with the utmost amity; and riding the three miles out to Euston, Wolsey reflected that all was to be as before; as the old proverb said, the falling out of faithful friends is the renewal of love.

The local gentlemen found their King a little less bluff and hearty than they had expected, for as he moved amongst them he was visualising the scene when he must break to Anne the news that for a few months she must be a little less . . . prominent. He was also thinking how horribly lonely he would be if anything came of this latest scheme. Even half a day's necessary absence from her now irked him almost unbearably.

CHAPTER
SIXTEEN

"And I heard it reported . . . that Mistress Anne Boleyn was much offended with the King, as far as she durst, because he so gently entertained my lord."
Cavendish. *The Life of Cardinal Wolsey*

GRAFTON. SEPTEMBER 14th, 1529. EVENING

Henry was aware that some ignorant, common people whispered that Anne Boleyn was a witch; and he had more than once said to her by way of a joke that he agreed with them, and that she had put a spell on him; but when, all duties done, he came to say good night to her and found her rooms stripped of her personal possessions and her women packing her clothes, he stood for a minute in the doorway and felt cold fingers on his spine. How could she have known what was said in a room on the other side of the house and overheard by no one?

He steadied himself: of course she couldn't know; she had mistaken the date for leaving Grafton. Women were notoriously vague about dates, which seemed strange, considering how much of their lives were necessarily concerned with them.

He said in a loud, jovial voice,

"Your poor wenches! All to unpack again. We've four days more at Grafton."

She said nothing; she made a sign with her hand and within five seconds they were alone, with both doors closed. Then she turned and looked at him, so coldly that her glance burned, as iron on a freezing day can burn.

"*We*", she said, "have no more time anywhere. I am going back to Hever tomorrow."

It was exactly what — in a few days' time, when his mind was settled — he was going to suggest himself. But that was unimportant now.

"You can't do that," he said.

"No? Well, I suppose not. You are King of England, I am your subject, I must be where you bid me But I think that by deciding to go home I merely forestalled your order."

Completely flustered, he said,

"You know very well that I never gave you an order, never would give you an order. How you knew ... Well then you must know that nothing was decided; I only said I'd think it over. And all the time I've been out there, remembering the old names and learning the new ones and talking about cows and wives and horses and children ... I knew I couldn't do it, sweetheart. Not even for a week, far less some months. I just couldn't do it. They can say what they like, do what they will; I need you, right here beside me, within hand's reach every day, all day."

He was talking about something of which she had no knowledge, and at the moment no wish to know. She said,

"So you *say*. That kind of talk has fooled me before, but it will never fool me again. The Cardinal is my open enemy, and your secret one. We're told to forgive our enemies and by God's grace I might perhaps forgive him for being mine, but we are nowhere told to forgive the enemies of those we call friend. I don't forgive him for what he did to you and you had no right to forgive him for what he did to me! You called him traitor in July. In September you help him to his feet, you put your arm about him and talk to him privately for hours. The man who could have set you free, and wouldn't."

"And for that you would leave me?"

"For that I *am* leaving you — with your permission, of course."

"But in God's name, why? Because I looked at a sick old man aged by ten years since I saw him last, too much overcome, too weak to get to his feet, and gave him a hand? And put my arm across his shoulders to draw him from the throng? And listened to what he had to tell me, something of great concern to us both. Sweetheart, be reasonable. He's a tool. I've used him before and I shall use him again."

"He failed you and he'll fail you again. Dally with him and you'll stay tied to Catherine until one of you dies. You yourself called him Cardinal Facing-both-ways. Leave the business of the Roman Court to him, as you left the one at Blackfriars and the Amicable Loan, and he'll manage it as he managed before. He hates me, I tell you, and would go to any length to prevent me from being Queen. And I am tired, Henry; tired of having no place, no security, no future. So let them have their way, Clement and Wolsey and Campeggio and Fisher. I'll retire and leave them victors in the field."

And he thought — Six years, I've waited six years.

He said, almost piteously,

"And what shall I do?"

She said,

"I think you must find someone who is willing to be your concubine; for that is all they aim to allow you. Or again, when I am gone, they may see fit to set you free to marry someone of their choosing."

He thought — That's it! Clement told Campeggio, and Campeggio told Wolsey. I was to ask her to leave Court and enrage her; and it wouldn't be a *rumoured* rift, it would be a true one. Crafty, slippery swine! For the first time in his life he felt a revulsion for churchmen — he, who but for Arthur's death, would have been one himself.

"I don't care what they want," he said, violently. "I know what I want. You, you, only you. I've done with Wolsey — you're right about him! I was a sentimental fool to mind his whipped-dog look and think about the past. I must look to the future. I'll find somebody wholly on my side to carry my case to Rome and show Clement plainly that he can't play fast and loose with me any longer. I'll cut Wolsey off, and by God, if Clement won't give me justice, I'll have done with him too. I'll show them just how far they can go with me!

Sweetheart, Anne, my darling, my darling, you're crying. But why? Here, come here."

It was true; tears of relief had filled her eyes and spilled gently over.

He took her in his arms and kissed her, her eyes, her mouth, the place where the black sweet-scented hair grew to a point from her forehead.

"They've tried everything, now, to separate us," he said. "I see it clearly now. They can't bear to think of a man being happy, as I am happy with you. And you must never, never, never speak again of leaving me. The very thought tears the heart out of my breast. You belong to me, and I to you and nobody, nothing, shall keep us apart."

CHAPTER
SEVENTEEN

"The King's sudden departing in the morning was by the special labour of Mistress Anne, who rode with him only to lead him about, so that he should not return until the Cardinals had gone — who departed after dinner."
Cavendish. *The Life of Cardinal Wolsey*

GRAFTON. SEPTEMBER 15th, 1529

Next morning, when Wolsey, who had risen early, rode into the courtyard at Grafton, all agog to continue his talk with the King and to lay before him some subtle suggestions, the fruit of a wakeful but happy night, he found the place all astir with horses and hounds, with huntsmen and servants busy with hampers and baskets. The King and the Lady Anne were off to hunt at Hartwell, and were taking their dinner with them.

The King was amiable, but in a curious, remote kind of way, considering how they had parted yesterday.

He said,

"I have seen Cardinal Campeggio and he is waiting now for you to take him to Dover."

Wolsey said, "But, your Grace . . . we were to continue our talk. Someone else can escort him and I will wait here until such time as is convenient for you."

237

"I should prefer, my lord Cardinal, that you escorted your fellow commissioner in the proper manner. I wish you both a safe and pleasant journey."

And having said that Henry swung round and with an agility surprising in a man of his weight got himself into his saddle. The gay, brightly clad hunting party trotted off, the Lady, all in bright tawny with a nodding feather in her hat, riding a dapple grey. As she passed the Cardinal who stood by his richly trapped mule, holding his cap in his hand, she gave him one look. There was no spite in it, no malice, merely the calm here-it-is expression of the player who at the end of a long game produces the winning card.

Henry, doting fool, must have told her of the plot to deceive Clement, and she had taken it as a serious attempt to sever her from the King. Nothing else, Wolsey thought, could have justified that look.

As for the King . . . Standing there, still with his cap in his hand, Wolsey thought — He was amiable enough. Evasive, because having thought it over, and talked it over, he had decided not to send the Lady into even temporary retirement, but disliked the idea of saying so. Yes, evasive. And there was something harsh to the ear about the words "your fellow commissioner". The night-crow had been at work, without doubt. Yet the King had wished him a safe and pleasant journey. It had been a hasty leave-taking, but amiable.

It was as well that he should think so; for he was never to see Henry, never hear him speak again.

CHAPTER
EIGHTEEN

"Whereupon the Earl of Northumberland and Master Walsh, with a great company of gentlemen, as well as of the Earl's servants as of the country, which he had gathered together in the King's name (they not knowing to what purpose or what intent), came into the hall at Cawood."

Cavendish. *The Life of Cardinal Wolsey*

CAWOOD. NOVEMBER 1530

Wolsey had almost finished dinner. It had in no way resembled the meals which were set before him in the days of his glory; nor was the dining chamber crowded with so-called friends, place-and-favour-seekers and sycophants. All was changed now, and he had changed, too. Since his final fall from favour, since Henry had mercilessly stripped him of every secular office and all his property, he had become ascetic in his way of life; he ate and drank sparingly, wore a hair shirt next to his skin, spent long hours on his knees and devoted all his energies and talents to the running of his diocese. To the few faithful friends who remained with him, and to his servants, he seemed to have taken on a quality of saintliness.

Cavendish, whose loving eye missed very little, could see a great difference between Wolsey as he had been during those two months before the visit to Grafton, and as he was now. Then he had wavered always between hope and dread; been, hard as he tried to conceal it, worried and fretful. Now that the worst had happened he seemed resigned, almost happy, like some sea-battered sailor come at last to a safe, if humble, harbour.

In London Henry was busy rearranging York House, which was now to be called Whitehall; and up river he was doing the same with Hampton Court, the lovely palace which Wolsey had made from a modest manor. Sir Thomas More was Chancellor, which was a sign of changing times, for More was not a churchman, nor a nobleman, but merely a good honest lawyer. In Rome the validity of Pope Julius's dispensation was still being debated, dragging on and on.

But Wolsey seemed no longer to care what happened outside whatever, as Archbishop of York, he might be held responsible for in the eyes of God.

In the old days a clatter on the stairs that led up to the dining-chamber would have meant that some lord and his attendants had come to pay court to the Cardinal and to taste his hospitality. In this remote and quiet place, the noise caused a stir, and Wolsey, chewing the last of his dried raisins, said,

"See who has arrived."

A servant hurried to the door, looked down the stairway and hurried back.

"My lord, it is the Earl of Northumberland."

Wolsey rose and crossed the room so swiftly that he met the Earl as he reached the head of the stairway. He embraced him with genuine pleasure. Young Harry

240

Percy, who had been sent to him to learn manners, now came, as a few other faithful friends had done, to pay his respects to the fallen favourite.

"Ever since I came to Yorkshire, my lord, I have hoped for a visit from you. I only wish that I had been forewarned, so that I might offer you a better welcome. I have just finished my dinner. But no matter. Come in, come to the fire. We will give you what we have."

Northumberland said stiffly,

"We have dined, my lord." He went to the fire, and his riding clothes began, almost immediately to steam in the heat.

Wolsey turned and greeted all the Earl's followers, shaking each by the hand, exercising his phenomenal memory for names and faces. Then he went to his guest by the fire, and studied him with a mounting feeling of disquiet. He'd been such a handsome boy, merry of face and glowing with health. Now he was thin and sallow; sharp lines ran from his nose to the corners of his mouth, others marked his hollow cheeks.

"I trust I see you well," Wolsey said, doubtfully.

"My health is excellent. And yours, my lord?"

He did not look at Wolsey as he spoke and the older man thought — He probably sees as sad a change in me.

"At the moment indifferent. A bout of the flux; but it will pass."

Northumberland said nothing. A nerve twitched in his cheek.

Wolsey said,

"I am glad to see that you have retained so many of your father's old servants."

"My father was reasonably well served; I saw no reason to make any change."

His voice was cold and flat.

"They say friends, wine and servants improve with keeping. And I am indeed delighted to see an old friend." As he spoke he put his hand on the Earl's arm, and it lay there for an instant, then Northumberland moved, muttering that he would dry his other side, and as he twisted the hand fell away.

Old, blind, egotistical fool, he thought. Had he no perception? No memory? Had he forgotten that only seven years ago he had rated him like a school-boy, called him willful and denounced his love for Anne Boleyn as a foolish entanglement: sent for his father and concocted the plan to marry him off to Mary Talbot and thereby ruined his life? How could he possibly think that now, when he was utterly disgraced, and all men of good sense were steering clear of him, Harry Percy should have come to Cawood voluntarily, or on any good errand?

Of course he couldn't. He knew! The friendly welcome, the assumption of friendship, even the greeting and the hand shaking for the servants, were all part of some instantly adopted plan, a kind of game of bluff for which, in his hey day, the old man was so renowned. He probably thought that by charm, by sentimental reference to past days, he might woo Percy from the performance of his errand and over to his side.

It was a wildly fantastic thought, but it was feasible . . . he, Harry Percy, might, if he wished, today start a rebellion in England. The North country was the most

242

stoutly orthodox of all districts, the most opposed to the new ways of thoughts, to the threatened breach with the Pope, to the divorce of Catherine. And the two most powerful men in the North, Darcy and Dacre, almost minor kings, were certain supporters of any move against the King.

The nervous tic in his cheek became more active as the Earl thought — I could do it, if I cared; but I no longer care for anything. Something, misery or sickness, has gnawed me hollow. Even revenge has no savour now. I shall merely perform my errand.

Standing there, in a haze of steam and the stink of wet wool and wet leather drying, listening with half an ear to Wolsey's talk, and making, now and then, a perfunctory answer, the Earl of Northumberland looked back over his brief, unhappy life, and was puzzled, as always, when he thought of the past. There was nothing so very extraordinary in what had happened to him. Almost all well-born men had their marriages arranged for them; and if they had fallen in love elsewhere, such fancies were soon forgotten in the realities of life. It had just been his misfortune — and he recognised it — to have fallen in love with a woman who would not *be* forgotten. He'd tried hard enough, God be his witness; he hadn't wanted to go through life heartsick for something he could not have. He was not romantic, he liked things to be easy and comfortable; he had wanted to live with his wife and rear a family, like any other man. But he was haunted, or cursed. Never once had he been able to approach his wife — or any other of the women he had tried in the three years following his marriage — without being unmanned by the memory of Anne; the promise in those black eyes, the scented silkiness of her hair, the clasp of her thin, immature arms. He was the one man in the world who fully understood his King's predicament; Anne cast a spell, and once you had fallen under its influence no other woman really existed as a woman, for you. You always remembered her at the wrong moment. He had, always. Sometimes he had been useless as a eunuch, sometimes he had taken his wife with a defiant savagery. In the end she had left him and gone back to her father and between them they had concocted a plan that surely out-rated anything in the world for irony. Mary had tried to divorce him because he was pre-contracted to Anne Boleyn!

He'd gone quite mad then. It was not that he cared whether his marriage to Mary stood or fell; but it was so typical of how old men tried to order things with their sly, false ways. Separate him from Anne by saying that he was pre-contracted to Mary Talbot and then turn about and try to separate him from Mary by saying that he was pre-contracted to Anne!

And there was more in it. Danger! For by that time the King had made plain his intention to have Anne. And for him, now Earl of Northumberland, to hint at any claim on her would have landed him in the Tower, which was, no doubt, what his spiteful wife and her father wanted.

Wyatt had written,

And graven in diamonds in letters plain
There is written her fair neck about:
Noli me tangere; for Caesar's I am.

Wretched as he was, the Earl had no wish to end in the Tower so he had harshly denied all knowledge of any pre-contract, and since there was no evidence of it, he had remained married to Mary Talbot. But in fact she was no wife to him; and he had no child; and nothing that he ate put any flesh on his bones, nothing that he drank lightened his spirits. Old before his time he cared for nothing except the preservation of some sort of dignity, which implied a carrying out of any duty.

And here, making conversation, and smiling paternally at him, was the author of all his misery. If only he'd said, seven years ago, "Silly boy, go ahead and marry your love with my blessing," then Harry Percy would now have been a whole man, happy and fulfilled, and his first-born would have been six years old.

The Earl turned himself again and eyed those who had come with him. Trusted men, all of them, but one could never be *sure*. There were many men who would do, or watch being done, something of which they did not wholeheartedly approve, so long as no one made a protest, so long as the victim of the proceedings seemed resigned, but once an appeal was made they lost firmness. Suppose, when the vital words were spoken, the old man turned and employed his honeyed, eloquent tongue in his own defence, in a demand for help. How many would then waver? It had better be done in private.

He shifted himself again and said,

"I am more thoroughly damp than I knew." Wolsey made the hoped-for response.

"Come into my bed-chamber, my lord. There is a good fire there and I have no doubt that I can find you a robe and a pair of slippers."

Cavendish opened the door to the inner room and would have entered to help with the finding of the clothes, but Wolsey checked him.

"We can manage," he said. "My wardrobe is small nowadays. Stay by the door."

The Earl's nervous and distrait manner had been noticed by Wolsey who suspected that he had something of importance to communicate and needed privacy.

The bed-chamber was plainly, almost austerely furnished, more like a poor cleric's room than the palatial apartments which Harry Percy remembered as part of the Cardinal's background. There was nothing of value in sight, even the candlestick was of pewter. York House and Hampton Court, the More and Tittenhanger had all been lighted by candelabra of gold and silver, set with jewels, and hung with chandeliers of Venetian work.

"Something is troubling you," Wolsey said, very kindly. "What is it? You can unburden yourself freely to an old friend. I have no power now, but I can listen, and as you know, I was ever prone to advise." He smiled and then turned to go to the clothes-press, knowing that some people found speech easier when not being watched.

246

Despite everything, despite even his own suspicion of the Cardinal's foxiness, Northumberland knew an instant of weakness, of distaste for the job he had been given, for the words that he must say. His cheek twitched so violently that it affected his mouth and made the words emerge in an unsteady, faltering voice. He laid his hand on Wolsey's arm and said,

"My lord, I arrest you on a charge of high treason."

Wolsey stood stock still. So it had come, after all. Falling not with the force of a blow entirely unexpected, but with the force of one so often expected and so often postponed that he had hoped to escape it altogether. Henry had stripped him of everything, and there had been a time, last year, when he had momentarily expected to be hauled off to the Tower. Instead he had been allowed to come to Yorkshire, and he had begun to believe that so long as he attended strictly to his ecclesiastical duties, he stood a chance of ending his days in peace. But it was not to be. The King needed a scape-goat for the latest delay in Rome, and he, blameless as he was, was chosen.

When he spoke his voice was as sure and judicial as it had ever been in his Court of Star Chamber; his own calm astonished him. Even the old flutter and jerk of the heart was absent now that the worst had come about.

"You have authority for this, my lord?"

"I have a commission."

"Permit me to see it."

"That I cannot do."

"Then you cannot arrest me."

In answer the Earl went to the door and said to Cavendish,

"Bring Master Walsh in here."

Walsh entered and before the Earl could speak, Wolsey said,

"Sir, my Lord of Northumberland attempts to arrest me for treason, but he cannot, or will not, show his commission. As a member of His Majesty's Privy Council, do you know of this matter?"

"I do, my lord. I assure you that we have a commission. But we may not show it, because it contains, besides our warrant, certain secret instructions."

"Then by you, sir, I will be arrested, but not by the Earl. A lord without a warrant, cannot arrest a ploughboy; a member of the Privy Council may, without warrant, arrest the highest lord in the land. Therefore I place myself at your disposal, taking God as my witness that I have never, by word, or deed, acted treasonably towards my King."

Walsh glanced at the Earl who gave a small, almost imperceptible nod of the head, and shuddering turned towards the fire.

"Then tomorrow, my lord Cardinal," Walsh said, "we will set out for Pomfret, leaving my Lord of Northumberland here to see that all is left in order."

"I shall be ready," Wolsey said. "His lordship was about to shed his wet gear; you also, Master Walsh, should change or you will be stiff tomorrow. Cavendish will see to you." He crossed the room and opened a door. "My stool room," he said. "There is no exit. You may safely leave me here. I should like to be alone."

The next day, though it was no longer raining, was so murky and overcast that even the morning was twilit. It was Sunday, and through the gloom the church bells sounded, muffled and mourning. Wolsey with the flux still on him, painful and humiliating, set out for Pomfret; and shortly afterwards Harry Percy, having hastily and perfunctorily seen all the fires out and the house at Cawood closed, rode away in the other direction.

Anne Boleyn rode with both of them. With Harry Percy, young and sweet, the ghost of a lost love, for lack of whom life had become so dry and desolate that even an act of revenge, so coincidental that surely in the whole history of the world it had no equal, was tasteless. With Wolsey, a cruel and malignant persecutor who at Grafton had snatched away his one chance to rehabilitate himself in Henry's esteem, and not content with that, had so worked and talked against him that this had happened.

The mule jogged steadily along towards Pomfret, Pontefract Castle, which was an ill-omened place. Many political prisoners and one King, Richard II, had died there in mysterious circumstances. Wolsey did not expect to die there; he was bound for London and the Tower and the block. He could not know that this flux, far from being a passing indisposition, was a symptom of a grave disease which was to kill him, mercifully, in a few days' time. But he did, as he rode, look back over the past, remembering how from humble beginnings he had risen to greatness and talked to Kings and their representatives as an equal. Henry's favour had raised him, his disfavour had cast him down. The Bible said, "Put not thy trust in princes", and that was a sound saying; for princes, like Samson, went and put their heads in the laps of strange women and were shorn of their strength. He thought, rationally, and without emotion — I should have done better to have served God with even half the zeal with which I served Henry; *he* would not, in my age, have left me naked to my enemies. The chief of whom is, and always has been, the Lady.

Harry Percy, riding North, riding faster, knew that nothing had changed. The Cardinal was doomed, but it made no difference. Nothing could restore the magic of those hours in the rose-scented garden. He had, he thought — mistakenly as it happened, for him, too, death was busy — years and years of life to get through. All those springs, with the trees in bud, lucently green, and flowers breaking and cuckoos calling and doves crying. One word only. Anne. Anne. Anne.

CHAPTER
NINETEN

"... the most virtuous woman I have ever known and the highest hearted, but too quick to trust that others were like herself and too slow to do a little ill that much good might come of it."
The Spanish Ambassador

GREENWICH. 1531

The worn quill was writing too thickly; impatiently Catherine flung it aside and selected a fresh one. How many quills, she wondered, had she worn down on letters which, for all the result they brought, might as well have remained unwritten?

Changing the quill had interrupted her flow of thought and she re-read the last sentence she had written. "Your Holiness should mark that my complaint is not against the King. I trust so much in my lord the King's natural virtues and goodness that if I could only have him with me for two months, as he used to be. I alone would be powerful enough to make him forget the past ..."

That, she thought, was absolutely true; she was completely certain that Henry had undergone no fundamental change; he was the victim of an ambitious, unscrupulous woman.

Now, how to continue? She brushed her mouth with its firmly closed lips with the feather of the quill. She wished to write vehemently, urging Clement to decide soon, and in her favour. The delay was inexplicable. It was two years since Campeggio had decided that the case must go to Rome, and no progress had been made at all.

Not for the first time Catherine faced the question — *Why* was Clement afraid to declare for her? He was afraid of angering Henry and driving him to Lutheranism. That must be the reason. There could be no other. And the truth was that by delaying Clement merely increased the danger. Wolsey was dead now. Catherine had never liked him, she had detested his pro-French, anti-Empire policy, but he was a sound, orthodox churchman. The men who had taken his place with the King were different altogether. Thomas Cromwell, once Wolsey's secretary, was the new favourite, a dangerous, worldly man; and there was the seemingly harmless little Cranmer, too, ear-marked as the future Archbishop of Canterbury. They were both prepared to do Henry's bidding without protest or question; if the delay went on too long, or if the verdict displeased Henry, Cromwell and Cranmer would assist in separating the English Church from the Papacy.

His Holiness should be warned. She dipped the quill and then hesitated. The Spanish Ambassador knew all these things and was in constant touch with Clement and with Charles; he would have reported the state of things in England. There was nothing for Catherine to *tell* Clement — he probably even knew how at

252

Christmas Anne had assumed the Queen's peculiar function and touched the silver rings which, being touched by the Queen, were supposed to have the power of relieving night cramp!

There was nothing to do but to appeal again, more humbly, more earnestly . . .

Griffiths opened the door and said, quickly, a little breathlessly,

"Your Grace, there is come a great deputation from the King. They ask immediate audience."

"It is late," Catherine said. "It must be urgent." Her heart leaped. News from Rome. And only one verdict was possible. Many disappointments had taught her caution, however, and she asked,

"Who are they?"

"I recognised the Dukes of Norfolk and Suffolk; the Earl of Northumberland, the Earl of Wiltshire . . ."

"Bring them in," she said. If Thomas Boleyn, Earl of Wiltshire, was one of the number, they did not bring any news she wished to hear.

She moved around the table, so that it was behind her as she faced the door. Her face had aged and her figure thickened since her appearance at the Court of Blackfriars, and tonight she was not dressed for show; but she had retained her dignity and even the ink-stained fingers of the hand she extended to each man in turn did not detract from the queenliness of the gesture. In addition to those Griffiths had named there were many of less importance, as well as Dr Gardiner, Dr Sampson and the Bishop of Winchester. It must be a matter of supreme importance. Mary!

She addressed herself to the Duke of Norfolk who had taken up a position that marked him as spokesman.

"My daughter, the Princess Mary . . . you bring me . . ." Even her resolution could not enable her to finish the sentence. Mary had never been robust, and now, just at an age when a girl most needed her mother . . .

"Madam, your daughter the Lady Mary is in excellent health. The matter which we have come to lay before you does not concern her."

"I thank your Grace."

"It concerns the matrimonial dispute, lately advoked to the Roman Court," Norfolk said.

Dear God, Catherine prayed quickly, lend me strength! For with that woman's father present they could only be about to tell her that her marriage was annulled, that the struggle and the shame had been borne in vain.

"His Holiness has decided that the case should be tried in a neutral court. He therefore suggests a French court, in Cambrai. His Majesty is agreeable to this and wishes the court to be set up with all possible dispatch. We have been sent to obtain your promise to acknowledge the jurisdiction of such a court and to attend it, either in person or by proxy."

The words came into her head, so suddenly and completely that she almost said them aloud — No French court could be neutral to me, a Spaniard! But that was a mere comment and she forced it back.

"My lords, I expect no favour of the Pope who has indeed helped me little and injured me much; but it was to the Pope that my lord the King first made his appeal to have our marriage looked at; and it is *only* from the Pope, Christ's Vicar on this earth, that I will accept a verdict."

She had been writing by the light of two candles, but others had been brought in and now the room was bright. The light wavered and the planes of the men's faces shifted, but their eyes stayed steady and it was at their eyes that she looked. Hostile some of them, indifferent some, but there were those that regarded her with respect, and a few with kindness. It was true, she thought; if you make no false claims but stand steadily upon your indubitable rights, keep your temper, refuse to give way to hysteria or self-pity, the honest man of goodwill will be on your side.

This was Henry's own picked deputation and she had given them the wrong answer, yet at least half of them approved.

The blood of her mother, Isabella, the warrior Queen of Castile, made itself felt for a moment. She thought — I could rouse this country against him; the common people love me and abhor Anne Boleyn. If I took up arms, not for myself, for Mary, I could overturn this new, shallow-rooted Tudor dynasty . . .

But to do that she would have to hate Henry and that was impossible. His image was fixed, immutable in her heart; the big strong handsome boy who had lifted her from her anomalous position of widow of the Prince of Wales and made her Queen of England, and had loved her and teased her, and made her laugh, so that the six years between them had seemed as nothing

255

. . . No, she could never take action against Henry; only against his determination to put her away.

"And that, Madam, is what you wish to tell His Grace?"

"That is my decision."

Thomas Boleyn said,

"You place the King in an intolerable position, Madam. Throughout the whole procedure he has been amenable to the wishes of the Pope. The Pope now proposes a neutral court, but if you refuse to acknowledge such a court what answer can His Majesty return?"

Catherine looked at him and thought — You are *her* father. One night, all unwitting, you lay with your wife and nine months later this monster was born, to be the ruin of us all. And now you tell me that Henry's position is intolerable!

She said,

"I love and have loved my lord the King as much as any woman can love a man. But I would never have been his wife against the voice of my conscience. I came to him a virgin; I am his true wife. Any evidence to the contrary is based on forgery and lies. He appealed to Rome and it is there that I wish the case to be tried."

They went away. It was another tiny triumph. There'd be no trial in Cambrai, with some cynical French Cardinal sitting in judgment. Neutral? When everybody knew that the French hated Spain and all things Spanish.

She sat down at the table and put her head in her hands and gave a sigh that was almost a groan. How long, oh Lord, how long?

The case would stay in Rome and sooner or later Julius's ruling would be upheld and she would be declared Henry's lawful wife. And what would that profit her? If Henry didn't hate her already, he would then. And who wanted to be tied, until death, to a husband who hated her?

Oh, how willingly, she thought, would I have gone to a nunnery and set him free and said, "Go play with your new toy, but think kindly of me." But for two things. My duty to the Church, in whose eyes we were legally wedded; and my duty to Mary, born in wedlock and indisputable heir to England's throne.

She looked at her unfinished letter to Clement and had her first, sickening feeling of suspicion of his intentions. *He* had suggested the court at Cambrai, and he must have known what that meant. He was weak, vacillating, unfit for . . . No, no, that was not the way to think, that kind of thought led straight to Lutheranism. Clement was Pope, by the will of God who was omniscient and omnipotent, and if Clement were weak and vacillating it was because God knew that the world, at this moment, *needed* such a Pope. One who would bend, but not break. That was it. A stronger, more brittle man would long ago have given way before Henry's determination. Clement had suggested Cambrai, trusting her to refuse the idea . . .

None the less, she did not feel like completing her letter to him. She pushed it away. She remembered the moment when she had feared that something had

257

happened to Mary. She must write to her, one of those bracing, heartening letters which since their separation had been their sole link. She took a fresh sheet, dipped the quill, and wrote, "Daughter . . ."

CHAPTER
TWENTY

"The timing of her surrender was masterly. Had she waited longer after Warham's death, Henry, whose infatuation for her did not exclude resentment at the way she had treated him, might have had leisure to reflect that once he had his divorce he would be free to marry a more docile and respectable wife." Garrett Mattingley. *The Life of Catherine of Aragon*

HAMPTON COURT. AUGUST 1532

The lime walk, leading from the house to the river, was one of the things which Wolsey had made and which Henry had allowed to remain unaltered. The lime trees were so trained and so cut that each tree linked arms with its neighbour, and overhead the branches made a roof impervious to all but the heaviest rainstorm. Between the boles of the limes lavender bushes had been planted, and on this August morning they were blue with flowers and all abuzz with bees. At the end of the walk, shaded by trees and near to the river, was a seat, cool on a hot day, and sheltered on a cold one. Henry and Anne had been making for it when he was recalled to give audience to a messenger.

One day, she supposed, some real news must arrive; but not today. She had hoped so much and been disappointed so often that words like message, messenger, despatch, important news no longer moved her. Waiting now for Henry to rejoin her she thought that waiting had composed the greater part of her life. On her tomb they could cut the words "She waited" and they would say all.

When Henry came into sight again, however, she knew that something had happened at last. The set, somewhat peevish expression on his face had lightened, and he moved swiftly for so heavy a man on such a hot morning.

"I have news," he said. "I'll give you three guesses."

"The Queen has agreed to come to terms."

His faced darkened as it always did at any mention of Catherine, and particularly when Anne referred to her by title.

"The Pope has agreed to set a date and a place."

He looked ferocious.

It was probably some small, homely thing.

"Your brindled hound has whelped."

"Wrong again. Warham's dead."

She saw no reason there either for jubilation or death's other attendant, grief. The Archbishop of Canterbury was past eighty, and of no particular consequence. Of late he had been out of favour with Henry because he clung to old-fashioned ideas, disliked the idea of the threatened breach with Rome, and kept advising patience.

Henry sat down and reached for Anne's hand.

"I welcome his death," he said. "It has saved me from having a serious quarrel with an old man in high office.

Now Cranmer can be Archbishop of Canterbury and our way will be clear at last."

This morning she found his optimism irritating. With every shift of the scene on the Continent, with every new delegation despatched, he had said much the same thing. Not long now, sweetheart. Now things will move.

"In Cranmer," Henry went on complacently, "I shall have a Primate prepared to acknowledge me as Head of the Church, and to declare that I am a bachelor, *and have been all along.*"

She said,

"Yes, Cranmer is very . . . pliable." She spoke in an abstracted tone, and did not look at Henry, but away, over the loop of shining river to the fields where the harvest was in progress, the harvesters burnt as brown as the sheaves they handled. She was suffering from one of her intermittent attacks of feeling insecure.

It was a long time now since Henry had first told her that he considered himself a bachelor. He had taken his stand on that, and gone ahead, like a bull, his head down, shoving aside this obstacle, and that. Suppose now . . . suppose Cranmer, the moment he was in office, said, "Yes, your Grace, you are a bachelor and have been all along," and Henry lifted his head, even for an instant, and looked around. What would he see? Not the girl with whom he had fallen in love, but a woman, worn thin and sharp by years of waiting and wariness and self-control and chastity in circumstances where chastity was difficult and almost misplaced. She thought of a dog, chained to a tree, with a bone just out of reach; he'd lunge and struggle, thinking that bone

261

the most desirable thing in the world, and never look beyond it. But suppose the chain snapped suddenly and he found himself free in a world scattered with bones, many more succulent than the one he had wanted so much? . . .

She looked back over their long association and realised that during its course she had given Henry everything except the ultimate favour. She'd been gay, and teasing, eager to entertain; she'd been serious, willing to listen and to try to master a knowledge of affairs — especially after the fall of Wolsey whose place, in a measure, she had tried to fill. They'd been together so long and so constantly that but for the fact that they did not share a bed, they might have been married for years. They knew one another almost too well.

And what was to stop him, the moment he was free, from finding someone young and fresh, whose moods and ways of thought were not as well known to him as his own?

With cruel honesty she admitted that throwing her over would be a most popular move. The ordinary common people had never accepted or approved of her. When she passed through the streets, or along the river in her barge, they came in their thousands to stare — and she knew why. They were everlastingly curious to know *what* there was about her that had caught and held the King's attention; men studied her face and figure, women her clothes. But they stared in silence, or broke it only to declare that they didn't want Nan Bullen for their Queen. And since Catherine had been virtually banished from London, antipathy had hardened . . .

For a moment she felt small, and lost and alone. In the pride of youth, flattered by the King's attention, she had thought that since she must make do with second best that second best might as well be apparently the greatest prize of all; but everything had conspired against her. She was twenty-five and her name was irretrievably sullied. They called her whore, and concubine, and paramour. If Henry threw her aside now the future would be bleak indeed . . .

Well, she had used every nail but one to hold Henry to her — and now she must use the last. It was ironic to think that an old man, who if he had lived would probably have gone to the Tower, had, by dying, forced her to take a step which all Henry's persuasions had failed to make her take . . .

"You're very quiet," Henry said. "This is not the time for your head to ache, is it?"

You see, she said to herself, he knows even the timing of your links with the moon's changes.

"Oh no. I was watching the harvesters and thinking . . . There's something sad about August. It is the turn of the year."

"I welcome the autumn," Henry said. "I like the grease season, when we hunt the fat deer, the misty mornings and evenings, and all the bustle and the moving from place to place."

Men weren't as conscious of passing time as women were. They didn't think, another summer gone! They didn't peer into a glass, reckoning the damage each year did.

She said,

"Where do you intend to make your progress this year?"

And he began to tell her where, and why, whom and what he hoped to see; and that gave her time for thought.

She'd take the last, most desperate risk of all. At once. She might be lucky and become pregnant . . . and Henry certainly wouldn't wish to risk having another son born out of wedlock. Yes, before Cranmer was ready to set Henry free, she must, if possible, be ready to offer Henry the one thing he wanted most in the world.

But the suggestion of altering their relationship must seem to come from him. And he must be provoked into making it.

"Would it be unseemly in view of the Archbishop's death to proceed with the entertainment that I had planned for this evening?"

"I didn't know you had anything planned," Henry said, all delight and expectation.

"It should have been a surprise."

"Never mind Warham. He had outlived his time; and had he lived on . . ."

But why speak of such things on such a bright morning? Death had saved Warham as it had saved Wolsey.

God's Blood! Why think of Wolsey *now*? He never thought of Wolsey. Not that any qualms of conscience were involved; his treatment of Wolsey had actually marked a change in his life. He was *right*, always and indisputably right; anyone who opposed him was wrong. The Pope, the Emperor, Catherine, Bishop Fisher, his daughter Mary . . . and More, he wasn't sure about More yet. But if they were against Henry Tudor then they were wrong and had only themselves to blame for what happened.

"What is this entertainment, sweetheart?"

"Oh, that is still a secret. And I should go now and busy myself with it. I was waiting to see what the day would do. Emma, my woman, who claims to be weather-wise, predicts thunder; and yet, it being so warm, I thought to have the mumming out-of-doors. It seems settled enough, don't you think?"

"I am, I think, as good a weather prophet as any old woman who spends her time huddled in bed-chambers; and I say it will be a fine warm evening. You go to your plans, I to my work; and I shall look forward all day to what you have to offer for my entertainment."

But it will surprise you, none the less, she thought.

An entertainment, and not just *any* entertainment, one with a purpose, to be made ready within a few hours. She sped into the house and sent pages running. Her brother George, Norris, Weston, Brereton, Wyatt and Smeaton, all to come at once to the chamber overlooking the Knot Garden. She ordered wine, dishes of ripe plums and pears, cold meats, cakes.

When the six men had arrived and the doors were closed, she said,

"You will have heard the news. Canterbury is dead."

"So perish all your enemies, my dear sister," George Boleyn said.

"He was old," she said tolerantly. She had not rated Warham very highly, even as an enemy, and her thought now was to use his death as an excuse. "He was out of favour, too. Nevertheless, to hear of a death is never pleasant, so I pretended to the King that I had an entertainment planned for this evening. That seemed to cheer him. The question now is, what can we possibly make ready in the time?"

She seated herself in the window, spreading her tawny skirts about her; topazes glowed in her ears and at her throat. Alert and intent she looked her very best, and the men crowded round, eager to please, anxious to make suggestions; all except her brother who stood a little to one side and gnawed his knuckle. Up to something, he thought, and more than likely mischief!

The relationship between them was a rare one. In their distant childhood days they had played together, he as the boy and the senior always the leader and instigator. Then they had parted, and when she had appeared at the English Court they had met almost as strangers. But they had quickly found that they were so much in sympathy that they could communicate in half-finished sentences, in the lift of an eyebrow, the flick of a finger. Once he had said to her, "If I didn't know otherwise, I should swear we were twins." And once his wife had snapped at him, in the middle of his recounting some tale about Anne, "If she weren't your sister I should suspect you of being in love with her. You talk of nothing else." Jane, like many other women, was very jealous of Anne, always demanding to be informed what in the world the King could see in her, and angry when given the answer, "Only a man can understand that."

He now said,

"We could do *The Man Leader*. It is largely in mime and what words there are matter very little." It was a clowning comedy, a caricature of the world, in which bears were the ruling race and one bear made a living by leading around a performing man.

"That wouldn't be suitable," Anne said.

"It's cheerful."

Norris said,

"Who wants to wear a bearskin in this weather?" and George saw her throw him a grateful glance.

"That is what I meant when I said it wouldn't be suitable. Think again. Here I sit, surrounded by the wittiest men in the wittiest Court in Europe, two poets and one musician; and all I ask is something easily prepared and suited to a hot summer evening."

"To be performed out-of-doors, by the river?" Weston asked. And he drew a grateful glance.

They were ready enough with suggestions, but nothing pleased her.

Finally George Boleyn said,

"Anne, saying 'no' is becoming a habit with you." They all laughed except Smeaton who thought the remark in poor taste. "But if you go on refusing every suggestion we shall end with no entertainment at all.

Or be left with" — he saw her look at him expectantly — "*Leda and The Swan*," he said.

Smeaton said quickly,

"Oh no! My lady disliked that piece and refused to have it performed. Did you not, my lady? more than a year ago."

"After George and I had sweated over it, too," Thomas Wyatt said, lightly. "It broke our hearts! One of the best things we ever devised and you called it gross and lascivious and altogether unsuitable. George and I cried ourselves to sleep night after night; didn't we, George?"

George made a sound of assent, his eyes still upon Anne.

"I wonder . . ." she said. "Did I judge too hastily? It was designed for out-of-doors, and made good use of the river . . . It would be better than something hastily devised and ill-finished . . . perhaps."

"I remember all *Leda's* touching words," Weston said eagerly. He was a very beautiful young man, most deceptively slim, almost frailly built, very fair of complexion and with eyelashes that all women envied. He was usually cast for the leading female role. "It is for George to decide," he added, "the Swan's outfit is almost as hot as the bears' skins."

"I'll suffer uncomplainingly, if *Leda* is what you want," George said.

"It is a vile piece," Mark Smeaton said. "And why should keeping have improved it?"

"Mark," Wyatt said, with some rancour, "has turned — what's the new word? Puritan? Your reputation will not be sullied, my dear fellow. Everyone will know that you are responsible only for the tunes."

Smeaton scowled. From the moment when Anne had appointed him, he had lived in a world of fantasy. His mind no longer accepted the fact that Anne belonged, or ever would belong, in any way, to Henry. She was not his mistress — every honest person about the Court admitted so much — and she never would be. Nor could she be his wife, circumstances would not allow it. Things would go forever as they were now, with Anne a goddess of purity whom all men might worship, but none touch. And her most devoted worshipper was Mark Smeaton, that man of genius.

And it was not fitting that she, so pure, so far removed from all fleshly things, should sit and watch — and by watching share, with Henry and other men, a vicarious excitement — while *Leda and the Swan* put up their lecherous performance. It might be a myth, it might be classical, it might be acceptable to these curled and scented young fops — but in the country, where he was bred, people had a word for such goings on, and not a nice one.

Smeaton would have been surprised had he known that George Boleyn's mind was running on much the same lines, though in a different direction. When he and Wyatt had first proposed the masque of *Leda*, pleased with themselves because it was spectacular and full of most ingenious devices, she had recoiled. Now she was in favour of it. Why? There could be only one answer. Where formerly she had feared to provoke Henry's lust, now she was willing to do so. Yet nothing

269

had changed in the situation; at least nothing that anyone knew about. But Anne was clever; so far she'd handled things well, and if she now changed tactics, she must have good reason. It might well be that Henry's passion was cooling; not to be wondered at. Few men had ever been tried so highly, frustrated upon one side by legal nonsense, and on the other by Anne's caution.

George said,

"Is it decided then? There's not a man who will not sit there, sweating, and envy the Swan his watery progress — and his capture." He looked into his sister's eyes and knew that he had guessed aright.

"I grieved to shut *Leda* away," Wyatt said. "And we can have it perfect by evening. There are few speeches. It was designed to appeal to the eye, rather than to the ear."

"To the eye?" Brereton murmured. "I'd have set it lower."

Mark said, "Shush" through his teeth.

"Shush yourself, Smeaton; and save your breath to blow your whistle." Smeaton turned dizzy with fury. That was how they spoke to him, contemptuously, as though he were of no account, simply because he was lowly born. Yet they would say things that no decent yokel would dream of saying in the presence of a woman he respected. He controlled himself and said,

"Whistle? There is no whistle in *Leda*, surely?"

"There is also," Anne said, "no sufficiently memorable song. Was that not one of the things I complained of, Thomas? It needs a song, a song of farewell from one of her human suitors, to be sung as the Swan carries her away. Could you make one, in the time? If you let Mark have the words an hour before supper he could set them."

"My small talent is always at your service," Wyatt said.

He was in love with her too, but realistically, even at times cynically; capable of writing poems inspired by her, and as he wrote, of thinking that a hopeless love affair was an excellent spur for a poet.

She had asked for a farewell song; and she should have it. Immortal words were already assembling themselves in his mind as he left her apartment. Yet, finding himself going along the gallery with George Boleyn, he grumbled a little.

"Make me a new song, she says, as she might ask me to pluck her an apple. Good songs don't come so easy." He took a few more steps and added, "And it's all very well to say that Smeaton can set the music in an hour. Given the words any musician could. I don't like Smeaton's manner lately. He has a swollen head."

"Anne spoils him," George agreed. "Poor oaf, he's in love with her." His sharp, not particularly kindly and yet tolerant eye had seen the truth about the musician's state, and he thought — If what I think is about to happen happens, it'll be such a shock to him to find that she's only human after all, he'll probably go off his head.

"It's damned presumption on his part," Wyatt said. "And he called *Leda* a vile piece. One of these days he'll provoke me into cuffing his ears."

They walked on. Within five minutes one of Thomas Cromwell's young men, in a hiding place cunningly contrived, had scribbled down every word that had been spoken. Cromwell had learned one lesson from Wolsey's fall — as you rose you made enemies and it was essential to know who they were. He had recruited and trained a little ring of spies, his very own; all young men who looked to him for preferment presently, and never questioned the orders he gave them. In every place where the Court was they had their secret posts, where they listened and scribbled.

"It may be the merest nonsense; but you need waste no time on trying to understand, or to discriminate. Merely write what you hear, as nearly as possible in the same words. And let me warn you," he looked at each recruit in the same hard way, "that any man who mentions his employment, or anything he has learned while pursuing it, will rue his indiscretion for as long as he lives — which will not be long."

Each evening they presented their day's gleanings and before he slept Cromwell sorted it through. Much was tedious meaningless rubbish; much was of interest. It was truly amazing what people would say at a stair-head to a friend who seemed trustworthy.

The scrap of conversation between Wyatt and George Boleyn fell into the category of rubbish, and was discarded.

Yet for some reason a few words — "Lord Rochfort said that Smeaton was a poor oaf and was in love with

272

the Lady" — stuck in Cromwell's mind and were one day to come in useful.

The evening remained fine, though in the West, against the scarlet and gold of the sunset, great slate-coloured clouds reared themselves into a fabulous city with towers and spires and minarets, and thunder growled somewhere in the distance. The entertainment was a marked success. All the little ingenious tricks worked and were applauded, particularly George's exit which called for skill, since he must carry Leda, still only half-willing, and board a flat little boat which had been moored just out of sight under the river bank, and with a single thrust against the bank provide sufficient impulse to send it gliding away, giving the impression that it was he, the Swan, swimming. That was, for everyone with inside knowledge, the trickiest moment of all; there'd been two practical attempts, neither very successful, in the afternoon. On the first George had failed to land squarely and the tiny boat had tilted; on the second his propelling shove had not been powerful enough and he had been obliged to try again, which detracted from the illusion of reality. But tonight all went well; in the eerie, cloud-occluded, sunset light the disguised god bore his human bride away while Sir Harry Norris, the most desolate of Leda's would-be lovers, sang, in his beautiful voice, Thomas Wyatt's new song.

"Forget not yet," the words mourned out on the evening air. Wyatt had written them out of love that he recognised as hopeless; Smeaton had put into the music

273

all the love whose hopelessness he refused to see, and Norris was singing, as always in Anne's presence, for her alone.

The heavy, sultry air, the strange light, the theme of the masque, the differing but potent feelings which three men had contributed to the perfection of the final song, even the soft noise of the doves in the trees, all had their aphrodisiac effect. Here and there in the assembly hand moved towards hand, eye caught eye; love was the thought in almost every mind; hopeful, sorrowful, confident, frustrated.

Henry thought — That song was written for me! "The cruel wrongs, the scornful ways, the painful patience and delays." Haven't I borne enough of them? "The which so constant hath thee loved, whose stead-fast heart hath never moved." Wasn't that true of him, above any man ever, anywhere?

And *she*, he thought, had arranged this entertainment. This was her sweetly subtle way of telling him that she knew how well and truly he loved her and realised how much he had suffered for her sake. How much more delightful an acknowledgment made in such fashion than Catherine's outspoken, "I love you, I have always loved you, I shall always love you." Anne knew, better than anyone else, how to put flavour into living.

After all, what was there left to wait for? He was sick and tired of waiting. Get Cranmer installed as Archbishop and the way was clear. He'd always insisted that he was a free man, hadn't the time come to prove it?

There was Anne to consider, of course. And his promise not to demand favours. But surely tonight, even she . . . He turned his head to look at her and found that she was regarding him with some expression which, before he could read it, had changed to her usual one of calm inscrutability.

"Did you enjoy it, my lord?"

He said, in a thick whisper,

"Sweetheart, if I could be granted one wish, I'd carry you off in just that way, and leave them all to stare."

She said,

"Why not?" but so softly that he could not be certain that he had heard aright.

"Not," she said quickly, and still very softly, "that we will have any staring or gossip. We must be discreet."

So she had said, "Why not?"; she was, after all this long time, surrendering. The blood began to move tumultuously in his body as though it had been damned for years and then loosened. He was momentarily frightened lest he should have a fit. A fine thing it'd be, he thought, half-humorously, to die of joy . . .

Afterwards he lay in the dark more puzzled, more disappointed, more depressed than he had ever been in his life. The great experience, so eagerly anticipated, so desperately sought and so hardly won, over and done with, and what was it after all? *Just another woman in a bed!* When he phrased it like that it sounded unbelievable, but there it was, it was true. All that promise, that hint of some peculiar and precious joy in store, was mere illusion. It was some trick of the eye. Between the sheets, in the dark, she was no different from Catherine, Bessie Blount, Mary Boleyn.

He lay there and knew that everything was wrong; even his sense of smell! For years and years, whenever he had been near her he had been conscious of the scent of her hair, not over-sweet, not musky, in no way obtrusive, a dry, clean fragrance, all her own; but now, nearer to her than he had ever been, he was only aware of his own freshly soaped odour and the scented oil which he had had rubbed into his hair and beard. He'd said to Norris — the only one in his confidence — "This is my bridal night, I must make myself fit." He could have cried when he thought of how he had soaked and scrubbed himself, put on his finest clothes and his jewels.

But that was all trivial nonsense. There were crueller thoughts. The mockery of the world, the words "the King's conscience" being made a joke, Catherine's tears, Wolsey's last look, the falling out with the Pope, and at the end, *just another woman in a bed*.

No. No. He fought off the thought as vigorously as he had ever parried the onslaught of a human opponent in the lists. It couldn't be true, for if it was, he had been wrong, and Henry Tudor was never wrong.

The iron weight which depression had laid upon his chest lifted a trifle. Henry Tudor was never wrong; he knew what he wanted and he got it, in the end, despite everything he got it. And if it seemed . . . No, never would he admit it. His mind flailed around and

276

eventually fastened upon something to which it could cling.

She was a virgin; that was it. His *first* virgin. (So much for Catherine's story!) It would be better later on.

As an explanation he accepted it; but it could not restore him fully. Even when he thought of next time, and next, there was none of that uprush of anticipation, the emotion which had sustained him all these years. The fact was that tonight marked a summit in his life; and from now on everything would be a decline.

No. No. He would not permit himself such thoughts. All would be well; it must be. He willed it so.

Then he realised that rightly he should not be thinking at all; he had imagined himself — a thousand, thousand times he had imagined himself, sated, brimful of content, falling asleep with his head on her breast. And now, here he lay, thinking . . .

And she? He never had understood her; the element of mystery had been part of her charm for him. But he had always thought that the moment of revelation would come . . . and here it was; no mystery had been revealed to him, no transcendental experience shared; just two bodies in a bed. And for this he had rocked the world!

Intolerable, he thought. He just could not lie here, wakeful, with his mind going round and round. He'd get up, go and find Norris, drink some wine, play a game of chess, divert himself. His premature return to his own apartments could be explained on the grounds of discretion. He had confided in Norris, Anne in her waiting woman. The truth, for many reasons should be kept secret for a month or two. Until marriage was possible.

And when he thought of marriage he had again that deadly awareness of expectation being lacking. Getting old? Nothing to look forward to, except decrepitude and death. Oh, nonsense, nonsense . . . A healthy man at forty-one was in his prime!

He left her kindly. It was no fault of hers; she'd been sweet, loving, perfect — if what you wanted was just a woman in a bed. And if that phrase kept recurring to him he'd go frantic, begin to shout and smash things! Nine years, nine years out of the best part of a man's life, and the whole order of things overturned . . .

Within half an hour he had another, even more comforting idea to offer himself; something he'd eaten at supper had disagreed with him and provoked a bilious humour which, as everyone knew, made its victim see everything askew. Otherwise there was something wrong with Norris, ordinarily such a gay, good companion. Tonight he looked gloomy, was short of speech, and when they sat down to play chess, he played a vicious game, as though something had upset him, too; as though he were prey to a bilious humour.

"Did *you* eat soused mackerel at supper?" Henry asked abruptly, leaning back in his chair after Norris had made one of his spitefully triumphant moves.

"I did, your Grace. Why do you ask?"

"Because I did. And it lies heavy. It makes a tasty dish — but have you ever seen mackerel freshly caught?"

"Not that I remember."

"It's like no other fish; its skin is like a snake's, and it isn't flat, like other fish . . . and as I say it lies heavy. You feel it too?"

"Maybe."

I'm eaten up with envy, Harry Norris thought, but if he sees and puts it down to something I've eaten, I should thank God. He is my King; I must not think of him as a gross, lecherous swine who having attained the very height of man's desire on this earth, can come away and discuss the processes of his digestion. If I think in that fashion, he thought, beating his fingers on his knees, I shall end like my grandmother, raving mad . . . How could I know? I'm a man solemnly betrothed, my future lay fair and clear; but I fell in love, as any man subjected to her company must do. But she belongs to him and tonight he took possession, and, God forgive him, comes back here to talk about mackerel and what it does to his belly! Let it swell till it bursts!

And then Norris remembered the countless times when Henry had been kind, understanding, amusing, admirable, worshipful. It was indeed typical of him at this moment to attribute his attendant's awkward mood to indigestion, when he was, in fact, suffering from a futile attempt to get drunk.

"Your move, your Grace," Norris said, in something of his normal manner.

"Is it so? Is it so, Harry? I'm afraid my mind isn't wholly on this business tonight. There! Move now, if you can."

* ★ *

She lay where he had left her; and when she lay in her grave she would not be colder, or more alone. She felt no disappointment, having expected nothing; she'd known, ever since her forced parting from Harry Percy, that from this part of life enchantment had gone forever. And she knew that to night she had only shared an experience common to most women — since only in the rarest cases were they allowed to marry the man they loved. But without love it was a cold and lonely business; the close intimacy only emphasised separateness.

She had an impulse to turn her face into the pillow and cry — but that would be to give way to self-pity, which in her situation would be absurdity, since everything she had done had been done deliberately and with open eyes. Every word, every gesture, every smile almost, directed to the one end. She deserved to be called, as she so often was, "calculating and ambitious". But it was impossible at this moment not to think how different everything would have been, had she and Harry Percy been allowed to marry.

A waste of time, even to think about!

Think that the deed was done now; the result still to come, to be watched for, waited for, prayed for. Let her be pregnant and Henry would speed up the final arrangements for his divorce, and make her Queen.

She thought again — *My child will be King of England*.

CHAPTER
TWENTY-ONE

"... we, by the consent of the nobility of our kingdom present, do make, create and ennoble our cousin Anne Rochfort ... to be Marchioness of Pembroke, and also by putting on of a mantle and the setting of a coronet of gold on her head do really invest unto her the name, title etc., and to her heirs male."

From the preamble to Anne's patent of creation

WINDSOR. SEPTEMBER 1st, 1532

Emma Arnett said in her firm yet unassuming way, "My lady should have a respite now. There is ample time." The ladies thankfully relinquished their little tasks; they had a certain amount of titivating to do upon their own toilettes, and refreshments would be welcome, too. Emma edged herself close to Anne's cousin the Lady Mary Howard and murmured,

"It is my lady's worst day of the month, most unfortunately."

Ever since Anne had come back to Court in the summer of 1527, Emma had taken pains to convey to somebody, month by month, by hint or direct statement, that Anne was not pregnant. Enemies naturally spread evil rumours; twice it had actually been said that she had been brought to bed. Such tales did no harm in places where Anne could be seen, but there was the rest of the world to think of, so every month Emma was careful to make it possible for someone to say, "Her own woman told me . . ."

As soon as they were alone, Emma said,

"Lie flat on the bed, now. What upset you? Isn't this a great day?"

Anne unclenched her teeth — it was the clenched teeth, the gripped hands and the grey pallor that had warned Emma — and said,

"I don't know! Nobody knows. That's the curse of it. I doubt if the King himself knows what he is doing, or why. It came over me as they fastened my petticoat. I should be robing for my wedding, not this, this empty senseless business . . . I'm frightened, Emma; I've lost all courage. I believe that now, after all, he intends to shuffle me off with a title and a thousand pounds a year." Her voice rose shrilly.

"Do you want them," Emma nodded towards the outer door, "to hear what you fear?"

"If I'm right, what does it matter? They'll be the first to say that my sister Mary did better — she got a husband!"

She put her face in her hands for a moment and sat, shuddering.

Emma regarded her without pity, but with genuine concern. The woman had now — had for a long time had — two sets of standards by which everything must be judged; her own inborn, ingrained sense of what was decent; and what was expedient for the Protestant

282

cause. To a great extent they overlapped, and where they did not, she was now satisfied to be governed by opinions of her Milk Street friends. Anne's admission of Henry to her bed before marriage had offended both codes; it certainly wasn't decent; it might be inexpedient. But the battle was not yet lost, and what small thing Emma Arnett could do to bring about victory would surely be done.

She tried with words.

"I know nothing of great matters," she said, "but to me it looks as though what His Grace is doing is good sense. He wants to take you with him when he goes to visit the French King and he wants you to have a high rank of your own."

"I know. I know." Anne jumped up, and hugging her arms around herself, began to pace up and down the room. She was already wearing the long inner robe of crimson velvet, trimmed with ermine, and as she made her swift turns the train of it swung and lashed like the tail of an angry cat. "So he says. But he knows his world well enough to know that it makes no difference. Twenty titles and fifty thousand pounds a year couldn't alter my status. All this day's work will ensure is that I shall take precedence of other men's mistresses; for no respectable woman will come to the meeting."

Her words, her voice, her movement about the room, were all indicative to Emma of a dreaded mood about to break. The Lady would work, patiently and painstakingly, towards her chosen aim, and then appear to give way to an impulse to destroy, to undo all she had done. She was capable, in another moment, of saying that she didn't want a patent of nobility, didn't want to be Marchioness of Pembroke, wanted to go back home and be left alone. She'd say that once too often — that was Emma's fear, especially now, at this very touchy time.

She said,

"I'm going to give you a little dose; just enough to steady you, my lady. The King is doing you an honour today and you *must* be calm and smiling. It's the waiting," she said soothingly, as she found and poured the poppy syrup, "but there're ruts in every road, my lady. Holding on is what counts, in the end. Drink that. And if you don't feel like lying down, I'll start on your hair so there's nothing to do when *they* come back."

Anne said,

"You're very kind, Emma. I don't know what I should do without you."

The remark evoked no compunction in Emma Arnett's breast. For one thing it was justified, few ladies anywhere had such devoted, watchful, cunning, tireless service as she gave Anne. And the motive behind it was a worthy one; shared by every Protestant in England; to keep Anne in favour; to see Anne made Queen; to see her produce a son. At all costs, for their purpose, the Princess Mary must be kept from the throne. She was a Papist. Henry was Papist, too, but a disgruntled one; in his threats and roarings and calling himself Head of the Church, there was *hope*. Under Mary there would be no hope at all; if the Pope said all women were to shave their heads, Mary would be the first to shave hers.

That was a natural thought to enter the head of a woman busy with her mistress's hair. It was long and black and glossy and seemed to have a life of its own; it curved under the brush, and then, as she threaded the strings of pearls through it, it clung to her fingers. Beautiful hair.

"You mustn't give way now," Emma said. "Things often aren't as bad as they look." In the glass her eyes met Anne's and wrinkled in their rare smile. "I learned that when I was no more than seven. My mother sent me to take some eggs and butter to an old woman who'd ordered them. She was well-to-do and scared of thieves, so she kept three great dogs and they were loosed at sunset. On my way I fell in with some other children, going birds' nesting, and I went off with them; so when I got to the old dame's house it was nearly dark and the dogs were loose. Before I got my hand on the gate they were leaping up on the other side, savage as wolves. I was scared. But I knew my mother was counting on the eight pence, and we might get no more orders. So I picked up a bit of branch and went in as though I was ready to clout them all, left and right. They knew my mind was set and kept well away. I got myself a name for being brave; but really I wasn't so much brave as desperate."

Glance met glance in the glass again.

"It was a good parable," Anne said, "thank you. And for the dose."

In the Presence Chamber Henry, gorgeously clad, seated himself in the chair of state. The two Dukes, the whole Privy Council, three ambassadors, most of the peers and all the courtiers ranged themselves on either side, forming a great half circle. Trumpets sounded and Garter-King-At-Arms entered, carrying the parchments upon which were written the patents; and after him came the Lady Mary Howard carrying the sartorial symbols, the richly furred mantle and the golden coronet.

The scene was set.

Anne's was not the only mind to entertain a suspicion as to the King's motives in according her an honour never yet conferred upon a woman. Several in the company imagined that what they were about to witness marked the zenith of Anne Boleyn's career. If Henry intended to make her Queen, why bother with this half-way stage? Even the people who took this view were puzzled, because if this were a gesture of dismissal it was also an admission that she had been his mistress; and that the King, and the Lady and all those nearest to them had always stoutly denied. It was unlike Henry to make so clumsy a move.

There were others who took the directly opposite view and thought that this elevation presaged marriage in the near future; the King, by this means, would avoid having it said that he had married a commoner.

There were a few who simply took the King's word for it that he wished to honour the woman he loved.

And now, here she was, walking between the Countess of Rutland and the Countess of Sussex, and followed by a bevy of ladies. And her worst enemy could not deny that she looked not merely noble, but

286

royal. Catherine at her most stately Spanish appearance, Elizabeth, Henry's mother, at her Yorkish best — which some old men remembered — had never surpassed the calm, the air of being set apart, of being made of some more precious substance than mere human flesh which Emma's dose, combined with Anne's own dignity, now presented.

With perfect timing, she made, as she approached Henry, three curtsys, and when she reached him, she knelt. Garter handed the patent to Henry, who passed it to his secretary who began to read it in the formal half-chant customary on such occasions. When he reached the "mantle" he paused long enough to allow the King to take the garment from the Lady Mary Howard and place it on Anne's shoulders; he paused again at the mention of the gold circlet, and the King took it and placed it on the shining, jewelled hair. The formal phrases rolled on and only those hearers with sharp ears and quick wits noted one significant omission. The title was hers in her own right, and would pass to her son. Ordinarily in such patents the words "lawfully begotten" were here included; in this case they were left out. Surely that was a clear indication that the King had changed his mind about marrying her, or doubted his power ever to do so with sufficient show of legality to make any child of their union fully legitimate.

Those who had been in contact with the King during the past few weeks had noticed a change in him. His temper had always been a little hasty; but his capacity to be pleased had been just as easily wakened. And on his visits to country manors he'd always been very tolerant of discomforts and shortcomings and delightedly conscious of any effort made to please or entertain him. This year a sourer mood had prevailed; more easily angered, less easily pleased. An endearing quality of boyishness, which he had carried with him into middle-age, had vanished, so that in both looks and demeanour he seemed suddenly to have aged, and as though he himself were aware of this, he had taken a perverse, almost savage delight in doing things that wore down younger men. A sudden change of plan which meant another twenty miles riding at the end of a long day in the saddle; unnecessarily early starts; dinners missed altogether, to be made up for by gargantuan suppers — "I don't know what's wrong with you young people; I can eat you all under the table." To some observers his behaviour was consistent with his being upon the point of making a break with Anne.

It was therefore in an atmosphere of curiosity and speculation, of hopeful hostility, or of frustrated hope, that Anne rose to her feet, the only peeress in her own right in England, and in formal phrases thanked the King for the honour he had done her, and retired.

Sir Thomas Wyatt, watching, remembered the lively, plain-faced little cousin with whom he had played in the gardens at Blickling and at Hever, a girl whose rather hoydenish ways had often earned her a rebuke from the strict French governess; he remembered, too, the charming sprightly girl who had come back from France and joined Catherine's ladies; a girl ill-provided for, always making up for the scantiness of her wardrobe by some ingenious innovation, so stylish that it was immediately copied. Well, she was properly provided for now. But it was somehow sad to see something so lively, so almost wild, tamed and put into a collar, even if it were jewelled. On the other hand, what would you? he asked himself. Would you rather see her married, a mother four times over, growing stout, raking the still-room shelves with an anxious or complacent eye? And remember, you yourself grow no younger, Wyatt. He wished suddenly that he might die young. Poets should die young . . .

Henry watched the new Marchioness retire and felt satisfaction mingled with a faint self-righteousness. He had just done the proper thing, and in a few minutes he would do another, when he would corner the French Ambassador and talk to him sternly about the arrangements to be made to receive Anne in France and the honours to be paid to her. He thought complacently of the presents he had made her to mark the occasion of her elevation, some exquisite miniatures painted by Holbein, in jewelled frames, to be worn as brooches and lockets, and a complete set of table-ware, all in gold or silver or silver gilt. The latter alone had cost him over a thousand pounds.

He would have denied angrily — and honestly — that everything that he had done for her since that sultry night at Hampton Court was merely an attempt to rear a wall between himself and a truth too intolerable to be faced. He did not suspect that he was behaving like a man with some grave disease who imagines that by behaving like a sound man, by ignoring every sympton, above all by keeping his own secret, he can *become* sound again.

He was, in fact, so busy concealing from himself the fact that he was disappointed in her, that now and again, he forgot that he was; and as soon as she had left the Presence Chamber, honoured as no woman had ever been honoured before, he began to think, What next? And during his serious talk with the French Ambassador, he had a brilliant inspiration.

He was, as Anne had told Emma, worldly wise; and he knew that the King of France, unfaithful husband as he was, would not bring his Queen to meet the King of England's mistress; so he forestalled that possible snub by saying,

"I have no wish to meet the Queen of France; in my present circumstance I would as soon see the Devil as a lady in Spanish dress."

A lady in Spanish dress; that made him think of Catherine; and of his wish to give Anne yet another proof of love and respect . . .

CHAPTER
TWENTY-TWO

"Anne was appeased by being decked out in Catherine's jewels."
Garrett Mattingley. *The Life of Catherine of Aragon*

THE MORE. SEPTEMBER 1532

Catherine was writing when Harry Norris arrived. She was always writing, rational, closely-argued letters, urgent and yet controlled, which were unanswered or answered evasively. This one was to the Emperor.

"Though I know that Your Majesty is engaged with grave and important Turkish affairs, I cannot cease to opportune you about my own, in which almost equal offence is being offered to God. There are so many signs of wickedness being meditated here. New books are being printed daily, full of lies, obscenities and blasphemies against our Holy Faith. What goes on here is so ugly and against God and touches so nearly the honour of my lord, the King, that I cannot bear to write it."

She halted her pen and looked up, staring through the window at the grey autumn day. Here and there a bright leaf still clung to the ravaged trees, bravely defiant, but doomed. Even the one which held on longest must fall at last and join the sodden mass which lay upon the lawn and the flowerbeds alike. Was she, too, destined to know defeat in the end?

The untended garden was symbolic of her life now. When The More had belonged to Wolsey it had been a gay place, a pleasant summer residence to which to retire when summer baked the London streets, a pleasant place to visit in autumn or winter for a short while with a large retinue, a host of visitors, a crowd of servants. As a permanent dwelling for a few people, living in what was virtually a state of banishment, it was lonely, over-quiet, dreary.

There was something eerie in the atmosphere, too. It had been taken, with all the Cardinal's other properties, by Henry, but it had remained much as it had been. Upon York House and Hampton Court Henry had immediately began to stamp his personality, exorcising that of his fallen favourite, but here something of Wolsey remained. Catherine was free enough of the more vulgar superstitions; Wolsey's body was coffined, his soul in Purgatory being cleansed of its sins, yet there were times when, along a passage, or on the stairs, she could almost believe that she heard a sound, that combination of the female rustle of silk and the heavy male footstep . . . All nonsense, and she regarded it as such. What was far more difficult to ignore was the thought that this had been Wolsey's house, that Wolsey had enjoyed Henry's trust and favour, displeased him, and died, disgraced and broken-hearted. Had Henry chosen The More as a dwelling place for her, with that in mind?

She had accepted her banishment without protest. Long ago she had declared herself willing to obey him, her husband and her King, in all matters not affecting her conscience and her conscience was not concerned with the site of her dwelling place. Also, the break with the life of the Court had been, in a way, welcome. Anne Boleyn was now supreme there, giddy, witty, pleasure-loving; and although her position was anomalous, inch by inch Catherine's had been made almost the same. There had actually been a time when Henry and Anne had taken supper together and then watched an entertainment, while Catherine, in her own apartments, had stitched away mending his shirts. A ridiculous situation, rendered all the more freakish by the fact that she and the Concubine, as Chapuys has named her, had never once come into open conflict. Catherine, fundamentally an honest woman, admitted to herself that here the credit was not solely hers. Anne had never openly flaunted her triumph over Catherine, and on more than one occasion had shown surprising tact — as though she knew what was due to an anointed Queen, because she aimed . . .

Don't think of it, Catherine now admonished herself, and took up her pen and wrote two lines, and then Sir Harry Norris was announced.

She had always held him in the highest esteem, faithful, discreet, resourceful, handsome and charming; and when, having greeted her, he said, "Madame, I have brought the written order," she heard the diffident, somewhat regretful note in his voice and hastened to put him at his ease.

"I was expecting it," she said. "Everything is ready."

On the previous day the Duke of Norfolk had come to her and asked her to hand over all the jewels which belonged to the Queen of England. His Grace, he said, wished to give them to the Marchioness of Pembroke so that she might be properly equipped for her visit to France.

Catherine had brought into play the subtlety for which her father, Ferdinand of Aragon, had been famous.

"But," she had said, "His Grace has expressly forbidden me to send him anything."

"And that, Madam, as you well know, meant no gifts at Christmas or New Year," Norfolk had replied with his usual bluntness.

She said,

"Also, it would be against my conscience to assist in the adorning of a person who is the scandal of Christendom."

Norfolk had thought, irritably, that he was sick in the belly at all this talk about conscience. He never mentioned his own, though it gave him trouble enough. He was a firm, orthodox Catholic, and he was also his King's faithful subject and with every passing day, every hour almost, the two things became more difficult to reconcile.

He was also — but this was incidental — the uncle of the person who was the scandal of Christendom, so he said shortly,

"Madam, you refuse to hand over the stuff?"

"Without the King's written permission, yes, my lord. After all, I hold them in trust and should not relinquish them upon a mere verbal request. Would you?"

Norfolk had looked at Catherine for a moment with envy and respect. With her no half-measures, no compromise; she was a Catholic and the Head of the Catholic Church had given her leave to marry Henry and she'd go to her grave believing herself his lawful wedded wife. Nor was she alone in her belief . . . And he had thought — If Darcy and Dacre and Fisher and More, if the Emperor, and the Pope . . . if they all came out openly in her defence, why then I . . . And so he had gone away bearing a heavier burden than the jewels of the Queen.

Catherine had known that Henry would try again. Not of his own will. Anne would never accept defeat.

And there, by some fantastic quirk of circumstance, was the similarity between the Princess of Aragon and the granddaughter of a London merchant.

Now, saying "Everything is ready," Catherine indicated a casket of sandalwood, the size of a small coffin, which stood on a table.

"May I see the order?"

It was written in a clerk's hand and signed with the King's unmistakable H R. The sight of the signature hurt her; but it was not Henry's doing. He'd been nagged, cajoled, persuaded. And because she could cajole and persuade and nag and sulk, Anne would go to France loaded with the jewels of the Queen of England — the diamond and sapphire necklace given to Anne of Bohemia by Richard II; the diamond and emerald necklace hung about the neck of Catherine of France by Henry V on the day of their son's christening — these Catherine had valued especially because they had been given to Queens whose husbands had loved them. There was a great mass of ornaments for which she had no particular feeling, and also one set, most magnificent, a head-dress, ear-rings, necklace, bracelets, brooch and rings of emeralds, rubies and diamonds which she had never worn because they had been given by Edward II to Isabella, the She-wolf of France who had proved to be a bad, false wife to him. There were some curious, almost worthless trinkets of great antiquity, dating back to the time when England was a poor country, a rosary of carved coral, a belt clasp of silver set with onyx and mother-of-pearl, a little fern-leaf brooch of jade. She had valued them all for the sake of their history.

But she now said, calmly,

"The inventory is there. And here is the key." Then she touched the massive gold collar which she was wearing. "This, Sir Harry, is my own, given me by my mother when we parted. His Grace will not mind, I think, if I retain it; it was never owned by any *other* English Queen."

Norris said,

"Of course, Madam, His Grace would never dream . . ."

Something in his voice encouraged Catherine to mention a piece of gossip that had been handed on yesterday by one of the Duke's attendants to one of hers.

"There is a rumour that the King intends to go through a form of marriage with Lady Pembroke when they reach Calais. Has it any foundation?"

"I have heard nothing of it, Madam." He wished it might be true.

"I have heard it, even here. Sir Harry, I wish you would carry a message from me to His Grace. Tell him I speak from love of him and from concern for his immortal soul. Tell him that I am his wife until His Holiness decrees otherwise, and if, before that time, he stands before God's altar and makes a mockery of the sacrament of marriage he must answer for his sin on the Day of Judgment. Tell him too, that he may be called to account for the imperilling of *her* soul. Every time he accedes to her, as in this matter," she glanced at the jewel casket, "he is encouraging her to demand more and more as the wage of sin."

Norris said,

"Madam, to my certain knowledge, the Lady has never asked anything of His Grace, except marriage. People lie about her. They'll say now that she asked for your . . . for the Queen's jewels, and I know she —" He broke off in confusion, not wishing to say, point-blank, to this woman who still reckoned herself the King's wife, that the King himself had had the idea of demanding back the Queen's jewels. He began again. "They malign her. There is no woman alive who cares less for trappings and trivialities. Whatever His Grace gives her, he gives. I assure you, she would die sooner than ask for anything."

Catherine was utterly unable to believe or accept that; it was in direct opposition to her view of Henry, the good, kind husband who had been seduced and was being exploited. She seized upon the obvious explanation; Harry Norris was another man who had fallen under the spell.

She said gravely,

"If you can believe that you can believe anything, and I pity your credulity. Take what you came for, and go."

CHAPTER
TWENTY-THREE

"The favourite diversion of Anne Boleyn and the King seems to have been cards and dice. Henry's losses at games of chance were enormous; but Anne . . . appears to have been a fortunate gamester."
Agnes Strickland. *Lives of the Queens of England*

WHITEHALL. JANUARY 1533.

Henry and Anne were playing cards as they so often did nowadays when they were alone together and no entertainment was taking place. Concentration upon the game served to hide the fact that they no longer had much to say to one another, that it was no longer enough for Henry simply to be in her company. Of all the words ever spoken by a human tongue none were truer than Mary's when she said, "And then . . . then suddenly it is all over. The things you did and said, that used to please so much, no longer please." Ever since August she had pleased him less and less, and her awareness of the change had made her nervous, and thus less likely to please.

She had one consolation; he had, so far, given no outward sign of lessened esteem; indeed the reverse was true. Her measuring stick was, oddly enough, Chapuys, the Spanish Ambassador: he was often at Court, he was

Catherine's friend and therefore her enemy, and he was independent. He had christened her "the Concubine", and though compelled to treat her with seeming courtesy, there was always in his eye an expression of enmity, tinged with contempt, and caution. Contempt for her as a person, caution for what she represented. Ever since August she'd watched him most carefully. He was supremely well-informed; if Henry had ever, by word or look, by the flicker of an eyelid, a movement of the lip, intimated that her reign was over, Chapuys would be the first to know, and the first to show that he knew. She had watched, taut, wary, to see that look of contempt flavoured with caution change to one of contempt flavoured with triumph. And the change had never come.

It was only when they were alone together; when jokes which had once amused Henry fell flat; when his eye wandered while she was speaking; when he did not notice a new gown or a fresh arrangement of the hair that she *knew*. And the knowledge dealt her a two-handed blow; on the one side a feeling of failure, of having gambled everything on one throw and lost; and on the other a feeling even more painful. She'd never loved Henry, because she loved Harry Percy, but Henry's love for her had saved her pride, flattered her, bolstered her, given her her opportunity to take revenge upon Wolsey who had ruined her life, justified everything she had done. Take that away, and what's left, what am I?

That, until lately, had been a question to which the answer had been unbearable. She'd known herself to be desperate, had mistrusted her own avid welcoming of every hopeful sign, said, anxiety, the cold weather, something I ate . . .

"Well, for once, I've won," Henry said. "You owe me two shillings."

The old geniality was lacking, and he did not look at her, his eyes were on the cards which he was gathering together.

"It's early yet," he said. "We'll play another game."

She said,

"I wanted to talk to you."

He looked up and said sharply.

"If it concerns Cranmer, there is nothing to be said. I've urged, begged, pleaded for speed in the acknowledging of his appointment, but in this, as in everything else, Clement is determined to keep me waiting. If I were drowning," he said violently, "going down for the last time and Clement stood there with a rope in his hand, he'd call a consistory to give him permission to throw it. And you know that as well as I do."

The last sentence held the note of impatient rebuke with which she was becoming familiar. And, by angering her, it solved the problem which she had been pondering all day — in what words exactly should she break the news.

She said,

"That is a great pity, because I am with child."

Once, years before, tilting with the Duke of Suffolk, Henry had taken a blow which had shattered his helmet and knocked him unconscious, and ever since he had been prone to headaches whose onset was heralded by a numbness across the front of his skull. He felt it now, and sat without moving or speaking just long enough for Anne to wonder whether, after all, she had fatally miscalculated and instead of pleasure he felt the dismay that such news might bring to any ordinary unmarried man. Then he said, and his voice shook,

"You are sure?"

"As far as one can be of such things." He rose, overturning the cardtable, came to her, put his arms about her body and his head in her lap and burst into tears.

She felt more tenderly towards him at that moment than ever before, and pressing her hands against the crisp russet hair, thought of the child, not as the long awaited prince, not as her foothold on security, but as a little boy, like Henry to look at, with all his good qualities, and none of his bad.

Presently he asked,

"When, sweetheart?"

"In September."

"Then we must be married at once. The day after tomorrow. St Paul's day. God in Glory! If only Clement . . . If only we could do it as it should be done! It'll have to be a hole-and-corner affair, my love, but I'll make up by giving you the finest Coronation ever seen." He gave her a great hug and a hearty kiss and stood up. "Cranmer's first act, once he's installed, shall be to declare my marriage to Catherine invalid. In an English Court. I've done with Popes. God is my witness that I have tried to keep in with the bungling fool, tried to do everything legally. I've been patient, humble, when all I asked was justice. And now, at the greatest moment of my life, instead of being able to cry the good news, I must . . ." Rage came up and choked him; he beat his fists together. "That's the end of the Pope in England," he said again. "But it'll be legal, sweetheart, never fear. Private, that's all, and kept secret for a little while. Half a dozen of our most trusted people. And your father and mother, if that would please you."

So the end of the tightrope was in sight at last; no farther away then the day after tomorrow. Married, safe, justified. Only now dare she look back and truly face the horror of fear that had gnawed at her all autumn, the fear that she had played her last card and still not won.

She said,

"I don't know whether to laugh or cry!"

"You must be calm," said Henry, the experienced father. "No excitement, no exertion. And I tell you this now, whatever you fancy, however fantastic, strawberries in February or green peas in April, just *tell* me and you shall have them, if I have to send to Turkey!"

His love had revived, as a rose, worn all day as a nosegay, will revive overnight in water. She was no longer the woman, who, after seeming to promise so much, had disappointed him so sorely and in such a mysterious way. She was the casket wherein lay that one jewel without which all his possessions were valueless. In September, God willing, she would justify him in the sight of all the world, by bearing his son, Henry the Ninth.

In the heart of the night Anne woke abruptly. She'd been dreaming, but the dream was already beyond

303

recall. It was an unhappy dream, that was all she knew. She'd been alone, frightened and unhappy, which was perverse, for surely tonight, of all nights, she should have slept easy. She lay for a while, remembering Henry's pleasure and thinking about the day after tomorrow — no, it was after midnight now — tomorrow, her wedding day. And a thought came, unbidden, unwelcome into her mind. Why, if a marriage, a legal marriage, could take place tomorrow, had it been delayed so long? Nothing in the general situation had changed since last August. Had Henry waited, deliberately, until he was sure that she was capable of bearing a child? Whatever the answer to that, one thing was certain: for this child's sake Henry was at last willing to cast off all Papal authority. Not for his own convenience, not for love of her, but for something which had as yet no life, no name, nor would have until September, he had said, "That's the end of the Pope in England."

She knew she should be glad: for the Pope had been no friend to her.

CHAPTER
TWENTY-FOUR

"The time and place of Anne Boleyn's marriage with Henry VIII is one of the most disputed points in history."
Agnes Strickland. *Lives of The Queens of England*

"The King's marriage was celebrated, it is reported, o†n the day of the conversion of St Paul, and because at that time Dr Bonner had returned from Rome some suspect that the Pope had given a tacit consent, which I cannot believe."
The Spanish Ambassador in a letter to Charles V

WHITEHALL. JANUARY 25th, 1533

Lady Bo said breathlessly,

"Tom, put your hand at the back of my waist and push me a little, please. Such steep stairs! And I don't want to arrive all of a fluster."

Wolsey, when he built what he had called York House which was now called Whitehall Palace, had built as he always did, proud and high. From the outside the turrets were impressive, inside they were full of attic rooms, reached by stairs intended for the active legs of young squires and pages, not for the ascent of middle-aged

305

ladies, roused untimely from bed, dressed in their finery, and flustered anyhow.

Thomas Boleyn had tried to explain to her over-night. The King, he told her, and Anne, were to be married, secretly, very early in the morning.

"Married? Properly married?"

"My dear, did you ever hear of anyone being improperly married?"

"Yes, indeed I did. The King himself, all these years."

He laughed. "An apt retort; but untrue. His Grace has been unmarried all these years. Tomorrow he will marry Anne and that will be his first legal marriage."

"Then why does it have to be secret? Oh, I know all about the Pope, Tom, it took a bit of understanding, but I did get it clear in my head at last. What I mean is, *if* as soon as the Pope says that Dr Cranmer is Archbishop, Cranmer and the King will go against the Pope over the divorce, *why* does it matter whether the Pope agrees to Cramner being Archbishop or not?"

"Now that is female logic and quite unanswerable in any terms that would have meaning for you. Look at it this way; suppose you and I fell out and to spite me you thought you'd sell Hever. The sale would be illegal. But suppose I fell ill and gave you something known as power of attorney; then you could act for me and it would be legal, whatever you chose to do. If Cranmer said the King was a free man before he was confirmed by Papal Bull, it'd mean nothing. When he does it, after he is properly installed, it will have some authority."

"Then why don't they wait?"

"I imagine that they are tired of waiting. Wouldn't you be? If you want a more definite answer," he said teasingly, "I suggest that you ask His Majesty that question, tomorrow morning.

"You know I would not dare. But I still think, Tom, that it's all a curious muddle; and if the Pope is to be thrown aside it might as well be done first as last."

"That is heresy, my dear. *Now*. In six months it won't be. The King clings to the Papacy as a man clings to an aching tooth. A clove will ease it, he says; I'll bite on the other side, he says. But the end is certain. Tomorrow morning will see the end of the Pope in England."

Lady Bo's mind abandoned its brief concern with great matters.

"Tomorrow," she said, "Anne will be married. And now I can confess that all along I've had grave doubts, and fears. I thought it all too likely that she had sold her good name for a mess of pottage."

"Your terms of exchange are wrong, my dear. It is one's birthright that one gives for that unappetising dish."

Now here they were, having been admitted by a side door, little used, to judge by the way its hinges squealed. There was no page, no squire in attendance, just that very pleasant young man, Harry Norris, who had indicated the stairs to be climbed. The stairs ascended in a spiral, and for a good part of the way there was a thick woollen rope, fixed by brass rings to the wall, and Lady Bo had hauled herself upwards by clutching at it; but at the last turn there was nothing save a stone wall worn shiny and dark by the touch of hands. Faced with that she had asked her husband's help.

At the top another of the King's gentlemen was posted, Thomas greeted him, calling him Heneage. He opened the door for them and they entered the plain white-washed room on the far side of which an altar had been placed. Nothing else had been done to cheer or beautify the attic and only the candles, burning bravely, mitigated the murky chill of the winter's dawn.

The King arrived, attended by Norris and Heneage. He was wearing dull tawny, heavily embroidered in gold. He looked nervous and Lady Bo's heart went out to him; such a great King, yet so human; so steadily faithful to Anne, and about to take a step which would not only restore her good name — sadly blown upon — but make her Queen of England.

Then Anne came in, with one of her ladies, Nan Savile, and her woman, Emma. Anne looked magnificent, but alarmingly pale, though that, Lady Bo tried to comfort herself, might in part be due to her dress, a dark cinnamon colour, furred with black.

Last of all the priest entered through a little low doorway behind the altar. He was a stranger, and at the sight of him Lady Bo remembered her own wedding where the priest had been an old familiar friend, part of her ordinary life. Later on, she was to hear a good deal of argument as to who, exactly, had performed the ceremony in this attic; some people said it was Dr Rowland Lee, one of the King's chaplains, others said he was an Augustinian Friar named George Browne. Nobody seemed to know for sure; though the King must have chosen him. And not too well, Lady Bo thought, her sense of this being a very odd wedding increased as she realised that the priest seemed not to know exactly what he was there for. He appeared to think that he had been asked to celebrate Mass; but before he could begin the King whispered to Norris, who stepped forward and spoke into the priest's ear; whereupon he folded his hands with a helpless, puzzled gesture and looked at the King almost piteously.

"The Pope," Henry said in a loud, firm voice, "has declared my former marriage invalid. I have that in writing, Sir Priest. I have also permission for this marriage. So, if it please you, proceed with the Nuptial Mass."

After a second's hesitation, during which a strange tension filled the attic room, and Lady Bo, despite the chill, felt sweat break out on her forehead and on her neck, the priest bowed his head; stood for a moment in a subservient attitude and then donned dignity and authority as though they were vestments and proceeded to speak the words that bound Henry and Anne together for life.

Lady Bo found herself inclining to melancholy. No choir, no bells, no hilarious guests, no presents. She belonged to a class where wedding presents mattered. And though Anne would not be setting up house and had no need for such practical tokens of goodwill as linen, blankets, pewter dishes and candle-sticks, churns and milk-skimmers, still her stepmother wished to give

309

her something, and last evening, going through her own possessions, had chosen a necklace of onyx and crystal beads which she herself considered very handsome. Tom had said, bless her soft heart and her softer head, what use did she think Anne would have for such a trinket; when she had accompanied the King to France she had been so plastered with gems of incalculable worth that one could not look at her without blinking. Lady Bo had made the answer that came into her head — that it was the spirit of the gift which counted, because she had learned that her Tom, except where she herself was concerned, was completely without sentiment, just as some people were colour-blind or tone-deaf. But she had not put the beads away; she had them in her pocket and if an opportunity occurred she intended to slip them into Anne's hand.

And then it was over; and suddenly cheerfulness blossomed in the cheerless little room. Henry's taut, fidgety manner gave way to geniality, and Anne, though still pale looked radiant. Lady Bo curtsied to Henry and would have curtsied to Anne, but before she could do Anne put her arms around her and kissed her.

"I wish you well, dear," Lady Bo said, and made her little gift. "And I pray God send you happy all the days of your life."

"And no good wish for me, Lady Wiltshire?" Henry asked.

"Oh indeed, your Grace, yes. Every good wish in the world."

He thanked her and said he could never regard her as a mother-in-law, she was too young and too comely; and he slapped Thomas on the shoulder, and cracked

310

jokes and hugged Anne, and gave for a little while such an impression of being young, transported with delight on the greatest day of his life that Lady Bo found herself thinking of country weddings she had known, and all the trappings, the worn old shoe thrown to represent the abandoned past, the herring, symbol of fertility, the expressions of goodwill, coarse maybe, but hearty and apt. She might even so far have forgotten her shyness as to have voiced one traditional wedding wish, had Henry not said.

"Come, sweetheart. You have been standing long enough. We must take good care of you now."

Oh dear, oh dear, Lady Bo said to herself; so *that's* the way it is! That is why there was so much haste that we mustn't wait for the Archbishop and a proper wedding.

Still, Anne had managed well; and this morning's ceremony constituted in Lady Bo's eyes the wished-for happy ending. And there was another thing too. Children conceived out of wedlock did tend to be boys. It was as though God knew that there was a risk of bastardy and thought the handicap of illegitimacy enough, without the added one of being female. So perhaps Anne had managed even better than she realised.

Going, with less effort, but with care, down the twisting stairs Lady Bo thought of one of the things country people, full of good meat and ale, said to bridegrooms, "Go to it, bor, and remember, God made Adam afore Eve."

CHAPTER
TWENTY-FIVE

"He sent yesterday the Dukes of Norfolk and Suffolk to the Queen to tell her that she must not trouble herself any more nor attempt to return to him seeing that he is married and that henceforth she is to abstain from the title of Queen.

The Queen's Chamberlain came to notify her that the King would not allow her henceforth to call herself Queen and that at the close of one month after Easter he would not defray her expenses nor the wages of her servants . . . She replied that as long as she lived she would call herself Queen . . . Failing for food for herself and her servants she would go out and beg for the love of God. Although the King himself is not ill-natured, it is this Anne who has put him in this perverse and wicked temper."

The Spanish Ambassador in letters to Charles V

AMPTHILL. APRIL 1533

". . . and it is his Majesty's express wish and command, that you should henceforth refrain from using the title of Queen and be known as the Dowager Princess of Wales." That was the end of a longish speech which the Duke of Norfolk had, with some effort, committed to

312

memory, and having delivered it he drew a long breath of relief.

Catherine said,

"The King's wish has always been, and will always be, a command to me."

That was capitulation at last. Norfolk and those who had come to support him congratulated themselves upon the ease with which their mission had been accomplished.

"Subject always," Catherine said, "to two over-riding authorities."

"And they are, Madam?"

Now let her mention the Pope and the Emperor and she was speaking treason; and if she were a traitor Chapuys, the busy body Imperial Ambassador, could cease his whining about how a helpless, inoffensive woman was being persecuted.

"God. And my conscience. God appoints to each of us his station in life, my lords; and He called me to be Queen of England. My conscience forbids that I should call myself by any other title."

Norfolk said,

"But, Madam, there can be but one Queen of England; His Grace can have but one wife."

"There we are agreed, my lord."

"His Grace married the Marchioness of Pembroke more than two months ago."

The room went dark. She was standing, as she had received them, dragging her sagging figure to its full height, attaining dignity. Now she wished she were sitting. Her legs were failing her. She might fall; she might faint. No, pride forbade. Never should they see how deep and fatal this wound was.

"Married? How? By some hedge-priest, under cover of darkness?" Her voice was bitter. "No proper cleric would have dared!"

"I can assure you, Madam, the ceremony was properly performed and duly witnessed. I was not myself present. But there are those here who were."

"Which of you?"

They stared at her, their faces noncommittal. Seldom in all history had there been so well-kept a secret. The marriage had taken place in the presence of the bride's parents, three attendants, one serving woman and certain members of the King's Privy Council; and only those who had been present knew who else was there. Even the exact date and place and the name of the officiating priest were secrets.

"It matters little who watched this masquerade. Marriage it was not. His Grace is my lawful wedded husband, and so long as I live he can have no other wife."

The Duke of Norfolk felt again that unease which the whole question of the annulment, and the consequences arising from it were bound to arouse in a truly Catholic breast. While he turned his eyes inward for a second the Duke of Suffolk said in his brutal way,

"Madam, your information is outdated. The Convocation of Canterbury recently decreed that Pope Julius had no power to permit His Grace to marry you and therefore that the marriage was null and void."

"I knew that. But I question the right of the Convocation of Canterbury to give judgment on the matter."

"Then, Madam, you question the validity of our English law; for Parliament has said that the English Church is sufficient to determine all statutes and that as Head of the English Church the King is the final judge of all things spiritual."

She wanted to say — These powers are self-assumed and mean nothing: I could call myself Queen of France, but that would not make me so. But bandying words was a waste of time. Once again she took her stand upon law as she understood it.

"My case is even now under consideration by the Roman courts and should not be tried elsewhere."

"Your case was lost years ago. And it is essential that you should recognise the truth, Madam; for Queen Anne is already with child."

Again their faces seemed to blur and recede into blackness. This was the end of all hope. No! The end of all hope if the child should be a boy. If Anne Boleyn could produce a prince the English would be so delighted that even the most conservatively minded of them would contrive to believe that the boy had been born in wedlock.

And Mary would be nothing. Worst of all, Mary would never have a chance to repair the damage which Henry — under the evil influence of *that* woman —

had done to the Holy Roman Catholic Church in England.

Not a glimmer of fear or doubt showed in her face, or her voice, as she said,

"Until the Pope dissolves our marriage, the Princess Mary will be His Grace's only legal issue and therefore heir to the throne."

It was no more than they had expected; and Norfolk was prepared.

"In that case, Madam, I must, with regret, inform you of His Grace's plans for you. The generous offers which he made in return for the withdrawing of your claim no longer hold good. Lord Mountjoy will no longer be your host, but your custodian; your allowance will be cut by three-quarters. You will be allowed to keep no state and your household will be reduced to a minimum."

"Then I shall feel no pinch," Catherine said calmly. "I need only my chaplain, my physician and two maids. They will continue to address me, and refer to me, by my proper title. I wish you to tell His Majesty that, and add that if such a modest household is a burden upon his resources, I am prepared to go about the country asking alms."

There was just a hint of a threat there. Catherine had retained the affection of the ordinary people, particularly of the women; if every man, married twenty years, could find some excuse for following his latest fancy, what woman would be safe? Catherine was Mrs Everywoman; and the world was full of interlopers, wicked women, would-be breakers of homes, like that

Nan Bullen. If it once got about that the King was being mean to Catherine over money, while loading Anne with gifts, there would be an uproar!

Norfolk said,

"That will hardly be necessary, Madam. His Grace meant only that since you are not Queen, if you refused the rank of Dowager Princess of Wales and the allowances that accompanies the title, then you must be content to be an ordinary gentlewoman."

"And that I can never be in this life," she said simply. "If it pleases God, and His Holiness to take away my title as Queen, I shall remain what I was born, Princess of Aragon."

To that there was no answer; the Dukes and the lords went away.

Now she could sit down and give way to the trembling which shook her like a palsy. She wanted to weep, but weeping did no good, it only made one's head thick so that clear thought was difficult. And she needed to think clearly; because one of the things which Norfolk had learned by heart and repeated concerned Mary. He'd said that Mary was to go to London and be one of Anne's ladies, by the King's wish. If that were true, Mary must go; for over a matter of such small consequence Henry was entitled to double obedience, as King, as father. But, however much humiliated, Mary must stand firm upon her unassailable right; she was Henry's daughter, born in wedlock, heir to the throne.

She must write to Mary. To encourage, not to admonish. Mary needed no admonishment; Mary was a rock. But she was only seventeen; and she was dreadfully alone.

As I am, Catherine thought. How eagerly *she* would have welcomed a letter of encouragement. None ever came. Clement went from procrastination to procrastination; making a little promise, withdrawing it; making threats against Henry and taking no action. And the Emperor Charles was just as bad. Nobody had ever come, fully armed and whole-heartedly to her aid. No! To think in that way wronged Fisher, Bishop of Rochester, who had never wavered, and her chaplain, Thomas Abell who had first pleaded her cause in Rome and then published a book defending the marriage. For that he had been imprisoned in the Tower. And she had, she was certain, many faithful, nameless friends. She owed it to them to fight on.

Her mind moved on to Henry. How displeased he would be by the answers she had returned him. She imagined how Anne, insolent in her hope of a son, must have nagged him before he — always so generous — would have agreed to cut down her allowance. Then another thought came, an icicle in the heart; how convenient for everyone if she — and Mary — died. Those who accused Anne of witchcraft also called her a poisoner. Bishop Fisher's supper broth had been poisoned one evening; several of his guests had died and he had been ill for a month. Mary must be warned of that danger too, and she herself must be very careful. Anne would become desperate now, knowing, as she must in her heart, that her marriage was no marriage and that her child would be a bastard.

As Catherine took her place by the table where she spent so many hours, and prepared to write, one of her women entered and hovered as though anxious to speak.

"You have heard the news, I daresay," Catherine said, wishing to forestall any lamentations over the reduced household, any veiled expressions of sympathy because of the marriage and the pregnancy. "I shall make my own arrangements, when I am ready. Nothing else has altered so far as I am concerned."

"I was wondering, your Grace, whether they told you about Bishop Fisher. I heard just now, in the courtyard."

"What about him?"

"They say he's been arrested and taken to the Tower and will have his head cut off."

Catherine thought of that noble, craggy old head; of that clear brain, dauntless courage, golden tongue.

"For being my friend," she said faintly.

"There was another reason given, your Grace. He found fault with something that Lord Rochford said, or did in France."

"And since when has it been treason to criticise George Boleyn? That is too flimsy . . . But if such a charge can take Bishop Fisher to the block there is no law left in England."

Suffolk had said, "*Then, Madam, you question the validity of our English law.*" The implication was — You, a Spaniard.

I may be next, she thought. If the English law can declare me unmarried it can behead me.

She began to write to Mary the kind of letter, urgent, full of advice, that a mother would write, thinking it to be her last.

She laid no blame on Henry. This was all the work of that wicked woman who held him in thrall, the cruel, ruthless, clever creature whom the London crowds called Nan Bullen.

CHAPTER
TWENTY-SIX

"He had been very much grieved that the arms of the Queen had not only been taken from her barge, but also rather shamefully mutilated . . . And whatever regret the King may have shown at the taking of the Queen's barge the Lady has made use of it . . . God grant she may content herself with the said barge, the jewels and the husband of the Queen."
The Spanish Ambassador in a letter to Charles V

LONDON. MAY 1533

Emma Arnett sometimes reflected wryly that if this prince were born straight-backed, with all his limbs in the right place, sound in mind and unmarked of skin, England would have *her* to thank for it. Often, in the middle of an emotional scene, or when she fell exhausted into her bed, she would think that nothing, nothing in the world except her anti-Papist beliefs and her recognition of the need to keep the Lady Mary from the throne, could ever have held her to her present employment. Now and then she'd remember, with ironic amusement, that the first thing she had ever admired about young Mistress Boleyn had been her self-control. Now she had none and almost every day gave way to some kind of emotional excess of the kind a breeding woman should avoid. None of her ladies — even the few of whom she was fond and who were fond of her — seemed to have any influence. The burden always in the end, fell upon Emma.

She had what Emma called "a wild turn" when she heard that threats had failed to move Catherine.

"She must be mad! There's nothing for her to hope for now. It's all over and done with, but she won't admit it. Spite, that's what it is, spite against me. And I never did her any harm. The King told me that he was a bachelor before I ever allowed him even to kiss me. That is true, Emma; I have letters to prove it. He called me cold and unkind. I didn't *take* her husband; he never was her husband. Yet there she sits, spoiling everything, calling herself Queen and turning people against me."

"Nobody's against you, your Grace, except the Papists."

"Then the streets must be full of them. Dumb, surly, staring. I'm beginning to dread my Coronation — if they behave as they have done . . ."

"They don't matter. Nothing matters, except that you should bear a sound child; and I've told you a hundred times that getting wrought up is bad, bad for you both. Put your feet up, now, and be calm."

"How can I be calm? Do you know the latest thing they're saying! That I asked for Prin . . . for the Lady Mary to be one of my maids-in-waiting. How does that sound? As though I would! Would I want that

322

glowering, pasty-faced girl always about me, reminding me . . .?"

She began to walk the room in the way Emma knew so well and now dreaded.

"It was the King's idea. He thought the mere mention of it would shock Catherine into agreeing to what he asked of her. And the truth behind that, Emma, is that he isn't easy in his mind. Far from it. The Bishops at Canterbury, the Parliament, the special Court at Dunstable may all declare that he never was married to her, but as long as she sits there calling herself his wife and Queen Catherine he can never be truly at ease."

"He'll be easy once the child is born — which it won't be if you go on stamping and shouting. Sit down now, and put your feet up."

Anne's behaviour worried Emma because it was so unnatural. She was now five months pregnant and ordinarily, by that time, a breeding woman had become placid and imperturbable. Emma had seen it over and over again; women who had been resentful — We've six now and hard-pressed to feed them, and the youngest hardly on his feet, and who'll feed the calves, and I meant to rear geese this year — But soon, before there was any outward sign, they'd be resigned, saying that where there were six to feed one more made no difference, and somebody would see to the calves, and geese could wait till next year. God knew His business . . . But of course, she conceded, she was thinking of ordinary women, concerned with ordinary things.

Anne's case was different. And thinking that gave Emma patience.

On one point no patience was called for; she, as well as Anne, was deeply anxious about the child's sex. A boy was *needed*. Even those resolute Papists who still held that only the Pope could give Henry permission to put away Catherine and condemn Mary to bastardy would hesitate when it came to choose between a Princess and a Prince to take the throne. But even here Emma took the long view, and when Anne said, "It must be a boy. She gave him a girl and I must do better," Emma retorted that a strong girl would be earnest of a boy to follow and that to get excited over this, as over any other matter, was bad. She called up all her old country lore.

"So far as I can see, so early, it is lying high which is said to be a sign of a boy. Boys they say, ride high from the start. And you haven't sickened, not since the first month. There's an old saying that wenches sicken you early, lads later. But if you go on acting so excitable you'll end with nothing, as I've said before."

"Nan Savile said that where she comes from they can tell with a needle and thread."

"A needle and thread," Emma said cautiously. "And pray, your Grace, how do they do that?"

"But the way it swings — held over the place where the child lies. To and fro for a boy, she said, round and round for a girl."

That, to Emma, unlike the riding high or the occurrence of sickness which seemed to her capable of natural explanation, savoured of superstition; but she was willing to do anything that would keep Anne calm.

So they tried; and the needle and thread, like most oracles, gave an ambiguous answer. It swung to and fro in a straight line; then it wavered and went round and round; then, controlled by Emma, it swung in the desired way.

"It must be a boy," Anne said, striking her fists on the bed where she had lain for the experiment. "It must be, it must be. A girl would ruin all."

"So would a miscarriage," Emma said.

She attributed a good deal of Anne's behaviour to the strain of the forthcoming Coronation. Henry was keeping his promise to make it the finest ever seen; and sometimes when he and Anne had been together, Anne would be pleasantly excited, speaking of how this street was to be hung all with crimson and scarlet, and the other with cloth of gold, of what she herself would wear, and how royally she was to be attended. Emma encouraged such talk, which was healthy and natural. All too often though it would lead on to Anne's bugbear, her nervous apprehension of how the crowds would behave.

"His Grace can order them to dress the streets and provide pageants, but he can't order them to cheer. Suppose I go down in history as the queen who rode through silence to be crowned. And why? What have I done that they should hate me so?"

"They'll cheer when they see you go to your crowning," Emma said. "It takes time for thick heads to get used to changes and up to now it's all been a bit of a muddle, with just a few stubborn people running round and saying you weren't even married. You'll see the difference now."

Nevertheless she took the precaution of mentioning Anne's fears to her Milk Street friends who undertook to have little groups of partisans posted at various important points to give the crowds a lead.

And then, as the preparations began to take shape, the King himself did something which made Emma long to box his ears, stupid, blundering, sentimental fool that he was.

She had seen immediately, when Anne returned from having supper with him that something had upset her. Her lips were so tightly pressed that her mouth was just a line, and her eyes were enormous and too bright. All through her undressing she spoke hardly a word and finally her ladies, discouraged by the silence or the monosyllables with which their chatter was received, fell silent too. The lack of conversation and the way the watchful Emma kept saying, "I'll do that," or "You can leave that to me," cut down the ceremony of disrobing by fifteen minutes.

When they were alone Anne said,

"Brush my hair again, Emma. I'm too upset to sleep yet."

"I could see something was amiss. But you should try not to upset yourself. Some silly little thing, I'll be bound."

"It was far from little. Nothing goes right for me. Nothing. I wish I'd never been born."

Emma brushed, steadily, soothingly. She'd hear all, in time.

"Whose barge would *you* suppose I should use for my river journey?"

"The Queen's — if there is such a thing."

"So I thought — not that I was consulted, but had I been I should have told my chamberlain to do just what he did do. There is a Queen's barge, and I am Queen; so my chamberlain took it and had Catherine's arms burned off and mine painted on. What was wrong with that?"

"Who says anything was wrong?" Emma's mind flew to Lady Rochfort, known to hate her sister-in-law, known to be a supporter of Catherine, known to possess a bitter, and rather bold tongue.

"The King," Anne said.

"That can't be true. Whoever said that was wanting to upset you. And really . . ." She paused on the verge of saying "you should know better" to the Queen of England. "You shouldn't play into their hands by getting upset over spiteful gossip."

"He said it to my face. He looked me straight in the eye and said my chamberlain had no right to take Catherine's barge, there were plenty of others quite suitable."

Emma halted her hand and said slowly,

"That doesn't make sense to me. Not after he took the Queen's jewels from her and gave them to you. Unless perhaps . . ." She was so practised in finding soothing things to say that she had thought of something that did make sense even as her tongue said that it didn't. "Unless it was her own, one she'd brought from Spain maybe; then he wouldn't want it used for such a journey. That must be it."

"The barge was hers in the same sense that the jewels were hers, and the title, and the crown. He can't quarrel with me for having them because he gave them to me; but over this he could. And did. I've suspected it for a long time; now I know. He hates me, Emma. He hates me."

Emma said,

"You mustn't say such things, Your Grace; and I shouldn't listen to them. It's a sick fancy, due to your condition, like wanting things out of season. I shouldn't think there ever was a lady loved as you've been loved. All those years of waiting, and all the changes — all for the good we know, but some of them went against the grain for *him*. And now, with your Coronation at the end of the month, and carrying his child, you pick on some little thing and say he hates you." She was about to say, "I call that wicked", but remembered herself in time and ended by repeating that it was just a sick fancy.

Anne said,

"No. I'm not given to fancies. He loved me — at least he wanted me. I wasn't brave enough or strong enough. I gave in too soon. And he's never really liked me since."

"He married you," Emma said bluntly. "He's giving you the grandest Coronation ever seen."

"Not *me*. The mother of the son he hopes for. But even to *her* he grudged Catherine's barge."

"Because he wasn't asked! Close to him, as we are, we see the man, with the same funny little ways all men have; but we should bear in mind that since he was crowned he's always had his own way — except over his divorce and even that he managed in the end. And by nature he's masterful; if he'd been born a blacksmith he'd have told his customers what they wanted, instead of taking orders. Over the barge he was put out because nobody asked leave. You mustn't take that to heart. Did you eat your supper?"

"No. How could I? I wanted to fling the plates on the floor and scream."

"That's the way to get a baby with no bridge to its nose, or one leg shorter than the other. Will you please, to set my mind at rest if for no other reason, eat a little now?"

Emma was annoyed with Henry for allowing his displeasure to show, but she thought she understood why he had been displeased. He had won, and having won he was sorry for Catherine and had been hurt to hear of her arms being removed from the barge. It was on a level with his religious policy. He'd won his battle with the Pope, but couldn't be wholeheartedly glad about it, felt bound to show some compunction, which took the form of trying to keep church ritual unchanged. Men were like that, always wanting to have things both ways. All the same, it was grossly inconsiderate of him to have upset Anne just now, and for a little while Emma wished that she were back in a simple merchant's household, where by virtue of long faithful service she would have had the privilege of speaking her mind.

And that made her think about her own driving ambition to better herself, an ambition which had, in the end, led to her being put in charge of a heart-broken girl being sent home in disgrace, which in its turn had led to her being the most powerful single influence upon the Queen of England. Truly the hand of God moved mysteriously; you didn't see it at the time, but when you looked back there was no mistaking. God had placed her, so that with a dose of poppy syrup, a sensible word, an encouraging word, she should keep Anne on *her* course. A humble instrument, Emma thought with pride.

She stood vigilant over Anne as she choked down the white bread and the beef which, because it was red was supposed to be good for the blood, as red wine was; and presently Anne looked at her, narrowing her eyes and said,

"I suppose I should be grateful to you for the care you take of me. And I *am* grateful. But you are like the King. You look on me as a brood mare!" She stopped eating and for the first time gave voice to the thoughts which tormented her if she woke in the dark of the night. "I often ask myself how this all came about. One thing led to another, and that to the next. I never did a thing without good reason. What went wrong? You always have an answer to everything, Emma. Tell me, what went wrong? You know, because you were with me, I was heart-broken over Harry Percy and then the King came, like a hound on a trail. I stood him off — that was reasonable, wasn't it? And when he said he would make me Queen, did I do wrong to accept such a dazzling prospect? Does the woman live who would have done otherwise? And now . . ."

"Now you are Queen. On the last day of this month you will be crowned. There is nothing wrong. Your Grace."

Except, of course, the unfortunate timing. The ceremonies, the wedding and the Coronation should rightly have been safely over before the pregnancy began. That was the root of the trouble. But it couldn't be helped, and there were people with worse troubles.

"If only it can be a boy," Anne said, placing her palms upon her just perceptibly thickening waist. "It must, it must be a boy."

"I pray to God it may be," Emma said.

CHAPTER
TWENTY-SEVEN

"The King's mistress was delivered of a daughter to the great regret both of him and the Lady and to the great reproach of the physicians, astrologers, sorcerers and sorceresses who affirmed that it would be a male child."

The Spanish Ambassador in a letter to Charles V

GREENWICH. SEPTEMBER 7th, 1533

It was a girl.

Anne never knew whose voice it was that broke through the half-swoon and said, "Your Grace has borne a fair lady," but she heard the words, she knew she had failed, and willed herself away, welcoming the enveloping darkness.

Emma Arnett said to herself,

"It is the will of God," and then suffered the mental confusion of all sensible, rational people brought face to face with an act of God which seems senseless and without reason. God surely understood the situation in England; He was omnipotent; He made everything; couldn't He just as easily have made a prince? Another girl was such a triumph for the Papists who in a few minutes' time, as soon as the news was out, would be saying that this was God's judgment on the King's new marriage. But, hard as it was to accept, it must be accepted; it was the mysterious will of God.

All through the palace; a girl! What a pity! Out into the streets: a princess! But we wanted a prince! The birth of the baby who was to grow into the woman who was to be the greatest ruler England ever knew, the woman of whom the Pope, hating her, was to say, "She is a great woman, and were she but Catholic, without peer", was regarded as regrettable by all but the very staunchest of the supporters of Catherine and Mary. The majority of the ordinary people, still Catholic at heart, had been reassured by the slowness and superficiality of Henry's reforms; his break with Rome had merely trimmed away some old and not particularly desirable customs, like the paying of Peter's Pence or the appointment of foreign clerics to English bishoprics; the core of ritual and belief had remained intact; and a prince who could be looked to to carry on his father's policy would have been welcomed by almost everyone in England.

So the little female creature was taken sadly and washed and swaddled and given to her nurse. And the one person who had a good word for her was her father, the person with most right to be disappointed. When he first saw her she was squalling; she was red in face, her eyes were screwed up and she had a frizzle of orange-coloured hair on her scalp. He touched it with a gentle finger.

"My hair," he said, "and my voice. She is indeed my daughter and she seems a lusty wench. I pray God will send her a brother in the same good shape."

He was disappointed, but less than he had expected to be, less than anyone would have foretold. He loved all his children; he loved Mary and was grieved that she had so decidedly taken Catherine's part; naturally in the circumstances he could not pamper or favour her, but he had always stopped just short of the positive persecution that commonsense suggested; he loved his bastard son and had done everything in his power to compensate him for his state; and now he was prepared to love Elizabeth, the first of his children to be born in wedlock. He intended her christening to give evidence of how highly he regarded her. Ambassador's might write home to their masters that the King was grievously disappointed, but anyone who ventured in his presence to imply sympathy, however tactful, met with a glower and gruffness. Henry Tudor had had his way and there was nothing wrong with his marriage, nothing wrong with his child.

Anne was slow to recover and he visited her often, taking presents and making heartening, bracing little speeches. The visits were a trial to him because her disappointment and resentment were so plain to be seen. Unwillingly he found himself remembering how often Catherine had faced a worse situation, a dead baby or a baby dead soon after birth. "It is God's will," she had said, every time, and her resignation had irked him. Now he was irked by Anne's lack of resignation. He chose to put that down to her state of health.

"When you feel stronger, you'll see things differently," he said; and he had his recipes for the rapid regaining of strength; she should eat well; stop fretting and look forward to being able to take advantage of the fine autumn weather and walk in the garden.

Emma gave much the same advice; she had known a black moment of doubt, thrown it aside and was now sternly looking forward again. Henry's attitude had impressed her and increased her good opinion of him; if he could be so cheerful, why should the Queen remain fretful? Since no one else seemed disposed to be frank, she was obliged to be.

"Your Grace, it is not the end of the world. The Princess is a baby to be proud of, a promise for the future. If you would be cheerful and make an effort, you could be up and about in a fortnight, and by this time next year, God willing, the mother of a prince."

But Anne's disappointment was the more crushing because it had followed upon — and ended — the happiest period of her life. June, July and August had been three wonderful months.

The Coronation had been — as Henry had promised — the most magnificent ever seen; and her secret dread, an unfavourable reception by the London crowds, had proved to be entirely without foundation. The ordinary people loved a pageant, loved any excuse to make merry, and from the time when she made her progress, in the disputed barge, to the Tower, until twelve days later when she rode in a litter to St Paul's, and thence to Westminster Hall, it had been one long pageant, one long merrymaking. There'd been no need for the pro-Anne patty to whip the crowds to enthusiasm. Heartened by the wine, red and white, which flowed in every conduit and fountain, they had stood and roared out their cheers and blessed her; and if there were some little silences it was because the people were momentarily struck speechless by the sight of her, clad in silver tissue, with her wonderful hair flowing free, so long that she could sit on it, and held back from her face by a circlet of rubies.

Ambassadors wrote letters which implied that the Coronation had been lack-lustre, knowing that such news would be welcome; but Anne who was at the centre of it knew differently and felt that she had at last been accepted. She was married, she was crowned, and she was going to give the English people what they longed for. Her inner fear of having lost the King's favour eased; Henry, like everybody else, respected success, and she would be a successful Queen.

The time which Emma had hoped for arrived, the peaceful ripening time of gestation. Even the weather and the season seemed propitious, the slow, warm days moving towards the inevitable harvest. The frantic anxiety as to the child's sex had ceased to nag; the physicians said it would be a boy, and so did all the soothsayers whom Henry insisted upon consulting. There was one wise woman living in the Welsh Marches who claimed to be a collateral descendant of Merlin, and who was said to be able to tell the sex of an unborn child from the mere handling of some garment worn by the expectant mother. She was too old to make the journey to London, or Henry would have had her fetched; as it was he sent a trusted messenger, with one of Anne's petticoats to be tested. The verdict was favourable; the messenger thought it unnecessary and

336

inadvisable to report that the old woman, more than half-blind, had hesitated a long time, fingering the silk, shaking her head and mumbling. Finally she had said,

"Trying to trick me, are you? Bringing me something two women have worn?" He had assured her that this was not so.

"Then why does my right hand say boy and my left, girl? In all my days such a thing never happened before. Queer, very queer."

She evidently took her odd calling very seriously; she held the petticoat in one hand, in the other, in both, and finally, folding it lengthways, hung it about her neck.

"A boy," she said then, but uncertainly. She was distressed, muttered that she was growing old, losing her skill; she'd never been confused before. But yes, it would be a boy.

So the assurances had poured in, and the good wishes; and Henry — if he had ever turned against her, as she had suspected last autumn — had dissembled so well, that Anne had faced the ordeal of childbirth happily and confidently.

And then — Elizabeth.

With more justification than ever she could now think — Nothing ever goes right for me; all the trappings, all the *possibilities* of success but nothing real and solid. And as she listened to Henry's, and to Emma's, exhortations to be cheerful and lively, to eat and be hopeful, to look to the future, she could only think, more waiting!

On the fourth day after her confinement she was at least spared the exhortations, for she fell victim to the complaint, possibly after childbed fever the most dreaded of post-child birth ailments; the one most unreasonably known as "white-leg". Your legs were no whiter than they had been before, but they swelled and swelled; and they ached with a dull grinding pain, as though they were between two millstones. There was no remedy; you lay and waited — waiting again — and you lived or you died.

Among her ladies some were sympathetic, some indifferent. Apart from the christening there were no festivities, and when the weather broke there was nothing to do but to huddle in little groups and exchange stories of cases similar to the Queen's which had ended happily or otherwise; or to express their amazement at the daring Catherine who had refused to lend the christening robe which she had brought from Spain and which had been worn by Mary, for the christening of the new princess. That, they said, had truly angered the King. They talked a good deal, too, about Elizabeth Barton, whom some people called The Mad Nun, and others The Holy Maid of Kent, like Joan of Arc a peasant born, and like her given to the hearing of angelic voices. Elizabeth's voices were all strongly pro-Catherine and had predicted woe to the country and death to the King should he marry again. Cromwell had recently had her arrested and examined by Archbishop Cranmer, not because he paid much heed to her prophecies, but because he hoped to find out who

338

had. But whatever the talk it always came back in the end to the Queen's state of health; and hovering meekly, as became a newcomer, on the fringe of each group, there was a young lady who, as she listened, wondered whether it would be so very wrong to wish that the Queen would die. Wouldn't it be the kindest thing that could happen to her?

Mistress Jane Seymour, because of her round face and flawless skin and demure manner, looked a great deal younger than she was; she was fresh to the English Court but she had served her apprenticeship in France and from under downcast lids had observed the world with some shrewdness. During the summer she had felt Henry's eye upon her, assessingly, and had blushed. When he had first made some excuse to speak to her she had blushed again and confined her replies to "Yes, Your Grace", and "No, Your Grace". He had not withdrawn his interest, however. What notice he had taken of her in public had been of a jesting, paternal nature, as when coming across her and some other ladies laughing at some joke, he had stopped and said that he hoped the joke, whatever it was, was fit for such young ears.

"Whose young ears, Your Grace?" one of them had asked, pertly vivacious.

"This child's," he had said, and lightly touched her sleeve.

To them it had been something else to laugh about, knowing her age; but to her it had been a sign.

And now Queen Anne had borne a daughter; and was ailing; she might never fully recover; and the King's eye had wandered. Would it be so *very* wrong to wish that she would die?

CHAPTER
TWENTY-EIGHT

"But she is so scrupulous and has such great respect for the King that she would consider herself damned with remission if she took any way tending to war."
The Spanish Ambassador in a letter to Charles V

KIMBOLTON CASTLE. JULY 1534

"I shall sit by the window for a while. You go to bed, Maria. God keep you."

"Your Grace should go to bed. It has been a full day."

"Yes. A day to remember. I shall sit by the window and remember it all."

They spoke in Spanish, Catherine and this, the favourite of her women; and they smiled at one another, sharing a joke which never grew stale. Maria, like Catherine, had lived in England for thirty-three years and had thoroughly mastered the language; but when, while they were living at Buckden, in the March of this year, a deputation had come from the King demanding that everyone take the oath that recognised Anne as Queen and Elizabeth as the only legitimate princess, Maria had suddenly become ignorant of any but her own tongue. She had waved her hands, and smiled and smiled, shaking her head and gabbling Spanish until they had decided not to bother about her. Others of the household had taken the oath, making the mental reservation which was permissible in such circumstances; some had refused outright. They had been hauled off. Catherine had also refused and it had looked as though she might be hauled off, too; but in the end she had been sent, this time definitely in the role of prisoner, to Kimbolton, which was a much more strongly fortified place than Buckden. The window by which she sat on this evening of lingering summer warmth was set in a wall four feet thick and it overlooked a wide moat.

The moat had, that day, been a setting for a curious scene.

It had, as Maria said, been a full day.

Catherine sat and remembered it, hour by hour.

The first intimation that this was to be different from any other interminable day had come just before noon, when Maria was making the fire over which she was to cook dinner. Catherine had always feared that she might be poisoned, and that fear had increased when, in March, Clement had finally given his verdict on her case. He had declared the dispensation allowing the marriage between her and Henry to be without fault, and that therefore the marriage was good and valid. After that she had not dared to content herself with the old rule which she had written to Mary, to cut only where others cut, and to drink only where others had drunk; she had had her meagre meals prepared by Maria in her own room.

So the place smelt like a peasant's hut when Sir Edmund Bedingfield, her new gaoler, came in saying that there was a messenger from the King.

He was young and raw, obviously chosen for his ability to ride fast, tiring out one swift horse after another; but for all that he was tired, and short of breath. He'd gulped out his message,

"Madam, the Imperial Ambassador is on his way to see you. His Grace has not given permission for this visit. He heard of it and sent me to overtake the Ambassador's train and turn it back. They took no notice of me, but are pressing on. I rode hard to tell you, Madam, that if you receive Messire Chapuys it will be against His Grace's express command."

"Which in all matters not concerning my conscience I am always ready to obey," Catherine said. She turned to Bedingfield and asked him to oblige her by sending a messenger to meet Messire Chapuys and tell him that she was forbidden to see him and that he should waste no time in riding on.

She longed to see and talk to Chapuys, always a most loyal friend; but just at this time she was not unwilling to proffer a good excuse for not receiving him. In the last two months — ever since Clement had decided that she *was* Queen of England — Chapuys had redoubled his efforts to rouse some of the old nobility to support her cause with armed force. He'd met with considerable success, especially in the North and West where the old ideas were strongly entrenched, and where the threatened dissolution of the religious houses was causing great alarm in a class from which Abbots

343

and Abbesses were largely drawn. The Emperor, Chapuys argued, could not now fail to come to the aid of a rising aimed at giving his wronged aunt and cousin their indisputable legal rights. All that was needed was that Catherine herself should agree to lead the insurrection. It was to urge her to do so that Chapuys had attempted to make this visit. Of that she was certain; and since her devotion to Henry and her rooted objection to being the cause of any bloodshed forbade her to make any move, she was relieved to have an excuse for not meeting Chapuys face to face and arguing about it.

She had eaten her modest dinner just after the drawbridge had been raised again behind the speeding messenger Bedingfield had despatched. Within an hour there was a commotion on the far side of the moat, and Catherine, going to the window, saw a group of riders whose clothes, and the harnessing of their horses, proclaimed them to be Spanish. The Ambassador was not among them. Chapuys was far too skilled a diplomat to risk Henry's displeasure by disobeying a direct order, but he had continued towards Kimbolton until he received Catherine's message; there he had halted, being now near enough to make it easy to hint that some young men should ride on to see the place where Catherine was imprisoned. There was no order against looking, he said; and if a Spanish-speaking servant should chance to look out and call to them, there could be no harm in sending the Queen a heartening message.

The young Spaniards did nothing to which Bedingfield could take exception. On the far side of the moat they gave a display of horsemanship in the Spanish style, making their horses dance and leap. Soon every member of Catherine's small *ménage* and all the Kimbolton servants were crowded at the windows or on the walls. Then the horsemen drew a little aside and rested while a professional fool took up the business of entertainment. He played all the traditional tricks, while under cover of the laughter and the applause a rapid exchange, in Spanish, took place between the horsemen and Catherine's servants. When the clown stood on his hands and walked backwards, or turned six somersaults in succession it was all the more entertaining because he did it on the very edge of the moat and was in momentary danger of tumbling in. In the end he did tumble in and appeared to lose his sense of direction, for he plunged away from the outer bank and ended in the middle of the moat, screaming that he was drowning, though everyone could see that he was as skilled in the water as out of it. He cried, "Lighten ship!" and began tossing things in all directions; his sodden clown's cap, his pouch, his belt, his shoes. Some articles he flung towards the outer bank, some towards the inner wall and the watchers yelled as the water-heavy, slimy, stinking things struck or passed near them. All but Maria whose eye the clown had caught and to whom he had said, in Spanish, "I have something for you," and to whom he had thrown a small locked casket. She had caught and hidden it, but held to her place, laughing and shouting, until the clown, plunging like a porpoise, had gone towards the bank and scrambled onto safety.

The casket, which had to be broken open, having no key with it, contained a letter which to Catherine meant a great deal, but, if intercepted, would only have informed the reader of what was already known, that the Spanish Ambassador was Catherine's friend and urged her not to lose heart, since God was just and would see justice done; and that Messire Chapuys considered the English an arrogant and boastful race. Only lately one English lord had told him to his face that he could at any moment put 8,000 men into the field, all his tenants and friends. "I said to him, your Grace, 'That may well be, my lord, but you must not expect me to be impressed by such numbers, serving as I do a master whose resources can hardly be numbered.' Nor is this old lord the only boaster I have lately had to do with. To me the English are an intolerable race, with one virtue only, they are sympathetic to anyone oppressed." The letter ran on in that way, garrulous, ambiguous, meaningful. Catherine burnt it on the fire which Maria made in order to cook supper.

The spoken exchanges across the moat were mainly concerned with lighter matters, in which Catherine would be interested and about which, probably, she had had no first hand information.

First and foremost, Mary. Attached to the household of her half-sister Elizabeth, Mary was contriving without too greatly affronting the King to hold her own. Whenever it was possible for her to do so she took

346

precedence. She had refused to take the oath, but had said that she was willing to call Elizabeth "sister", just as she had called the Duke of Richmond "brother".

There was news of the Concubine, too. She had given proof of her Lutheran leanings by writing a letter to Secretary Cromwell asking him to be lenient to an Antwerp merchant accused of bringing in and distributing copies of the New Testament in English. She had made overtures to Mary, which the Princess, rightly suspicious of their motive, had rejected. When Anne visited her baby daughter Mary invariably retired to her own room in order to avoid meeting her; but some of Anne's ladies, noticeably Lady Rochford, had always made a point of going to Mary's room and talking with her. Surprisingly, the Concubine had never rebuked them for doing so, or seemed to bear any resentment because of it. There were, so far as anyone knew, no signs of a further pregnancy and around the Court there were rumours that His Majesty's passion was on the wane, though he still gave her his attention.

In Cambridge a serving man named Kylbie had been arrested for calling the King a heretic. Kylbie had been grooming his master's horse and got into an argument with an ostler who had said there was no Pope, only a Bishop of Rome, the King's Grace had said so. Kylbie had retorted, "You are a heretic, and the King another. And none of this business would ever have happened if His Grace had not lusted after Anne Boleyn."

"And then, Your Grace," Maria said, recounting this piece of gossip, "they set about one another with sticks and the man Kylbie was arrested. But he said the truth.

She is to blame for all." She threw out her hands to indicate the cheerless room, the humble pan on the smoky fire, the loneliness of the flat countryside. "I pray God to curse her and bring her low with madness in her head and the gnawing sickness in her body."

"Oh no," Catherine said. "Don't curse her. Pity her rather. Her bad time is yet to come."

She spoke sincerely. She knew what happened when Henry's passion waned. It had waned for her, but she had been upheld by her rights, by her religion, by her connections. What would Anne have to support her? Nothing. Nothing at all.

CHAPTER
TWENTY-NINE

"But one thing, good master Secretary, consider, that he was young, and love overcame reason . . . I saw so much honesty in him that I loved him as well as he did me . . . I saw that all the world did set so little by me, and he so much that I could take no better way . . . If we might once be so happy to recover the King's gracious favour and the Queen's."
A letter from Mary Boleyn to Cromwell

"The Lady's sister was banished from the court three months ago; it being necessary to do so, for besides that she had been found guilty of misconduct, it would not have been becoming to see her at Court enceinte."
A letter from the Spanish Ambassador to the Emperor

WHITEHALL. DECEMBER 1534

The Mercer, with a splendid careless gesture dropped the roll of amber-coloured velvet to the floor, whence his acolyte apprentice retrieved it and began to smooth and refold it.

"This, your Grace," the mercer said, reaching for another roll, giving it a twist and a shake so that the material spilled down, a waterfall of sheen and colour, "is straight from France and a complete novelty. So woven that . . ." He pivoted so that the light changed on the silk; in one light it showed fleur-de-lys of dark blue on pale, in pale fleur-de-lys on dark. "There!" he said, in a tone of deep satisfaction.

"Would your Grace consider it impertinent of me to ask why not? Blue is not, I agree, the colour for everyone; and in my experience it is the very ladies for whom it is least suited who favour it most. Ladies of insipid colouring. Your Grace could wear anything."

"Not blue," Anne said firmly, but she smiled so that the little man should not feel that he had been impertinent. "It is beautiful, and a novelty, and if two shades of yellow could be woven in the same skilful way I should be pleased to have a gown of it."

"I'm sure that could be done, if your Grace wishes," the mercer said. But before dropping this piece to the floor he held it a second, admiring it, regretting its rejection.

Anne said,

"Wait. I'll have it. Not for myself, as a gift for someone to whom that shade is immensely becoming."

Mary should have it for Christmas.

Mary's husband, William Carey, had been one of those who had died during the Sweating Sickness in one of the manors the King had just abandoned and for the last three and a half years she had lived an aimless, rather unhappy life. She spent a good deal of time in the houses of various relatives, particularly with an aunt at Edwarton in Suffolk. Every now and then Sir

350

Thomas would send for her to keep Lady Bo company, and then, in a short time, quarrel with her, scold her for wasting her opportunities and complain that she was a burden to him. She had refused, with the stubbornness of the weak, to come to Court until Anne was married; then at last she had accepted invitations and made quite protracted stays. But she had changed; her sweetness had soured into a whining self-pity, and, most surprisingly, she often gave evidence of having inherited Sir Thomas's facility for planting verbal barbs.

But she would be pleased about the blue silk, Anne thought; and it would suit her, though her looks, like so many of their kind, were fading early.

The dresses must be ready for Christmas wear, so as soon as the mercer had gone, Anne sent for Mary and they retired to her bed-chamber, attended by Emma and two sempstresses, one of whom, an expert fitter, was armed with a measuring tape.

Mary eyed the blue silk with no sign of pleasure.

"It was a kind thought, but I don't wish for a new gown."

"But it was to be my Christmas gift to you."

"I don't want it. One can get accustomed to anything and I am accustomed to shabby clothes."

"Then why not have a change? Come along, Mary, don't be silly. Off with that drab old thing, and come and be measured."

Anne was already in her petticoat and submitting to the touches of the dry, cold, dressmaker's hands of the woman with the measure, who had a pretty little problem of her own. Should she say, what was true, "Your Grace's measurements are exact to an inch to

351

what they were last time." Or would that be tactless? So many ladies would welcome the remark; but when the lady was Queen of England, mother of one girl child, it might not be quite the thing to say.

Anne looking over her shoulder at Mary saw that at the word "measured", a wild, almost frantic look came into her blue eyes.

Mary said,

"When I had gifts to give I never forced you to accept them, did I?"

Anne thought, as she had so often done before, excusing Mary's behaviour — She's jealous, and that is natural enough. Who wouldn't be in her place? If only she knew how little there is to be jealous of!

But all the same she shouldn't make such remarks before Emma, and two sempstresses; sempstresses were notorious gossips, they had to occupy their minds with something while their fingers were busy. She could imagine how this little exchange would be magnified and over-coloured in the retelling. Quarrelling like fishwives, they would say. So she shot Mary what Lady Bo would call an old-fashioned look and then spoke sternly to the woman with the tape.

Mary said, rather sulkily,

"If that was all you wanted of me, I'll ask leave to retire."

"You have it," Anne said and turned back so that she faced the glass on her table. In it she saw Mary move towards the door. A flaw in the glass? Imagination? Oh God, not that. Just now when nothing was going well.

352

She said sharply, "No, Mary, wait a moment. I want . . . I want your advice upon another matter." To the sempstresses she said, "There, that will do. My usual hanging sleeves, and a curved neckline instead of square," and bustled them away. She invented an errand for Emma. Within five minutes the sisters were alone, as once they had been in the bedroom at Blickling.

Anne said,

"You're pregnant!"

Mary made a moaning sound and dropped on to a stool, pressing the back of her knuckles against her face.

"Just when we're all in such bad odour," Anne said, furiously. "George acting like a frivolous fool and being rebuked, Father falling out with Cromwell; and now this. This is worst of all! Mary, how could you? How could you? You've brought disgrace to us all just at the very moment when we needed bolstering up." Once she began her tongue lashing old grievances sprang to mind. "All my life," she said bitterly, "I've suffered from your shame. In France nobody could ever distinguish between the two of us; or if they did it was only to think that a trollop's sister must needs be a trollop, too. I've spent my life trying to prove otherwise and now . . ."

The old Mary, moaning, abashed, gave way to the new one.

"And you did prove it, finely, did you not? Married on April 12th and brought to bed on 7th September. You should rail at me!"

"We were married before, privately."

"So we were told," Mary said.

"But it is true. Believe it or not, as you wish. It is not *my* behaviour we are discussing, it's yours. And you have shamed us again. And without the excuse you once had," she said cruelly. "You're old enough now to know better."

Mary said,

"But I . . ." and then stopped open-mouthed for a second. She took a breath and said more calmly, with something approaching dignity, "You'll be sorry for the things you have said. One day. When you know all."

The most hateful suspicion shot through Anne's mind. Henry so plainly dissatisfied, his attentions more and more perfunctory; Mary still besotted with love for him, undemanding, sloppy-minded, as comfortable to fall back upon as a feather bed. And it would account for the change in her, the flashes of sharpness, the new confidence, the occasional smugness.

"Is it Henry?"

Mary's expression showed fright again.

"No. Oh no. Anne, I swear it."

"Then who?"

"I can't tell you."

"But you must. He must be made to marry you. The King must compel him . . ."

"Anne, if you mention this to the King I'll never, never speak to you again. Please, please leave it alone. I'll go away. You need never see me . . ."

"Oh, don't talk like a fool! Where could you go! In a week or two there'll be no hiding your state." Mary acknowledged the truth of that by beginning to weep and the sight of her, so helpless and silly, muddled,

354

shabby, tearful and stubborn, exasperated Anne and at the same time roused that old protective feeling. She went over and shook Mary's shoulder.

"He must marry you. If he can. Is that it? Is he married already?"

Mary choked. Then she said, with a courage which Anne could only recognise later,

"Yes, he's married. So you see there's nothing you, or the King or anybody can do about it."

The hateful suspicion struck again.

"You must tell me his name," Anne said, tightening her grip on Mary's shoulder.

"I can't. I won't. What right have you?" She flung off Anne's hand and stood up, sobbing more violently, so that of her next words only a few were enunciated clearly enough to be heard. "Just because . . . Queen of England . . . skin of your teeth . . . prying into my affairs . . ."

She ran, crying, from the room.

That evening, in the hall at supper, Anne was conscious of something in Henry's mood, boisterous without being pleasant; and of a suppressed excitement, a watchfulness; and of Norris looking at her as he often did these days, with a grave, almost pitying expression, maddeningly similar to the expression dogs wore when they saw you crying. It increased the raw-nerved feeling with which the scene with Mary had left her, and finally she snapped at him,

"What's the matter, Sir Harry. Is my headdress awry?" He then looked like a dog slapped for something it had not done, and said, "Your Grace, on the contrary, if I had a thought it was how well it became you."

Towards the end of the meal Henry's new jester came in. She detested him; he was almost, not quite, a dwarf, big-headed, squat and ugly, but he had been born like that, so although his appearance evoked repulsion in her, she did not hold it against him. What she hated was the slyness of his patter, the innuendos which he produced under cover of near idiocy. Henry doted upon him and allowed him the utmost liberty. She had once voiced a protest about his jokes, "They are an attack upon your dignity." Henry said, "After supper, at my own table, my dignity can take care of itself."

Tonight he did his tumbling and his juggling and his acrobatic tricks, interspersed with stories and comments which were, or were not, amusing, depending upon whether you were aware of their reference. At one point he said, in the bucolic drawl he sometimes affected,

"Life's funny, ain't it? Funny but fair. Oh yes, you must admit, everything work out very fair. Fr'instance I know a man, got a nice kennel, but not dog to put in it, and I know another man, got a nice dog, and he ain't got no kennel."

There was some scattered laughter, a little over-hearty, laughter that said — Oh yes, we see the joke; we're in the know! Anne wondered what was amusing there. Was her sense of humour defective, or

356

was this little freak too subtle for her understanding, as Henry had once suggested?

An accomplice of the jester threw three wooden hoops in such a way as to form a spinning tunnel, through which he dived, turned a somersault, stood up and said, "I'm off! This 'ere Court life is too wearing for me. I'm gonna retire to the country, Staffordshire!" He ran off as though he were being pursued by someone aiming blows at him.

There was another burst of the same kind of laughter, followed by titters from those who, like Anne, had failed to see the joke, but did not wish to seem lacking in appreciation.

Henry laughed as heartily as anyone; and then, turning to Anne said,

"Ah, that reminds me, my dear. I hadn't time to tell you before. I've sent your sister and her husband packing."

His face blurred; behind it the hall, the fire, the candles, the hangings, the gay-coloured clothes, began to tilt and spin. She put out her hands, like a blind woman, and found the solid table edge and held on to it.

Henry's voice, coming from a great distance away, said,

"Silly young cub! He came to me six months ago and spoke of a wish to marry . . . But this is probably an old tale to you."

"No," she said, and was relieved to hear her voice sound so ordinary; surprised, interested, but quite controlled. "Her husband, you say? She never even hinted. Who is he?"

357

"Sir William Stafford. You hadn't missed his innocent rosy face this evening?"

She had braced herself to hear that Mary had made some shocking *mésalliance*. Mary's own behaviour . . . But there was no reason why she and William Stafford should not be married. He was rather young for her, and not well-to-do, but he was of good family. Why the mystery? And why had Henry sent them packing? Before she could speak, Henry went on, and something in his voice betrayed the fact that he was enjoying himself.

"I most strongly advised him against such a match. In fact I downright forbade it. Notwithstanding which he married her. Or so he told me late this afternoon. And one can only hope that his tale is true! When did you last see her?"

"Early this afternoon. But what I . . ."

"Sh!" Henry said, raising his hand. "Here is the Welsh harpist who was so warmly recommended to me."

The man — he was old, with long shaggy grey hair and beard, and a robe of homespun of the same grey — played superbly, but she could pay him no attention. She understood now why Mary had been so secretive, so distressed; but why had Henry forbidden the marriage in the first place? He'd never, so far as Anne knew, suggested any other match for her; he must have realised, as Anne herself had done often enough, that a woman of Mary's character and nature, left unattached, was always a potential source of scandal.

She could understand his anger at finding himself disobeyed. Even if he had merely *advised* against the marriage and then it had taken place he would have been affronted. He was becoming more and more autocratic over small things as well as large; but he didn't sound displeased. He wasn't in the hearty, rip-roaring rage which one would have expected: and he'd laughed at both the slyly relevant jokes.

The explanation came to her; distasteful, but it must be faced. So she faced it to the accompaniment of the limpid ripple of music that was like the sound of a waterfall. *Henry was making Mary his whipping boy.* That accounted for his action, and for his manner. And he'd have been even more pleased had Mary done something more shaming than make a clandestine marriage; then he could have said "your sister" with even more venom.

She'd cried to Emma, before her Coronation, "He hates me." She had believed it then; but everyday living, some acts of consideration, even of kindness occasionally, had taken the sharpest edge off her awareness of his hatred. Faced with this fresh evidence of it she felt weak, drained and hollow. Emma's Bible said, "Whatsoever a man soweth, that shall he also reap." What had she sown that the harvest should be so bitter? Used his love for her as a ladder to climb by; used it as a salve for wounded pride, hurt self-esteem. That was all. She'd never done him any harm. She'd failed him in bed, in some obscure way that she would never understand; and she'd borne an unwanted daughter instead of the longed-for boy; and she had not yet conceived again. In the eyes of a man like Henry these were, no doubt, offences, but they were not deliberate ones. Nothing to justify the tone of voice in which he said, "I've sent your sister and her husband packing."

But she mustn't retaliate; mustn't make the obvious retort, that her sister Mary in making a clandestine marriage behaved in precisely the same fashion as *his* sister Mary had done. She mustn't quarrel with him. Because her only hope was to bear his son. Unless she could do that the past was all waste, the future without prospect.

The last sound of the plucked strings vibrated, shivered on the air and died. She moved her hands and joined in the applause. The old man bowed, more grave and stately than a bishop, towards the King, and spoke a few words in a strange tongue. Henry, genuinely moved, both by the music and by this contact with Wales — he was sentimental about his Welsh lineage — leaned forward and shouted down the hall a phrase in the same tongue, which to the listening ears of the English sounded like abuse. The old man smiled and bowed again.

"He thanked us for listening, and wished us good night," Henry said, beaming round with pride and pleasure. "I thanked him for playing for us and wished *him* good night."

Anne said,

"I am glad that you could thank him in his own tongue. He played very beautifully. We are all indebted to you for bringing him to London."

Henry accepted the implied compliments; then his look as it dwelt upon her, darkened.

"We were talking about your sister," he reminded her. "You say you saw her this afternoon? Did you make her cry? That silly young whelp found her, blubbering in a corner, took her by the hand and burst in on me to make a full confession. While I was having my beard trimmed!"

She gripped her hands together under the shelter of the table's edge and prayed, God give me patience. She said,

"He chose his time badly."

"He chose his wife badly. Years too old. And shop-soiled."

Everything in her, except her common-sense, cried out against that. She'd have given everything, except her hope of a son, to have been able to stand up and shout — And who had a hand in her soiling? Who used her and threw her aside? Isn't there for every bad woman in the world a man, equally bad? Am I any better than she? No better; less lucky. When he found her crying, he braved you and your barber. If you found me crying, you'd gloat, you'd gloat, you'd gloat . . .

But truth, and honest speaking, and Mary, must all be sacrificed to something that had as yet no existence, no shape, no form, no name.

So she smiled and said, amiably,

"They displeased you, and they are punished. So . . ." She spread her hands. I can dismiss Mary. She's married; she's loved. Any man who dare break in

361

with such a confession upon Henry and his barber, is a man indeed. She'll be safe with him.

Henry had hoped for a scene. An exchange of verbal buffers. But it was like tilting at one of those scarecrows farmers put in their fields. Unresponsive, cold. Cold as a fish. Her own sister and not a word of protest.

What could a man hope for, with such a wife? Nothing.

The past was all waste; the future without prospect. Unless . . .

CHAPTER
THIRTY

"Alas, it pitieth me — to think into what misery she will shortly come."
Sir Thomas More speaking of Anne Boleyn in 1535

WINDSOR. JULY 1535

The Duke of Norfolk was not particularly quick-witted and it took him a moment or two to catch the drift of what the King was saying. When he did so, his first thought was that it was wine talking; a justifiable thought for it was growing late, and Henry had not gone sober to bed on any night since Sir Thomas More's execution. Then, as Henry talked on the Duke thought, Why consult *me?* His strong self-preservative instinct came into play. How could he possibly answer without offending the King or encouraging him in what he was proposing, a plan which the Duke most thoroughly disapproved.

He felt Henry's eye upon him and hoped that he didn't look as shocked as he felt, and hastily composed his features into an expression of respectful attention.

When Henry had finished unburdening himself, the Duke said,

"There is no one in the world who more wishes to see you happy and content and the father of a prince, your Grace."

But not a prince who was Jane Seymour's son! Jane Seymour, another commoner! Another girl like Anne Boleyn, with a wildly ambitious family! A family, too, as near Lutheran as anyone dared to be in these days when the English Church was so precariously balanced, in an attempt to avoid both Papacy and Lutheranism.

Henry sensed some reserve and said rather awkwardly,

"Of course, I realise that Anne is your niece."

The Duke made a gruff, repudiating sound. "That doesn't bother me. If you send me on an errand with Wiltshire and his popinjay son I put up with their company as I would with toothache; but the Boleyns are nothing to me."

"Yet you object?"

"No. No. I can see . . ." He cracked a knuckle, then another and stirred on his chair. "Your Grace, I'm no lawyer, just a plain man. If I knew what to say I shouldn't know how to say it. Cranmer's your man, or Cromwell . . ."

"All in good time. I'm talking to *you*, now."

"Then, Your Grace . . . There's a country saying about the fox that got away with the rooster being caught if he comes back for the hen. I'm against playing the same trick twice. We've heard enough about consanguinity in these last years. The word stinks. To go raking over all that old business of Mary Boleyn as an excuse for getting rid of Anne, that'd be like wiping your nose on a mucky rag. I don't say don't do it, but I do say, don't do it that way."

364

Henry looked into Norfolk's earnest, beefy face with something approaching affection. Norfolk had always been his loyal, active servant, but in the last year he had become more; one of the few people whose religious views exactly accorded with Henry's own. Too many people were either backward-looking Catholics, secretly regretting the breach with Rome, or forward-looking reformers, anxious for more changes. Norfolk, like Henry, managed to be Catholic without being Papist; and Norfolk understood why, in the end, having been given every chance to conform, More, whom Henry had truly loved, the wittiest, most charming man in the world, had had to be beheaded. More had insisted upon regarding the Pope as Head of the Church, and Catherine as Queen of England; and since it was treason for an ordinary man to hold such views, it was doubly treasonable for one whom the King had called friend, and made Chancellor, to do so.

Therefore Norfolk's opinion mattered now.

"Maybe you're right. Well, there is another way out. A pre-contract. Years ago Anne was on the point of marrying the present Earl of Northumberland . . ."

His voice trailed away as he realised what he was saying. God in Heaven, what happened to people to change them so much? He remembered himself how desire and determination and worship had welled up in him, and he had thought — She is too good for him! Now he could speak of it like that.

"That hare won't run," Norfolk said bluntly. "Mary Talbot tried to bring that up when she was sick of Northumberland and ran back to her father. I happen to know because Shrewsbury consulted me about it. Northumberland said he never was betrothed to my niece, or anybody else."

"Oh," Henry said. He thought for a minute. "Do you reckon he'd say the same if he knew that it was my wish that he admitted to the betrothal?"

"You know the Percies. Born awkward. And if you said you'd behead him if he didn't he'd most likely laugh; he's so sick and full of pain it'd be a merciful end." He cracked another knuckle. "And pre-contract is another word that stinks."

"So that leaves me where I was, tied to a woman I no longer love."

"That's not so uncommon. I should say that nine out of every ten men hate their wives — after a year. But they use them, as God meant women to be used."

Henry said, with an almost touching simplicity,

"I have tried."

With matching simplicity Norfolk said,

"Try again, sire. I'll be blunt. What this country needs is a prince, not another long, drawn-out wrangle about who is married to whom or, if not why not."

"In fact you advise me to do nothing, except," he laughed a little, "my duty in bed?"

"For a time, anyway. As for Mistress Seymour . . ." He broke off, decided that he might never again have such an opportunity to speak his mind, and went on, "My niece set an example, keeping her legs crossed till the crown was in her lap, but that's not to say that every girl must set her price so high."

Henry treated his old friend to one of his most ferocious scowls. Jane was the sweetest, dearest, most innocent little maiden in the world, completely without ambition. Different in every way from Anne, who had always seemed to be offering a challenge or promising something, egging a man on. Different too from Catherine, whose wifely attitude had been imposed upon a fundamentally strong character, which, combined with her greater age and her piety, had always slightly awed Henry. Jane was a child, a kitten, a plaything, Henry thought fondly, unaware that he was thinking as only a middle-aged man could do. Norfolk, he decided was entirely lacking in the finer feelings. Still, he was a man of sound sense and his advice, if nothing else, was at least sincere.

Norfolk accepted the scowl as the price of plain speaking, always a luxury in the Royal presence. He was, on the whole, rather pleased with himself. The King's trouble was that he was not properly grown up where women were concerned; too soft, too sentimental. With all women, not merely, like most men, with the love of the moment. Look at Catherine, who had quietly defied him for years; and Mary was worse. My God, Norfolk thought, if she were my daughter I'd bang her head against the wall till it was as soft as a baked apple!

The silence lasted until Henry broke it, speaking on some other subject; and so slipped away, unremarked, unrecognised, one of those momentous occasions which later can be seen to have been pregnant with tragedy.

CHAPTER
THIRTY-ONE

". . . Jane Seymour's shameless courtship of Henry VIII was the commencement of the severe calamities that befell her mistress, Anne Boleyn. Scripture points out as an especial odium the circumstances of a handmaid taking the place of her mistress."

Agnes Strickland. *Lives of the Queens of England*

GREENWICH. JULY 1535

Anne lay on her bed with her skirt pulled aside and one foot, stripped of hose and shoe, being poked and prodded for evidence of possible injury by Emma Arnett. Her cousin, Lady Lee, stood near the head of the bed, holding a flagon of grated hartshorn. Other ladies fluttered about suggesting remedies, suggesting calling Dr Butts, suggesting — this with faint sly smiles and significant glances — running to tell His Grace.

It was a warm day, but Anne was shivering and her privet-flower pallor had the grey tinge which Emma knew. It was consistent with the pain of a twisted ankle, yet Emma was puzzled, for there was no sign of swelling, nor had Anne flinched under the probing fingers.

Anne said,

"You stay, Margaret. Send the others away ..."
When the room was cleared she moved her foot, "Let
be, Emma. I did not twist it. I had to think of
something quickly and that was the best I could do."

"I never saw such presence of mind," Margaret Lee
said, looking at Anne with admiration, and then
changing the look immediately to one of pity as she
remembered what had provoked the display of presence
of mind.

Anne pulled herself up against the bed-head.

"Who else saw, Margaret?"

"No one. I'm certain. You were so quick and so
clever." But it mattered so little — except to Anne's
peace of mind — who had seen and who had not.
Everyone knew that the King was in hot pursuit of Jane
Seymour, and she so indiscreet, or so stupid, or so
powerless to control him, that the sight of him kissing
her in a corner or holding her on his knee, could
surprise no one, except Anne. Anne, until this morning,
had been in ignorance, the centre of a conspiracy of
silence which stemmed from various causes. Malice —
because a good many people derived pleasure from
seeing her made a fool of; affection, which sought to
spare her any knowledge of what might be unimportant
and transient; fear of the King's anger, for though
Henry had on several occasions been careless before
others he had, so far, acted discreetly before Anne.

This morning, however, he had been caught. Anne
and a party of about a dozen, most of them carrying
some musical instrument, had been making their way

to a pleasant, shaded spot, enclosed by a quick-thorn hedge and furnished with stone seats. One path ran in on the side nearest the palace, another immediately opposite. Anne and Margaret had been walking ahead, had reached the opening in the hedge and seen Henry, with Jane Seymour on his knee, on one of the seats. Anne had stopped abruptly and cried out and then seemed to fall backwards, so that all those following were thrown into a momentary confusion. She had clutched Margaret's arm and said, "I twisted my ankle." Mark Smeaton had thrust his lute into someone's hand and run forward and lifted her and carried her to the seat which had emptied as though by a wave of a magician's wand.

Just for a second she had thought of how often she and Harry Percy had used this very spot for a trysting place, and occasionally been obliged to retire just as hastily. Then she had forgotten the past in consideration of the present and the future. She was glad that she had feigned a slight accident, it excused the shivering, the incoherence, all the symptoms of shock.

"Jane Rochfort," she now said, "she was immediately behind me. If *she* saw, half London knows by now."

Would it, Margaret wondered wretchedly, be the truer kindness to admit that half London knew already? It was very difficult. Anne's friends had all said — It's nothing; he's forty-four and at about that age most men fall in love for a little while with some young pretty face. It'll pass. Why worry her?

And she thought, Why should I be the one to tell her? And how would she take it? Explode into terrible rage?

Freeze into silence? Or laugh? She realised, with a faint shock of surprise, that close as she was to Anne, and fond as she was, she really knew her hardly at all.

"Is it?" Anne asked. "Known by everyone? Was I the only person surprised, just now?"

Margaret glanced at Emma.

"Never mind Emma," Anne said. "I expect she knows."

Emma's hard-featured face turned an ugly brick-red which after a second deepened. The first flush was caused by an unaccountable feeling of guilt, the second by anger at herself for feeling guilty. She had known all along and had been one of those most eager and active in concealing the truth from Anne, one of those who prayed earnestly that this latest fancy of the King's might wear itself out, with no harm done. She had never doubted that once Anne knew she would fly into a rage; and the sorry truth was that Anne was now in no position to give way to her temper and quarrel with the King. If she did anything might happen.

Emma had come very near to falling out with the baker and his group who had taken the new rumour without any dismay, saying that Jane Seymour and her family were on the Lutheran side of the fence and that Jane, if she stayed in favour, would be another prop to the cause.

"What she gains the Queen will lose," Emma had declared, "and Mistress Seymour couldn't help much even if she would, which I doubt. She's got no wits. You have to be subtle to have any influence!" She knew, she'd been very subtle herself and one of the things that Anne had done to help the Protestant cause had been the direct result of Emma's subtlety. For it was Emma who had persuaded Anne to read the New Testament in English; and so, when some merchants were in trouble for bringing English Testaments into the country from Antwerp and were threatened with expulsion and the confiscation of their goods, Anne had been sympathetic. She had also been able to say that she herself had read the Testament and she was no heretic.

Emma had reminded her circle of this, and also of how Anne had intervened on behalf of Hugh Latimer when he was in danger of being prosecuted for heresy; she hadn't merely saved him, she had had him appointed as her chaplain and given a bishopric. For these reasons, and no others, Emma wished Anne to remain the unchallenged influence in the King's life; and she had prayed that he might tire of that pudding-faced little doll before Anne knew anything about it. But here, once again, there had been no direct answer to prayer. And now, here she was, feeling guilty of disloyalty for not speaking out, and angry at herself for feeling guilty, because speaking out might have increased the damage.

She was at this point fully entitled to say,

"I don't know what Your Grace is talking of, exactly." And she said it.

Anne said,

"Jane Seymour. You knew. And you, too, Margaret! You could have spared me this morning's humiliation." Margaret's eyes filled.

"I have wondered . . . But it's nothing, really. It's just a . . . a temporary infatuation. We all hoped it would pass over without your knowing."

Anne swung her feet to the floor, pushed her bare foot into her shoe and folding her arms about herself began the rapid pacing and turning that Emma knew so well.

"I've no doubt that Catherine's friends said that to her!" She spoke with quiet bitterness; and then, on a rising note, cried,

"But the cases are not comparable! He is my husband, he never was Catherine's. We were troth-plighted and had exchanged rings before ever I came back to Court. And even then I never shamed her publicly, enemy as she was to me."

"There's no likeness at all, your Grace," Emma said. "You were always to be Queen. This is just a romp. His Grace is forty-four and men about that age often go foolish over some silly young girl."

"Young? She's as old as I am. We were in France together. And I'm not so sure about her being silly. I'd say sly. Still whatever her age and nature, she may be about to take my place. And if so, I'd like to know!"

Margaret Lee cried,

"Oh, Anne, that is ridiculous. How could she? You are Queen; you were properly married and crowned. You're taking this altogether too seriously."

"I know the King. If he wants to put me away, he'll find a way to do it." She made one of her rapid turns. "And I'd go," she cried. "I've failed. Wishing and willing and hoping and praying got me nothing but a

373

girl, so I've failed, just as Catherine failed. But *I* shan't sit about demanding to be called Queen. If he thinks he can get a son by Jane Seymour — and a splendid prince that would be! — he's welcome to try, I shall tell him so this very day."

Margaret Lee said, with great earnestness,

"Anne, you are Queen, and it is not for me to advise my Queen; but you are my dearly loved cousin, too. To *her* I say that to take that attitude would be to throw him into Jane's arms. You must act as though nothing had happened, and be charming to him, and join the rest of us in hoping and praying that he'll tire of her, quickly."

"With everybody laughing at me and pitying me behind my back; and my enemies gloating; and Henry thinking that I'm too blind or stupid to notice. I suppose he has been thinking so. I'll undeceive him!"

The shock tremor had now merged into the tremor of fury; even her voice was shaking. Her face had grown small and sharp and shrewish, her great eyes shone black, and jet-hard. Emma said,

"Your Grace, I'm going to give you a dose. It was a shock, and you're upset. But you must not do anything hasty, or go on tearing yourself to pieces in this way."

"Emma's right," Margaret said. "Take a dose and lie down — I'll sit and fan you. You'll see presently that it means nothing; it happens in almost every marriage, sooner or later." She was hurt by Anne's ravaged look and added, impulsively, "That damned, pudding-faced little humbug! I could kill her!"

Suddenly, rather shockingly, Anne laughed.

"Oh no, my dear. Not you. I should do that! I'm supposed to be the one so expert with poison. I'm such a clever poisoner that Catherine prevented my marriage for years, her daughter refuses to acknowledge me and sends me rude messages when I try to befriend her and calls my daughter The Bastard. I've dealt so cleverly with them, I'm well-equipped to deal with Mistress Seymour."

"Here," Emma said, holding out the dose.

Anne took it and said,

"This is the only poison I know!"

"This, Your Grace? It's absolutely harmless. Would I bring you anything . . .?"

"Of course not, Emma. That was a poor joke — like my reputation as a poisoner."

And a witch! The words slipped into her mind; and she remembered that night at Blickling when she had felt the upsurge of power; and the next day when she had viciously pricked the laurel leaf and with a vehemently worded ill-wish, buried it. Childish nonsense. Wolsey certainly had come to no good end; but he'd lived for seven years after that leaf had rotted. Too slow. Too slow for Jane Seymour! Also, and she came to this realisation slowly and with some surprise, the sheer hatred was missing. She was angry with Jane, even more angry with Henry, but she was no longer capable of the concentrated hatred that would strike its target dead if it had its say. It, like one form of love, was a thing of youth, lost as the years gathered.

"Sit down, now," Margaret said, "give Emma's dose a chance to soothe you."

It had already begun. The hurt was a little less raw; and out of all that Emma and Margaret had said, her mind was selecting the grains of comfort, saying temporary infatuation, saying forty-four and foolish, saying it will pass . . .

As her mind eased her body relaxed until at last she was lying on the bed. Margaret produced a fan, and its movement, the regular touch of the stirred air and the slight sound of its passage had an almost hypnotic effect. Presently she said drowsily,

"A son, that's all he wants now. And I can't see why. Women can't ride in tourneys, but there are plenty of knights to be hired. What is so wrong in being a woman?"

Margaret thought — If I don't answer her she'll talk herself to sleep.

"Elizabeth, if she were brought up to be, could be Queen . . . Catherine's mother was, and a good one, they say. And in Norfolk they still remember a Queen . . . the last person to stand out when the Romans came. Her name was Bo . . . something . . ." Her voice seemed to trail away; and then with a final effort at clarity she said, "Not Lady Bo. I don't mean her. She'd never stand out against . . . anything."

Still moving the fan, lest the cessation should disturb, Margaret Lee looked down at the face of her cousin where all the marks of strain and tension were smoothing themselves away. She thought to herself that Anne, in the last few words, had answered her own question. Lady Bo would never stand out against anything because she would always do exactly what her husband told her to do. And that was why women couldn't be Queens in their own right; to ensure the succession the woman must be married, and then, naturally, the husband had ascendancy.

No. The cure for this whole situation was for Anne to bear a son. She must have a good rest, rise refreshed and restored, make herself look beautiful and be charming to Henry. He'd been so nearly caught this morning, thought Margaret Lee, who combined a fundamental sweet innocence of character with a good deal of worldly wisdom, that he would be more than ordinarily anxious to be amiable.

Somehow, between us, we'll put that Seymour's little snub nose out of joint, she thought.

Henry had enjoyed his supper, giving way yet again to the temptation to eat too much. Now that he was once more in love he was trying, somewhat half-heartedly, to reduce his bulk, thinking that it aged him. He could usually find some good excuse for eating well today and sparingly tomorrow, and his excuse on this evening was that he was feeling cheerful because it seemed that he had, after all, escaped in time that morning. At intervals all through the day the thought had recurred that Anne must have seen; and though he did not care much and had his answer ready — not a defence, an answer; he meant to tell her flatly that she must learn to bear what Catherine had borne from her — it was preferable this way. He had no liking for scenes; and he had a great liking for the little extra flavour which secrecy gave to his love affair. It made him feel like a boy again. He had been pleased when she came to supper, especially finely dressed in amber silk, banded with black velvet, and in a mood which was not merely amiable, but positively gay. He blessed the little unevenness in the path which had made her turn her ankle, even while he inquired kindly about the extent of the injury.

The music during and after supper pleased him, too. Mark Smeaton was certainly a most gifted fellow, and the choir boys whom he had selected to sing, had sung several of Henry's own songs, some of which he had written as a young man, in love with Catherine, some from a later period when he was in love with Anne. Hearing them now, when both the loves that had inspired them were dead as burnt-out candles, caused him no regrets, no remorse, no grief over the mutability of all things human. Listening he thought that they were good songs, and it was a pity that of late he had had so little time to give to such pleasant ploys. He must make a song for Jane, something very subtle . . . mentioning Spring, because that was the year's youth and she was young, mentioning perhaps apple-blossom, because her skin was so like it, pink and white. When he thought of subtlety he remembered how while he loved Catherine, he had ridden in the lists as "Sir Loyal Heart"; and then, when he transferred his affections he had changed his motto to "Declare I Dare Not". And again he felt nothing, except the pride in his subtlety. He was in love again, and his old loves were of no more importance than last year's roses to a fresh-flowering bush.

He was pleased to see Anne happy and gay, because presently he must take her to bed and go through the

378

flavourless business of trying to beget an heir for England. After this talk with Norfolk he had set himself a limit; the end of this year, 1535. A man had only one life. If she wasn't pregnant by Christmas he would know that God had given a sign that this marriage was wrong too . . .

He thought how marvellous it would be if she could be pregnant by the end of August. That was the beginning of the grease season, which took its name from the fat which the deer carried after the full feeding of summer. It lasted until October, and that was the time of his country visits. If only, he thought, Anne could be pregnant and queasy and bound to stay in London while he rode out . . . Wolf Hall in Wiltshire, the home of the Seymours, could be one of his stopping-places. Jane could be there . . . Once again anticipation, the drug upon which, waiting for Anne, he had lived so long that he had become an addict, and of which, since late summer three years ago, he had been deprived, tingled along his veins.

He looked sidelong at Anne. He no longer thought her beautiful. That, like the indefinable joy that she had seemed to promise, had been a delusion, part of the unaccountable spell that had wasted so much of his life and cost so dearly; but she was comely and she was a woman, and tonight he felt potent. Tonight, God willing, he would get a son . . .

And at last they were alone.

She had taken all the advice offered by Margaret and Emma. Margaret's so incongruously sophisticated,

Emma's so downright and bucolic. Emma's final word had been, "Your Grace above all things needs a son and nobody has ever thought of another way to get one."

Margaret had said, "If Anthony's eye ever wandered, I'd try to catch it back. I'd darken my lids and redden my lips and . . ."

"End by feeling like a painted harlot whom nobody cared to hire! It's useless, Margaret. If a man loves you, he loves you, and you could go barefoot, in a dirty shift, and still be beautiful to him. When it's over, it's over. Whatever I do won't make me, to Henry, look as comely as Jane Seymour."

Margaret said sagely,

"He's vain. All men are, but he is vainer than most. I always thought that one reason why he never forced Catherine to renounce her claims — and he could, you know, he could have starved her into submission had he been so minded — was because deep in his heart he was flattered by her determination not to let him go. If you put up a fight . . ."

"There's some truth in what you say," Anne said, and sat down before her glass.

And all the advice, she realised, had been good, sound, based on centuries of female experience; for here he was; and the sight of him, standing there, so big and smug and confident, a husband about to exercise his conjugal rights, fired something inside her, unexpected, unplanned, insane.

"Keep away from me," she said, "I'm not your hireling. If you feel amorous go find the little bitch who sat on your knee this morning and give England another bastard!"

He said, in a rather helpless way,

"So you saw."

"I saw. So now everybody knows. You seem to find maids-of honour irresistible! Or is this another quirk of your conscience?"

Stung by that taunt he found it easy to make the remark which he had planned, but he said it more unkindly, saying "your betters" instead of "Catherine".

"Put up with it," she threw back at him. "I have no intention of putting up with the kind of thing that happened this morning. I shall leave Court! Catherine is my better, in patience, if nothing else. But I shan't follow her example and hang on until I'm ordered away from Court. You can find some excuse to get rid of me, as you got rid of Catherine, and marry your pudding-faced charmer."

Nothing could have suited him better; but the Duke of Norfolk had quietly closed both doors that offered a possibility of escape. And it wouldn't do to let Anne go, a deeply wronged and very angry woman, anxious to blacken Jane's name at every opportunity. That would make him look so light-minded and frivolous — which God knew he was not — wasn't he here at this moment with the express intention of doing his duty and trying to get a son? Moreover Anne's going would leave him in the exact position which he had occupied so uncomfortably for so many years, poised between a wife he couldn't use and a sweetheart he couldn't marry. And ill-minded people would say that the place was littered with his cast-off wives.

He changed his tone and said reasonably,

"You're making much out of very little. Men have impulses of which women know nothing. She's a plump, soft, cuddlesome little thing, like a kitten, and like a kitten I cuddled her. No harm was intended, or done. Come to bed."

"If you stumbled on me, hugging one of your gentlemen, would you say no harm was done and wish to bed with me a few hours later?"

Suddenly he was swept by a perverse emotion. She was saying "No" again, and that set the old will-o'-the-wisp dancing.

"Let's not quarrel or argue," he said. "She's a kitten and I stroked her. But you are my wife, my angry, railing fish-wife, and I will take you to bed and stop your mouth with kisses."

She stood still and silent, looking at him in the way which he had once found so fascinating, and now for a moment did again, her look of seeing something invisible to anyone else. She was thinking that, despite losing her temper and acting in opposition to all advice, she was being offered another chance. With a son in her arms she could laugh at Jane Seymour and a hundred like her. And as Emma had said, there was no other way . . .

She had never known exactly when Elizabeth had been conceived, but tonight was different. This child would be born in April; and would be the boy for whom

England had waited so long. She was thinking this when Henry, still a little breathless, said, in a sudden access of goodwill,

"You may send the girl home for all I care."

It demanded an effort to think backwards, to think — *I* was sent home, and he followed; better that she should be here, under my eye.

She said,

"No. I think the time may come when I shall need *all* the services of *all* my ladies."

CHAPTER
THIRTY-TWO

"In the autumn of this year, 1535, the queen was once more flattered with the hope of bringing a male heir to the throne, to the great joy of the king." Agnes Strickland. *Lives of the Queens of England*

GREENWICH. SEPTEMBER 1535

"It is not a miscarriage," Emma Arnett said.

"Give it another name, then!"

"You missed a month. Women do; even those who have never been near a man."

The need to scream, scream, scream, came upon her. She only just mastered it by turning furiously upon Emma.

"How should you know? I tell you I felt it. I knew. I was sure. Why else am I here and not on progress? I was with child, I tell you; a child who should have been born in April. Now I have miscarried. It's like a blight; girls and miscarriages! And I was so pleased. So was he when I told him. Fool that I was to speak so soon. I know what he'll say! Another cursed marriage. The first one cursed because the Pope let him make it, and this one cursed because the Pope forbade. That'd be comic, if it wasn't so . . ."

Something that seemed to have no part of her decided that it *was* comic and she sat down on the bed and rocked to and fro in a gale of hysterical laughter.

Emma, acting from some motive not yet clear to herself, laid her hard square hands on Anne's shoulders, and said urgently,

"Stop. Your Grace, stop it! Do you want them to hear? Lady Rochfort coming to see what's amiss."

Anne seemed past caring; she laughed on. Emma shook her, not gently, and then, moving one hand, placed the palm of it squarely over Anne's mouth. As she did so she said, through the sound of the now-muffled laughter,

"I'm sorry, Your Grace, but you forced me to it. Listen, I beg you, I beg you. Let this be between you and me, till we have had time to think."

Anne made some gulping sounds and then was quiet; cautiously Emma removed her hand. The hysterical bout had passed. Anne said quite calmly,

"And what will thinking do? Put it back?"

"It might save the situation," Emma said, her Saxon eyes as cold and hard as flint. "I was loth to own that it was a miscarriage, knowing how the very word would set you off. But suppose it was . . .?"

"I tell you I know that it was."

"Then it proves one thing." Emma's attention seemed to detach itself. She looked thoughtfully about the luxurious bed-chamber.

"What does it prove?"

Emma said, with seeming irrelevance,

"I've come a long way from the farm . . . But close to the soil, there's a kind of wisdom. On a farm, if a cow slips her calf *once*, which is to blame, her or the bull? Nobody can tell. Try her with another bull, him with another cow and then the fault is fixed and the bad breeder goes straight to the shambles and is beef." She paused for a second, gazing into Anne's eyes. "I'm thinking this proves that His Grace is a bad breeder."

"He fathered the Duke of Richmond."

"Did he? His mother *said* so. But what company had she kept?"

"Emma!"

"It would bear thinking on."

As she spoke Emma had a curious feeling that it was for this moment that she had been born. She was doing, or was out to do something that nobody else in all the world could do.

She thought of the fear which haunted all Protestants — that something should happen to the King before the reforms were properly established, and that all the backward-looking Papists, all the people who were neither one thing nor the other would rally to the cause of the Lady Mary who was old enough to take control, sit a horse, wear the Crown. The baby Elizabeth would stand no chance against Mary; but a boy would; from the moment he was born he would be unchallenged.

Emma, from reading the New Testament, had progressed to reading the Old which was crammed with proofs that if the *heart* were right, acts mattered little. Look at Jacob, cheating his old blind father, cheating his brother, and his father-in-law, and yet *chosen*, beloved of God, and the founder of all the tribes of Israel. There must also be taken into consideration Christ's attitude towards adultery; He'd dealt very gently with the loose-living woman at the wells of Samaria, and had protected the other woman who was about to be stoned . . .

Not without an inner amazement, Emma Arnett, that decent woman, realised that if Anne, to bear a prince who would save the country from Mary, must commit adultery, she was willing to be an accomplice, even an instigator.

"It should be thought about," she said, "and nothing said yet. This news would dishearten your friends, and delight your enemies. And His Grace would take it very hard."

Her lips were framing the simple-seeming, obvious remarks, while her eyes, looking into Anne's, made their own communication. We know how it could be managed . . .

The room seemed to grow smaller, closing itself in around the secret; the scented air seemed to vibrate with words which must not be spoken, need never be spoken.

Then, suddenly, Anne's innate secretiveness took fright. This was too close! It wasn't that she did not trust Emma who had always been loyal and close-mouthed, and who had dealt admirably with the situation which had existed in the months between her yielding to Henry and her marriage. But then the worst danger had been scandal, in which Henry had been himself involved. This was different. If, as a last desperate resource, she took this perilous road, she would walk it alone.

Still eye to eye with Emma she said,

"That advice is sound. I'm grateful for it. And for your restraining me when I was distraught. I'm too anxious. I think too much of Catherine. A slight show and I go screaming about a miscarriage because it is a thing I dread, and always in the forefront of my mind. Now I'm no longer sure. Somehow, despite everything, I don't feel that I have shed my load."

Emma's gaze remained steady, but behind it she, in turn, retreated. Oh, she thought, so that is the way it is to be. You don't trust me. Very well, go ahead, do it in your own fashion. I shall stand by and pretend to be deceived with all the rest. The end is what matters, not the means.

Yet she was more hurt by Anne's lack of trust than she would admit, even to herself. It was a poor reward for all she had done, and especially hard, coming as it did just when she had saved the situation

She looked at the door and thought, but for me they'd have all come crowding in when they heard the laughter; they'd have asked what was the matter and she, just then, would have blurted it all out. And then suddenly to be put in my place like that!

Still, she had averted certain disaster, she had made success possible, she had served the cause. And for what other reason was she here?

CHAPTER
THIRTY-THREE

I do not say that this is how it happened; I only say that this is how it could have happened.
Your Author

GREENWICH. SEPTEMBER — OCTOBER 1535

The pretty maid-of-honour said discontentedly,

"Masked again! And that is the third time running. I could understand it if Her Grace were swollen about the face or pop-eyed as women in her state so often are, but she looks as usual. So why?"

The plainer one wanted to say that the masked balls were immensely enjoyable. She'd enjoyed herself more during the two in the past ten days, than at any other time in her life. Safely masked she had been equal to the greatest beauty in Court, and had had as good a time. But to say so would have been to decry herself, so she joined in the lament.

"It makes so much work," she said, falsely. "Still any kind of gaiety is welcome. I always used to hear how clever the Queen was at devising entertainments, but since I came to Court I've found life rather dull."

You always will, poor dear, the pretty one thought. She said,

"Ah, being pregnant again has made a great difference. *And* the change in His Grace. He's acting like a lover again; sending in a courier every day to ask after her health. And all those deer! I'm growing tired of venison however dressed. We shall have it again this evening, without doubt."

"This evening," said the plain one, "I am going to wear a wig."

How wise, how very wise, thought the pretty one, with a swift glance at her companion's lustreless, mouse-coloured hair.

"Where in the name of goodness could you get such a thing at a moment's notice?"

"I borrowed it. From my aunt Talbot. She went bald, years ago, when my youngest cousin was born, and she used to wear a cap. But when my uncle died and she had money to spend she bought two wigs; beautiful ones, bright brown and curly. When Her Grace announced that this evening we were to be masked again and to appear as we would wish to appear, I asked leave and ran out and begged the loan of one of my aunt's wigs."

"Bright brown and curly? Then I know one thing. You are not intending to pay Her Grace the compliment of imitation. Nor am I. I did think of it; I think I was the first to do so. Appear as you would wish to appear. As soon as I heard that I thought it would be a pretty compliment . . . but six other ladies had the same notion, so I abandoned it."

"Six?"

"That I know of; so there will be twenty most likely."

The plain girl's heart gave a little ecstatic leap of anticipation. Ladies who intended to pay Her Grace that compliment would be obliged to wear head-dresses which concealed their hair, for her hair was unique; therefore aunt Talbot's beautiful wig would be all the more noticeable. She remembered with pleasure the last masquerade when they had all been rural characters, shepherds and milkmaids, thatchers, plough-boys, goose-girls, and a very fine upstanding plough-boy had attached himself to her and finally taken her to a small dark room that smelt of horses and of harness, and had kissed her with enthusiasm. He had suggested that they both remove their masks, and she had been able to say, "The Queen forbade that anyone should," and so escape unshamed. That was what made these masked balls so different and so wonderful; usually, on the stroke of midnight everyone unmasked and there you were with your almost lashless, gooseberry-green eyes and snub nose, yourself again. Unwanted. It was such a pity, she thought; nobody wished to be plain, or could be blamed for being so. In all other respects you were just like any other girl. And at the very back of her mind there lingered a hope, frail yet lively, that tonight somebody, momentarily caught by the masked, anonymous face and the beautiful wig, might pause, look a little deeper and realise that a face wasn't all . . .

She felt so warmly towards the Queen, who had made this possible, that she almost wished that her aunt Talbot had chosen to invest in wigs of straight black hair so that she too, in response to the order to appear as she wished to be, could have impersonated Her Grace.

Her little contribution was not missed. Not twenty, but forty-three ladies had paid Anne the ultimate compliment, and had shown considerable ingenuity; breasts tightly bound to flatten them; waists tightly clenched in; almost unmanageable high heels to lend stature; dresses of the colours she favoured, yellow, white, tawny, orange and cinnamon and black. Some ladies had even had their hair dyed; others had made shift with head-dresses. Gold and silversmiths must have worked all through the night on hasty copies of her favourite trinkets.

Forty-three versions of her, of varying validity; some had entered into the spirit of the game and imitated her manner, sprightly yet a little aloof.

It wasn't easy to tell one from another; it was impossible to know where they went, or what they did, or with whom.

That was — to the regret of the plain maid-in-waiting — the last of the masked balls. The Queen would dance no more until April had come and gone. The King came back from his progresses, perceptibly heavier, for everywhere he stayed he had been offered the best the house afforded and it would have been churlish not to eat and praise, the food.

He was settled in his mind, too, content to wait and see what April brought. If Anne bore him a son then he would do what kings had done from time immemorial, give all outward honour and respect to the mother of his heir and enjoy himself with his mistress. Jane would accept that, once she saw that there was no alternative. But if the new baby should be another girl then he would *know* that this was another marriage cursed by God and he would get out of it somehow and marry Jane as speedily as he could.

Winter settled down over England and all life seemed attuned to the slow, inevitable process of gestation.

CHAPTER
THIRTY-FOUR

She won't live long. Go to her when you like.
Henry VIII to the Spanish Ambassador

KIMBOLTON CASTLE. JANUARY 4th–7th, 1536

Catherine was dying.

Nobody knew exactly why. Some said that she was dropsical, but there was not much sign of that disease; she had for years suffered from rheumatism, but rheumatic people were usually long-lived; there were those who believed in the local rumour that Kimbolton stood in the centre of an area where the very air was inimical to any but the native-born. Those closest to her said that she was dying of heart-break, occasioned not by her personal misfortunes, which she had borne with fortitude, but by the terrible things which were taking place in England as a result of Henry's break with Rome.

Whatever the reason, she was dying and she knew it; and when, on the fourth of January, a day of grey, weeping skies, Messire Chapuys arrived at the castle and was admitted promptly, she knew that her death was regarded as imminent by Henry, for otherwise the visit would not have been permitted.

From the bed she extended her hand and Chapuys went down on his knees, cautiously, for they were stiff in damp weather, took it and kissed it.

She said,

"You have come. Now I can die in your arms and not like a beast, abandoned in a wet field."

Chapuys, like most normal men, found the mention of death by the dying, embarrassing, and made some awkwardly evasive remark about hoping that her health would improve.

"Not on this earth, my friend. That is why I am so relieved to see you at last. My women are loyal and kind, but powerless, and my present chaplain is timorous and pliable. To tell them my final wishes would be like telling the wind. But you . . ."

"I shall do my utmost to carry out anything you wish done," he said soothingly, and settled himself to endure some discomfort of body — for he was damp and muddy from his journey, and of mind — for she was certain to mention the Emperor fondly and with hope, and just before he had left London he had heard that Charles, anxious for Henry's help against the French King, had agreed to ignore Catherine's rights, and Mary's. It would be a mercy if Catherine died before she learned of that.

"Material things first," Catherine said. "'I have no estate and fear I may die in debt. My allowance has been small and prices have risen steeply of late. I have a gold collar which my mother herself fastened around my neck when I sailed from Corunna; I would like Mary to have that. And my furs. They are old and worn, but while the Concubine lives she will get no new ones and in cold weather may be glad of mine. Do you bring me any news of my daughter?"

"Nothing of much mark. She is pursuing exactly the orders you gave her; obeying the King in all matters save those of conscience. She has rebuffed the Concubine's overtures on several occasions. You may be proud of your daughter, your Grace."

"I am. But I pity her, too. All her best years . . ." Even now she would not say "wasted"; but there were times when she felt that all the suffering, all the stubborn standing upon rights had been in vain. She had begun to feel so when Henry started to demolish the religious houses and, give away, or sell cheaply, their vast estates. It was bribery, ensuring the continuance of the breach with Rome. Even if something unforeseen happened and Mary came to the throne she would find it very hard to pry men away from their ill-gotten acres.

Still, having done what she could, she must leave the outcome with God.

"As for me," she said, "I wish to be buried in some place belonging to the Observant Friars, my favourite order."

He opened his mouth to say that there were now no Observant Friars in England. The Friars had been among the first to go. Even here in the middle of this dismal swamp she must have heard . . . But at the hour of death the mind tended to look backwards. He said,

"I will remember that."

"And I should like five hundred Masses to be said for my soul."

396

He nodded, and let that pass too.

"That, I think, disposes of everything." She lay for a moment mustering strength and then said, in a more vigorous voice, "One thing troubles me. You always urged me to take action. Was I wrong not to give you more heed?"

There was only one answer to that. But it was useless, worse than useless, cruel, to point out to the defeated and the dying just where they had gone wrong.

So he said, gently,

"Your Grace has always acted in accord with your conscience, so how can you have been wrong?"

She gave him a faint smile. "That was a diplomatic answer. I am . . . no, not troubled . . . perplexed about the workings of conscience. You, I am sure were acting in accordance with yours when you went about rousing people to my cause, and trying to persuade me to take up arms. Then whose conscience was right, yours or mine?"

"Only God can judge of that."

"Now, at the end of it all," Catherine went on, "another thought troubles me too. Was I wrong years ago? If when the King first questioned our marriage, I had complied and gone into a nunnery — it was Cardinal Campeggio, I think, who suggested that — then Clement would have, or might have given way to the King and England would have remained part of the true Church. Is not that an appalling thought to visit me now? I have always been so sure, so certain. Always I felt that I was acting as God willed. Now I am sure of nothing and sometimes I feel that I drove Henry to sin in the first place, and by ignoring your advice, rejected the chance to save him. And to think that way, is, I assure you, to feel the pains of Purgatory prematurely."

Chapuys was at a loss. He was a diplomat, not a theologian. His glib tongue and supple brains were more at home dealing with worldly things. But out of pity for her, he tried.

"Such thoughts," he said, "are a temptation to despair, which is a sin. You say that you have always felt sure that you were acting as God willed; that being so you have never before been tempted to despair. Such thoughts may be of the Devil, who having failed with you in other respects, tries this. And remember too, that while faith is confident, it is not truly faith . . ."

He warmed to his task, surprising himself. He spoke of the *apparent* triumph of evil and of heresy and of God's power to reverse it at any moment He chose. Referring to her concern over Henry's spiritual state he reminded her that ultimately every soul was responsible for its own salvation. And then, moving with some relief on to more familiar ground, he spoke of Mary, exaggerating a little as was his habit. Hope of Mary's succession must on no account be abandoned, he said. If anything happened to Henry, Mary could count on the support of everyone in the country except convinced Lutherans, of whom there were but few. And as for the Concubine's latest pregnancy — the delight in gossip shone in the Ambassador's eyes — there was something extremely odd about that. The child was supposed to be due in April; well, in his time he had seen a good many *enceinte* women, and he'd seen Anne only last week, and if she were six months gone with child, so was that bedpost. And everybody said the same. Gossip — not to be relied on, of course, but often showing which way the wind blew — said that she had been pregnant but had had a miscarriage in the autumn, dared not tell the King, would begin presently to pad herself out as much as her overweening vanity would allow, and planned, in April, to have a newly-born male child smuggled in . . .

Catherine felt vaguely that it was wrong to derive comfort from such talk, but in fact she did, and presently she said,

"I think I could sleep now. In the last six days I have not slept as many hours, and that explains my melancholy, for which I apologise. You have brought rest to my mind."

Chapuys, completely exhausted, and very stiff, rose and tottered away.

Catherine slept. And while she slept there arrived another old friend, the Dowager Countess of Willoughby, who, as Maria de Salinas, had come to England with Catherine. She brought with her no order for admittance from the King and at first Sir Edmund Bedingfield was dubious about letting her in; but she shouted at him in the masterful well-born Englishwoman's voice which she had acquired, that the weather entitled her to ask hospitality of any inhabited place: And since the dangerous Spanish Ambassador had been allowed entry there seemed no reason to exclude a comparatively harmless woman. So when Catherine woke it was to see another friendly face, and pleasure in the reunion revived her a little. She was strong enough to sit, well-propped with pillows, and write the last of her innumerable letters.

It was to Henry. It began, "My most dear lord, King and husband," and went on, without a word of reproach, to beg him to consider the good of his immortal soul. "For my part, I pardon you everything . . ." And she did; she looked upon him as a fellow victim; he was easily led, he had been badly advised, he had fallen prey to an evil woman. "For the rest I commend unto you our daughter Mary, beseeching you to be a good father unto her." She mentioned her three remaining maids, asking that they should be paid their wages and provided with marriage portions and ended the letter with the words, "Lastly I make this vow, that mine eyes desire you above all things."

Three days later she died in Lady Willoughby's arms.

In London, when he heard the news, Henry rejoiced. It meant the end of that always-just-hovering-threat that somebody might take up cudgels on Catherine's behalf; it ended, even in Catholic eyes, his state of being a man with two wives. And it gave him elbow room for the future . . .

CHAPTER
THIRTY-FIVE

"It was said she tooke a fright, for the King ran that tyme at the ring and had a fall from his horse, but he had no hurt; and she tooke such a fright withal that it caused her to fall in travaile, and so was delivered afore her full tyme."
Wriothesley

"... the King had said to somebody in great confidence ... that he had made this marriage seduced by witchcraft, and for that reason he considered it null; and that this was evident because God did not permit them to have male issue, and that he believed he might take another wife."
The Spanish Ambassador in a letter to his master

GREENWICH. JANUARY 1536

The rain had cleared and everything was washed with the peculiarly lucid light of a sunny winter's day. It was fine enough for most of the ladies to go, well-furred, to watch the King and his friends at exercise in the tilt-yard. Anne had stayed indoors, careful always to remember that she was supposed to be farther advanced in pregnancy than she actually was; and Margaret Lee had stayed with her. They were busy with an almost completed piece of tapestry. It was heavy and bulky, and Emma Arnett insisted upon standing by to help with handling it.

Anne, as she worked, worried away at the problem which had confronted her, day and night, ever since the autumn. She had told Henry that the child would be born in April. Unless it was prematurely born — and who could count upon that? — April would come and go and she would not be delivered. How late could a child be without causing comment and question? She had managed to inveigle Dr Butts into discussing that. First babies, he said, tended to be tardy, anything from a fortnight to three weeks, though, he had added, often the baby was blamed for the mother's fault. Women reckoned so ill. The average for women was about two hundred and seventy days; in his experience; second babies — he had smiled at her as he said this — were usually more considerate than first ones, they were often three weeks early and that was why second confinements seemed easier.

Margaret said,

"Have you yet received an answer from Mary?"

"I have indeed. Rude and contemptuous, as always."

She had been particularly anxious to come to terms with Mary. Mary had been the one who had said — at least so it had been reported and never contradicted — the vilest possible thing about Elizabeth. "And does she resemble her father, Mark Smeaton?" If Mary could say that, about Elizabeth so obviously Henry's child, what might she not say next time? Mary simply must be won over.

Anne, rebuffed so often, had not tried the direct approach; she had sent a message through Lady Shelton. She had asked Mary to let an old sore heal; she had said that she would be a mother to her, and promised that if she would come to Court and be one of the family that she should take precedence of everyone, she might, if she wished walk, on all formal occasions, side by side with Anne herself. Never had a Queen made such an offer; but Anne reflected with frank wryness, never could a Queen have had quite such reason.

"She said that she would sooner die a hundred times than change her mind."

"I hope you sent her back a sharp answer," Margaret said. She was constitutionally incapable of making a sharp answer herself and one of the many things she admired about her cousin was her ability to wage verbal warfare, if need be.

"I wrote to Lady Shelton," Anne said, a little wearily. "I asked her to tell Mary that from now on what she does and how she acts are of no interest to me. I told her that I hoped to have a son and was merely trying to establish her beforehand. That was sense. If this is a boy, within six months the Lady Mary might lie in Peterborough beside her mother for all any one will care."

"In less than six," Margaret said, happily. She, as much as anyone in the world, was counting upon this child's birth, counting upon it being a boy. She loved Anne and wished to see her properly re-established. The King had been a little more discreet of late, but he had not yet tired of Jane Seymour; and although Anne seldom spoke of it, Margaret knew that she was troubled. She had never been quite the same since the day when she had discovered Henry with Jane on his knee, and no wonder. Still a boy would right everything. In the joy of being the father of a prince at last Henry would forget the trivial pleasure of dalliance.

Margaret spared a moment to breathe yet another swift prayer for a safe delivery, and a boy baby: and then, seeing Anne's hands idle and her eyes fixed in an inward, unhappy look, set herself to rouse her.

"Now, blue would you say, or purple? Of blue we have plenty, the purple is running short. If it is to be purple we shall need more."

Before Anne could answer there was a clatter outside the door; it opened and the Duke of Norfolk burst in. Except for his helm, which he carried in his hand, he was clad for tilting; his long heavy face was the colour of tallow.

"The King," he gasped. "He took a great fall . . . He may be dead!"

In one piercing second she saw exactly what would happen to her, bereft of Henry's protection. Mary on the throne. Herself hurried away and disposed of; for Mary would never let this child be born. Then she swayed on the stool, and would have fallen but for Margaret's supporting arms.

Emma dropped the ends of wool she was sorting and ran forward.

"You take her feet," she ordered, pushing Margaret away and putting her own arms under Anne's. "We

404

must get her flat. Open the door," she said to the Duke, "you blundering fool! You clown! If he's dead, all the more reason . . ." O God, she prayed, more earnestly than she had ever prayed before, let the child be unharmed, let her go her full time; this is the prince, dear merciful God, who is to set thy people free!

They laid Anne on her bed, loosened her clothing and wrapped her warmly. Emma put a pillow under her feet, too; and when Margaret took the flagon of grated hartshorn to hold to her nose, checked her.

"I'm not so sure. If he's dead . . . At least she isn't fretting now. What did that old fool say, 'may be', didn't he? Run and find out. We might have good news to bring her round to."

Margaret ran, and Emma went down on her knees by the bed and laid her hands gently upon Anne's body, as though warding off some threatened, physical attack. O God, dear God. The prayer ran through her mind, as repetitious, as stylised as the telling of beads against which her kind railed so bitterly. This was the child who would keep Mary from the throne, keep England from slipping back into the Pope's clutches, a child whose very begetting was proof of God's secret, mysterious ways of working His will on earth.

Margaret, less than half-way to the tilt-yard met the ladies swarming back. The King was not dead, merely unconscious and suffering a small wound in the leg. The doctors were with him.

Armed with this cheering news Emma set to work with the hartshorn, with cold water, with wrist rubbing.

405

She yielded place to no one, and when Anne moaned and stirred it was Emma's voice which said, bluntly and briefly,

"He isn't dead."

"He was stunned," Margaret said, "and his leg is hurt a little. The doctors are with him."

"I should go to him," Anne said.

"Oh no, Your Grace," Emma said firmly. "That you'll not do. You've had a bad shock and a swooning spell and you must lie and rest."

"You could do nothing," Nan Savile contributed. "We shall hear when he comes round. Perhaps you can go then."

She was content to be persuaded; her limbs felt boneless, and the child lay heavy, heavy, like the weights they placed on prisoners who refused to plead, the *peine forte et dure*.

"I'll rest a little then — though I'm well enough."

"Small thanks to his Grace of Norfolk," Emma said grimly. "I've never before in my life wished myself married, but I'd give something to be *his* wife for just half an hour."

Within two hours they had news that the King had regained consciousness and suffered no more than a headache and a scratch and what promised to be a remarkable bruise on the leg. Emma, reasonably sure now that what she dreaded most had been averted, allowed Anne to get up, and clad in a loose robe, go along to his apartments. He made light of the headache, but seemed concerned about his leg.

"It's on the very spot where I had a most troublesome ulcer, until Thomas Vicary cured it. A fine thing it'll be if this knock opens it up again."

She said that she hoped that would not happen. She said that she was glad that so severe a fall had not injured him more. She looked at him with a dreary feeling of guilt because her first thought had been for herself. She'd felt no grief, nothing but fear. It was an outstanding example of the way in which circumstances could corrupt people.

"Dr Butts has applied a plaster," Henry went on complaining, "to draw out the bruise, he said. By the feel of it it's drawing the flesh from the bone."

I should pity him, she thought, knowing as I do how anything less than perfect physical health disgusts him.

But another thought swung out in counter-balance; *he* should spare a thought for me, just a question; he must know what a shock I sustained; and I am with child. Not his, but that he does not know. The feeling of something badly amiss, of having lost herself, of having mismanaged everything, of being alone and on the wrong road, a feeling that reached back to that thundery night at Hampton Court, came upon her as it had so often lately, and with even more force. Their whole relationship was wrong; and was she much to blame? She'd only done what most women, placed as she had been, would have done. Every single move in this blind-fold game had been forced upon her; and the root, the real root of all the trouble lay with him, with what Mary had once warned her of, his inability to love anyone who loved him. On that night at Hampton

Court he had thought she loved him, and he had begun to hate her then. After that she'd been nothing but a brood animal, and knowing that she had not dared to tell him last autumn that she had miscarried. She'd been compelled to find her own way out of that predicament; and she had; and for the last few months whenever she had these dismal thoughts, she had been able to think about the boy whom she might bear. But not tonight. Tonight the child was just a leaden weight, dragging down so that her back ached.

Henry, with the headache like a leaden cap, with spikes inside it, bearing down on his head, and his leg throbbing, a pendulum of pain, thought that it was civil of her to have come, but oh, how he did wish she'd go away. She looked so unwell that the sight of her filled him with foreboding. Something wrong with this pregnancy? He'd asked himself that when he came back from his progress in October, expecting to find her sleek, filling out and had found her hollow-cheeked, a little wild of eye. Later she had seemed to settle down, but not completely, not as she had before the birth of Elizabeth. And maybe, he conceded, for that he was a little to blame. She was jealous. She knew about Jane. And she hadn't Catherine's good sense in that respect. Catherine had known about the Stafford girl, about Bessie Blount, and Mary Boleyn . . . but she hadn't gone about looking . . .

Still, there was a belief that a really healthy vigorous child leeched strength from its mother. If that was true this child should be exceptional. Cheered by that thought, he asked a little belatedly,

"And is all well with you?"

She forced herself to smile.

"All is well with me. And I hope that all will soon be well with you. I wish you a good night."

"That I most certainly shall not have," Henry said, reverting to egotism, "unless I can persuade Butts to remove this damned plaster."

She went away, moving slowly, very conscious of her burden which had, since the shock, ceased to seem like a part of herself.

Six days later, after a long agony that surpassed the pangs of ordinary birth, she bore what would have been a boy.

Over the tiny scrap of carrion which should have been the saviour of his country, Emma, who had not wept for forty years, almost wept, would have wept, had there been room in her shocked and angry mind for any soft emotion.

Her faith, the new faith, founded upon reason and shorn of superstition, faltered and failed. Really, she thought with furious despair, it looked as though God didn't know His own business!

They brought the news to Henry, where he sat with his leg supported by a stool. It was very swollen, very black and very painful, but that was only to be expected; what distressed him was to find, every time the bandage was removed, that the trivial wound, instead of drying up and healing, remained moist and seemed to be widening. The old ulcer waking again?

That the child was dead brought him no surprise; nothing good could be expected of so premature a labour; that it would have been a son filled him with impotent fury which for about the space of an hour swamped every other feeling. Then it began to recede, leaving, like an ebbing tide, some stark and alien things stranded and exposed.

First, the hope that she would die and thus put an end to this marriage, as cursed as his former one. Second, the determination should she live, he would rid himself of her. Third, a pondering of the means. And fourth, this for comfort, the certainty that soon things would change and begin to go well for him.

Passionately he willed her to die. It would make everything so simple. There'd be a splendid funeral, as befitted one who had been Queen of England, a little time, a very little time of mourning, and then, because the succession was of such paramount importance, marriage with his darling little Jane. The most captious critic of his acts and motives could find no fault with that.

Let her die, and by dying make good the fraud she had practised, the fraud which he would never, to his dying day, understand. All those years of longing and waiting. For nothing. Die and wipe out the false promise, the wasted years, the letters, the garden at Hever, Catherine's tears, Wolsey's last look. Die and make all good . . .

She did not die. She clung to life as stubbornly as Catherine had clung to her title. In the whole of God's creation there was nothing so tough, so resilient as a woman.

He could justifiably have pleaded his lameness as an excuse for not visiting her, but something impelled him to go. Supported by Norris and leaning on a stout staff he hobbled along to her room. Her drained face looked very sallow against the whiteness of the pillows, and her hair was limp and damp, like the coat of a drowned animal. He felt nothing but disgust and hatred, and his first words were brutal,

"So you lost my boy!"

"It was the shock my uncle of Norfolk gave me. He told me that you were dead."

"And if I had been, wasn't that all the more reason for holding on to the child?"

"If willing could have done it, I would. You should know that."

"Well, you'll get no more boys from me!" That was what he had come to say. He wanted to hurt her, wanted to see her wince and begin to weep. She merely looked at him and with out any perceptible movement of lip or eye, contrived to convey an expression of mockery. He turned away abruptly and limped from the room.

In the ante-room of his own apartments he found the Duke of Norfolk, Cromwell and Sir Thomas Audley, his new Chancellor, awaiting him; he'd summoned them earlier in the day. He greeted them gruffly and passed on into his audience chamber where he sat down heavily in his chair and stuck his injured leg straight out, waiting until Norris had arranged the stool.

"You'd better all sit down," he said. "I have something of some importance to communicate to you."

The Duke of Norfolk, ever since the day of the King's fall, had lived in a state of acute apprehension. Sooner or later, he was certain, he was going to bear the brunt of the blame for the catastrophe. Emma's words still rang in his ears, if nobody else had seen the connection, she had, and she'd talk; rung by rung that talk would mount. It would come to the King's ear, and then . . .

It might be now. In the presence of his Chief Secretary and his Chancellor, the King might point the finger and say, "*You* killed my son!"

And what the punishment would be was past the mind of man to imagine. The King enraged could devise fearful punishments. Norfolk had never, in these few days, ceased to think about what had happened to a few Carthusian monks in the previous year. They had merely asked Cromwell for advice on what attitude they should take to the Oath of Allegiance; and for that, by no standards a crime, they had been taken to Newgate, put into iron collars, and fettered, and so stood, without food or water until they died. Norfolk carried, in his pouch, ready to hand, three pills, each one guaranteed to kill a man. There had been four, but he'd tried one out on an old servant who was always complaining of the stiffness of his joints. Take this, he'd said, and see what it will do for you. He'd been dead before his master had counted to two hundred and twenty. When the finger pointed, Norfolk would swallow the pills.

"This latest disaster," Henry said, "has shown me where I stand. This marriage is as cursed as my former one."

There was a silence. To Audley and Cromwell the announcement came as a surprise, to Norfolk as a relief. Vengeance was to be wreaked, not upon him, but upon his niece.

Cromwell, the lawyer, said in a tentative way, "Your Grace, it was regarded as a legal marriage."

"By some!"

He remembered, unwillingly, a few of those who had refused to acknowledge its legality. Fisher, More whose heads had rotted on Tower Bridge, and Catherine . . . But the memory, instead of softening his temper hardened it. They were all fellow victims.

"A man is the best judge of his own marriage, and this I *know*! I was seduced by witchcraft into making it, and it has brought me, and this country, nothing but woe."

Cromwell thought — Last time it was his conscience, and my master, Wolsey, fell, tripped on his conscience. I shall not trip over this superstitious rubbish. Put into plain English, he wants to marry Jane Seymour and that suits me well. We're related by marriage, and if I help with this the whole family will have reason to be grateful to me.

Audley thought — Wolsey held the Seal and opposed him, and was disgraced; More held the Seal and opposed him and was beheaded. They were both brilliant men, while I can claim no more than my share of good common-sense; whatever he proposes, I shall go with him.

Norfolk thought — I've had a lucky escape; he's blaming circumstance, not me. But this talk of witchcraft, no, I don't like that. Open to ridicule.

Henry looked at their faces, all at that moment bearing a strong resemblance to one another, well-fed, moulded by self-interest, calculating, shrewd and wearing expressions of consternation.

He said,

"Well?"

A ghost with a very similar face moved in the shadows.

Nobody wished to be the first to speak; nobody knew what, exactly, to suggest. Only Norfolk, with his plain man's ability to focus attention on one thing at a time, ventured to decry the King's suggestion without offering an alternative.

"I must beg your Grace to abandon the thought of witchcraft. Nobody believes in witches nowadays, and to mention the word in such a connection would make us all the laughing stock of Christendom."

"No new experience for me," Henry said sourly. "And why *nowadays* when everybody has a smuggled Bible. Witches are mentioned *there*. It says distinctly enough — Thou shalt not suffer a witch to live."

So that was it! He wanted her dead.

For a little while nobody spoke and no man looked at another.

Then at last Norfolk said,

"I am sorry, Sire, but as a reason that will not do. It would be such bad policy. I beg you to consider. There are so many things these days, things people have believed in for hundreds of years, contemptuously dismissed as superstition. Our Lady's blood at Walsingham — that is superstition; how can we turn about and ask people to believe that a girl, by witchcraft, cast a spell over the King of England?"

Henry glared at him.

"Not so long since when I talked with you on the matter, I suggested two other reasons, and you scoffed at both. I'm beginning to suspect that, despite all your protests to the contrary, you are interested in keeping your niece where she is.

"As God is my judge, that is not so. Rid yourself of her, but let it be for some reason which any man of good sense can accept. And," he added, remembering their former conversation, "one that does your Grace's reputation no damage."

"Name one," Henry said challengingly. He looked from one face to another. "Name me one."

Cromwell said,

"I beg your Grace's indulgence, but it seems that I — I do not know about Sir Thomas Audley — am not fully informed. Your Grace and his Grace of Norfolk have formerly discussed this matter?"

"I know nothing of it," Audley muttered.

"I spoke of it, last summer. To *you*," Henry said, swinging his stare to Norfolk. "And you opposed me and gave me a lot of advice which I followed to the letter. And with what result? Another still-born boy! Is that, or is it not, plain proof of God's displeasure?"

A great dark wave of depression swamped him and he looked at the three men with hatred. His premier Duke, his Chancellor, his Chief Secretary, and not a glimmer of understanding among the three of them. How would they feel in his place? A king without an heir, with a wife he hated, a sweetheart he longed to marry. And a bad leg!

He said, suddenly malicious,

"I shall retire now, and have some attention from Dr Butts. This plaster is worse than the wound. I've told you what I want. You sit here and thresh it out. When you hit upon something that my lord of Norfolk can bring himself to approve, come and lay it before me."

Cromwell, the lawyer took charge.

"My lord, this conversation which took place last summer, the remedies for his case which His Grace suggested and you scoffed at, could you enlighten us thereupon?"

Norfolk gave as detailed an account of the conversation as he could. His feeling of guilt over the miscarriage, and the King's accusation about his wishing to keep Anne as Queen, had shattered even his monumental self-confidence and he was pitiably grateful when, at the end of his account, Cromwell said,

416

"And you were right. As you were right about the witchcraft. And right, too, about any damage to His Grace's reputation. These are tricky times. The country is in a state of ferment, one false move now?" He made a movement of his hand.

Audley said,

"But the Queen was never popular, not as the Princess Dowager was. I think, given adequate reason, the people would accept her disposal. I agree with my Lord of Norfolk that witchcraft is ridiculous, and that nobody wishes to hear any more about pre-contract, or consanguinity. So what have we left?"

The answer formed itself, out of thin air.

Adultery!

Not one of them had actually moved, yet they seemed to have drawn together, and Norfolk when next he spoke did so almost in a whisper.

"Against a woman one charge is always feasible, and as often as not, justified."

"It means naming a man," Audley said. "What man?"

"There," Norfolk said, "is the irony. My sister is dead, so I will only say that she was notoriously flighty; Mary we all know about; but Anne, though they call her witch and poisoner, has never, so far as I know, been accused of laxity."

"That need be no stumbling-block," Audley said. "A simple matter of accusing some man and then extracting a confession. Someone of small importance for preference. Less fuss."

At the back of Cromwell's mind a memory scratched, like a dog seeking admission at a closed door. Shy though, and elusive, sidling away as he sought to call it in. It would come back, as such things often did, just before he fell asleep.

He said,

"Such a scheme involves the King admitting to being cuckolded. I doubt if that will be to his liking."

"Rats caught in traps have been known to gnaw off a leg to get free," Norfolk said brutally. "What other way is open that involves no long-drawn-out litigation, or, and this matters more, loss of popularity for him. The Princess Dowager's death has stirred many memories, the still-born boy has started tongues clacking. Now this! Next time he draws attention to his matrimonial affairs it would be strongly advisable that he should appear as the injured party, *deeply* injured and compelled to take action."

Audley said,

"With that I agree."

Cromwell said,

"It is indisputable."

Audley was also trying to remember something; a bit of kitchen gossip, little minded at the time. It came back to him; he exclaimed, "I have it!" and then, as the other two men looked at him as though in expectation of a solution of the whole problem, what he had heard seemed so small and frail that he hesitated to expose it. It was a reported speech, and so out of character with the speaker that it seemed very little to go upon. On the other hand, plainly they were here to make a case out of

418

nothing, and this, frail as it was, was better than nothing. Still, he framed what he had to say as a question rather than a statement.

"Did you ever hear something that the Lady Mary is reported to have said when informed of the birth of Princess Elizabeth?"

Instantly the thing which had been scratching at the door of Cromwell's mind came trotting in and settled. But in accordance with his usual policy of caution he said,

"It has momentarily escaped me. What was it?"

Norfolk answered.

"I remember it. She said, 'And whom does she resemble? Her father, Mark Smeaton?' Is that what you have in mind, Audley?"

Smeaton. Cromwell could see the name and the few words before and after it, standing out from thousands of words that he had read on that same day. "Lord Rochfort said that Smeaton was a poor oaf and was in love with the Lady."

He said,

"Ah, yes. I remember that too. But a querulous question, asked in a moment of chagrin, is not evidence, you know." And nor were a few words exchanged by uncommitted persons and overheard by a spy.

"It's something to start with," Audley said. "I think we must bear in mind that within a short time His Grace has suffered a severe disappointment over this still-born boy, and a physical injury. He told us, just now, what he wished, and left it to us to find a means of attaining his wish. I think that we should give some proof that we are endeavouring to do so."

"I agree," Norfolk said. "But even you must see that it would be worse than useless to go to him now and say that we have decided that the best thing for him to do is to play the cuckold. He's like me, a blunt man, no good at dissembling. We must play for time. Say that we are on the track of something that will set him free and lose him no jot of popularity. That should content him for a little. Then the day will come and he will ask, 'What?' and then we tell him that it may be possible to prove the Queen an adulteress. What he says then must determine our course." He added cynically, "My niece may in the meantime have recovered her health, dressed her hair in some new fashion and renewed the spell he spoke of. We mustn't be hasty."

No, they were agreed there; a show of activity, of willingness, but no haste.

Yet something had been decided, without debate, without a moment's consideration. Mark Smeaton was the man.

CHAPTER
THIRTY-SIX

"Ah! Mark . . .
A time thou hadst above thy poor degree,
The fall whereof thy friends may well bemoan.
A rotten twig upon so high a tree
Hath slipped thy hold, and thou art dead and gone.'
Sir Thomas Wyatt

STEPNEY. MAY 1st, 1536

Mark Smeaton, dressed in his best, arrived at Cromwell's house in Stepney, exactly on the stroke of noon. He had been invited to dine with the King's chief minister, an honour which fell to few men and which was a tribute paid to his genius.

Delighted as he was by the invitation he did not imagine that Cromwell had asked him solely for his company. He was probably planning some grand entertainment for the coming summer and needed expert advice about the music. But — and this was the delightful part — any ordinary musician of lowly birth would have been told to wait upon the Chief Secretary at nine in the morning, and if he were lucky, be given leave to refresh himself at the buttery on his way out. Mark Smeaton was asked to dine. That was the first token of recognition that had ever come to him from the outside world; it would not, he felt, be the last.

It was the Queen who had first seen in him something out of the ordinary, and for that, as well as other reasons, he loved her. He could not, of course, still worship her as goddess of purity; her first pregnancy had destroyed that bit of fantasy, but he had quickly — to save his reason — built himself another. She was Henry's unwilling wife; her changing moods, her silences, her wistful looks all stemmed from unhappiness. She was actually in love with him herself, as he was in love with her. But it was a secret, never to be acknowledged even when they were alone together. Once, and once only, he had attempted to speak to her about it and she had rebuffed him; he'd wept over the rebuff until he had thought about it enough to convince himself that she was right. She was wise, she knew the value of silence and secrecy in a love affair which must always remain a thing of the heart and mind.

To walk along ordinary streets made him feel strange. For years now his life had consisted of his music, and his dreams; he was out of touch with reality. Around the Court he was known and nobody wondered if sometimes he stood stock-still, staring into space; if necessary they'd say, "Wake up, Smeaton," or joke, "Thinking of a fine tune!" Here in the noisy streets he was jostled; and once a woman with a basket of fish said, "Look where you walk, can't yer?" in a railing tone.

The great house, when he reached it, seemed oddly deserted. He had heard that Cromwell, warned by

Wolsey's fall from high estate, lived comparatively modestly; still everyone had servants, and a man of such importance, in a house of this size, must have many. The tall doors, as was customary, stood open, and beyond them the entrance hall was unattended. Surely an invitation to thieves. But while he stood, hesitant, for a moment, a man appeared, from nowhere it seemed; a steward to judge from his black clothes and gold chain. He asked, "Master Smeaton?" and then led the way upstairs, through several well-furnished rooms, none of them occupied, down a few stairs and into a passage, and finally into a room of very moderate size, bare-walled, stone-floored and meagrely furnished with a table against the wall and a few chairs. It had one small window, so high, ill-placed and thickly barred that on this bright May morning the room seemed full of chill twilight; it was a second before Mark realised that Cromwell was in the room, on the side away from the window, and in his dark clothes, almost lost in the shadow.

The steward said, "Master Smeaton, my lord," and went away, closing the door behind him.

Cromwell came forward a little; he did not smile, or offer his hand. He stood there looking at his visitor with that most disconcerting of all stares, the one that travels from head to foot and back again, seeming to assess the quality of one's clothing, to measure one's height, judge one's status.

The stare unnerved Smeaton, especially when across the hard face that looked as though it had been carved from mutton fat there drifted a look of pity. I've made a muddle, come on the wrong day, at the wrong time, Smeaton thought. He said, with the little stammer that came upon him when he was nervous,

"Y-you were expecting m-me, my lord?"

"Oh yes, I was expecting you," Cromwell said in a heavy voice which did nothing to put Smeaton at ease.

And then suddenly he had what he thought was the explanation, of the deserted house, of the strange reception. Of course! May Day, when all servants expected to have leave to go and gather garlands, if female, to wash their faces in dew, to attend the many May Day Fairs. And perhaps a gentleman accustomed to dining out would know that on May Day one should not be too punctual. By arriving before the board was set he had betrayed a lack of worldliness — and that accounted for the pitying look. Poor fellow, he doesn't know the rules.

"I h-hope that I am not t-too early."

"Oh no. Not by a moment. We are ready for you. Be seated."

He had been asked to dine, and one chair stood near the table, so diffidently, he began to move towards it.

"No, not there," Cromwell said. "Here!"

It was like one of those sleeping dreams when everything seems a little wrong, out of shape. The chair Cromwell indicated was the best in the room, a big chair with carved arms and legs. Taking it, Smeaton carefully spread out the skirts of his new tunic. Cromwell seated himself in another chair, almost opposite, and as soon as he had done so the door opened and the steward came in, followed by two men of inferior sort, coarse looking fellows in buff breeches and jerkins. They brought no dishes. The steward carried writing equipment which he placed on the table before sitting down on the chair nearby.

Cromwell said,

"I asked you to dinner, Smeaton, and that was no empty invitation. A good dinner is preparing and you will be very welcome to it when you have answered a few questions which I am compelled to ask you. I hope you will be frank because this is a distasteful business to me and I shall be glad to have it over as soon as may be."

It was at this point that Smeaton remembered that Cromwell had been very ill. He had taken to his bed, seeing no one, and for one period of four days had refused all food and drink. Maybe his brain had been affected.

"I shall be pleased to answer anything you ask — that is if I have the ability," Smeaton said.

"Good. Now, your name is Mark Smeaton. Are you known, or have you ever been known by any other name?"

A crazy question; but he answered it with truth, reluctantly. "A few people call me Marks. They are ill-natured or jealous and it pleases them to pretend that I am a Jew. But my true name is Mark Smeaton."

"And you are the Queen's musician?"

"I am. But that you know, my lord."

From behind him there came the unmistakable sound of a quill at work. He twisted his head and saw the man he had thought a steward writing quickly, finish a word and pause, quill poised.

Cromwell said, "As you shall presently see, this conversation is of more importance than may at first appear. The gist of it is being taken down."

Smeaton was becoming more and more confused. He was accustomed to finding the outer world — the world outside his music and his dreams — a strange and alien place and other people's behaviour unaccountable, but now he felt that he was the one sane person in a world gone crazy. He'd been asked here to dine; he had expected to discuss music.

"Now a moment ago," Cromwell began again, "you used the word 'jealous'. Who is jealous of you? And why?"

Smeaton had watched, always from a distance, a number of petty Court intrigues and jostlings for place. It occurred to him that before Cromwell asked his advice he was, like a cautious man, making certain that he was not involved in anything, such as a quarrel, which might bring difficulties later on. It seemed a round-about, ponderous way of getting at the truth, but then Cromwell was a lawyer and they had their peculiar ways.

"Maybe I exaggerated in using that word, my lord. The fact is that I am a professional musician; many gentlemen about the Court are musicians too, gifted, but amateurs. There is a difference which they are sometimes reluctant to recognise."

"Naturally. And who are these gentlemen?"

He saw no reason not to give their names. Everyone knew. The grubbiest little page after six months at Court could have answered that question.

"Chiefly of the King's household. Sir Harry Norris. Sir Francis Weston, Master William Brereton — and perhaps most of all Her Grace's brother, Lord Rochfort, Sir Thomas Wyatt, too. I often set his words to music and there is the usual dispute as to what makes a good song."

"There is then, some jealousy; and a certain element of competition?"

"Yes. But it does no harm. It . . . it improves the standard of all our work."

"And the aim of it all is to please her Grace?"

"It is indeed!"

"Should I be correct in saying that of them all you please her best?"

"That, my lord, is what gives rise to the dispute. We are all most anxious to please her. And often, yes, often my performance does give her most pleasure. Which is not to be wondered at. I am able to devote my whole time and attention to my music; the others have other duties."

"And you all desire to please her because you love her?"

"That is so."

"You love Her Grace?"

"With all my heart. She has no more devoted servant than I . . ."

Suddenly he had another idea as to where all this might be leading. There was no ignoring the fact that

427

since her miscarriage the Queen had been out of favour, and some people had begun to drift away; there'd been fewer visitors, almost no gifts lately. Did Cromwell think that he, Mark Smeaton, was likely to desert Anne and run after the rising star of Seymour? He, who if she were left with only one friend in all the world, would be that one!

"Does anyone question my loyalty?" he asked, dropping his diffident manner. "Tell me his name, my lord, and I'll throw the lie in his teeth, whoever he is." Cromwell noticed for the first time the size and power of the hands which had guided a plough, the powerful peasant shoulders under the silk tunic.

"Gently," he said, rather as a man might speak to a restive horse. "Your devotion was never in doubt. How does the Queen feel towards you?"

"She approves of my music. She appointed me to be her personal musician."

"Does she love you?" The little question was slipped in with such a casual air that it seemed of no importance at all.

"As much as a Queen can ever love a mere musician."

Cromwell shifted a little in his chair. For a second Smeaton thought that he was preparing to rise, that this odd little inquisition was over. And he had, he felt, established his exact status. Now for dinner and the real business of the day.

But the Chief Secretary had settled again.

"So far, so good," he said. And even into Smeaton's unrealistic mind was borne the impression that up to now they had been merely skirmishing. Now what? The whole room seemed to close in, to grow darker, to wait.

"Now tell me, Smeaton. How much can a Queen love a mere musician?"

This question verged upon that secret, private life; he must be careful.

"She is always gracious and kind."

"Never more than kind?"

"I don't know what you mean by that, my lord?"

"I think you do. You are reputed to be reasonably intelligent. I hasten to assure you that everyone in this room has been chosen for his discretion, so you may speak freely and without embarrassment. I asked — Never more than kind?"

"Never. As you mean it."

"Ah! So you do know what I mean? So that there may be no doubt, I will put the question in another way. Have you and the Queen ever had guilty intercourse?"

"Never! It is unthinkable! Whoever imagined it possible is my enemy — or, or hers!" And what a vile, what a deadly enemy.

"I can understand that you have been about the Court long enough to have acquired some notions of chivalry. One does not betray a lady. I advise you to abandon that notion — it is little more than a myth, anyway. I realise, too, that a man's memory can be faulty. So will you look back and try to remember and bear in mind that to tell the truth cannot harm, and may benefit you. Has the Queen ever committed adultery with you, Smeaton?"

"Never. As I hope for Heaven hereafter. Never."

"Then your memory is at fault." As he spoke Cromwell nodded and the buff-clad men moved forward. Smeaton struggled with them, with the desperate ferocity of a wildcat, but they were two to one, and in a few seconds they had him helpless in the big chair, his arms tied to its arms, his legs to its legs. Then one of them placed a ring of thick knotted cord about his head; an exact fit until a stick was pushed between it and his skull; then it was tight.

And now the whole wicked scheme was plain before his eyes. Well, they had chosen badly. He would never blacken her name, whatever they did to him. He'd die first.

He would have died. Had they taken a sword and threatened to run him through, or held a club ready to dash out his brains he would have died, saying, "No. Never."

"I will repeat the question. Has the Queen ever committed adultery with you?"

"No."

Another nod; the stick was twisted and the cord tightened. The knots bit home, and pain ran, in little pointed spears, down into his eyes, his nose, his ears and the back of his neck.

"Has she?"

"No."

A nod; a twist. He heard the skin split with little explosive sounds under each knot, and the blood began to flow, slow and sticky.

He was big and strong but he had never been able to bear pain, either his own or other people's. And this was more than pain, it was agony.

"Think again; think well," Cromwell said. "You seem to be a stubborn man, but we have other means, should this fail. And all your endurance is wasted. There will be a confession, signed by you, before we have done. And if you confess, fully and freely, you may escape, as being young and not in a position to resist advances. Can you hear me?"

"I can hear," Smeaton groaned out.

"Then confess."

"It never happened."

The pressure increased, became intolerable. He screamed. And then the peak of pain was passed and he began to spin down into darkness. Cromwell's voice followed him, just a senseless noise now, and even that dying away. He was dying, for her.

Then pain again and consciousness rushing back and Cromwell's voice speaking words again.

"There is no escape for you, Smeaton. Except by confession. Would the rack loosen your tongue? I tell you again, there will be a confession, signed by you. If you die it will make no difference."

He could not save her. He might die of torment, after hours and hours of torment, suffering every pain that the inhumanity of man had devised, and at the end it would make no difference. There would be a confession, with his signature, forged.

He said, sobbing,

"What do you want me to say?"

"I want the truth. Are you ready?"

"I'll say what you want."

"Then you are not ready."

The cord tightened again; this time judged to a nicety, so that the pain stayed at the screaming peak and his brain tilted.

"I'll say it. I'll say anything."

"That's better," Cromwell said, and he must have made the sign for the cord to be loosened. "Now begin."

Once he had started it came easily enough, because it was really all part of his dream and therefore had a truth of its own. For almost four years, ever since she had submitted to Henry, he had dreamed of possessing her. He was able to bring out a dozen small corroborative details, the gleanings of watchfulness and of a vivid imagination. She had a mole on her neck, always hidden by a necklace or a collar; her breasts were so small that the hand could cup them; at the moment of climax she . . .

On and on it went until even Cromwell, who had lain on his sick-bed and devised this approach to the final solution of the problem was slightly shaken. Was it possible that fumbling round in the dark he had hit on a hidden truth? The most he had expected had been the admission, extracted under torture, "Yes, I bedded with her." He'd got that, and more. Much more. This did not sound like a grudging admission of guilt, but the real direct-from-the-heart, almost boastful reliving of a love affair, it was all there, even his envy of Norris,

Brereton and Weston and George Boleyn who had been, he said, favoured more than he had been.

Finally he had told all, everything that he had wished were true, everything that he had almost convinced himself was true, because otherwise how could he have lived, loving her as he did and seeing her every day?

"And that is all?"

"Is it not . . . enough?"

"The paper, Edward."

Cromwell ran his eye over it almost perfunctorily. This was not the first interrogation which this particular secretary had reported; he knew exactly what to omit.

"Now, if you will sign."

Smeaton signed. Cromwell regarded the signature with satisfaction. If anyone said "rack", which was what everyone thought of as a means of persuasion, this signature would be a refutal.

"Keep him here," Cromwell said. "Give him anything he wants to eat or drink and wash off the blood. As soon as it is dark enough take him to the Tower. Sir William Kingston has been warned of his coming."

CHAPTER
THIRTY-SEVEN

"Ah! Norris, Norris, my tears begin to run
To think what hap did thee so lead or guide,
By which thou hast both thee and thine undone,
That is bewailed in Court on every side."
Sir Thomas Wyatt

WHITEHALL. MAY 1st, 1536

Henry looked at Cromwell and said,

"If only Norris had not been involved! He's slept in my chamber, been closer than a son. It cuts me to the heart that he, whom I trusted . . ."

"Smeaton's statement was taken down just as he made it, Your Grace."

And why, in God's name, shouldn't the King suffer? Smeaton had suffered this morning, and would suffer more. The others would suffer. And Cromwell in the last three months had suffered more mental distress than most people bore in a lifetime.

First of all he had had the task of breaking to the King the news that one way to free him had been thought out, a way that would free him swiftly and completely, since in a Queen adultery was treason and punishable by death. Henry had instantly dug in his heels and demanded, "Am I to clap the horns on my own head?"

Cromwell had pointed out that it was the only alternative to legal action on the plea of consanguinity which would revive the old scandal of Mary Boleyn, or on the plea of pre-contract, which would rouse echoes of the case against Catherine. No, Henry said, he had abandoned both those ideas last summer, after his talk with the Duke of Norfolk. He'd have no consanguinity, no pre-contract and no cuckolding.

Cromwell, ambitious, self-seeking and cynical, could, if pushed too far, turn like a cornered rat. He had done so then.

"Your Grace, all that you leave open to me is to have her poisoned, or pushed downstairs."

Henry had quite seriously considered that suggestion, and then, rather regretfully, said,

"Difficult to achieve and open to suspicion. God's Head! Is that the best you can do? I tell you I want some means of ridding her that will leave me with the goodwill of my people."

"Her adultery, could we prove it, would do that."

"And bring their mockery, too."

"Not necessarily. The ordinary man whose wife betrays him is mocked because he has been a blind fool. He's been home to supper every evening, he's slept in the same bed with her. He must be a blind and unobservant ass. But Kings have matters to attend to that demand the removal of their minds and eyes from domestic matters. I am positive, your Grace, that if you proceed with this, there will not be a man in the country who will not sympathise with you, nor a woman who will not think that the Queen has taken advantage of her opportunities."

Arguments like that had gone on and on, and Henry, wasting time, had fretted against its wasting. And the sore on his leg had grown worse, and his temper with it. He had demanded the impossible, and finding it unobtainable had thrown hard names, a cushion, a stick and the three-legged stool at his advisors. At one point Cromwell's health had broken down under the strain and he had taken to his bed.

Then, suddenly, Henry had veered around and agreed to proceed against Smeaton. So if, now, he had a little more than he had bargained for, and was cut to the heart, Cromwell was glad.

"I rode with Norris in from Greenwich this afternoon," Henry said in a self-pitying voice. "I begged, I pleaded with him to confess. I'd have forgiven him if he would but have confessed. I know her ways. And there's enough here to condemn her without mentioning his name. You could have blotted it over. But he was stubborn as wood. He had a guilty look though, and I've been thinking. He was long ago betrothed to a Mistress Shelton; he's made no move to get himself married. Now we know why!" He narrowed his eyes and looked hard at his chief minister. "Give me an honest answer. You knew of all this. You suggested a charge of adultery because you knew you were on safe ground. And if you knew, so did others. In God's Name, why didn't you tell me?"

Cromwell felt a tremor in his bones. His flesh stayed solid and steady, but his marrow quivered. Whatever you did, he thought bitterly, was wrong; pitfalls you never dreamed of opened suddenly under your feet.

He knew a moment of envy for his blacksmith father. If a horse were properly shod it put its hoof down and walked away, the owner was satisfied and paid you and that was that. In the world which he had chosen to inhabit no job was ever really done and finished with.

"I do most earnestly assure Your Grace that until this morning I *knew* nothing. What Smeaton revealed in his confession was as great a surprise to me as it is to you. We fixed upon him as a *likely* man. Close to the Queen, and the subject of two casual, quite unrelated remarks which might have meant nothing. He was therefore interrogated . . ."

"Did you rack him?"

"Your Grace. I questioned him in my own house where I keep no implements of torture. And the signature, does that look like the hand of a racked man."

Almost unwillingly, Henry said,

"No. Not that I care about him. He should be torn in pieces! But Norris . . ."

"Naturally I am grieved that anyone for whom you had an affection is implicated. At the same time I feel it my duty to advise you to let things take their course. In a way this is all to the good. The very magnitude of your wrong will divert attention from its nature. This shows her as such a monster of iniquity that no man

437

could possibly have been on guard against her. From our point of view things have worked out well."

"A little too well," Henry said and gave Cromwell a searching look which he met with one of calm and candour. Then, as though seeking some flaw, Henry read the confession again and found, not a flaw but a hateful unpalatable truth. This damned tinkling musician had *enjoyed* her, just as he himself had dreamed of doing and never had. And the others, doubtless, had had equal joy.

"I sent Norris to the Tower. Where is this wretch?"

"On his way there."

"Good. And the others?"

"Arrested or being arrested."

And then, deep inside the bulky body with its ulcerating leg, inside the mind hard-shelled with egoism and corrupted by power, the young Henry Tudor, gay and just and high-hearted stirred once, perhaps for the last time.

"I never wanted this," he said. "What happens to her I do not care, for whatever Norfolk may say I know she did bewitch me; she's wasted the best years of my life. But I meant to pardon the man when he had served his purpose. I meant to pardon him . . ."

CHAPTER
THIRTY-EIGHT

"I was cruelly handled at Greenwich, with the King's Council and my Lord of Norfolk who said 'Tut, tut, tut,' shaking his head three or four times. As for Master Treasurer he was in the Forest of Windsor. Master Controller was a gentleman. But I to be a Queen and to be so cruelly handled was never seen! Master Kingston do you know why I am here?"

Anne's own rambling words on arrival at the Tower

THE TOWER. MAY 2nd, 1536

She took possession of her senses again by a process that was not unlike waking from a light, troubled sleep; but she had not been asleep; she knew that because she was standing upright with her hands clasped before her. She was in her right mind, could see and hear, felt no pain; yet something was wrong, and there was a gap . . .

Slowly she looked about and recognised the room. It was the one she had occupied during her stay in the Tower immediately before her Coronation. Except that now there were no flowers, nothing had changed; even her chair was there, still under the canopy. This side of the gap the Queen's Chamber in the Tower. And on the other? She remembered perfectly; her uncle Norfolk's voice saying, "We have orders to arrest you on a charge of treason; and are taking you to the Tower."

Dinner. Yes, they'd been at dinner. Not a lively meal. On the previous afternoon, at the jousting, the King had suddenly risen, wearing a look of dark displeasure and gone away with out a word: and he had left a feeling of uneasiness behind him. She had lived in a state of apprehension ever since January and all her women had shared her nervous mood. Henry would, she was sure, get rid of her somehow, and anything unusual could make her feel that the moment had struck; and it was unusual for him to leave in the middle of a joust. So she was prepared for something, had long been so prepared. But treason!

When Norfolk said the word she had begun to laugh, the senseless, painful laughter that would come upon her at the most unlikely moments and which she was powerless to control. Her women looked frightened and even her uncle and those with him had drawn away a little. Then Emma had come running with the poppy syrup, a massive dose, and had forced her to drink it, saying, "Your Grace must be calm and bear up." Soon she had stopped laughing and had said to her uncle. "If that be His Majesty's pleasure, I am ready to go." After that she could remember nothing; not even how she had made the journey.

Still, here she was; and not in a dungeon as one would expect. And not alone. There were two women at the far end of the room. She blinked her drug-laden eyes, and then narrowed them, staring and trying to make the women look like Margaret and Emma — the two people most likely to have insisted upon accompanying her; but they weren't the right shape.

She said,

"Who are you?"

One woman said,

"You know very well who I am; What trick are you up to now? I'm your aunt, Elizabeth Boleyn. And I must say that when I married your uncle and took that name little did I dream that the day would come when I should have such cause to be ashamed of it."

"I'm Mrs Cosyns," the other woman said.

"Why are you ashamed?"

"Ashamed to be related to you, even by marriage," her aunt said, with a look of utter loathing. "You heard the charges."

"Treason, they said. But that isn't true. How could I commit treason?"

"I don't know what you hope to gain by pretending to be a half-wit. The two women who came with you said you'd heard the charges."

"Are two of my women here? I'd like to have them with me. You are both excused."

"What you like isn't law any more; you'll have what's ordered. Mrs Cosyns and I are to attend you."

"And it is not," Mrs Cosyns said, "a job I fancy. I can tell you that."

"I shall remember your manner towards me, Mrs Cosyns, when this farce is ended."

"Farce," Elizabeth Boleyn snorted. "Tragedy more like. Tragedy for the decent members of the family."

"You know very well that I have not committed treason. It is an excuse. The King is tired of me and wants to be rid of me. I was willing to go. I would have said so had he given me the chance. There was no need to fabricate a charge against me . . ."

"Fabricate!" Her aunt's voice was almost a scream. "How you can stand there and say such things, when you know . . ."

"I know I never did a traitorous thing, spoke a traitorous word. Apart from that I know nothing. When they came to arrest me I had a hysterical fit and Emma gave me a dose. I may have stood there and appeared to be listening to the charges. I may even have replied, but I remember nothing at all. I'd be obliged to you if you would tell me exactly what I am said to have done."

She moved to the chair under the canopy and sat down, folding her hands in her lap.

"I'm not going to soil my mouth with an account of such evil doings," Lady Boleyn said.

"*I'll* tell you," Mrs Cosyns said, and came forward. She had no particular cause, no personal reason for hating Anne; she was human in shape, had, presumably, been once an innocent-hearted child, but life in some way had warped her, made her coarse-minded, spiteful, unkind. She said, with real relish,

"You're charged with adultery; with five men, your own brother one of them."

"Oh no! Nobody could be so wicked!" She meant that even Henry in his hatred couldn't have stooped to invent such a charge.

"*You* could!" Mrs Cosyns said. "Your pet, Mark Smeaton, made a confession. And he involved all the others."

She said in a thin, faint voice,

"What others?"

"Sir Harry Norris; Sir Francis Weston; William Brereton; and your brother."

"They'll deny it."

"Naturally. But they can't get away from what the Chief Secretary has written down, just as Smeaton said it. And signed."

"Mark went to Cromwell's house yesterday. He was invited for dinner. He did not come home. He was taken, and with no rank to protect him, tortured. On the rack a man will say anything."

The conversation had now reached a point at which Elizabeth Boleyn felt she could take her share.

"The Duke says otherwise. The confession was signed in a hand no racked man could have written."

"Then it was spite," Anne said. "He affected a great devotion to me, and I offended him once. This is his revenge."

She had a passing vision of an impotent, offended girl planning vengeance on a great Cardinal; and it matched exactly with an impotent, offended musician planning vengeance on a Queen.

The two women had been instructed to spy and pry, to listen and report anything, anything at all that might be useful. So Lady Boleyn threw in a brisk question,

"And why, pray, should so petted a lap-dog as Smeaton turn and bite his mistress?"

443

"He was jealous," Anne said, "and just a little mad. And I know why he named those he did. On ordinary days, when they came to my apartment, they kissed my hand; at Christmas, or New Year, or on a birthday, they kissed my cheek. My brother always kissed my cheek and embraced me. One evening . . . Mark came in and played the virginals for me. He played very well and when he had done I put my hand on his shoulder and thanked him. He turned and took my hand and twisted it and kissed my palm. I withdrew it sharply and said, 'You may not do that.' Then he said, 'Mere friends may kiss you, but I who am your slave, may not.' And he began to cry; he cried very easily. I said to him, 'Mark you are not my slave, you are my musician, and I cannot allow you such liberties as are allowed to gentlemen of His Grace's household.' And that hurt him, I could see and was sorry. He was very conscious of his humble birth." She thought how she had been, too, and taken such pains to spare him whenever possible. And this was how he had repaid her. If it was indeed his doing.

She jumped up. "I must refute this charge. But how? If I cut my body open, I could not prove it clean." She put her hands to the top of her bodice and for a moment the two women watching thought that she meant to rip it down and expose the body about which there had been so much fuss — and would be so much more. But she dropped her hands and said again,

"George and the others will deny this preposterous charge."

They must; out of honesty as well as self-interest.

444

There wasn't a man living who could truthfully say that he had sinned with the Queen. She'd taken such meticulous pains during those weeks when she had been set on getting herself with child again. She'd been one of the masked, anonymous dancers; one evening a character from Pope Julius's game; another evening one of three dozen milkmaids; on the third one of forty-three versions of herself. She had hardly spoken, and when she did she had not used her own voice, or the French accent which came so easily to her; she'd sounded rustic, just a girl up from Norfolk or Suffolk, invited to a masked ball at Court and completely dizzied, ready to go the whole way. She had made absolutely sure that no man could look at her next day and think . . .

"Lies won't save them. Nor you either," Mrs Cosyns said. "You'd do better to make a full confession and get ready to die in a state of grace."

"To die?"

"Traitors do," the woman's voice was relentless. She had a purpose; if Anne could be driven to confess it would greatly ease the whole procedure.

She tried to stave off panic by reckoning her resources. Her most powerful relative, her uncle Norfolk, was plainly against her; but surely her father . . . And that thought brought Lady Bo to mind.

"My poor mother," she said. "She will die of sorrow!"

"Your mother has been dead these four and twenty years," Lady Boleyn snapped. "If you mean that Norfolk clod, your stepmother, such people

445

don't die of sorrow. Your blood kin are more likely to die of shame."

"Most of them," Anne said, with a flash of her old spirit, "have too much sense! The charge is false and nobody not poisoned with hatred would believe it for a minute." But the King believed it. He hated her now as much as he had once loved her. And he had the power of life or death.

"All those poor young men," she said.

"Poor indeed; seduced by your wiles, and doomed to die for their foolishness."

Anne stumbled to her chair and sat down again, and thought about death. It came to everyone. With your first breath you began to die and every breath thereafter brought you nearer to the last. But in order to live at all people pushed that thought away, or otherwise life would be just a hopeless waiting. Death happened to other people, and would one day happen to you, but you didn't face that truth; even at the end, the last desperate remedies, the last rattling breaths were all attempts to evade the truth, to stave death off.

Henry would act fast; he was hot for Jane and he'd want his next marriage to be legal beyond all question.

In a short time, a few days perhaps she would be dead. She looked at her hands, felt the terrified fluttering beat of the heart in her breast and imagined the stillness, the chill, the irrevocability of death. And after death, the judgment.

She sat for a long time, looking back over her life as it would appear when she stood before God to give an account of it. At the end she was comforted. God knew everything, the sorry little shifts, the self-seeking, the many faults, the sins: but He would know, too, and could be trusted to understand, that everything would have been different, she herself would have been different, if only they had left her alone and allowed her to marry Harry Percy.

CHAPTER
THIRTY-NINE

"Know that we, the said Abbot and convent . . . for the many benefits conferred upon us by that excellent man Thomas Cromwell Esq., the principal Secretary of our Lord Henry VIII . . . have given and conceded and by these presents do give and concede, to the said Thomas . . . our annual rent or annuity of ten pounds sterling . . . and in our manor of Harlowe and its appurtenances in the county of Essex . . ." Extract from a grant in the *Collectanea Buriensis civitatis*

WESTMINSTER. MAY 10th, 1536

All that could be done to freshen the atmosphere had been done; the windows stood wide and somebody, within the last few minutes, had burned some lavender; but the stench was still so perceptible that Cromwell, who was feeling queasy, stopped upon the threshold of the chamber, took out his handkerchief and applied it to his nose. Then he realised that such an action might have given grave offence, so he contrived a series of small tittering sneezes, snick, snick, snick!

From the bed where he lay, fully dressed save for his hose, Henry asked,

"Have you taken a cold?"

"No, Your Grace. No. It is the hay-fever. A nothing. How are you feeling?"

"Better. But low. Low. They opened my leg and undoubtedly saved my life. I was nearer death this morning, Cromwell, than ever in my life since I fell in that ditch at Hitchin and almost drowned in the mud."

Some ten or twelve days earlier Dr Butts had succeeded in closing the open ulcer: Henry, with joy, had discarded his bandage and presented Dr Butts with the title-deeds of a manor in Ewhurst. But the poison, denied outlet, had turned inwards and combined with mental stress and his determination to go about as much as possible and show himself to his people as the innocent, injured man, had had a frightening result. He'd wakened in the early hours of this morning, deranged, incoherent, shouting for Norris. His new Groom of the Stole had fetched Dr Butts who recognised high fever when he saw it and inspected the leg, horribly swollen and inflamed. He had sent for the barber-surgeon who made the incision; almost instant relief had followed; the King was so much better that later in the evening, bandaged again, he intended to go out, but for the moment he was resting.

He looked unwell; and so did Cromwell. Cromwell was being driven by that thing most unwelcome to lawyers, haste. Evidence took time to collect, it had to be verified, sifted, correlated, and the King refused to allow for these lengthy processes. He would listen to no protests, the whole thing was distasteful to him and he wanted it over and done with. So for the last ten days Cromwell had been in the uncomfortable position of a normally careful-marketing housewife compelled to do her shopping in the last minute. In what evidence he had so far collected there were contradictions and discrepancies which sickened him to think of.

Standing by the bed, feeling far from well himself, he commiserated with his monarch upon his lapse from health and proffered his good wishes.

Henry said,

"Did it ever occur to you, Cromwell, that I might *die?*"

"All men must die, Your Grace, eventually. Of your demise I have certainly never considered since it is unlikely that I shall have the misfortune to survive you. I am six years older."

"But a whole man; which I at this moment am not. I've been thinking. Suppose I died. Suppose I died this morning. Who is my heir? Elizabeth — that witch's get! Is that not so?"

"The Dunstable Court declared your former marriage invalid and the Lady Mary illegitimate; it follows then that the Princess . . ."

"That must not be. Now you listen to me. I'm mortal. The moment this business is over I shall marry again. If she'd died in child-bed, or from any other cause, I'd have made the gesture of a two months' mourning, but no man can be expected to mourn for an adulteress. I shall marry at once. But a child takes nine months to breed and if I should leave Elizabeth as my heir, God knows she would have friends powerful enough to make her claim good. And that wouldn't suit me. Mr Secretary, I want this marriage wiped out, made as though it had never been."

Cromwell knew that when Henry addressed him as Mr Secretary there was no escape.

"But Your Grace, on what grounds? It was a legal marriage; the Dunstable Court . . ."

"Damn the Dunstable Court. I can't tell you what grounds. I can tell you the means. She'll be tried and she'll be condemned. The sentence is burning or beheadal, according to my pleasure. Give her a little time to think over what burning means, and then offer her the merciful alternative, one clean stroke of the sword of a skilled headsman brought over from Calais, in return for her admission that she was never my wife. She can plead a pre-contract or any other obstacle she cares to name. Anything so long as our marriage is declared invalid and the way to the throne left clear for my next child, even supposing *that* to be another girl. You understand me?"

Cromwell pondered. Then, pressing his finger-tips together he said,

"That, Your Grace, brings up an interesting point. If she were never your wife she cannot be an adulteress, nor a traitor. At worst she's guilty of fornication, which is not a capital offence."

Henry said,

"By God's Holy Name, you are a shrewd fellow!" And having said that he had a feeling of horror, as though he had suddenly found himself on the very verge of a steep cliff. *He'd* always been the one with the keen mind, the quick perception. That had been his one advantage over Wolsey's subtler brain; on hundreds of official documents his scribbled, pithy comments testified to his ability to see into the very heart of things at a glance. And he'd missed this. Worry and illness between them were destroying his mind.

"What small wit I have is always at Your Grace's service," Cromwell said, flattered by the compliment. "And the point, though interesting, is not of importance. As Queen she will be tried, as Queen she will be condemned. Afterwards, in a private session with some reliable authority, she admits a pre-contract. It may well be that one or two of these street-corner lawyers in which London abounds may fasten upon the point which we have recognised," he tactfully gave Henry more than his due. "But there remains the charge of incest; that is a thing from which the mind of the ordinary man shrinks. It runs counter to every decent instinct. The rabble-rousers, even if they fasten on the *No Queen, no adultery* cry, as they might well do, would stop short at siding with an . . . Your Grace, I think there is no name for it . . . a partner in an incestuous relationship. If only," he said a little plaintively, "that can be proved. What little evidence I have been able to collect in so short a time has no bearing on that aspect at all."

"Have you tried his wife?"

"No, Your Grace. Surely the wife would be the last person . . ."

"Ah," Henry said. And he felt as though, playing tennis, he had missed one ball — the point about no Queen, no adultery — but was now given the chance of slamming one home. "Lady Rochfort, if I remember rightly, was one of those ardent supporters of the late Princess Dowager, who, when the French emissaries insisted upon visiting the Lady Mary, stood in the streets and cheered. It sent a whole gaggle of them to the Tower. She certainly has no fondness for her husband's sister. She may be the last one to know, but she'll be the first one to squawk, if you handle her rightly. And I'll tell you how to handle her. Tell her the Tower is still there and that there are within it several less comfortable apartments than the one she occupied on her last visit. Then ask her a few questions; the answers may be . . . enlightening."

"I will do that immediately, Your Grace."

He could have withdrawn then. He'd got his orders. Run away little errand boy and do your master's will. Handle filth, outwit the law, forestall any fair-minded Londoner who might stand up and say in the voice which, off and on had rung through England for a thousand years, "Look 'ere, this ain't fair!" Yes, he was prepared to do this. It paid him to please the King.

But now and then little boys, hardly borne down upon by their master, will place a tack, point upward on his chair.

Cromwell, hard borne down upon, hating his master, had a little tack ready.

He said,

"With the trial so soon upon us, and much evidence still to gather, I am likely to be much occupied, Your Grace, until the end of the month. So I wonder . . . Do you feel well enough to consider another matter?"

453

"I told you," Henry said, "I feel better. What is this other matter?"

"The dissolution of certain of the larger religious houses. All the subjects of very unfavourable reports from the commissioners. Setting other considerations aside, Your Grace's exchequer could well do with their revenues."

The argument there was as nice an adjustment as the knotted rope around Smeaton's head.

Henry hated the dissolution of the religious houses; it smacked of Lutheranism; yet to leave them alone in the state in which some of them were, was to encourage precisely the kind of scandal that bred Lutheranism. They were also, and this must never be overlooked, places where loyalty to the Papacy still flourished. And, as Cromwell said, the money was extremely useful.

Still, so far, he had dissolved only a few, the smallest, the uneconomic units, or those with the most scandalous reputation, and he'd dealt fairly, kindly even, with such of the monks and nuns as had been willing to acknowledge him as Head of the Church; they'd been given generous pensions, or, if qualified, installed in secular livings, one or two were now bishops.

"I have a list here," Cromwell said, drawing a roll from inside his robe. "Most of the incomes stated could, I think be multiplied twice, or even three times. They most consistently underestimate their revenues." He unrolled a list and held it towards the King who knocked it aside with a sweep of his hand.

454

"Five doddering old men or women in a crumbling house, a lame horse and four sheep with foot rot! Am I to be bothered with such nonsense now. Do as you like about them!"

"The houses such as Your Grace so exactly describes have all been done away with," Cromwell pointed out. "These are larger, and rich . . ."

"I said do as you like. Does hay-fever make you hard of hearing?"

The tack had been well placed, and the prick administered. Cromwell retrieved the list, rolled and replaced it.

"I shall set to work on Lady Rochfort immediately," he said. "I trust that Your Grace's health continues to improve."

Outside the room Cromwell breathed deeply of the uncontaminated air. And he deliberately removed his mind from all thought of the Queen and her coming trial and all the nasty business in connection with it. On the list in his breast there was the name of one enormously wealthy Abbey, the Benedictine house at Bury St Edmunds. Abbot Reeve who ruled it, had just offered Cromwell a gift of ten pounds a year and a fine house at Harlow. He was trying to buy immunity for himself and his Abbey.

I've just been told to do as I like. Cromwell reflected; I shall take the bribe, and give Abbot Reeve a respite, two or three years for being so obliging. The word will spread; others will follow his example. And God knows I need some reward for all the dirty work I am required to do.

CHAPTER
FORTY

"The Earl of Northumberland, Anne's first lover, was named on the commission for her trial."
Agnes Strickland. *Lives of the Queens of England*

"Another curious fact emerges concerning Cromwell's activities . . . On May 13th he sent to the Earl of Northumberland, then residing at Newington Green, Sir Reynold Carnaby, who was known as a friend of his, to try to extract from him an admission that Anne had been pre-contracted to him."
Philip Sergeant. *The Life of Anne Boleyn*

NEWINGTON GREEN. MAY 13th, 1536

Harry Percy, Earl of Northumberland, was having one of his bad days. Of late they had come more frequently, sometimes three or four of them in succession. At such times he was unable to eat without nausea and the pain in his body, ordinarily a dull gnawing, became so sharp that nothing but pride prevented him from crying out.

Nobody knew what ailed him. He had suffered many things at the hands of various doctors; he had consulted wise women, especially in the North country where doctors were rare, and drunk their mixtures, tried their ointments, applied their plasters. Nothing eased him, and that, he perversely chose to believe, proved that there was nothing much the matter with him. Fussing about made the thing seem important; and there was nothing important about a belly-ache.

On this particular day, however, he was behaving like a sick man; yesterday he had sent for his doctor, and today rising at noon, he had not bothered to dress. Wrapped in a robe he sat in a chair by the window, just above a little knot garden whose colours shone in the sunshine; he had his feet on a stool and a folded rug over his thin knees.

He was husbanding his strength; he must be well by Monday.

On the previous day he had received the information that he had been one of the twenty-six peers chosen to act as "lord triers" in the trial of the Queen.

He was only thirty-three, but women no longer meant anything to him — a fact which, had he examined it frankly, might have hinted to him that he was more seriously ill than he chose to admit. He could not have been said, with any truth, to be in love with Anne any longer; there was too great a gulf between the girl who had kissed him in the Greenwich garden and the woman who had married Henry Tudor. But the girl still lived in his heart; he felt sentimental about her and the news that she was to stand trial for her life had been a sickening shock. He was sure that the charge was a rigged one. At sixteen she had been prudish, when by being not-prudish she had nothing to lose and much to gain; and a girl like that didn't suddenly turn madly

457

wanton at twenty-nine, when she was in a position where wantonness could gain her nothing and could lead to certain disaster.

As soon as he had received the message and absorbed its meaning he had begun to feel ill. He had noticed in the past that his worst attacks often followed upon a fit of anger or any kind of excitement. He had felt vilely ill when he had gone to arrest Wolsey. On this occasion he almost welcomed the pain and the nausea. I'm a sick man, he thought. I can't go and sit through a trial. There are fifty-three peers in England, let them choose another.

So he had sent for his doctor, who had clystered him, and he had fully intended to stay in his bed and to write a letter, in shaky, infirm hand, pleading disability.

He'd slept very little until it was almost dawn. The window was pale, and the birds were beginning to make tentative little calls. Then he fell asleep and dreamed that he was riding in a wild and desolate place in his native Northumberland; riding his favourite sorrel horse. Suddenly the fog had come down. He thought, I'm a long way from home still, but no matter. Rufus can pick his way. He'd let the rein go slack and the horse, as though responding to this gesture of trust, trotted briskly and confidently into the murk. And then it had stopped, so abruptly that he had jerked forward. Some obstacle in the road, he thought; and speaking soothingly, he had leaned forward and tried to peer ahead. And there she was. Anne, just as she had been years ago except that above the black waterfall of hair she wore the ruby coronet in which she had gone to her

Coronation. She looked at him and held out her hands, appealingly. He thought — She's lost in this fog; how lucky we came along. He leaned and reached for her hands to lift her, but a swirling cloud of fog came between them. He cried, "Anne!" And woke.

The window was yellow with sunlight and all the birds were shouting.

He lay there and thought — There will be twenty-six lords there and some must be honest. The King has made himself greatly feared, but even he could not contemplate a mass beheadal of half the peers in England.

He thought — She isn't guilty. If they'd named *one* man I could have believed that after all these years she had found another love; she never loved Henry, of that I am sure. But she might, perhaps, have found one love. Not five, one her own brother, and one her musician, once a ploughboy. That is ridiculous. And whoever framed this charge knew nothing about her, nothing at all.

He thought — She was always quick-witted and words came to her easily. She could confound the witnesses, hostile, bribed, scared, that they'll bring against her.

He thought — All the lord triers are men; she'll charm them.

He thought — I must be there, to give my vote in her favour and to give a lead to the waverers.

So he must be well by Monday.

Bent on getting well, full of buttermilk which he detested but which seemed the only thing his disordered stomach would tolerate, he was sitting in the reclining position his doctor advised, breathing the fresh air from the open window when his friend Sir Reynold Carnaby arrived.

It was three months since they had last met and the Earl was furious to be caught in this invalid guise.

"A trifling indisposition," he said. "I over-ate and am paying for it. But it gives me great pleasure to see you. Sit down. What happy chance brought you this way?"

"An old cousin of mine, a woman, somewhat infirm, lives nearby, and I visit her from time to time and try to order her affairs. She was at odds with her cowman. Having settled that I thought I might look in on you and beg a proper meal. Old women, I find, fall into two sorts, those who delight in food, those who despise it. My cousin, alas, is one of the latter kind. My dinner this day was a soused herring, a small one, a slice of black bread, a month old, and a glass of home-made wine that tasted like horse-piddle."

"You recognised the taste?"

Well, Carnaby thought, thank God Percy could still crack one of his unsmiling jokes. His friend's appearance had been a shock to him; the eyes fallen back into dark hollows, the skin stretched so tight over the face bones that the skull seemed to be about to break through.

"You shall have a meal," the Earl said, and rang his bell. "My cooks *cook* whether I eat or not. You shall have a good, if belated dinner, I only wish I could join you; but I must get the better of this attack by tomorrow, so that I can take my place on Monday."

"Oh, have you been chosen?" He thought of the question which he had been sent here to ask. ("You're a friend of the Earl's," Fitzwilliam, one of the commissioners, had said, "and he's more likely to speak frankly to you than to anyone sent expressly for the purpose of asking." Carnaby, no fool; had asked some apparently artless questions designed to discover why the inquiry was being made at all. Fitzwilliam had said that the answer might have some bearing on the procedure, and added that Carnaby need not worry; whatever the answer, the Earl would not be affected. The commissioners merely wanted to know what truth there was in the rumour. "Put the question as casually as you can," he said.)

Now he waited till the table was set up and several choice dishes set before him. Then he said, casually,

"I suppose you know that among the rumours this affair has revived is one which holds that you and the Queen were once betrothed. Is it true?"

"No. It's a tale my wife invented when she had a notion to divorce me. She and her damned father put their heads together and thought of getting rid of me on a plea of pre-contract. I denied it, naturally."

"Why?" Carnaby's voice held nothing but friendly interest. "It would have made you a free man."

"It happened not to be true," the Earl said. "We never were betrothed. How could we be? Mary and I were pledged from childhood. And I saw no reason to tell a lie in order to let Mary have her headstrong way. Would you?"

"I might have, in your place. I'm afraid I should have thought a lie a small price to pay for freedom. You could have married again."

"I'd had my bellyful of marriage by that time. And frankly, given the choice between the truth and a lie I choose the truth, which is why I never made much success at Court. I claim no credit for it," he said, looking at Carnaby who was young and ambitious and had his way to make, and possibly many lies to tell in the process, "it's as personal a foible as a taste for oysters."

Carnaby was convinced; he could go back and tell Fitzwilliam confidently that there was no truth in the rumour. But his own interest was aroused; and having cut himself a slice of brawn and peppered it, he said,

"You knew her well?"

"The Queen? Yes, thirteen years ago. She came from France and joined Catherine's ladies. I was attached to the Cardinal's household. Comings and goings to and fro. You know how it is."

"What was she like, then?"

"Oh, it's hard to say. Young. Gay. And she never had any money. Her father — well, you know him, avaricious and mean, he never could realise that a girl at Court needed clothes. So she used to contrive things; she could do marvels with a yard of ribbon . . . and never sorry for herself about it; she'd laugh, particularly when other women copied her tricks."

He had never spoken about her in that way to anyone and was astounded at himself. Carnaby listening thought — You may not have been betrothed to her, but you were in love. And hearing of her plight made you

462

ill. How horrible it must be to be chosen to sit in judgment, in such a case, when the accused was someone you have loved. And when only one verdict was possible . . .

He was tactful; he finished his meal, expressed his thanks, sat for ten minutes giving a vivacious account of his old cousin's dispute with her cowman, and then rose and said he must be getting back. Then, as he took his leave he said,

"If I were you I'd excuse myself from the trial. A . . . a bilious attack lasts three days, the place will be crowded and very hot. I'll carry a message for you and explain. It'd be no trouble at all."

"That's kindly. But I shall be well. And I shall be there."

When he was alone again he sat by the window, thinking of this and that, and among other things about courage. Once, not so long ago, either, it had been a very simple thing. A matter of risking hurt to your body. You dealt blows and accepted them. Now that kind of courage was not enough; you had to face disapproval, possible disgrace, obloquy. Knights rode into the lists proudly displaying their chosen lady's favour, a glove, a sleeve, a flower. He faced a combat of a different kind. On Monday he would give proof of his belief in Anne's innocence. When he had said, "I shall be there," he had spoken as the heir to a long line of fighting Percies, formidable men, each in his generation.

I shall be there, he thought, and mentally he girded himself for battle.

CHAPTER
FORTY-ONE

"Either there was evidence for these things, or there was none. If there was evidence, it must have been close, elaborate and minute; if there was none, these judges, these juries and noblemen, were the accomplices of the King in a murder perhaps the most revolting that was ever committed."
Froude. *Henry VIII*

"I could not observe anything in the proceedings against her, but that they were resolved to make an occasion to get rid of her."
The Lord Mayor of London, who was present at the trial.

THE TOWER. MAY 15th, 1536

Carnaby had been right about the heat. As the Earl of Northumberland reached the entrance of the room in the Tower which had been converted into a courtroom, a wave of warmth and the smell of close-packed bodies rolled forward to meet him and his feeling of nausea quickened. Still, he was reasonably certain that he could not actually vomit; for finding the attack persistent, he had subsisted all Saturday on buttermilk, attempted to eat on Sunday morning, sickened, and

464

since then had taken nothing except tiny sips of well-watered wine. Abstinence seemed to have increased the pain rather than lessened it and he felt more ill than he had ever felt before.

He was worried, too, for in the room where the lords had assembled he had had an opportunity of learning the temper of the peers who constituted what was, after all, a jury, and who should have come together this morning with unprejudiced minds. There wasn't one — or at least there wasn't one who spoke in his hearing — who didn't seem convinced of the Queen's guilt. No, that was not quite true; not one who didn't seem convinced of the necessity of a conviction; and from recognising that need to being convinced of her guilt was only a short step. And the Duke of Suffolk had struck an alarming note when he had said brutally, "The adultery is only part of it, as you will shortly hear. There was a conspiracy against the King's life, and talk that would amount to treason even had she been locked into a chastity girdle."

Northumberland had tried to stand, to move about among the rest, but weakness had compelled him, after a few minutes to take a seat in the window, and watching from there he had gained an impression that the Duke of Suffolk — and the Duke of Norfolk, too — had concentrated their attention upon such of the lords as might possibly be open-minded, those who as a rule took little part in affairs, were not often at Court and might not be fully informed of the King's wishes. Some of Suffolk's approaches were not unsubtle. To Northumberland for instance he had said, "I am glad to

465

see you sufficiently recovered to attend. It must have cost you an effort. His Grace will be appreciative. At such a moment every sign of loyalty is comforting to him." He had added, "It should not take long. From what I hear the evidence is overwhelming."

Only a village idiot could have failed to hear the message; it rang as clear as a crier's bell — Unless you vote her guilty you too are a traitor.

And traitors died horrifying deaths. That was a thought fresh in everyone's mind, for only three days previously Norris, Weston, Brereton and Smeaton had been condemned to be hanged, drawn and quartered. Smeaton had already confessed; the others had been offered a free pardon if they would do so. Their confessions could then have been used as evidence against Anne. They had all refused. Brave men. Could he match them? Distress of mind seemed, as it often did, to incease the pain in his body. When he stood up to take his place in the shuffling line entering the hail he found himself unable to stand erect. He felt as though a great needle threaded with red-hot cord were stitching his ribs to his hip-bones. He was obliged to walk bent over, like an old man. He was aware of attracting glances of curiosity and sympathy, and Lord Oxford immediately behind him murmured,

"This won't be long drawn out."

There was something sinister in this general belief that the verdict was a foregone conclusion and that the trial would be brisk. How could they know? Was there to be no defence?

466

* * *

The King, or his advisors, had decided to give the trial an open-and-above-board look by admitting some members of the public. They were much the same as those who had been present at the Cardinals' Court at Blackfriars; the Lord Mayor of London, some representatives of the City Companies and a crowd of ordinary citizens, many of whom, just three years earlier, had stood and watched Anne go in beauty and in triumph to her Coronation.

The Duke of Norfolk, appointed Chief Steward for the trial, took his seat on the chair under the canopy; the other lords moved to their appropriate places and a tense hush fell.

He had intended to watch her arrival, to judge in that moment when she was first confronted with the Court, whether her demeanour showed any sign of guilt or not, though, and he admitted it to himself, he had no notion of what he would look for. If she were guilty of such terrible things, she must be brazen and capable of out-facing her judges; and the most innocent creature on earth, accused of such crimes, might well blench and shrink. Yet he had an obscure feeling that he would know; some chord, long untouched, would wake and respond, and he would know. But at the very moment a wave of nausea hit him and everything wavered and shook before his eyes. He thought — I am about to die! And waited, limp, resigned, for the cloud to thicken. But it cleared, and presently he saw her, standing on the platform, well in front of those who had escorted and attended her. She was curtsying towards Norfolk, towards her peers, and then towards the citizens. She looked ill, worn, haggard, haunted, but calm, and extremely dignified. He had a sharp, sudden mental vision of her as she had been, so young and pretty and gay. Another person altogether. Then he looked down and saw his own yellowish, claw like hands tense on the sharp ridges of his knees. He, too, was a different person. And he thought — Is this life which promises so much and gives so little, and handles us all so roughly, worth clinging to? I'm willing to die.

But not as a traitor.

Then he found himself listening to the arraignment, read out in the dispassionate, official voice. It was horrible, as he had known it would be. It was so horrible that no man present could feel anything save disgust and shock and revulsion. But when, at its end, Anne raised her hand and said in a clear, firm voice, "Not guilty," and sat down, the Earl of Northumberland knew that the moment of revelation which he had missed earlier had come. As he had felt, from the first, she was innocent. However brazen, no guilty woman could possibly have listened to that arraignment and preserved that remote look, as though what was being said concerned some other person.

What was terrible was to think that there could be, in England, a mind depraved enough to concoct such charges, and at the same time so careless.

One woman stood up and testified that the Queen had misconducted herself with Sir Harry Norris in the first week of October in the year 1533, just a month after the birth of the Princess Elizabeth. How many people, people within this hall must remember that after the birth of her daughter the Queen had been afflicted by one of the child-bed ills, white-leg as it was called? It was not so dreaded or so fatal as child-bed fever, but it would be a powerful deterrent to adultery.

Had that thought struck any other of the peers? Covertly, the Earl looked about; there were faces that looked sickened, faces that showed disgust, a few — most horrible of all — which betrayed the fact that these salacious details had roused a vicarious excitement. Nowhere could he see what he sought, the dispassionate, judicial, *weighing* expression which bespoke the open mind and the desire to return a just verdict.

A garrulous, incoherent old woman offered as her contribution the fact that the Queen had invited Sir Francis Weston to violate her — and *that* word had obviously been put into her mouth — on Holy Innocent's day of this very year, 1536. The Queen was then carrying the Prince of whom she had miscarried. Would any woman in that condition have wished, have dared? Would Weston, handsome, young, happily married, have desired . . ."

And the evidence concerning George was not only obscene, it was ridiculous, dealing with one detail which no one could possibly have known, even if the incestuous act had been committed under some close-watching eye.

But there was no comfort to be gained from the obvious falsity of so much of the evidence; it announced too loudly and clearly that the King and his friends were determined upon her death, and so sure of obtaining a verdict of guilty that they could afford to dispense with logic, reason, likelihood.

And time was running out. She would soon be called upon to speak in her own defence, and then, one by one the peers would give their verdict, beginning with the lowest in rank. And since, muddled in with the evidence of the various adulterous acts there were accusations of conspiring to bring about the King's death, and of saying that when he was dead she intended to marry each of her paramours, and of declaring that she had never loved the King, and that he was impotent, it was plain that what Suffolk had said in the ante-room was true. She was accused of treason and anyone who supported her risked sharing her fate. Dare he, who had once loved her, who had always remembered her kindly and often with longing, stand up and say "Not guilty"?

At the thought he burst out into a profuse perspiration, so hot, so unstaunchable that his immediate neighbours, the Earl of Arundel on his right, the Earl of Oxford on his left, stirred and drew away from him as far as they were able, thinking of the Sweating Sickness. Harry Percy thought of it, too, and wished that he were smitten, wished that he could be one of those who fell into coma and died quickly. He sat there, willing himself to die before the moment of decision came. But although his heart raced and his ears roared and his sight was blurred and the drenched satin of his doublet gave off an acrid, charnel stink, he was still conscious enough to hear some of what she said when it was her turn to speak.

As he had expected, she spoke well: her voice, though low-pitched and soft, carried clearly. She had missed no flaw in the evidence; nor had she missed, poor woman, the weight of the forces ranged against her. Yet every now and then the old wit flashed.

"My lords, I stand before you accused of such crimes as surely never were brought against any one woman before. I cannot claim to be without fault, or sin — being but human; but I do declare myself, before Almighty God, to be innocent of *the crimes set out in the arraignment* . . . Adultery is, of its very nature, a difficult charge to refute; a murderer might call a witness to say that he was elsewhere at the time of the crime; a thief might say, 'Search me and see if I have stolen goods about me.' These things I cannot say; but this I do. I am Queen of England, well aware of the penalty that awaits those who cuckold Kings. To have behaved as some who have stood here today and said that I behaved, I must have been lunatic, and that, surely, would have been noticed earlier, and in some other respect . . . On one date mentioned as a day of sinful indulgence, I was abed and in a state to provoke no emotion in any man save revulsion, or, had he a kind heart, pity: on another I was with child. Women at such times are careful, and I assure you, that since it was my great hope to present you with a living Prince, I was more careful than most. Something that Lady Wingfield said to my discredit was mentioned. My lords, Lady Wingfield has been dead and gone to her account these many years; whatever she said is hearsay, and by English law hearsay is not evidence. I mention these things because they are samples of the evidence brought against me, and reasonable men, if there are flaws in a sample of cloth, suspect the whole roll and scrutinise it with especial care . . . I am not asking you for mercy, mercy is for the condemned. For justice I do beg, that being the prerogative of the King's most humble subject."

Once during her speech, when his sight cleared a little, the Earl of Northumberland found himself looking at the ordinary people in the body of the hall. They were with her; their faces showed their feelings. Briefly he envied them, these solid simple citizens who could reach their own conclusions and go home to their families and voice their views.

The faces of the peers wore the stony, stubborn look of those compelled, against their will, to listen to words which might, given any thought or attention, undermine their preconceived decision; here and there an uneasy look, an eyelid flickering, a twitch in the cheek, but on the whole a look of rebuttal tinged with boredom. No hope, he thought. No hope at all.

Traitors died horrible deaths. You were strung up, half choked, taken down while still conscious, your heart and entrails were cut out, then you were cleft into pieces.

Now they were getting to their feet; he tried but he couldn't stand. He had the absurd thought — If I can't stand, I can't vote. But Arundel took one elbow, Oxford the other and heaved him up. The stitches that knit his ribs to hips screamed and broke. Near swooning with pain he hung there and heard the voices.

"Lord John Mordaunt?"

"Guilty."

"Lord Thomas Burgh?"

"Guilty."

On and up; Wentworth, Wyndsore, Sanders, Clynton. He thought of Norris and Weston and Brereton, condemned to torture before death, and offered free pardons if they would confess. God strengthen me, give me courage! He thought desperately of the long line of brave men whose name he bore; he thought of his dream . . .

"Henry, Earl of Northumberland?"

He mumbled,

"I can't, I can't," and sagged like an empty sack between the two supporting arms.

"How say you?" the inexorable voice demanded.

The Earl of Oxford jerked him by the arm and said, "Speak up, man!" And then, when no answer was forthcoming, gave it himself.

"Guilty."

Then Arundel answered, and Exeter, and the Duke of Suffolk; and it was over. They hauled him into the ante-room and laid him by an open window.

So he was spared the ordeal of hearing Anne declared guilty and being sentenced to be burned or beheaded as the King willed. He did not see her stripped of every sign of royalty, not hear her last speech which included the stinging sentence —

"I am willing to believe that you have sufficient reasons for what you have done, but they must be other than those which have been produced in Court, for I am clear of all the offences which you then laid to my charge."

But he heard, because the peers grumbled about it, what one simple brave man, the Lord Mayor of London, had said, "I could not observe anything in the proceedings against her, but that they were resolved to make an occasion to get rid of her."

For the month or so of wretched life that remained to him, he was haunted by those words and by the knowledge that he, of all men, should have been the one to say them.

CHAPTER
FORTY-TWO

"If the reports of the Queen be true, they are only to her dishonour, not yours. I am clean amazed, for I never had better opinion of woman; but I think Your Highness would not have gone so far if she had not been culpable . . . I loved her not a little for the love which I judged her to bear towards God and the Gospel"
Archbishop Cranmer in a letter to Henry VIII

"On the 17th of May, she received a summons to appear, on the salvation of her soul, in the Archbishop's court at Lambeth, to answer certain questions as to the validity of her marriage with the King . . . her proctors . . . in her name, admitted the pre-contract with Percy, and every other objection that was urged by the King . . ."
Agnes Strickland. *Lives of the Queens of England*

LAMBETH. MAY 17th, 1536

Even on this warm evening the little low crypt in the Archbishop's house struck chill and damp. Cranmer, the Duke of Suffolk, Lord Oxford and Sir Thomas Audley were already there when Anne, accompanied by

Margaret Lee, Sir William and Lady Kingston and three guards arrived.

Margaret had stopped crying when Lady Kingston had come in to announce that Anne was to be conducted to Lambeth for an interview with the Archbishop. "Oh," she had said, "that can mean nothing but good. What is it about, Lady Kingston?"

"That we must wait to know," Lady Kingston said. Her manner was calm and impartial. Since the trial Anne had seen less of her aunt Elizabeth and the hateful Mrs Cosyns, more of Margaret and Lady Kingston, and actually she preferred the latter's company. Margaret was so deeply distressed, so unable to control her tears.

"I think I know what Cranmer, somewhere in the conversation will ask of me," Anne said. "A confession."

"Then make one," Margaret cried eagerly. "There'll be a . . . a bribe attached to it. They offered George and . . . and the others a free pardon if they would confess. They must offer you as much."

"They died, four men, this morning, protesting their innocence to the end. Am I to turn about now and say that they were guilty?"

"Nothing can hurt them now. Say anything, anything at all that would save you; please, Anne, I beg . . ."

Anne, not too steadily calm herself, looked at Lady Kingston who said quickly,

"Lady Lee, if you are to accompany us, it would be as well if you made ready. Sir William and the guard will be waiting."

Margaret hurried away and the dreadful, hysterical atmosphere of the room lifted a little. Anne's own behaviour was varied and unpredictable, Lady Kingston thought, but she did at least have periods of apparent resignation. Poor Lady Lee just could not accept the inevitable and many of Anne's worst outbreaks were the result of her cousin's behaviour.

"I shouldn't have mentioned making a confession in front of her,' Anne said. "I should have known how she would take it. And if that is what the Archbishop wants, how can I comply? I am innocent of all the charges they named, Lady Kingston. I am innocent."

"It may be something altogether different," Lady Kingston said, avoiding the issue in her practised way. She looked Anne over, marvelling once more at her ability to remain not merely neat, but elegant. "You look fit to appear anywhere."

Margaret had then returned, having hastily splashed her swollen face with cold water and brushed back her hair.

"I am sure this means something good," she said. "I was always certain that the King would never . . ."

"I think we should go," Lady Kingston said.

So here they were, and Cranmer came forward to meet them, nervously rubbing his hands together, as though washing them. He greeted them gravely and then said,

"I have something to say that is for Lady Pembroke's ear alone; so I must ask you to leave us together. If you wish, Sir William, you may examine this room and assure yourself that there is no other exit."

Perfunctorily, Sir William examined the place. He had never suspected that this excursion was a trick to help the prisoner to escape. He could guess its purpose. Cranmer had been given the job of trying to extract a confession; for the truth was that since the trial nobody had been quite easy. The perverse London populace who had accepted Anne so reluctantly, had, the moment she was condemned, turned about and espoused her cause; the amateur street lawyers had fastened on three points. One piece of evidence brought against her had rested upon the word of a Lady Wingfield, dead for some years, and "that ain't evidence. Anybody can put what words they like into a dead woman's mouth. Hearsay ain't evidence." Then there'd been two specific dates for misconduct which the sharp-witted London women made mock of. "October that year she was still a-laying in with the white-leg; whoever said that didn't know much about white-leg nor adultery." And they said, "January this year, when she was five months gone! Tell that to somebody that never had a big belly. The last thing you think of such times . . ."

And if the evidence could be so obviously contrived in three places, how much of the rest could you believe?

That was the talk in the London streets, and Sir William, aware of it, had no difficulty in guessing what Cranmer had been ordered to procure by some means or another.

Inside the little crypt Cranmer said,

"Please be seated, my lady." He waited until she was seated and then sat down himself. "I wish you to

478

believe that what I am about to say is said from a most earnest desire to spare you pain."

That was simple truth. The idea of anybody being burned appalled him. They could say what they liked about the smoke deadening the senses before the fire reached the living flesh; that was all a matter of chance, what the fire was made of, which way the wind blew. No matter how heinous the crime, burning alive was a punishment out of all proportion . . . who ever it was. And with this woman he was involved. He owed her so much. If the King had not been determined to marry her, where would Cranmer have been? Not here, not Archbishop of Canterbury.

Anne looked at him, and thought of Catherine. In her cold, calm moments — this was one of them — she thought often of Catherine. Catherine had had a chaplain, a Thomas Abell who had gone to the block for his loyalty to her. Cranmer, once her own chaplain, was so much a King's man that he had not uttered a word of protest at the way she had been treated, and sat here now, plainly about to divulge some distasteful little scheme . . .

"I wish," Cranmer said, "I wish with my whole heart that none of this had ever happened. I was incredulous. When I first heard of the business I wrote to the King. I said 'I am clean amazed, for I never had a better opinion of a woman.' I wrote that, my lady."

"But since, you have altered your opinion."

He washed his hands violently.

"I am not a lawyer; I cannot judge. You were tried by your peers, my lady, and they condemned you . . ." He looked at her and imagined to *what* they had condemned her; that living flesh, that hair, those eyes . . . Oh God, help me to help her to avoid such a fate. "You must listen," he said urgently "You must listen to me and agree. His Grace demands it and only he can spare you now."

"If it is a confession you ask of me . . . my lord, I cannot make it. I never did commit adultery with any of the men named. When I think of burning . . ." She clasped her hands together against her breast. "I try not to think of it, but it's there. All the time. They say that the smoke chokes you before . . . but . . ." She gave a great convulsive shudder.

Cranmer leaned forward and took one of her wrists, circling it between his finger and thumb.

"I'm not asking a confession," he said quickly. "Oh no. It is easier than that. The King says that you shall have a quick, easy death if you will agree that you were never his lawful wife. A specially skilled headsman, brought over from Calais . . ."

What a nightmare situation; to sit here and offer a healthy young woman, once his friend, his patron, the choice of two forms of death, both horrible.

"I should prefer the block to the faggot. Anybody would."

"Anybody would," Cranmer echoed; and his flesh shuddered too, as though, from a distance of twenty years, it had felt the lick of the flames that were to consume it.

"But you, at the Dunstable Court, ruled our marriage good and valid. And to deny that now will make my child a bastard."

"That will be done, I fear, with or without your consent. His Grace has set his mind upon that."

Pliable as he was, he had a feeling of dismay as he contemplated the manner of man whom he must serve or face ruin.

"Then I will agree. On what grounds?"

"Pre-contract."

"So I was never married!"

"That is the argument."

She jumped up and began to walk the little room. "But that I fear the fire, I would *never* agree. The Concubine. That is what the Spanish Ambassador always called me. The Concubine did this and said the other. I always hated it; but I could laugh then, knowing it untrue. All those years and years of waiting. This makes mock of them." She stood still, struck by a thought; for five months she had deserved the name; and now it would be hers forever. And she had committed adultery, so secretly that the sin was known only to God. Yet she would be remembered as an adulteress, too. She swung round on Cranmer and said, "God is said to be a stern yet merciful judge, my lord. I only pray that His mercy matches His sternness!"

"His mercy is infinite," Cranmer said. And it had need be, with men so sinful. His own conscience was far from easy.

Anne resumed her pacing.

"And how do we go about this making void of a marriage?"

"A mere formality. Those gentlemen who were here with me will constitute a Court. Dr Sampson will stand proctor for the King, Dr Barbour and Dr Wootton for you. I shall conduct the inquiry. You through your proctors will admit to a previous betrothal which invalidates your marriage to the King."

"To whom was I supposed to be betrothed?"

"To Lord Harry Percy, now Earl of Northumberland."

She was at the end of the small room, and turning, faced him, leaning back against the wall.

"Oh no!" she said.

"If you prefer to name another gentleman . . ."

"Harry Percy will do," she said and began to laugh. The crazy sound filled the crypt, bouncing back from the low ceiling and stone walls.

"Please," Cranmer said, "my lady, this is no matter for Lady Pembroke, I beg you . . . I'll call your women . . ."

But to reach the door he had to pass her and she put out her right hand and caught him by his full sleeve. Without engaging in an unseemly struggle he could not release himself and was forced to stand rocked by the laughter that shook her. She made a fist of her left hand and beat with it upon her chest. "It will stop," she gasped, between gusts of laughter, speaking as though it had nothing to do with her. And presently it did stop. She said, breathlessly,

"I'm not mad. There is a joke — such a one as only God could have devised. I had to laugh or cry. And jokes are meant to be laughed at, even the cruel ones."

Cranmer regarded her miserably and without understanding.

"It all began with him," she said. "We were in love, we would have married, but they parted us. Thirteen years ago they would not allow us to be betrothed, now to destroy my marriage they claim that we were. When I was young and able to love they took him away; now, in this guise they give him back to me. Did he laugh, too?"

Cranmer thought it best not to say that Northumberland had not been consulted or that he had twice denied the betrothal. He said,

"Evidence of the betrothal was given by George Cavendish who was gentleman-usher to Cardinal Wolsey at the time. He affirms that Lord Harry Percy told the Cardinal that he was so bound in honour to you that he could not in conscience marry another woman."

"If only they had heeded him *then*," she said bitterly, "none of this would ever have happened."

And again the little self-seeking strain in Cranmer came uppermost and he thought the inevitable thought — And I should not be Archbishop of Canterbury. He said,

"Will you agree that there was a pre-contract?"

"I would deny it, but I don't want to burn. I thought just now of Catherine, how stubbornly she stood upon her rights, but she wasn't threatened with burning. My lord of Canterbury, threatened with burning anybody would agree to anything."

"Then this business should take but little time," Cranmer said. And then, thank God his part would be done.

It took about fifteen minutes to unmake the marriage which had taken so long to make: which had brought the Reformation to England; which had produced Elizabeth.

WHITEHALL, GREENWICH, RICHMOND, HAMPTON COURT, WINDSOR, MAY 17th, 1536

In all the royal palaces the needlewomen were working late. With red eyes, aching backs and tired fingers they were working at bed-hangings and covers, at chair backs and cushions and tablecloths, everywhere where the H and the A had been worked in interlinking stitches, the A was to be removed and a J put in its place. A lot of work to do in a little time. The woman the A stood for was to go to her death on the day after tomorrow; the woman the J stood for would be married that evening or next day, and all must be in order.

One old woman could remember the time when all this stuff was new and everybody was busy embroidering H and C on everything. The new king was then being free-handed with the money his tight-fisted old father had saved. They'd been the days; everything young and full of hope and promise.

Yes, she'd worked H and C; and then, her sight still good, thank God, she'd picked out many a C and

484

worked A instead, and now here she was, her sight still good, thank God, picking out A and putting J in its place.

Some of her neighbours had a lot to say about the rights and wrongs of it, but she didn't bother. She was glad the King was so changeable in his mind. He could change again next year, for all she cared, if only her sight remained good. It all meant work for such as her.

CHAPTER
FORTY-THREE

"... who, whilst I lived, ever showed yourselves so diligent in my service ... as in good fortune ye were faithful to me, so even at this, my miserable death ye do not forsake me."

Anne Boleyn to her attendants

THE TOWER. MAY 17th, 1536

The guard at the gate eyed Emma Arnett and thought — Drunk; disgusting! Her black gown had been decent once, but now the whole front of it was plastered with mud, she must have fallen flat on her face, and one sleeve was half ripped out. Her cap was awry on her head and from one side of it the grey hair tumbled. There was mud and a graze on her face and her whole manner had the demented kind of confidence that came from too much liquor.

"Orders," he said. "Nobody to come in or go out."

"But I have the King's own permit. Look, read for yourself. Or can't you read?"

The guard could not read; but he knew a trick when he came up against one. He took the paper and held it so that the smoky light from the torch fixed in the wall fell on it. A plain piece of paper, no heading, no date. Some writing done in ink, very level and nice and

486

across the bottom, huge and sprawling, the letters H R done in, well, for all the world they looked as though they'd been done with a burnt stick.

"If I let you in with that, old woman," he said, "my back'd smart tomorrow."

"It'll smart if you don't," Emma said. "Can't you recognise the King's hand? All right. Go fetch somebody that can read."

"You go home and sleep it off. You should be ashamed."

"I'm asking you for the last time," Emma said — but her voice was still breathless and excited — "to fetch somebody with some sense. All right then, I will!" She threw her head back and screamed. The noise she made was not quite so loud and piercing as that which she had made a little time ago at the Westminster landing steps because with one thing and another her voice was wearing down, but it was a loud noise and it carried. In no time at all two other guards and a young officer were at the gate.

"Sir, sir," Emma said, singling out the officer. "I beg you look at this. Signed by the King not an hour ago."

"Stand back," the officer said. They'd been warned that there might be trouble, even an attempted rescue, and though the old woman looked harmless enough one never knew. He looked right and left. All quiet.

"Bring me the paper," he said.

When he had it he held it under the torch and read, "His Grace, the King gives permission for Emma Arnett to go to the Tower and remain with her mistress, Lady Pembroke, until she is needed no more." That much was neatly written in ink. Then, in what looked like charcoal, were the letters H R which, if not from the King's hand, were remarkably good forgeries.

"Come here," he said. "Now, how did you come by this?"

"I wrote it," Emma said. "I took it and a piece of charred wood, so he could sign anywhere, and I've been following him about. I'd tried other ways but everybody was against me. And it wasn't easy to catch up with him and get close enough. Tonight I did. I was roughly handled, but he did hear me and he signed. You'll let me in?"

"This could be a trick."

"Of course it was a trick. How else could I do it? They knew very well that if I'd been let to speak . . . I've been under restraint till the trial was over. Once it was I was turned loose and I wanted to come to her, but I couldn't get leave. Till tonight. There it is, and if you don't believe me, send and ask. He's at Westminster."

The young officer looked right and left again. Nothing stirring.

"You must come in and wait," he said. "I'll make inquiries." Emma was shown into a small bare room, and the officer went to find Sir William Kingston who, not wishing on the one hand to ignore an order which seemed to be signed by the King's hand, nor, on the other, disturb His Grace at supper, sent someone along to Westminster steps to ask if there had been a scene there, earlier, and if anyone could remember an old woman being given the King's signature to her paper.

There were upwards of two hundred. It had rained in the afternoon but the evening was warm and fine and people had gathered, as they had lately, to stare at their monarch and wonder.

Every evening he'd gone out to supper in this great house or that, or had entertained guests, behaving like a man with nothing on his conscience and absolutely no shame. Cuckolded five times over, by his brother-in-law, by his closest favourite, by a low-born musician and two other men; and he behaved as though nothing had happened at all. What a man!

An ordinary citizen, suspicious of his own wife, would go to stare and think — How well he wears his horns; may be I take things too much to heart.

Another, tired of his wife, would think — Lucky fellow, he's worn out two and is ready for the third.

Some, happily married, had comfortable thoughts — I'm poor and humble but I'm lucky. I wouldn't change my Joan, Alice, Margery, Mary for any woman alive.

Several sober decent citizens described the scene when one of their own kind, sober and decent, had screamed and tried to get near His Grace, and had thrown herself face downward at his feet and been hauled up again so roughly that her sleeve had been torn. Yes, but she'd had her way. The King had written on a paper she had and muttered something about loyalty, and she had then picked up her skirts and run — they pointed the direction — as though the Devil himself was after her.

The torn sleeve was identification enough. Also, one man who had pushed near, vouched for the act that His

Grace had signed with a bit of burnt stick; some of the black had come off on his hand and he'd sworn and rubbed his hand on his tunic.

The messenger sped back to the Tower and presently Emma was admitted.

And she, that tower of strength, that rock in an emergency, that unemotional woman, gave way at last. She went down on her knees and took Anne's hands and kissed them again and again, and wept. The tears came with difficulty, accompanied by harsh, chest-rending sobs.

For when Anne had been taken away, Emma Arnett had at last faced the truth. A terrible truth. For thirteen years she had served Anne, on this excuse, or that, always deceiving herself, telling herself that Anne was a mere instrument, to be used for the furtherance of a common cause. She'd thought about the Bible in English, the protection of Lutheran merchants, of Latimer, of the prince who would save England from Mary.

And it was all lies.

The truth was that she loved Anne Boleyn; always had, always would; and now it was too late. Anne Boleyn was to die on the day after tomorrow.

THE TOWER. MAY 18th, 1536

The headsman, imported in advance, Henry being so certain that Anne would choose the easier death, said,

"For all Calais is reckoned part of England, it's really part of France; and we do things differently there."

490

CHAPTER
FORTY-FOUR

"The day before she suffered death, being attended by six ladies in the Tower, she took Lady Kingston into her presence chamber and there, locking the door upon them, willed her to sit down in the chair of state . . . Then the Queen most humbly fell on her knees and . . . charged her . . . that she would so fall down before the Lady Mary's grace and in like manner ask her forgiveness."

Speed

THE TOWER. MAY 18th, 1536

Margaret Lee, in one of the calms between her storms of weeping, spread out the writing things and tried to persuade Anne to the table.

"I do beg of you, write to him. I'll take the letter myself and wherever he is I'll find him, and go on my knees and present it. Anne, you must, you must. He can't mean this to happen. But you know what he is, he's waiting for some sign from you. And the time is so short. Do, I beg of you, write a letter."

"I wrote once. He took no notice."

"Dear Anne, that was before the trial. He had his way. You aren't even married any more. He can marry Jane now, without . . . without . . ."

She could not bring herself to say the words.

Margaret could understand Henry's motives, up to a point; he was an ageing man, wildly in love with a girl, he wished to marry her and being a man who put no consideration before his own pleasure, he had entered into a wicked plot to rid himself of Anne. She prayed that God would punish him for that. But now that he was free again, why must Anne die?

"He wants me dead," Anne said. "Nothing else will do. He hates me."

"That is no reason . . ."

"It is for him. He has hated me for a long time. I think he hated me even while he still believed that he loved me. I made him wait. He's taking revenge for that, now."

"He might still relent, if only you would write. You write such a good letter. You must write and beg for mercy."

"He has none. Last evening proved that; he didn't say — Admit a pre-contract and live; he said — Admit a pre-contract and die quickly. He is determined upon my death. Besides, to spare me now, when five men are dead for their supposed sin with me. On their behalf I did write; I begged him to be merciful to them. We know how he answered that plea! For myself I asked only a fair trial, not to have my enemies sit in judgment on me; but they did, with the verdict given before a word was spoken. He has shamed me, and he'll kill me, but he shan't humble me."

The reservoir of Margaret's tears had replenished itself and she was crying again.

"Margaret, please . . . Don't make it harder. I am resigned now. I dread the moment, but it will be only a moment. Think of it this way . . . What would life hold for me after this?" She thought of Catherine, living out the empty hopeless days in the Huntingdonshire marsh while in London another woman wore the crown and was called Queen. Bad enough; but Catherine had had an easy mind; her name had never been blackened; she had not been instrumental in sending five men, young, gifted, handsome, to their deaths. "I was fond of them all, in different ways," she said aloud. "Their faces haunt me. Their faces and the horrible things that were said in Court. But for the actual doing, I shall be almost glad to die."

"So would I," Margaret sobbed hysterically. "So would Emma. How are we to go on living?"

"You must try to forget. When you do think of me, remember me kindly. And remember that in my trouble you stood by me, and greatly comforted me."

"He's a bad man. The wickedest man since Judas Iscariot. I pray God will punish him. I pray that Jane will bear him nothing but monsters, and that his leg never heals, but grows worse until the stench of it sickens him. I pray God he never has another happy moment."

"Sometimes I feel like that — full of hatred. But there are other times . . ." Her eyes took on a faraway, mystic's look. "Times when I wonder, no, more than that, I almost *see* that the things we do, the things we think we *choose* to do, and the things that seem to happen to us by chance, were all arranged for us,

493

beforehand. It is a hard thing to explain, especially when you don't fully understand it yourself. But . . . You see, Margaret, I was once warned that I might die in this manner."

In an awed voice Margaret said,

"A soothsayer?"

"No. A book. A book of pictures. It was some time ago, before the Cardinals' Trial at Blackfriars. I went back to my room one evening and the book lay on a stool. Just three pages. There was the King and the Queen and me, without my head."

"How horrible!"

"I didn't think so then. Nan did; she was with me, and when I showed her she said that if she thought it was true she wouldn't have the King even if he were King ten times over. But I laughed, and called the book a bauble, and said I *would* have him, even if it meant losing my head. You see, I was set on my course. And lately I have been thinking. If it were my fate to be beheaded, then it was Henry's fate to bring it about . . ."

But Margaret refused to grant Henry even that much of exoneration.

"That makes it sound as though he isn't to blame. And he is. He is! He arranged all this so that he could marry Jane Seymour without people saying he was always chopping and changing. And he could pardon you now, this minute, if he chose. He might, if only you'd write to him. Dearest Anne, I beg of you to write."

494

"If he pardoned me he'd always be afraid that some people still considered me his wife — as some people always thought Catherine was. He'd never risk putting himself in that position again. We must face it, Margaret. It is necessary for me to die."

Margaret began to cry again.

Somewhere a clock chimed. Another of the few remaining hours had run its course. It might, she thought, seem strange to wish away what was left of life, but this waiting, without hope, shut in with weeping women and never sure how long one could stay calm oneself, this was the worst part of all, except one, the moment of which she willed herself not to think, the moment when the blade would fall. However skilled the headsman, however swift the blow, there would be some pain. Could she face it without flinching?

The door opened and she was relieved to see that it was Lady Kingston, come to take her turn. Lady Kingston was pleasant, civil, even kind, but she was blessedly uninvolved. Not a friend who suffered and wept, nor an enemy who gloated. She ignored Anne's situation, still addressed her with respect, and without any obvious effort always contrived to introduce some topic of conversation that was neutral and of mild interest. She was a good needlewoman and they talked on the subject of embroidery, of Lady Kingston's difficulty in making a truly satisfactory garden, of cures for freckles and brittle finger nails. Lady Kingston's hours in the Queen's Chamber were much in the nature of a social visit. One lady calling upon another and engaging in amiable chatter. Lady Kingston, a modest woman, rather prided herself upon this as an achievement, for in talking with Anne's other attendants she had learned that Anne was seldom so calm with them; and she had often heard weeping, hysterical laughter and almost demented raving coming from this very room. I manage better, she thought to herself, and wished that her husband could realise how well, in a quiet way, she assisted him in his far from easy office.

Her husband might under-rate her, but Anne had realised her worth; she was like a piece of good sound, closely-woven cloth, with nothing showy about it, but with a strength and substance that once shaped would last almost indefinitely. And for this reason she had chosen Lady Kingston as the repository of two messages. Both Margaret and Nan would have undertaken their delivery, but their own emotions would have impeded their utterance and detracted from the force of what they said. Emma would have been the perfect messenger but her status would make access difficult. Lady Kingston was next best, and Lady Kingston must be used.

When Margaret, still sobbing, had gone, Anne said,

"Lady Kingston, please sit there," and pointed to the chair under the canopy.

"Oh no," Lady Kingston said. "Rightly I suppose I should not sit in your presence at all, much less use the Queen's chair."

"At the moment there is no Queen. I wish you to sit there, Lady Kingston, and hear me out. I have one thing upon my conscience and cannot rest until I have cleared it."

Lady Kingston took the chair and then looked at Anne with some misgiving. She had no wish to be made to listen to some revolting confession. Behind her professional, impartial manner she concealed certain doubts, being a believer in the adage about no smoke without fire. There'd certainly been a great deal of smoke. Also, from her observation of Anne's behaviour during her imprisonment, Lady Kingston had come to the conclusion that she was a woman likely to say or do almost anything; she moved from tears to laughter, from talkativeness to silence; from raving against the injustice of her sentence to the most dignified acceptance of it, all without reason. She might now, on the eve of her death, have decided to tell the whole story.

"Madame, I do not think that I am the proper person. You would do better to send for your confessor."

"It concerns something that you, as a woman, could better do."

Lady Kingston's fears were confirmed: some woman-to-woman talk of illicit love. Her distaste showed on her face.

"It concerns the Lady Mary."

"Oh, well in that case . . ." Lady Kingston relaxed and prepared to listen.

"I want you to go to her, as soon as is convenient for you, after my death, and carry a message. If I could go myself, I would; but I am . . . I mean I shall be represented by you. See, I go on my knees to you, as I would to her." She dropped to her knees and stayed there. "Will you do that, go on your knees to her, as my proxy?"

"If that is your wish." Lady Kingston's manner had stiffened again; there was a touch of melodrama about Anne's action which made her feel uneasy.

"Say to her that I am sorry, from my heart, for the way I behaved to her, and to her mother. I was set on having my own way, and felt that they were thwarting me. I deeply regret it now and I beg the Lady Mary's forgiveness. Will you tell her that?"

"Most willingly."

Lady Kingston was puzzled. She had never heard of any specific act of unkindness done by the Queen to Catherine or her daughter; and she had heard Lady Lee, weeping over the injustice of things, say that Anne was so kind, always kind, so kind that she had several times offered friendship to Mary, and every time been repulsed. And surely, whatever had been done to the old Queen and her daughter had been the King's doing. Lady Kingston had never by word or deed exercised the slightest influence upon her husband's behaviour and privately doubted whether any man ever did anything because his wife asked it. Anne was probably exaggerating. Poor soul, Lady Kingston thought, if *that* is the worst thing on her conscience . . .

And then suddenly the light broke. Of course, Anne was thinking of her child who would almost inevitably fall into Mary's keeping. Jane Seymour would have little time and attention to spare for the two bastard

498

step-children; Mary was so much older, and after all this would be in so much better odour that she might well be put in charge of Elizabeth. This message was intended to soften Mary's heart and influence her behaviour. Quite clever, so much more likely to be effective than a direct appeal which would betray its purpose. Lady Kingston remembered that Anne was always said to have had a good head on her. And oh, she thought, at times like this, how the most ordinary expression can be misplaced; now I am bound to think about her head and what will happen to it tomorrow.

Anne stood up, and in a different manner said,

"I have a message for the King, too. Will you carry it?"

"Oh, I think perhaps my husband . . . He is the Keeper of the Tower."

"And as such will have other things to see to. Please, Lady Kingston. It is not a long message, but it must be remembered exactly."

"Very well." If it were in the same contrite tone as the message to Mary, delivering it would not bring disfavour upon the messenger. And having thought that, Lady Kingston saw by the way Anne's eyes suddenly flashed and her mouth curled, that this would not be a contrite message.

"Tell him," Anne said, slowly and distinctly, "that I commend me to him and thank him for so constantly advancing me: from a private gentlewoman he made me a Marchioness, from a Marchioness a Queen, and now, having no further honour to bestow upon me, he gives me the crown of martyrdom."

"And then," Lady Kingston said, reporting to her husband over their supper table, "she began to laugh. I tried to calm her, but couldn't, so I fetched her women. And I came away. I don't like the way she laughs . . . It wouldn't sound quite right anywhere, and here it is downright unnatural."

"It's unusual," Sir William agreed.

"She isn't like anyone I ever knew, or heard of. And if people ask me . . . after — What was she like? I should be hard put to give an answer. So changeable, and all in a minute. When she spoke of the Lady Mary she looked sweet and sorrowful, when she spoke of the King she looked . . . vicious, and then she was laughing."

Sir William gave a little grunt; all women were like that; didn't she realise that she herself was variable as an April day?

"Just at the minute it's all music, playing the lute, old songs and new ones. You'd hardly think this was the time. Or do you think that she still has some hope, for a pardon at the last minute, or a rescue?"

He raised his head and looked at her with attentive narrowed eyes.

"What put that idea into your silly head?"

"Nothing." His look dismayed her. "Nothing, except the way she behaves."

"You've heard no rumour? No gossip?"

"None. How could I? I've seen no one."

"You've seen her women. Were they more cheerful? Whispering in corners?"

500

"Oh no. Poor Lady Lee was crying her heart out again. Why? Are you expecting something?"

He almost confided in her, but that would have been to break the habit of a married lifetime, so he told her curtly to mind her business and leave him to his, and went on chewing the food which would, he knew, lie in his stomach like red-hot lead, it always did when he was worried.

He had just received his final instructions from Cromwell. They showed clearly enough that the Chief Secretary thought there might be trouble. The scaffold was to be set up inside the Tower precincts, and to be very low, so that nothing would be visible outside. Only a few, carefully chosen spectators were to be present, and as a last precaution the time of the execution had been changed to mid-day, a fact which was to be kept secret. London which had refused to doff its cap or raise its voice for Nan Bullen, now talked of Queen Anne, of her wrongs and her virtues, quoting the vast sums of money she had distributed to charities in the last months of her life and the interest she had taken in the education of poor boys of promise. Fickle as the wind, public opinion had now swung round so definitely in her favour that an attack on the Tower was likely and a riot in the streets possible.

It was, Sir William thought, a unique occasion — apart from the rights and wrongs of it. A woman on the scaffold, and that woman a Queen. In the last two hundred years or so, two Kings of England had been deposed, and were dead soon after; Edward the Second mysteriously at Berkeley Castle, Richard the Second

501

mysteriously at Pontefract; but it was one thing to let the London crowd learn of a dark deed done at some distance and irrevocable, and quite another to ask them to stand by and tacitly give their consent to the execution of one who had been crowned.

"I shall be glad when this is all over," he said, grumpily.

"It's just on ten o'clock, now," Lady Kingston said. "In ten hours it will be over."

He did not correct her.

In ten hours from now . . .

Emma Arnett thought about death-beds; when you tended the dying you might know that the hours were numbered, the end unavoidable, but there was something you could *do*: you shifted the pillows, rearranged the covers, moistened dry lips, wiped sweat-dewed brows, and such simple doings distracted your mind. This was altogether different. You sat here, within a few feet of a living, healthy young woman and could think of nothing except that in a few hours this beautiful living body would be a hideous mangled corpse.

Beyond the dead body she could see nothing; no hope of resurrection, immortality or reunion. Her belief in Purgatory she'd lost with her belief in priest and Pope; Heaven and Hell had vanished, never to be recovered, on the evening of Anne's miscarriage, when she had lost her belief in God. Once her shock at God's apparent stupidity had subsided, she had tried, with all the force of her resolute nature to drive herself into

502

humble acceptance, to admit that God knew what was best, that His ways, though mysterious, were right. She could never do it; she might as well have tried to restore life to a tree blasted by lightning. Night after night she had lain, her mind going round and round, coming back always to the same hopeless conclusions, the mental exercise as futile as a snake eating its own tail. Even her desire to believe defeated itself, for it was inevitable that sooner or later she should think to herself — If I believe it is because I want to, because I can't bear not to. And once that thought was thought there was no going back.

So, when she thought of Anne as dead, it was as dead for ever; and under the grief and misery and horror lay the even more dreadful hopelessness of a mind which was homesick for the days when it had seen, beyond the grave, the life everlasting, a world of beauty and plenty past all imagination, peopled by angels and saints and all the hosts of Heaven, basking in the presence of God Himself.

After her one emotional outburst Emma had not cried again; hers was a grief past tears.

Margaret, with short intermissions, had cried all the time. She tried not to; she knew that it made things worse for Anne, and did no good at all, but she could not help it. When Anne suggested that they should spend an hour singing she had gulped out, "Oh, how can you?" almost as though it were she, not Anne, who tomorrow morning must kneel at the block.

Anne said,

"Margaret, I should like my songs to be remembered. And there is only you to commit them to memory. In days to come I shall be remembered as one of the wickedest women that ever lived. Henry must justify himself and to do that he will see that my so-called sins are remembered. My child will never know the truth and will be ashamed of me. They'll find me a nickname — all too easily: The Queen without a Head. But if you will remember my songs, Margaret, and teach them to your children and ask them to teach them to theirs, sometime in the far future, I may be remembered for them, when everything else is forgotten."

"I'll try," Margaret said, though the mention of the nick name, and the thought of any future without Anne in it, had started a fresh spate of tears.

And the songs that she must particularly master the tunes of, because no one else had heard them yet, were ones written and composed in the Tower, and quite heart-breaking in their sadness.

Defiled is my name, full sore,
Through cruel spite and false report,
That I may say for evermore,
Farewell to joy, adieu comfort.

And the other,

Oh death, rock me asleep,
Bring on my quiet rest,
Let pass my very guiltless ghost
Out of my careful breast.

Ring out the doleful knell,
Let its sound my death tell;
For I must die,
There is no remedy,
For now I die!

Anne thought — This is the last time I shall use a lute, the last time I shall sing; but the thought did not have, in her mind, the awful finality that it would have had in Emma Arnett's, for she could add — On this earth. As the dreaded moment drew nearer she became more and more certain of God's understanding and forgiveness. She'd been a sinner, but on earth she had been punished beyond her deserts, in the world to come that might count in her favour. There would be music in Heaven, and one day she would be there to join in it.

She said,

"But Thomas always made the best songs; and this is apt." She began to sing,

"Farewell, my lute, this is the last
Labour that thou and I shall waste,
For ended is what we began:
Now is the song both sung and past,
My lute be still, for I have done.'

She laid the lute down for the last time.

CHAPTER
FORTY-FIVE

"I have seen men, and also women executed, and they have been in great sorrow, but to my knowledge, this lady had much joy and pleasure in death."
Sir William Kingston in a letter to Cromwell

"No person ever showed greater willingness to die."
The Spanish Ambassador in a letter to Charles V

THE TOWER. MAY 19th, 1536

Sir William was a man hardened to his job and willing to face the responsibilities of his office, but he had dreaded the task of telling Anne that her execution was to be postponed for four hours. He was afraid that she would see in the delay some promise of reprieve, or that hearing that she must endure the extra four hours of waiting would provoke tears.

He broke the news in his official, emotionless manner and braced himself to meet what followed.

Something that in almost any other circumstances he would have believed to be a flash of humour crossed her face.

"All my life," she said, "seems to have been spent in waiting, and now I must wait, even for death." Her face became sombre again. "Not until noon? I am sorry for that. I hoped by that time to be dead and past my pain."

"With such a skilled headsman there will be little pain," Sir William assured her. "The sword is sharp, and his use of it very subtle."

"And I have but a little neck," she said, putting her hands to it, and laughing. Sir William wondered what his wife had found so disturbing about her laughter. It was, as he had said, unusual. He reflected that he had seen a number of people executed, but none so cheerful.

He had found her with her chaplain, and, his errand done, was about to leave them alone again, but Anne halted him.

"I have made my confession," she said, "and am about to take the good Lord into my mouth for the last time. That is a solemn moment and not one for the telling of lies. I would like you, Sir William, now to witness that I solemnly declare myself innocent of the crimes of which I was accused. I did not sin with my brother, nor with Norris, Weston, Brereton nor Smeaton. That is the truth before God in whose presence I shall shortly stand. I trust you to make it known."

A little earlier she had confessed the truth to her chaplain, admitting to three isolated acts of adultery, "not through any lust of the flesh or any desire whatever save to bear His Grace a living son". That confession would go with her chaplain to the grave and no one would ever know. But she hoped that what she had said to Sir William in one of the last hours of her life would be spread abroad; it was her final attempt to clear the names of the five men who had died, most of all her brother George . . .

"I shall report what you have said, Madam, as I report everything," Sir William said. And that meant that he would write it in his next letter to Cromwell. It would go no further.

Sir William had long ago forsworn the luxury of speaking freely, even his thoughts and his feelings were governed by expediency more often than not, but for a moment he found himself wishing that this last statement of the condemned woman's might be made public, if only because it would comfort the relatives of the dead men; particularly the wife and mother of Sir Francis Weston who were so devoted, so certain of his innocence, that they had offered the King a bribe of 100,000 crowns in return for his life.

It was reasonably certain, Sir William's mind ran on, that Anne would not repeat this statement from the scaffold. To do so would be to question openly the justice of her sentence, and risk a more painful form of death. Speeches from the scaffold were almost as stylised as responses in Church. He'd seen dozens of executions, and known dozens of prisoners who, protesting their innocence up to the very steps of the scaffold, had, once they had mounted them, spoken in fulsome terms of the King and admitted that they deserved to die. Everyone knew that unless this formality were observed there might be an unfortunate hitch, a last-minute postponement, and then death in an uglier guise.

He gave a little mental shrug. That was the way the world was and there was nothing he could do to change it.

Anne said,

"Thank you. I am grateful, too, for the courtesy you have shown me while I have been in your care."

"I have done nothing but my duty, Madam."

She was holding out her hand. As he took it he felt the hard shell of habit and stern thinking begin to fail him. He said,

"I will see . . . expeditious . . . easy as possible. God be with your Grace, then . . . and hereafter."

He felt as though an iron hand had him by the windpipe, and the words came out indistinctly jerkily.

She smiled at him; and he who had always been one of those who had wondered what on earth the King could ever have seen in her, reeled for a second under the impact of that vagrant, unpredictable charm. He turned and went blundering out of the room, and once beyond the door stood for a moment blinking and swallowing. When he had himself in hand again he walked on, thinking — I am the last man at whom she will ever smile.

The added four hours of waiting, longer than any lifetime, were coming to an end at last. It was a warm morning, and the air in the Queen's lodging was still and heavy, yet the four of them, waiting there, shuddered and trembled as though blown upon by an icy wind. Anne in a desperate attempt to comfort Margaret and Nan and Emma had spoken of her certainty of their reunion in Paradise, but her voice was unsteady as she wove her last spell with words, attempting to describe the indescribable the gardens at Greenwich on an unclouded summer day, but more beautiful, with music of which earth's music was nothing but a faint false echo. "And all whom we have ever loved, even, I think, our little dogs. Think of it so. Tonight and tomorrow, whenever you think of me, think — she has done with pain and trouble; and look forward to the day when we shall again be together."

Margaret and Nan wept, Emma sat with a face of stone. For her no future either here or hereafter; Anne Boleyn, whom she had loved, better than she had loved her family, or her old master, Richard Hunne, would be dead; and she, forever bereaved, growing older and stiffer in the joints, would go on down a road that grew narrower and darker until it ended in the grave. For her no heavenly gardens, or music, no reunion. She thought, almost angrily — You start by not believing in a mass of superstitions, and you end by not believing anything. It's like falling down a well, you can't pull up half-way.

Her big, work-worn hands trembled as she held them in her lap, hiding something there. She was waiting for it to be half past eleven; and presently it was. Time to render the last service of all.

She moved her hands, revealing a small wooden bottle.

"I daren't bring anything bigger than what I could hide in my bodice, your Grace," she said. "I was afraid what I had in my pocket or my hands they might take away from me before they let me in. So there isn't much, but enough to calm you and take off the sharpest . . ." She was going to say edge, but that brought the sword to mind, the cold cruel steel.

Anne looked at her, for a moment unable to speak.

"Emma, that is a miracle! All along I've so feared that out there, all eyes upon me, I might, at the last moment . . . fail."

It was one thing to be resigned to death, another to face with dignity the sight of the apparatus.

She hoped that the dose Emma had smuggled in was as large, and would act in the same way, as the one she had given her on the day of her arrest. After her trial, when she was allowed the company of her own ladies she had asked about that day and been told that all the way to the Tower she had behaved with the utmost dignity. To a group of spectators, gathered to stare, she had said, haughtily, "You cannot prevent me from dying your Queen." Yet she, Anne Boleyn, the conscious I, had not been there at all. If she could go to the block in that same tranced way . . . Then there would be no fear of her screaming, or crying, or laughing. Ever since she had gone to France and left childhood behind she had been — yes, she would use the word now — vain, greedy for admiration, had early learned how to make much out of little, had realised that while girls more naturally pretty could rely upon the impression their faces made, she must cultivate style, manner, charm, a good carriage and taste in clothes. For her last appearance before the public eye she had chosen her manner, too. She wished to make a calm, a dignified, an impressive exit, so that people, remembering later, brooding over the horrid details of her supposed offences, might say, "At least she died like a Queen," and wonder perhaps whether her manner at the end could be consistent with the frivolity, the light-mindedness, the unspeakable behaviour of which she had been accused. Now, thanks to Emma, she might perhaps achieve this last ambition.

Emma's shaking hand poured the dose and Anne's shaking hand took the cup. It was a good deal larger than the doses Emma had so often administered, but smaller than the one she had offered on the day of the arrest. Still, it would serve.

Then, with the cup half-way to her lips she halted her hand; Margaret and Nan, red-eyed, faces swollen from crying, Emma her face taut with misery.

"We'll share it," she said. "Like a loving cup."

She offered it to Margaret whose mind was so sodden with wretchedness that she would have drunk, without thinking, from a cup of poison just then. She took a mouthful and swallowed it before Emma could say,

"I brought it for you!"

"And I said we would share it. Nan?"

"I couldn't swallow anything," Nan Savile said.

"I brought it for you," Emma repeated. She threw a look of reproach at Margaret and added, "There was little enough."

512

"There is plenty to keep me from making a spectacle of myself," Anne said, and drank. And she had again, more vividly than ever, that sense of destiny of which she had spoken to Margaret. She thought, even this simple thing has played its part, and no negligible one, in bringing me to this moment. That evening of my first quarrel with Henry, when I was planning to go back to Hever and Emma spoke of her friend the apothecary and gave me the first dose, so that I was almost asleep when he came back and in no mood to carry on the quarrel; but for the dose I should still have been angry and told him that insults were not wiped out by gifts.

She doubted whether she had drunk enough to produce the tranced state in which she had come from Greenwich to the Tower, but she waited for the feeling of calm, of nothing mattering very much, which had so often been the syrup's gift to her. Today, of all days, and for the first time, it failed her. She might as well have drunk water.

I might have known, she thought; nothing is to be spared me. I go to the block sustained only by my faith in God, the master who arranged this puppet show, and who will not be too hard upon the puppet who all along has responded to each pull of the strings, and all the time believed that she willed every move.

Then, in various courtyards and towers the clocks chimed and in innumerable sunny gardens all over England the hands of the sun-dials touched the figure twelve. And it was noon of Friday, May 19th, in the year of our Lord 1536.

It had been decided to admit about thirty carefully chosen members of the public, headed by the Lord Mayor; their presence, it was felt, would prevent any accusation of furtiveness; and it would be useful if, as was hoped, the condemned woman made a confession from the scaffold.

When Anne appeared, escorted by Sir William Kingston, and followed by her women, something like awe laid hand on all present, even her avowed enemies. Only a few people had ever thought her beautiful, most had denied that she was even pretty; today she glowed with a beauty that was almost unearthly. She was well-dressed, as always, but nobody noticed the gown of black damask, dramatically in contrast with the huge white collar, or the black velvet hat under which her wealth of glossy hair was closely folded and pinned tight. It was her face that held the attention, the great eyes glowing as though from some inner light, the creamy skin, the mouth, its pinched look gone, sweetly curved, composed.

She moved, with all her unmatched grace, to the scaffold steps and mounted them. Directly ahead of her was the block, with the straw spread about it; on the extreme right the heads- man, masked and clad in skin-tight black, stood, holding the sword behind him, a futile, formal gesture of consideration.

She faced the little crowd, recognising some faces; the Duke of Suffolk; the Duke of Richmond, Henry's bastard; Cromwell, whose eldest son was married to

514

Jane Seymour's sister and who would rise now to greater heights; certain ambassadors; the Lord Mayor.

Emma's dose had, after all, had some effect; she was no longer shivering, and when she spoke her voice was clear and firm.

She said,

"Good Christian people, I am come hither to die, according to the law, for by the law I am judged to die and therefore I will speak nothing against it, as I know full well that what I could say in my defence cannot concern you, or give me hope of life."

The words held the quintessence of something which Henry had always — though sometimes unconsciously — resented in her; the ability to strip a thing down to its bones. In civil, almost amiable terms she was telling them that, the law being what it was, she was helpless, *and so were they*; they had titles and high office, but they must do the King's bidding or perish. Even the least sensitive of them understood; in England now there was no law but the King's will; and he had rigged and they, by active participation or passive acceptance, had helped him to rig an infamous charge against one who had once held his heart in her hands; he had disposed of an unwanted wife, how much more easily would he dispose of an unwanted favourite, or minister?

Her next sentence played, as skillfully as ever her fingers had played upon the lute-strings, upon their fears. In a changed voice, a voice that everyone must recognise as sarcastic, she said,

"I pray God to save the King and send him long to reign over you, for a gentler and more merciful prince there never was." Then her tone changed to one of warning.

She said,

"To me he was ever a good and gentle sovereign lord." And she looked at the block, and then at the headsman. *Take heed; this is what a good and gentle sovereign lord can bring you to.*

Then she said,

"Thus I take my leave of the world and of you, and I heartily desire you all to pray for me."

It had been arranged between them that when she said those words, a sign that she was ready, Margaret should come forward and remove the hat and the deep collar which might impede the headsman. But Margaret, distraught and bemused from her one mouthful of the poppy syrup, had collapsed, and was upheld only by Nan's straining arms. Emma, racked with grief, was still, from long habit, conscious of her place; she waited for a second for Lady Lee to recover herself and to do what she should. Then she moved and it was too late. Anne had taken off her hat and her collar and Emma was just in time to receive them.

With the hat off, and the collar, and her hair pinned so close her neck was exposed, longer by two inches, smaller by two than any other woman's neck. The headsman eyed it with professional satisfaction; one clean stroke, he thought, and he'd have earned his £23 6s. 8d. and also established the claim for the superiority of French headsmen over all others.

Anne turned and embraced Margaret and said, "Remember my songs," and pressed into her limp hand a tiny book, bound in gold and black enamel, containing some verses of the psalms written on vellum. She then kissed Nan and said, "Be happy. Remember the picture; this had to happen." And then she came to Emma. "You have been my best friend. Pray for me."

Then she knelt by the block and arranged her skirts so that her feet were covered and said,

"Lord God, have pity on my soul."

Nan should then have come forward with the handkerchief to cover her eyes, but she, like Margaret, seemed incapable of movement. Again Emma waited for a second, and then, thrusting the hat and collar into Margaret's hands, she took the handkerchief from Nan and went forward and tied it into place.

The headsman came forward on noiseless feet, raising the sword as he came. It fell and the little neck was severed like a flower stem.

CHAPTER
FORTY-SIX

"Yes, — four-and-twenty hours had not elapsed since the axe was reddened with the blood of her mistress, when Jane Seymour became the bride of Henry VIII . . . The wedding cakes must have been baking, the wedding dinner providing, the wedding clothes preparing, while the life-blood was yet running warm in the veins of the victim, whose place was to be rendered vacant by a violent death."
Agnes Strickland. *Lives of the Queens of England*

RICHMOND. MAY 19th 1536

The boom of the gun informed Henry that after twenty-seven years he was free of all matrimonial entanglements.

He was dressed for riding and a horse, chosen for speed and strength, and crammed with corn, stood waiting. Others were posted at convenient stages all along the road that led to Wiltshire, to Wolf Hall, where Jane waited. Pack horses, carrying his finer clothes and gifts for his bride and her family, were already well on their way.

All morning he had felt nothing but impatience, mingled with regret that circumstances had made it necessary to change the hour of the execution; four hours of daylight wasted: and when the gun sounded he felt nothing but relief. It was safely over; he was a free man; he could go.

Swinging himself into his saddle he was convinced that the latest attempted remedy was curing his leg.

Everything was in tune with his mood; the trees hung with translucent green, the fields lively with young corn, the hawthorns in bridal white, meadows rich with buttercups and cowslips, the woods awash in a tide of bluebells. He was a young man again, in love for the first time and on his way to his wedding. All that he genuinely believed, for amongst many other things, he was a poet and possessed the poet's ability to create his own world.

Matrimonially, he thought, he'd been ill done by, two cursed marriages, one contrary to God's law, the other brought about by witchcraft. But now he was free and his real love would make up for everything.

He rode swiftly, happily in the May sunshine. And no ghosts ran alongside.

CHAPTER
FORTY-SEVEN

"Her father had declared his conviction of his daughter's guilt at the trial of her reputed lovers."
Encyclopaedia Britannica

HEVER. MAY 19th, 1536

"Now mark this," Thomas Boleyn said, eyeing with distaste his wife's face, disfigured from crying, "I never want to hear her name, or George's. Not from you. Not in this house. Outside I shall hear plenty."

Lady Bo took on an expression of true East Anglian obstinacy. She said again what she had said dozens of times in the last nineteen days.

"I simply don't believe it. Even if they've somehow found a way to make her confess . . ." She bit the inside of her cheek sharply to control her mouth which was beginning to quiver, "I still shouldn't believe it. Only somebody wrong in the head could have carried on in that fashion. And she wasn't wrong in the head, far from it."

"What she did wasn't done with her head," Anne's father said coarsely.

Lady Bo looked at him with more than distaste, with positive dislike.

Oddly matched as they might seem to any observer, they had been a very happily married couple, until nineteen days ago when, as soon as they had the dreadful news, Lady Bo had begun to urge action. After all he was the father of George and Anne, he couldn't just stand about and let such things happen without protest. Harsh words had passed between them for the first time.

"Why, my own father," she had exclaimed, "and he nothing but a simple yeoman, God rest him, wouldn't have let such a thing happen to me! He'd have come to London with his fowling piece and brought his labourers and all our neighbours, armed with pitchforks and sickles and made a row even the King would have noticed."

"And got himself hanged, drawn and quartered for his pains."

An unpleasant thought, but it lacked some ultimate of horror, some inhuman element which she detected in her husband's behaviour.

"Your father, my dear, is safely in his grave, you can afford to play fast and loose with him. I'm alive. Two of my children are accused of treason; and if I so much as look askance God knows I may be sent to join them. Perhaps you would like that!"

She thought that over in silence for several minutes. Then she said,

"Well, they're not my children, and I've never had any hand in any affairs. And stepmothers aren't supposed to be overly partial. *I* shall go to the King and tell him that I'm certain a dreadful mistake has been made."

If a rabbit had suddenly roared like a lion, the Earl of Wiltshire would have been no more surprised, or shocked.

"That," he said, "you will not do. I forbid it." He still was not annoyed at her; she was an innocent, unworldly creature to whom her obligatory contacts with the great world had taught nothing. "We must walk very warily," he said, "if we are to come out of this with our lives, our freedom and our goods."

He had then argued that nothing could be done until after the trial; the truth would all be sorted out then; they could depend upon English justice. As soon as the trial was over he argued that no protest could possibly avail; they had been condemned by their peers and to question the verdict or ask for mercy upon two such flagrant offenders would simply be to court danger.

Lady Bo had wept, had sometimes argued back, had said unkind things, such as, "All you care for are your goods!"

Their pleasant relationship, adoring on her side, indulgent on his, was shattered past repair. When she was excited her voice became loud and her Norfolk accent very marked.

"To say *that* about George and Anne is plain daft. I know it does happen, in lonely places where brothers and sisters don't see anybody except each other for months on end. But they're both married. And if it was going to happen wouldn't it have happened when she was at home and free. I've seen them together enough to know, I should reckon. Laughing and teasing each other, or making songs. Besides all which, where was the King while all this was going on? That's what I should like to know? Norris, too, there's another bit of nonsense. He came with the King on all those early visits; did he ever show any interest in her then? The whole thing was made up, by the Seymours. *And* the King. He didn't dare talk of getting rid of Anne in any ordinary way. *Another divorce*, people'd have said. So he did this, God rot him!"

The Earl did not question the rightness of her judgment; but he knew his world. Year by year, ever since Wolsey's death, the King had assumed more power and grown more tyrannical. Anyone who dared to oppose him could begin to count his days. Any move to help Anne, or George, would have been as futile as, and a good deal more dangerous than attempting to storm their prison with your bare hands. A situation of this sort was like a hurricane, you couldn't fight it; all a wise man could do was to lie low, let it sweep over, and hope to escape mortal damage.

On this Friday morning Lady Bo had a fresh horse to flog. What about decent burial? The King had had his way now, and surely, surely, to a bereaved father — or if he didn't care to ask, to a stepmother — he wouldn't deny permission to take and properly inter the body of the woman whom he had once loved, and who had been Queen of England.

"They're buried where they fall. That is the law. What difference does it make?"

"It would make a difference to me. George I never knew very well; but I was very fond of Anne."

He then made his remark about not wishing to hear her name again.

It had been a matter of bewilderment to Lady Bo *how* Henry, who had loved Anne so frenziedly, could have come to hate her, as he must have done. Now she had a faint glimmer of enlightenment. Feelings *did* change. She would never feel the same towards Tom again, after this. Still, even had she the power, and even if her feeling of dislike increased to hatred she would never bring unmentionable accusations against him, or have him done to death. But the King . . .

"There's one thing," she said, in the new firm voice that had developed in a fortnight, "I shall never be under the same roof with *him* again! I warn you, if ever he comes to a house of mine, as he walks in, I shall walk out."

Thomas Boleyn said sourly,

"I wouldn't worry about *that*, if I were you. I don't think we shall be honoured by any more visits from His Grace."

CHAPTER
FORTY-EIGHT

STAINES. MAY 19th, 1536

Mary Stafford ceased crying for a moment and said for the twentieth time,

"Whatever she did — and I don't for a moment believe that she did all they say — it was his fault. He drove her to it. I know, because I know what he's like."

William Stafford felt again the twinge of distaste which any reference to his wife's past evoked. He had known all about it; he had accepted it; he had looked upon her as a sweet innocent creature of whom all men she had known — except, of course, Carey — had taken cruel advantage: he had wanted to cherish her and compensate for the way in which the world had treated her. But that was in the past. His attitude had changed as soon as they began to live together, an ordinary married couple. He had become retrospectively jealous, wished her past out of existence, hated anything that brought it to mind. And this affair by focusing Mary's mind upon the King, the one of whom he was most jealous, had given him some painful moments.

"I did my best to warn her," Mary went on, too thoroughly miserable to notice his lack of response. "I told her no good could come of it. I told her she wasn't pliable enough."

He said, with some malice,

"I'd have thought the evidence showed otherwise."

Mary missed the point — he'd noticed during the last year or so that she did often miss the point; she said,

"Oh no. Not pliable enough to take neglect and unkindness without trying to hit back. She was always like that. She was the only one who would ever try to stand up to Father. She once . . . Oh, poor Anne!" Tears threatened again. William said quickly,

"Then you do believe her guilty?"

"Not the way they said. Not George! That was unthinkable. I could never believe . . . His wife invented that filthy tale; she was jealous of Anne and eager to be rid of George. And not Smeaton. Of that I am sure. Anne had taste, and Smeaton, when he wasn't playing some instrument, was just a plough-boy. But the others . . . Yes, I think she may have tried to console herself, or was trying to make Henry jealous, and so revive . . . But I'd warned her of that, too. Once his interest wanes there's nothing to be done. She may even have been trying to retaliate for Jane Seymour. We shall never know." The exact reason for their not knowing came uppermost in her mind and she began to cry again.

William said, and this time he spoke from a desire to comfort, not from spite,

"You must remember that she was hard and cruel to you, Mary."

526

"She was not! She was always trying to give me things. That very last time . . ." She became incoherent, sobbing out words about a blue dress and not wanting to be measured. This was the first time that the exact circumstances which had brought about the crisis had been mentioned, and Sir William indulged in a few sourish thoughts about the duplicity and the complexity of women. Then he took his stand upon firm fact.

"She never," he said, "lifted a finger to help us. To get me reinstated. Did she?"

"How do we know? Didn't I want to do something only the other day, and didn't you forbid me?"

"You wanted to make a spectacle of yourself. And to no good purpose."

"There again, how can you know? He has moods. If I'd just chanced to hit on a good one, he might have listened to me. And I could have told him about George's wife being so hostile, and how strict Anne always was with Smeaton, and about the dates being so silly. I could at least have *tried*. I don't suppose anybody ever thought to say those things to him. Kings do rather . . . well, live in glass cages and hear only what people want them to hear and see what people want them to see. I know. I was inside once — the cage, I mean. And you can't blame Anne for not influencing him, when *I* can't even influence *you*. Till the day I die I shall always regret that I didn't try."

"Then I hope that you will also bear in mind that I acted for your final good. We are both banished from Court. And for you to go weeping and wailing, bursting in, would have been fatal to our hopes."

527

"What hopes?"

"Our hopes of being taken back, my dear silly girl. Leave aside whether it was her influence or not that kept us away from Court; the fact is that from now on everything will be reversed. Whatever was done, or liked, or approved in your sister's time will now be undone, disliked and disapproved. And on that turn of the tide we may yet reach harbour. You'll see. You'll live to thank me, my dear, for restraining you."

Mary Stafford was silent for a moment. She was measuring things up, as scrupulously as her tradesman ancestor had ever measured the cloth or the corn or whatever it was that he had sold; and then she said,

"No. I shan't be grateful, William. I was grateful to you for marrying me, but I have borne your child and by obeying you sacrificed the one chance of saving my sister. So I think you are repaid. If you are offered a chance to return to Court, take it. I shan't go. I'll never make obeisance to Jane Seymour. When the whole thing is sorted out, *she murdered my sister.*"

"If we're going to use such fanciful terms," William said, "let's say that your sister committed suicide. She knew the risk she was taking, and she knew what the penalty was. If she had her due, she'd be buried at a cross-road . . ."

CHAPTER
FORTY-NINE

"God provided for her corpse sacred burial, even in a place as it were consecrate to innocence."
Sir Thomas Wyatt

THE TOWER. MAY 19th, 1536

No change of scene in even the best-planned masquerade had ever been made so swiftly, Emma Arnett thought grimly, looking around the place; one minute a crowd, the next nobody but themselves; one minute the law taking its course in ordered ritual, the next everything abandoned and in confusion.

She had always known that the world was a cruel, heartless place, but even she could hardly believe that it would be left to Anne's women, almost senseless with grief and shock, to deal with the mutilated corpse of their mistress. What happened, she asked herself, when the executed person had no faithful friends?

She waited a moment for Lady Lee to take charge; she was by every standard the one to do so; a lady born, cousin to Her Grace, a dear, close friend. But Margaret, shaking, weeping, leant against Mistress Savile, who, shaking, weeping, leant against her; and the May sunshine beat down upon the headless body, the severed head, the bloody straw.

Emma said,

"There must be a coffin," and waited a little. There was no coffin. Inside the Tower everything was done to order, and no one had ordered a coffin. The King who had decked his darling with jewels, with furs, brocades and velvets, who had crowned her when she pleased him, and killed her when she ceased to please, had made no provision for decent burial. There was a grave — if you could call it that — Emma said to herself, a shallow hole scooped out alongside the place where George Boleyn and the others had been laid; and there was an old man, more than half drunk, leaning against the wall, waiting to shovel . . .

"There *must* be a coffin," Emma said again. She ran about, to the guardroom, to the Keeper's lodgings where Sir William, thankful for once for his wife's attentions which included the provision of strong beef broth well laced with red wine, said,

"I have carried out my orders. No coffin was mentioned. Tell the woman to go away."

Emma ran back to the room Anne had occupied and snatched a sheet from the bed, and took a damp cloth from the washing-stand.

Back by the scaffold she said,

"There's nothing; no coffin, no arrangements. You'll have to help me. I can't do it all single-handed." The last words came out bitterly; she wished she could. But time was short. The old man with the shovel was already mumbling about his dinner and the two graves he had to dig in the afternoon. Unless they were quick he'd be dragging this corpse, as Emma guessed he had dragged a good many, un-coffined, by the heels, into the makeshift grave.

"If you could brace up, and wash her face, and wrap her in this sheet, I'll find something," she said.

And finally she found it; an old arrow chest; too short, oh good God! And why, why, why, should I still, at such a moment call on that name? But too short, good God, for any one who had . . . who had died a natural death. Long enough for what remained of the body which had housed the brave defiant girl, the gay woman, the anxious woman, the crafty, the honest, the kind, the cruel, the altogether puzzling and contradictory human being whom Emma Arnett, without knowing it, had loved for thirteen years. And lost.

The old man, though unsteady on his feet, was obliging and helped them to carry the makeshift coffin to the grave.

Margaret said,

"We must at least say a prayer."

"Not too long, lady, please," the old man said. "I want me dinner. And I've got two to dig for this afternoon."

Emma knelt with the others, and folded her hands, but she did not pray. She thought — This is a dog's burial. Worse. When our old Nip died my father laid him by the foot of his favourite tree in the orchard and I put a bunch of gully flowers there.

They left the old man to his task and stood aimlessly for a moment.

"We must tidy up," Emma said, and they went back to the Queen's lodging where fresh pain waited. Her

531

clothes, still bearing her body's imprint, still fragrant with her scent; the pillow with her head's pressure visible; her brush, her comb, her handkerchief.

"I'm not sure," Margaret said thickly. "I believe that when people are . . . when people . . ." She pressed her hand to her mouth. "I think all their belongings are confiscated."

"Property," Nan Savile said, "and titles. Not things like . . . Who'd want her poor little clothes?"

They started crying again.

"Come along now," Emma said. "We'll pack. What happens after is not our business."

And when, tearfully, fumbling, all trace of Anne's occupation had been folded away, Emma said,

"There's your own gear, too. I brought nothing. I'll help you."

They went along to the room which Margaret and Nan had shared. Instinctively they kept together, three people against the world. Nobody came near them; it was as though the stroke that had severed the neck of their mistress had severed their contact with the world.

And at last there came the moment when all was ready, not a hairpin left. Nothing to do but go away and leave her there, in the traitor's unhallowed grave.

Margaret sat down on the bed and said,

"Her chaplain, what happened to him? And her aunt, Lady Boleyn. Wouldn't you have thought that she . . . I know that those who were outside," she was thinking of and excusing her husband and her brother, "it was difficult for them. But her chaplain and her aunt, they were here, couldn't they between them have tried . . .

532

She was a Christian: she should have had a Christian burial."

Nan Savile said,

"Yes. So she should. Even if . . . We *know* there was no truth in the accusations, but even if there had been she had made her Confession and taken the Sacrament; she died in a state of grace, and she should have been buried decently, not like a dog."

"Oh, I've known a dog buried with more ceremony," Emma said. She told them about old Nip.

Margaret said, in a musing tone,

"Under his favourite tree. *Her* favourite place was Norfolk."

"Not Blickling," Emma said quickly. "I know for a fact that she was once very unhappy there."

They looked at her questioningly.

"It's a long time ago, and she was young and things had gone wrong with her. But she was brave, just as she was today. Nobody will ever know just how often things went wrong for her, or how brave she was. Most people thought she was lucky. But I knew."

"I was jealous of her once," Margaret said. "My brother could never speak highly enough of her. I could never see why — until I came to know her."

"Did you?" Nan Savile asked. "Did you ever know her? Was there ever a moment when you could say with any certainty what she would do, or say? She confounded me time and again."

"But that was part of what I liked, the not knowing. *He* may not realise it," Margaret said, with a sudden vicious note in her voice, "but he'll miss her. To the end of his life! And so shall we."

They wept again. Emma watched and wished that she, too, could weep.

Margaret suddenly stopped crying, mopped her eyes and said,

"Salle! That is in Norfolk. Her father's people lie there, her grandparents . . ."

"That would be seemly," Nan said. "Could we do it? It's a long journey?"

"We'd need a cart," Emma said. She did not add, as most women would have done — And a man to drive. She was still capable of driving a horse.

"Our gear justifies the use of a cart," Margaret Lee said. "But could we lift her? The old man helped."

"We were unstrung and doing what we had no mind for," Emma said. "If I thought that it'd please her . . ." But she was dead, dead, dead and nothing would ever please her again; and yet . . . "I could lift her myself, myself alone."

"Oh no. We'd help," Nan said. "But at the other end . . . we must think of that. It must be properly done, and the priest there would need to know."

"We could never tell him," Margaret said. "People who . . . people who die as she died, can't be moved without the King's permission. I don't think he'd give it. So we couldn't say . . ."

Emma said,

"We could use my name. Salle is where I was born. There've been Arnetts there since the time when the wild men, with horns, came in raiding. To hear my

534

grandfather talk you'd have thought Arnetts had driven them back with their bare hands. But we've been gone from there more than forty years. The sheep drove us out. So there's none left to question. One, of us Arnetts fancied to be buried in the old place and had money enough to pay for the journey, would that sound reasonable? I know it isn't what she *should* have had. But she'd be with her own."

And she thought to herself, Why bother? Deny God and what was the difference between man and dog? Why not be content with the shovelling away of something which left about would become an offence to eye and nose, and an attraction to flies? Why not?

She had a sudden blinding flash of something there was no name for; a feeling that all along, as a Catholic in her youth, as a Protestant in her maturity, as rebel against it all, when God seemed to have failed her, she had been misled and mistaken. There was something behind it, the un-named, unrecognised source of all virtue. Some people were honest and kind and loyal, dogs were faithful, donkeys were patient, flowers were beautiful . . . and nothing could ever come from nothing, so somewhere there must be a source of perfect honesty, kindness, loyalty, faith, patience and beauty . . . And the future that had stretched before her, barren and narrow, wouldn't, she felt, be like that, it would be a search for the real truth, the hidden thing which had just revealed itself for a moment, and then vanished. But she'd find it again.

Nan Savile said,

"If we could do that I should feel so much easier in my mind."

"We *will* do it," Margaret said.

"I'll ask for a cart to be here at about eight o'clock; it will be growing dark by then," Emma said.

Their voices were steady; they could look at one another dry-eyed. They had stumbled, by chance, upon the oldest solace for the oldest of mankind's sorrows — the decent laying away of the beloved dead.